P9-EFI-905

Pedro
&
Daniel

PEDRO & DANIEL

Federico Erebia

Illustrated by
Julie Kwon

LEVINE QUERIDO

Montclair | Amsterdam | Hoboken

This is an Arthur A. Levine book
Published by Levine Querido

www.levinequerido.com • info@levinequerido.com
Levine Querido is distributed by Chronicle Books, LLC
Text copyright © 2023 by Federico Erebia
Illustrations copyright © 2023 by Julie Kwon
Library of Congress Control Number: 2022916277
ISBN 978-1-64614-304-7
Printed and bound in China

FSC
www.fsc.org

MIX
Paper | Supporting
responsible forestry
FSC™ C144853

Published in June 2023
First Printing

For Daniel, my brother.
And for all children who aren't seen for their worth,
beauty, and potential.

Recordar es volver a vivir.
To remember is to live again.
Origin unknown

contents

INTRODUCTION

THIS NOVEL IS a work of fiction based on my memorable relationship with Daniel, my brother. Other characters, and some scenes, are composites and/or fictional. All other names are fictional.

Many of the stories in this novel are difficult to read. They were difficult to write. Those who have known any of the many forms of abuse depicted in these stories may experience triggers. Please see the resources listed below. There is help either a click or a call away. Please ask for help.

After Daniel's death in 1993 at age thirty, the seeds of this novel were planted within the fertile grounds of the controlled chaos of my mind, where they germinated — constantly calling out for the light of day, to be written down, to be shared with others.

Now, in what would have been Daniel's sixtieth year, my memories have brought him back to life within these pages.

Recordar es volver a vivir.

Part One of this novel is a series of sixteen stories told in slightly differing third-person narration. Perhaps you might imagine the voices of the family doctor, priests, police, neighbors, or any of the many adults who were aware of Pedro and Daniel's circumstances, but chose not to intervene on their behalf.

Parts Two to Five are told in Daniel and Pedro's voices, in alternating chapters.

Pedro and Daniel use dichos throughout this novel. There is a full index at the end of this book with details about their translations, and their origins when identifiable.

RESOURCES

CHILD ABUSE

https://ChildHelpHotline.org
https://www.ChildWelfare.gov/pubs/reslist/tollfree/

DOMESTIC VIOLENCE

National Domestic Violence Hotline: 800-799-7233
https://www.TheHotline.org
https://www.ChildWelfare.gov/pubs/reslist/tollfree

LGBTQIA+

https://www.LGBTHotline.org
https://www.TheTrevorProject.org

RACISM/COLORISM

https://www.LinesForLife.org/racial-equity-support-line
https://NAACP.org

SUICIDALITY

National Suicide & Crisis Lifeline: Dial or text 988
https://988LifeLine.org
https://www.ChildWelfare.gov/pubs/reslist/tollfree

Part I
May 1968–August 1969

Más vale pájaro en mano que cien volando.
Piensa en toda la belleza en tu alrededor y sé feliz.
La rueda que chilla consigue la grasa.

MAY 1968

A bird in hand, two in a tree,
If all were yours, you would have three.

When you are happy and content,
If none are yours, you won't lament!

I

CAUTION IN THE WIND

Mom hurls hurtful slurs at Pedro and Daniel,
names for sissies,
the brothers cannot,
    should not
    yet understand,
words which nevertheless stab their young hearts,
    when they are thrown with precision between clenched teeth,
    like venomous dart rockets,
    trailed by tails of spittle spray,
her eyes bulge, her chest heaves, her breaths rasp,
    as she approaches them,
    with eyebrows arched, nostrils flared, lips in a sneer,
her left hand reaches,
    her right hand struggles to touch the ceiling for one clear
        objective,
    to produce the maximal velocity and impact
    when it accelerates down to strike their little bodies,
preferably their heads,
    with a sharp, staccato, knuckled, coscorrón,
    and its sweet, sudden pulse up her arm,
or their faces,
    with an opened-palm slap,

and its bitterly short-lived pins and needles in her hand,
or any other meaningful contact resulting in the small boys' injury,
    no, not lethal, or necessarily serious,
which would bring her some satisfaction, some alleviation, some
    antidote,
    to help settle her unbridled rage and rancor,
    brought on by their deviant deeds and delinquencies. . . .

• • •

She has a fleeting thought. . . .

'Quisiera matar dos pájaros en un tiro.'

But she has her preferred target when she can't hurt two with one
strike.

• • •

The boys avoid waking the demon, always simmering just below
Mom's surface.

It constantly sniffs for scents of weakness, joy, or folly,
listens for sounds — whispers, and especially laughter —
which nurture the embers, and coax them to ignite,
so that this demon might erupt from Mom once more.
She is in constant search of the next fix that might calm it
    within her.

• • •

Of the five senses,
only *touch* can grant Mom the satisfying sensory sequence of:
    the smell of fear,
    the sight of tears,
    the sound of suppressed sobbing,
    and the taste of victory.

• • •

They have three sisters and an older brother, but Pedro and Daniel are very much alike, as if they are twins born fifteen months apart.

'Son tal para cual.'
They are two of a kind.

Daniel often plays with their sister's doll. He brushes, then combs her hair; he dresses her in outfits with high heels, or sometimes he prefers to give her slip-on slippers; he pretends to apply mascara, eyeliner, blush, then lipstick. His lips bite an imaginary tissue to remove the excess lipstick on the doll's lips.

Pedro really likes the doll's handsome boyfriend — the one with the sky-blue eyes — but no one knows, and no one can ever find out. He remembers the last time he held a doll: he had been touching the subtle and enviable dimples on the blue-eyed boyfriend's angular face when Mom walked in. He will not risk releasing her wrath once more for the same crime. He won't ever touch a doll again. The associated beating and vulgarities were a warning that the next time would be much worse. Pedro must live in this fantasy world with her, where he cannot be himself.

His real truth must stay hidden at all times in his cluttered head.

So Pedro suppresses speech, glances, gestures, and every other movement. It consumes him. He is known for being quiet and still. Mom interprets these as symptoms of his low intelligence and overall laziness — es un pendejo y un huevón — more labels he must work to dispel.

When he does speak, he struggles in both languages.

Their problems don't end there.

Neither Pedro nor Daniel likes sports. Mom says all her boys must like sports, play sports, and be good at sports. There will be no exceptions!

On an athletic field, Pedro bumbles, fumbles, stumbles, then tumbles.

On the other hand, Daniel sees no reason to hide his disinterest with insincere attempts at playing sports. He has unanswerable questions about Mom's drive to make them athletes.

They are each destined for displeasure and disappointment in this delusional demand for athleticism.

* * *

The children get themselves ready for school every morning. Sara and Juan will take a standard yellow bus to their elementary school in town, about five miles away. Pedro's kindergarten bus travels a few miles in the opposite direction, to an unincorporated community—it's not big enough to be a town with its own elected officials.

His school is across the street from a small airport, which caters to wealthy fishing enthusiasts, and those with summer homes in the area. Next to the airport is the cemetery where their baby sister is buried. Pedro's enduring image of the only time he saw her was when she was in the little white casket on a card table in their living room. She was an unusually large baby doll, with a wrinkled face and closed eyes. He longed for someone—anyone—to pick her up so she could open her eyes like the doll in Sara's room, whose internally weighted eyes open when *it* is picked up. The doll's eyes close again when it is laid down.

* * *

Pedro had long ago promised Daniel he would take him along to school someday. Daniel is terco and necio about promises, so he has stubbornly not forgotten. He believes,

'Querer es poder.'
Where there's a will, there's a way.

So naturally, Daniel pesters Mom as well. He thinks to himself,

'¡El que no llora, no mama!'
The child that doesn't cry doesn't suckle.

Daniel remembers every dicho, or proverb, he has ever heard, and he finds opportunities to use them to his advantage. Dichos are useful tools for a precocious five-year-old. They are wise old sayings, on par with a wise old man or woman who should not be ignored or disrespected.

'A canas honradas no hay puertas cerradas.'
There are no doors closed to wise elders.

Now, the last day of kindergarten has arrived. Pedro won't have another chance. He must throw caution to the wind and fulfill his promise *today*. But Pedro is afraid to ask Mom for anything. He should choose his words carefully.

He opens Mom's bedroom door a few inches, peeks into the dark room, and repeats in a loud whisper the words that Daniel just fed him, and helped him practice: "¡Mom, la maestra dijo que lo tengo que llevar!"

Pedro believes in his heart these words are true, but he knows others, maybe even his teacher, would disagree. He has heard:

'Media verdad es media mentira.'
A half truth is a half lie.

So, he holds his breath for Mom's response.

Unexpectedly, the darkness says in exasperation, "¡Ándale, llévalo!"

Pedro nervously uses his foot to help guide the door closed, resisting his treacherously shaking hand that would sabotage everything by slamming the door shut.

Now, Daniel has to calm down, get dressed, and have breakfast. Pedro needs to get him on the bus before Mom changes her mind. With any luck, she's gone back to sleep, and won't get up until one of their baby sisters wakes and starts to cry — if even then.

• • •

Every night, Pedro and Daniel whisper in their bed until they fall asleep. Daniel loves hearing Pedro's stories about school. Everything is new to them:

"Sheets of colored plastic magically make a new color, if you put one on toppa the other!" Pedro whispers.

"Wow," Daniel says, and his big eyes open wider.

"Play-Doh and glue paste and crayons smell good enough to eat! One boy was even told to stop eatin' 'em!"

Daniel giggles!

"The cafeteria has sloppy joes, corn dogs, jello 'n fruit, 'n brownies!" Pedro teases.

"Yum!"

"The teacher tested us to make sure we're ready for first grade," Pedro says, sounding serious.

Daniel feels uneasy about this. He's heard tests are hard.

"I showed her I can name all the colors of the rainbow 'n the letters of the alphabet. I can count to ten. I can color inside the lines. I can use scissors."

Daniel has been practicing these at home with Pedro. He knows Pedro can do them all well, and he has been a good teacher to Daniel.

"But I had trouble sayin' some words."

"Uh oh." Daniel knows Pedro stutters when he's nervous. And Pedro gets nervous a lot.

"¡¡¡Tartamudo!!!" Mom has yelled.

"Mrs. Walker wonders if it's 'cause we speak Spanish at home."

Daniel rolls his eyes and says, "Really?"

"Then, she's surprised I won' skip for her!" Pedro laughs.

Daniel giggles, too.

"What if somebody saw me skippin'?"

"Why would skippin' be part of a test?"

"Who knows? Remember Mrs. Torres, who works in the cafeteria? She tol' Mom I won't eat spinach."

"Mrs. Torres is a metiche chismosa with all her gossip," Daniel claims.

"Somebody's always watchin'," Pedro warns.

Daniel knows there are lots of metiche chismosas—and chismosos too! You can't forget about the men who love to gossip. They may be worse than women, since they try to be macho about everything.

"The other boys skipped 'round and 'round the whole room! They couldn't've been happier. They didn't seem to care who saw 'em skippin'," Pedro says with wonder. "Mom told us skippin' is just for girls. That boys can't skippa 'round like a 'maldito maricón de mierda'!"

Daniel still skips when he wants. He can't really help it—it just happens, all by itself. And, Daniel doesn't care too much, because he's used to being called a maricón . . . even if it hurts the way Mom says it to them.

"Mrs. Walker looked at me 'cause I wouldn't skip. I just stood there, like La Momia Muda."

The mute mummy.

Mom has words to describe everything Pedro does.

"What else could I do? I couldn't really esplain 'maldito maricón' to her. I don' even know what those words mean—in English *or* Spanish!"

Pedro is used to being judged at home, but he had never been judged before at school by his teacher. It had been a safe place; she had been a safe person. He believed he had always done things well for her, the way he had been asked to do them.

"I felt like I was stuck inside a plastic container, where I couldn't see or hear normal," Pedro says. "But finally, Mrs. Walker said I can go to Our Lady of the Immaculate Conception School next year!"

• • •

Pedro rushes Daniel to the bus stop. Mom didn't ask any questions; she just stayed in bed. If Daniel isn't home, it will be one less child for her to look after.

The bus stop is on the other side of the main road around the corner from their house. It's a rural road where the speed limit is an often-ignored suggestion. The traffic is sparse so the neighborhood children can usually time their running across the road without getting hit. The road is flat and straight. They can see their yellow bus at least a mile away, with its red lights flashing at every stop it makes.

The bus driver's bushy brows lift when he sees Daniel climbing the stairs in a moth-eaten brown cardigan over a fully buttoned, white shirt; oversized corduroy pants cinched around his mid-chest with a long belt; and worn leather shoes with short strings tying the top eyelets together. Pedro hurries him to the empty front bench where Pedro always sits — with the expansive window, showcasing the world in front of them. The driver gives them a side-eye glance, then his wispy whiskers whistle along with the song playing on his transistor radio.

All the kids stare and point at Daniel when they see him on the bus. Pedro avoids their eyes. Daniel is too excited to care what others think. In a few months, this will be his morning routine, so he takes in every tiny detail.

When the bus arrives, the children run toward the school building. Their joyous chatter echoes off the brick façades, producing a deafening effect that exaggerates the number of children.

The kindergarten class is on the lower floor where the large windows are level with the playground just outside. Mrs. Walker's eyes and mouth open a little when she sees Daniel from across the room. Pedro avoids her gaze, and he sits Daniel in the first available seat.

After the kids settle down, Mrs. Walker tells each of them to go to the front of the room, one after the next. She had told her students to bring their one true treasure today.

The other kids are eager for their turn, but Pedro is nervous.

The girls display dolls, dresses, and diaries.

The boys brag about baseball cards, cars, and cartoon comics.

Then Mrs. Walker looks at Pedro, who is the last to present, and says, "What one true treasure did you bring today Pedro?"

Pedro takes Daniel by the hand. They go to the front of the room, and Pedro says, "I brought my brother, Daniel."

'La amistad sincera es un alma repartida en dos cuerpos.'
True friendship is one soul shared by two bodies.

**Más vale paso que dure, y no trote que canse.
Lento, pero seguro.**

JUNE 1968

Choose a step you know will last,
Not one in which you'll tire fast.

Much like the tortoise and the hare,
The tortoise won, with time to spare!

2

A HIGHLIGHT FOR PEDRO

PEDRO AND DANIEL wait for Mom in the doctor's office lobby. She is going to have another baby! The boys love having new babies in their small house.

> 'Apretados pero contentos.'
> *Cramped, but content.*

They love when the baby gives a toothless twinkle, or a gurgling giggle. They love when the baby starts saying silly words. They love smelling the baby's head, and the aromas of the special lotion, powder, shampoo. They love watching the baby sleep. But they know the consequences for waking a napping newborn.

Dr. Fritz holds a special place in Mom's heart. He has delivered all her children, except Pedro, for whose birth Dr. Fritz was late. Mom has forgiven, but not forgotten this infraction. It reminds her Dr. Fritz is only human. He is only a man. He is not really like God.

Pedro and Daniel have heard Mom say:

> 'No se puede tener todo.'
> *You can't have everything.*

After her last visit with Dr. Fritz, Pedro announced he is going to be a doctor when he grows up. For a few minutes, he was actually Mom's favorite child. At any moment in time, Mom both announces and shows who her favorite child is, but that can change often each day. Pedro can't remember any other time he was Mom's favorite.

Today in the doctor's office, Daniel is grumbling about the few crayon fragments he has available to him; then he notices some travieso has mischievously used different colors to slash at all of the pictures inside the coloring books, with no attempt to stay within the lines. He starts sorting through stacks to seek other options.

Pedro picks up *Highlights* from a table crammed with magazines. Every page is full of puzzles and pictures and riddles and stories. He always looks at *Highlights* at school. He tries to do only one thing in the magazine, so he can enjoy it over many days. It takes a lot of discipline for him to stop after only one puzzle or story, and he frequently fails. He'll promise himself he'll only do one more. . . .

Today, he wants to do all the activities in the magazine! He won't give up until he discovers every hidden object in the drawing. He looks closely to spot the differences between a pair of pictures that seem identical. He reads about the good boy and the not-so-good boy; he wants to be like the good boy. There's a maze, and a word find. . . .

I hope I can finish everything before we leave!

Then Pedro notices a book club advertisement that had been torn from a magazine. It says,

THE FIRST BOOK IS FREE!

The boys don't have books, or paper, at home.

A few weeks ago, Pedro took a free calendar pad from the bank so he could draw on the blank back of each page. Sometimes, he cuts envelopes open so he can draw on the clear paper inside. He doesn't like envelopes with windows.

There is a small postcard at the bottom of the ad that he tears away at the perforations. The front says:

NO POSTAGE NECESSARY.

Daniel notices Pedro's concentration on this sheet of paper, crosses the room, and sits down next to him. He puts his hand on Pedro's shoulder and looks at him with his big brown eyes.

"You should ask that lady to help you," Daniel says.

"Can you please ask her for me?" Pedro replies, sheepishly aware of his limitations.

The receptionist is happy to help the boys fill out the form.

Pedro decides which book he wants for free. Someone will need to pay for the others that will come monthly until he cancels, but he ignores that detail for now. He wants to focus on the brand-new book he's getting for free.

Every day, for weeks, Pedro prays the postman will provide.

One day, Mom exclaims, "¡¿Y qué es esto?!"

Pedro has never received a package before.

Mom opens it—and there is Pedro's beautiful red book!

Pedro can't believe Mom lets him keep it when a crying toddler distracts her. He will hide it in his room, just in case.

'Fuera de vista, fuera de mente.'
Out of sight, out of mind.

This brand-new, beautiful book has a dustcover, and underneath, there's a textured, fabric case. It tickles his fingertips when he runs them back and forth. The title and names of the author and illustrator are in gold. The book has a distinct smell. Pedro buries his nose into the middle of the open book and inhales.

It's clearly like heaven, if heaven has a smell.

He squeezes his eyes closed and fairy-tale images dance around in his cluttered mind.

"I wanna see it!" cries Daniel.

"Okay, but don' get it dirty!" Pedro says, as he puts the dustcover back on.

The pages are crisp and stick together a little. They make a funny noise when the boys try to grab one page to separate it from the next.

Squeak!

They read every word on every page, and look at the wonderful illustrations.

Squeak!

Sometimes they ask Sara what a word means, or how to pronounce it.

Squeak!

Then there is a word they don't know. Sara doesn't know it. Juan doesn't know it. And when Pop comes home, he doesn't know the word either!

Pedro's head fills with questions and thoughts and wonder.

What does this word mean?
What other words don't I know?
What are other words no one else knows?
How can I learn all the words in the world?

This is suddenly a new game, a new challenge, like those in *Highlights*! Now Pedro realizes he needs more books — and more ways to learn.

"Maybe if I keep readin' and learnin'," Pedro muses, "I really *will* be a doctor when I grow up!"

"El que la sigue, la consigue," Daniel says. "*Where there's a will, there's a way.*"

Quien más mira, menos ve.
Vísteme despacio que tengo prisa.
Más de prisa, más despacio.

JULY 1968

The more you look, the less you see,
You'll see the forest, not the tree.

Stop and smell the scented rose,
Breathe in deep, delight your nose!

3

HERMANOS DE DOBLES SENTIDOS

DANIEL MAKES PEDRO laugh when they're supposed to be quiet. Pedro will laugh quietly, until he's spasming, with tears running down his cheeks. No one would know if he were laughing, crying, or having a medical emergency!

Daniel rolls his big brown eyes when he knows he shouldn't say what he's thinking. He contorts his face and uses his hands and hips for added flair and flamboyance. Mom calls him El Perico, the parakeet—the imitator. He knows she doesn't mean it in a nice way, but he still takes it as an overall compliment. The reactions he gets from his caricatures confirm he has capacity for talent.

The boys will have a rare respite while Mom is in the hospital with the new baby. They've been looking forward to this since they found out she was pregnant, which means she'll be in the hospital four or five days before she and the baby come home. It's like getting a pair of perfect presents.

Their siblings are outside with the daughter of a neighboring comadre. She's a high school senior who knows all the cool things happening in the outside world, plays music on her transistor radio, reads the kids their horoscope, and says, "That's groovy!" a lot.

Pedro giggles as Daniel mimics the actress in the movie they saw last night. Daniel has clothes, shoes, and jewelry from Mom's closet which he mixes in a myriad of combinations. He especially loves drop-and-dangle clip-on earrings. He can put lots of them on all at once, around his ears. He even clips some to his hair in a type of tiara formation, à la Elizabeth Taylor in *Cleopatra*.

Daniel wears one of Mom's wigs, which are in fashion these days. Her prized, strapless, full-skirt, azul-celeste silk gown is a wrinkled cloud under his arms and all around him. Her long white gloves are puffs at the ends of his shirtsleeves.

Daniel's unsteadiness in steep stiletto shoes makes Pedro snort. He can make noises when he laughs today because no one is here to yell at him!

"¡Otra cosa, mariposa!" Pedro cries out.

Do something else, butterfly!

He's unaware of the doble sentido of the word mariposa.

Daniel bats his eyelashes, pretend-applies lipstick, and air kisses all his fans in his make-believe studio audience. He cackles when he catches himself in the mirror, then he bats some more and pouts his lips. He dramatically wraps a scarf around his neck, the way women wear scarves in other movies the boys have seen.

Daniel stumble-walks in high heels, and he exaggeratedly wiggles his bum as he has seen countless women walk in both English and Spanish movies. Seductive shimmying and shaking is a universal language known to men, who stare with their mouths open when wiggling women walk by, hypnotized by the swishing back and forth, back and forth, back and forth—mimicking a pendulous, ticking clock a hypnotist might use.

Pedro's face felt warm when the two men smiled in the movie last night. His tummy tickled too. It felt like they were smiling at Pedro, and no one else. Their handsome faces filled the screen with lots of big white teeth and blue and green eyes and dimples on chins and cheeks.

Pedro remembers one of the actors was a gallant gladiator in a guts and glory movie. The other was a secret spy with lots of girlfriends in a different movie. When he snaps out of his pequeño ensueño, he quickly looks to see if Daniel noticed. He is awkwardly aware he was staring off with his mouth slightly open, like the maldito pendejo de mierda Mom says he is.

Pedro thinks he and Daniel are the same because they're different from other boys. But they're also different from each other. They are:

'El mismo perro con distinto collar.'
Same dog, different collar.

Mom stopped getting mad when Daniel plays with dolls or dresses, because he keeps doing it anyway. Pedro would never risk playing with either.

Without thinking, Daniel has people laughing with funny quips. Pedro is mute, except with Daniel.

Daniel is a travieso who would hurl a whirling dervish out of whirl so he could whirl on center stage all by himself. Pedro mostly sits quietly.

Pedro doesn't like going to Mass. He doesn't like that he was born with Original Sin and will always be a sinner. Jesus died for Pedro's sins a long time before he was even born. Since God is all knowing, and He already knows Pedro is going to do all his sins, what's he supposed to do? What's the point of trying to change what can't be changed?

On the other hand, Daniel loves going to Mass. He loves singing. He loves when the bread and wine become the body and blood of Jesus Christ.

"It's like a miracle!" he declares. "Most of all, I really wanna talk to Jesus like the priests do!"

In a little more than a year, Daniel will be in first grade, and he can go to Mass every morning before classes start.

Mom is so happy Daniel wants to be a priest!

When her comadres mention the boys are skinny and don't play sports, Mom says Pedro wants to be a doctor and Daniel wants to be a priest.

And, it has the intended effect.

She has found an unexpected source of pride in her disappointments.

"Hay que hacer de tripas corazón," she says to herself.

What can't be cured must be endured.
When life gives you lemons, make lemonade.

Cuando en duda, consúltalo con tu almohada.
Duerme en ello, y tomarás consejo.
El que no oye consejo, no llega a viejo.

AUGUST 1968

When you wonder what is right,
Consult your pillow overnight.

In the morning, in your head,
You'll know what's right, not wrong instead!

4

FAMILIA EN
MÉXICO LINDO

PEDRO AND DANIEL'S family drives down to Mexico every summer. Pedro secretly feels sorry for everyone in the whole wide world who hasn't been to Mexico. He wishes he could live there all year round.

"El amor y la felicidad, no se pueden ocultar," Daniel says on the way down from Ohio. *"You can't hide love or happiness."*

"I love bein' happy in Mexico!" Pedro says.

"I think the dicho is talkin' 'bout love-love," Daniel says. "You know, kissy kissy love love."

Pop drives the whole way with only a few stops for gas and for them to use the bathroom. They go from Ohio into Kentucky, Tennessee, Arkansas. Then, it takes twelve hours just to drive through Texas to get to Mexico!

The back seat of the station wagon is down, so there is a flat bed behind Mom, Pop, and the babies in the front seat. It is full of boxes, bags, blankets, and lots of children.

They won't have to stop for any food or drinks. Mom packed tortillas stuffed with fried potatoes and scrambled eggs, bologna and cheese sandwiches, chips, fruit, and water in mason jars.

The boys are supposed to pee in a large bottle, but Pedro holds it in until they have to stop for gas. If he can't pee outside on a tree, how is he supposed to pee in the back of a wobbly car, on a bumpy highway, when he's kneeling with his head bent down because it's hitting the roof of the car, with his shirt tucked under his chin, while he's holding the bottle with one hand and he's holding down his shorts and chonies with his other hand, and everybody inside and outside the car are looking right at him the whole time?

Mom is not happy, but she seems to think it was worth a try.

At the border, everyone must get out of the station wagon so it can be searched. It always takes hours. The amount of time, and the level of inspection, depends entirely on the amount of money Mom is willing to give the guards as bribes. There is a hierarchical system for discreet cash disbursement. It's hard to tell who is most stubborn about it: Mom or the various men with palms open behind their backs. Each man holds a key that allows advancement to the next phase of this painful process.

Mamá and Papá are Mom's parents. Papá is a night watchman. He is at the end of his duty when the sleepy family finally crosses the bridge and enters his border town in the early morning hours. They drive through the business district looking for him.

"¡Allí está!" Daniel's eagle eyes spot Papá checking the doors of the shops on his route. He's got a quick step, with his left arm swinging and his right hand cupping the butt of the pistol in its holster. His lips are puckered in a whistle.

Pop pulls up next to Papá. The gold front tooth shines in his toothy smile. "¡Hijos, bienvenidos!"

Mamá is feeding the chickens when the family arrives with Papá at their house on a dusty dirt road. She wears a short-sleeve dress with a sunflower pattern made of thin cotton, and her huaraches squeak as she runs toward them. The reunion is loud and joyful.

Mamá nurtures a magical garden with a maze, which an untrained eye would mistake for unkept and overgrown bushes, weeds, and vines. Birds of every color visit throughout the day. The children have to keep their clothes clean, but when they play hide-n-go-seek, they can use the large bushes, except for the one with tiny thorns that ruin the day with snagged fabric.

Papá teaches the kids how to peel the abundant fruit in the pomegranate tree to release the juicy, tangy seeds, whose nectar stains hands, faces, and clothing. They pick limes for the refreshing limonada they drink in the hot, sunny afternoons. The avocado and mango trees are full of ripe fruit ready for plucking.

The kids enjoy watching and feeding the chickens. Mamá shouts daily for them to *stop feeding them honey locust leaves, they'll get constipated!* But the chickens seem to relish the leaves. Only Juan is brave enough to fetch the eggs under the hens each morning.

Pedro prefers the flour tortillas Mom makes over corn tortillas. But the corn tortillas made at the tortillería near Mamá are so different from those they buy in a package. As the boys walk, they start to smell a buttered, roasted corn aroma from around the corner. Everything running around in Pedro's mind magically pays attention to the flavor of a warm tortilla, right off the machine.

"I'd love to live next to a tortillería," Pedro says, "here in Mexico."

"Me too," Daniel agrees. "I love Mi México Lindo."

• • •

Every morning, the kids wake to the sounds of

"¡¡¡EL MAÑANA!!!"

The man selling the morning newspaper.

"¡¡¡PAN!!! ¡¡¡PAN DULCE!!! ¡¡¡GALLETAS!!!"

The man selling fresh bread, cakes and cookies.

"¡¡¡CAFÉ!!! ¡¡¡CAFÉ CON LECHE!!!¡¡¡CHOCOLATE!!!"

The man selling coffees and hot chocolate.

Daniel thinks it's the best way to wake up.

Then he remembers to check under his pillow. "Una peseta!"

All the kids wake to find a coin or two under their pillow.

Papá won't let Mom take the coins away from his grandkids. He supervises as they buy cookies and candies from the passing street vendors. Mom protests, but Papá raises a finger to his lips, so she watches with an angry face and a half-circle frown. The boys have never seen anyone control Mom, and Papá does it without yelling or violence.

It's like magic!

Daniel avoids Mom's face, which secretly sends a message: *don't you dare spend all that money on candy and cookies!* Pedro tries not to look too happy, just in case she remembers for later.

• • •

Papá sleeps during the day, but it's hard with all the kids acting like kids. A few times, he yells at them, but he can't get angry at grandkids he only sees a couple weeks each year. When it's hot and humid, poor Papá lays on top of the covers in his chonies. The fan sitting on a chair a few inches from his face swirls the soupy, suffocating air around him.

• • •

A day or two after they arrive, all the kids are told to gather in the front room. Mamá takes out the key hanging from a chain around her neck: she looks at her grandkids until they're all sitting quietly with full attention. She opens the big wardrobe, and faint, delicious aromas of rose water, makeup powder, stored fabrics, and oiled wood waft out over them.

Mamá makes a show out of taking out hidden gifts she's squirreled away here and there for this very moment. She laughs a girlish laugh when she forgets a present or two. Last year, Daniel got a colorful spinning top that makes swirling shapes when it spins, and Pedro got a silver ring with his initials. This year, Sara gets an embroidered shawl, Juan receives a Mil Máscaras wrestling mask, Pedro has a miniature harmonica, and Daniel collects a colorful kaleidoscope. The younger kids are soon rewarded for their patience too.

. . .

Mom is yelling at Mamá in the kitchen, and wakes Papá in the other room. Some kids rush in, while others watch from a safer distance.

"¿Ave María Purísima, qué pasa?" Papá cries out as he rubs his eyes and enters the room in his white tank top and chonies. He tries to calm Mom, but she won't stop yelling at Mamá, who is crying—not with angry coraje, but with deep sentimiento—and Pedro's heart breaks for her. He knows the way Mamá is feeling: as if Mom has laid bare and broadcast her every defect or deficiency with a sneer.

Then Mom yells at Pop when he tries to take her into the other room.

Then Mom breaks a Jarritos soda bottle over Pop's head, and there is glass and blood and coraje everywhere.

. . .

Papá gets up around three in the afternoon. The kids watch him get ready for work from behind curtains and furniture. Papá sits in front of another chair in the large front room, near the open windows where the bright sunlight illuminates his face. He places a mirror on the back of the chair, behind the large wash basin on the seat. He has a musky smelling brush he wets with water, then swirls against an aromatic bar of soap in a cup, making a thick cream he smears all over his face.

Papá knows he's being watched, so he puts on the shaving cream with dramatic flourishes until the kids giggle. It reminds the boys of feeding their siblings as they make airplane noises, the spoon flying in wispy patterns until the baby opens their mouth so the spoon can land. Papá even dabs a little cream onto the top of his head! It looks like a dollop of whipped cream on a piece of pie!

Then Papá takes an odd-looking razor and shaves his face. Sometimes, he shaves the top of his head as well, because he's basically bald. Daniel imagines his head feels soft and smooth and cool, like a small, ripe watermelon. Papá shakes drops of aftershave onto one hand, rubs both hands together quickly, then he taps all over his face and head:

tippity tippity tippity - Tap.
tippity tippity tippity - Tap.
tippity tippity tippity - Tap.

Papá doesn't wear chonies like Pedro and Daniel; they are more like the white boxer shorts Cary Grant and Rock Hudson wear in the movies. He puts on olive-green pants and a matching shirt with two buttoned pockets. He shines his black, military-style boots before he pulls them on. He adds a pale yellow, woven, leather belt.

Then he puts on his holster with individual bullets in their compartments. All the kids have been warned to stay away from Papa's pistol, which he puts on top of the armoire, without bullets, when he gets home from work in the morning. Pedro squints his eyes so he doesn't have to see when Papá reaches for his gun and places it in its home.

Last, Papá puts on his wide felt sombrero that's the same color as his belt. Papá is so handsome with his big smile and gold front tooth and his night watchman uniform.

• • •

Mom is tired of all the kids sniffling in the back of the Pontiac station wagon. She tells them that they'll turn around, go back, and spend one more day with Mamá and Papá: they just have to go to sleep, and when they wake up, they'll be back in Mexico.

But when the kids wake up, they still have about two hours before they leave Texas and enter Arkansas. They have *not* turned around to spend another day with Mamá and Papá.

Daniel wipes the tear on Pedro's cheek and whispers into his ear, "Desgracia compartida, menos sentida."

Shared misery is felt less.

And, Pedro gives him a weak smile.

Para tonto no se estudia.
No estudio para saber más, sino para ignorar menos.
Dios nos libre del hombre de solo un libro.

SEPTEMBER 1968

One need not learn to be a fool!
So listen well when you're at school!

Read, write, and add; learn to subtract;
Don't be a dunce, to be exact!

5

WRITINGS ON THE WALL

COUNTLESS STORMS HAVE shaken Pedro and Daniel's house from within. They always seem to hit full force in the middle of the night, but the rumblings begin hours before.

There will be howling winds, scattering debris, and raining glass, followed by thunderous, rhythmic wailing from the crushed stone driveway that wakes the neighborhood, combined with lightning flashes of red and white that illuminate the night sky.

Then all will be suddenly quiet.

Pedro thinks of these storms and is reminded of oil and water that have been shaken in a jar: each component struggles frantically to disentangle and repel the other, as their true nature demands, dispelling the forces of energy that had led to their kinetic ensnarement.

Tonight, Pedro wakes up to cyclical rumblings nearby: they are loud—Mom is yelling—then soft—Pop is trying to calm her—but they both get louder with each new cycle.

A storm is coming in fast!

Pedro comforts Daniel who is whimpering next to him in their bed. They both know what to expect: it will get much worse before it's over, hours from now. They know it will be several days before a peaceful sun will rise in the east and their Pop will be allowed to return home.

Juan is probably awake in his bed nearby.

Sara is ten years old; she has her own room across the hall.

There is nowhere to hide in their small house. The children are *usually* safe if they stay in their rooms, but safety is not assured. Injury is imminent within the dangerous eye of the storm.

'Entre padres y hermanos, no metas tus manos.'
Don't get involved in family arguments.

They must wait for it to pass.

Only time will tell what lies ahead.

• • •

Earlier that evening . . .

Pedro notices Mom is in a good mood. She is never in a good mood. Not like this.

She is chatting with Pop. He is sitting on the floor in front of her as she knits. He looks back at her lovingly, gently teasing her, trying to coax a laugh out of her.

She just giggled!

Pedro knows something is not right.

Is not good.

Is likely bad.

He studies Mom closely from across the room.

The TV show is ending. The laugh track has longer and louder bursts of laughter. Then there is clapping in the television studio audience. The music starts and the credits begin to roll.

The show is over.

Mom's anxious hands work faster.

click - clack, click - clack, click - clack.

Time is urgently accelerating, out of time with the pendulum of the hanging clock.

tick-tock, tick-tock, tick-tock.

This syncopated discord furrows Mom's brow.
Creases form on her forehead.
Uncertainty distorts her face.
Subtly.
Mom's eyes lose their luster, but she keeps working.

click - clack, click - clack, click - clack.

A darkness falls over her. It's so obvious to Pedro, but no one else seems to notice the writing on the wall.

There is a severe, suffocating, sogginess in the air. The room is closing in on Pedro. His head fills with cloudy thoughts, sad recollections, and a sense of doom. His small body weakens. He vanishes into his head, and its expansive, dank darkness, and despair.

He has no memory of going to bed.

• • •

The storm is quite intense when Sara throws open their door, "Please come to my room! Please, hurry! I need you!" she says in an urgent, loud whisper that can't hide her fear. She's holding her pillow against her belly.

Without looking down the hallway, all four of them run into her room, then jump on her bed.

"Do you see them?" she asks, pointing at her wall, before the boys can seek comfort under her blankets.

They turn to look — and gasp!

On the wall, opposite the window, are moving images. They are not flat against the wall, but rather they are three-dimensional, colorful cartoon characters suspended in air: four animals in costumes playing instruments, dancing to their soft beat, playing their music for these four siblings. There seems to be one character for each child.

"What are they?" Pedro asks in confused amusement.

"I don't know," Sara replies, sounding less scared. "They just showed up! I'm glad you can see them too!"

"I like 'em!" Daniel says with a big grin. "They're funny!"

"Are they for real really real?" Juan asks.

Two are playing guitars, one is a drummer, and one is playing a keyboard. They are each the size of a soda can. Pedro focuses on the bear wearing a hat, a wide polka-dotted tie, and a sleeveless open shirt; he is playing a bass guitar hung low. His right arm is barely bent as he plucks the strings.

The siblings watch them in a trance, no longer aware of the raging storm outside Sara's room. They are lulled into calmness, and tranquility.

Then they are asleep.

And all is quiet.

The next morning, the four siblings can't explain what happened last night. The characters engaged them, but left no evidence of their visit other than indelible visions and feelings that cannot be erased or easily forgotten.

The kids have seen movies about Bernadette of Lourdes, the children of Fatima, and Juan Diego of Mexico. None were believed when they had visions of Mary, the Mother of God.

These siblings have *not* seen Mary, so they decide to keep their unusual occurrence a secret.

The children find comfort in knowing someone is watching over them.

"But will they also protect us?" asks Pedro.

"Donde hay humo hay fuego," Daniel reassures.

Where there's smoke, there's fire.

"Quien espera, desespera," Juan notes.

One who longs finds despair.

Más vale gotita permanente que aguacero de repente.
La mejor salsa es el hambre.

OCTOBER 1968

I'd rather have a steady drip,
A waterfall would make me slip!

Enjoy the lesser things in life,
When there is rife, it can cause strife!

6

TELLTALE TRICKS AND TREATS

PEDRO AND DANIEL love Halloween. It's the only time of year they get to keep candy for themselves, after they go to dozens of houses and open their bags to raining sweets and chocolate bars.

Easter is a close second favorite holiday for Daniel, whose sweet tooth has a bottomless root.

Pedro doesn't like Easter, or its candy: yellow, overly sweet, marshmallow chicks; odd-flavored jelly beans; funny-tasting, hollow-bunny chocolate that gives him a headache; and the absolute worst: malted-milk Easter eggs.

Last Easter, Mom smashed an egg onto Pedro's head when he walked into the living room. She had been savoring her wait with a building anticipation, hiding by the doorway with her arm straight up before she brought it down with a forceful wallop. She thought it was the funniest thing ever: Pedro standing there with a stupefied look, shards of eggshell and mucousy yolk and eggwhite dripping down his face onto his clean Easter shirt, shorts, and shoes, unable to register the appropriate reaction that would lessen the likelihood of an additional slap or coscorrón.

Through bitter tears, Pedro saw Mom struggle to say—through laughter, wiping away her own tears—that it is a special Mexican tradition, and it will bring him good luck in the coming year. Pedro noticed she failed to share this tradition, its good luck, and its humiliation with anyone else.

This Halloween, Pedro would love to have a store-bought costume. A superhero or a Disney cartoon character would be awesome. On the other hand, Daniel is happy to create outfits from old clothes, cosmetics, and costume jewelry. Mom lets him use throwaway makeup just for this one occasion.

Sara becomes a fortune teller with a red bandana tying her hair back, hoop earrings, and her new embroidered shawl over a loose white blouse. Daniel adds a touch of rouge, eyeliner, mascara, and lipstick. Pedro makes her a crystal ball with construction paper and crayons.

Juan becomes a pirate with a dark scarf over an eye, a kerchief around his neck, and a drawn-in mustache; it's the only makeup he'll allow, putting a damper on Daniel's creativity. Pedro has made a pirate hat with folded newspaper and a blue jay feather. They couldn't figure out how to give Juan a wooden leg or a parrot on his shoulder. It will have to do.

Pedro and Daniel are Freddie-the-Freeloaders with the secondhand clothes they get at church that are too worn and torn for regular use. Daniel attempts a Red Skelton–inspired makeup application with smears and smudges, but neither are happy with their costumes.

"Can I be a ghost?" Daniel asks.

"Mom won't let us make holes in a sheet," Pedro replies.

"Whatta 'bout a mummy?"

"How you gonna do that?"

"With toilet paper!"

"Are you kiddin'? Mom won't let you waste that much toilet paper!"

"Let's just put on more layers of clothes, and an old hat," Daniel mutters with no enthusiasm.

"And let's make more holes in the old clothes. That'll help!" Pedro adds half-heartedly.

They each get a pillowcase to hold their candy.

Mom will stay home with the infant and the toddlers. She enjoys the newness of a newborn, particularly the smell of their heads that wanes over time, but she prefers when they are *all* sound asleep.

Pop arranged to stay home this evening so he could accompany his kids as they make their neighborhood rounds.

"¡Hijos, qué ingeniosos disfraces!" Pop exclaims as the kids enter their living room. "You really did a nice job with them. I barely recognize *any* of you!"

"Thanks, Pop!" Pedro says with a beaming smile.

"I did all the makeup!" Daniel declares.

"I only have a mustache, no makeup!" Juan confirms.

"I can tell you your fortune if you want!" Sara offers.

• • •

When walking from house to house, Pedro noticed kids weren't wearing their store-bought masks because they couldn't see and couldn't breathe with them on.

"'Y, ¿tú qué eres?'" Daniel retorts in exasperation as they leave Doña María's house. "Really people, you can't tell what we are?"

"Sobre gustos no hay nada escrito," Sara declares. "I *love* my costume!" She twirls to make her skirt and shawl billow around her in a flurry of colors.

At the end of the night, it didn't matter about their costumes. They all got loads of chocolate bars, lollipops, sweets, a smattering of pennies, and an apple they won't be allowed to eat because of the news warnings.

"Who gave us apples?" Pedro asks. "Don't they know anythin'?"

"A beber y tragar, que el mundo se va a acabar," Daniel chants, stuffing a chocolate next to the ones already in his mouth.

Eat, drink, and be merry because the world is ending!

"That sounds like something a pirate might say," Juan's full mouth mumbles, as his chocolate-covered fingers adjust his pirate hat.

**Un hombre sin alegría no es bueno o no está bien.
Una manzana al día para mantener alejado al médico.**

NOVEMBER 1968

When it is said, you are not well,
It means you're sick, under a spell.

When it is said that you are good,
You are not bad, it's understood.

If you're not glad, I've heard it tell,
You are not good, or are not well.

7

SHADES IN OUR COLORS

PEDRO AND DANIEL are standing in their yard with Mom when a nice neighbor lady says Pedro is a spitting image of Pop. Pedro thought she said "splitting image," as if Pop had been split, and Pedro is a smaller piece of Pop, like a mini-Pop. Pedro likes this idea, and smiles inside — not outside where Mom might see it.

But the neighbor said "spitting image."

Spitting? Yuck! Why would it be spitting *image?* Pedro wonders. *What's spit got to do with anything?*

Then the neighbor adds, "And they're both so handsome!"

Pedro's face suddenly burns hot. There is an urgent fullness in his throat, of cotton balls, sawdust, old rags.

Mom abruptly spits out, "¡¡¡Yo tuve novios *mucho* más guapos que estos dos!!!"

Mom punches Pedro on the arm to snap him out of his stupor: he must translate her words. He coughs to dislodge the detritus and debris in his throat, looks at the oblivious woman, and says: "Mom had boyfriends who were *more*-more han'some than us!"

• • •

Pop is han'some, Pedro thinks.

When they go to the Mexican cinema in Toledo, men in the movies who look like Pop are called *moreno* or *prieto*, because their skin is darker than güeros: lighter-skinned men.

43

All kinds of men in those movies lovingly sing to their morenita or prietita. Both are terms of endearment for women with darker skin.

These aren't meant to be bad words.

Pedro thinks: *All those women are beautiful, and the men are han'some — even somma' the villains! It doesn't matter if they're moreno or güero, morena or güera!*

• • •

Pedro has learned a word can have two — or even more — meanings. It all depends on the speaker's intentions. The inflections — the accents on words in a sentence — can make a difference.

For instance, his uncle in Mexico once looked at Pedro and said to Mom with a curled-lip sneer, "¡Salió prietito!"

He came out dark!

Uncle's intention was clear, and it hit Mom and Pedro like a snake bite to the face — but for different reasons.

The way Mom looked at Pedro, he knew she was mad at him, not at her own brother who said *those two words* with venomous malice.

Salió prietito.
How can *two little words* cause so much pain?

She was mad Pedro came out prieto like Pop, not güero like her other kids. Mad she had to claim Pedro as a son.

And Tío Bigot was happy to irritate his sister, who shared his beliefs. He knew she could be easily triggered.

"Es un San Martín de Porres," she said with her own sneer, taking everyone off guard, deflecting scrutiny.

Tío Bigote, a bigot with a large, handlebar bigote mustache, was suddenly at a loss for words at the mention of the mixed-race Catholic saint from Perú who was black of skin.

When the nice neighbor lady leaves, Mom is a spitting kettle of boiling anger. Unlike other times, this tempest will not wait until the middle of the night.

Pop is tinkering with the kitchen faucet. He had not heard the neighbor outside. He is not aware there is a problem, until Mom storms in.

"¡¡¡Vete de mi casa!!!" she screams.

Get out of my house!

"¡¡¡Y llévate este renegrido contigo!!!" she snarls. She takes a startled Pedro by the arm and pushes him out the door with Pop. Then she slams the door at their irksome existence.

Renegrido is a word Pedro would never dare translate for anyone, not even Mom. You're not supposed to say the N-word *ever*; he hates it when he hears it in movies.

He hates *those two words* as much as he hates *two other words*: *maricón* and *joto*.

• • •

Pop caresses the front door, addressing it with Mom's pet names. Pedro stands next to him, head down and motionless. Pop wants to figure out what happened, how he can make it better. He apologizes to the door for whatever it is he might have done. He declares that he did not mean to upset her, that she is his love, now and always.

Pedro tries to explain to Pop what the neighbor said. He's embarrassed to repeat that they both are handsome. He doesn't understand why it was such a bad thing for the neighbor to have said it.

But Pop appears to understand. And he seems to know why Pedro has become the perfect punching bag—his surrogate double—when he's not around.

• • •

Now it's cold and dark. Pedro is hungry, and he has to pee. He's sobbing as he pounds on the door and yells, "¡¡¡Mom, te amo!!! ¡¡¡Te amo, Mom!!!"

A mucus-filled cough startles him. His sobs stop, and his vision clears.

Pedro suddenly realizes Mom has never said, "¡Te amo!"

He's never heard her say *those two words* to anyone: not to Pop, not to his siblings, and certainly, not to him.

Te amo.

How can *two little words* be so powerful?

Pedro remembers he learned those words at the Mexican cinema, mesmerized by two people showing affection toward each other like he had never seen before. He doesn't remember who they were, if they were prietos or güeros. It didn't matter.

• • •

After his siblings have gone to bed, Mom lets Pedro in, but she tells Pop to stay out. He will sleep in the car tonight. She believes he is guilty of being handsome in the eyes of a neighboring woman, which means all of the neighboring women think he's handsome, which means Mom does not deserve Pop, which is both preposterous and beside the point.

Mom sits on the sofa and holds Pedro against her bosom. She rocks him as she quietly sobs and mumbles, then cries con coraje, like after one of the bad storms when she has had Pop hauled away for being too good for her, so he should rot in a jail cell for the night.

Pedro is scared and self-conscious. He can't remember if Mom has ever held him in her arms.

Ever?

Maybe, as a child, so that's why he can't remember?

He thinks: *It would really help if she only said:*

Lo siento.

How can *two little words* heal so much pain?

He'd rather be in his bed, safe with Daniel, than in her awkward embrace. He thinks to himself:

'Es peor el remedio que la enfermedad.'
The cure is worse than the problem.

It just makes things worse.

No dejes para mañana lo que puedas hacer hoy.
En la tardanza está el peligro.
El perezoso siempre es menesteroso.

DECEMBER 1968

If you put off what's due today,
Procrastinate, and/or delay,

Then you should know, when it's tomorrow,
You will be sad, and full of sorrow!

8

LA VIRGEN DE GUADALUPE

PEDRO AND DANIEL know La Virgen de Guadalupe is the most important Mary, Mother of God for Mexicans, and for so many other Catholics around the world. She was one of the first and most famous apparitions endorsed by the Vatican as an authentic appearance of Mary, and it happened in Mexico.

Pedro and Daniel are familiar with the story of Juan Diego, an Indigenous Mexican who saw Mary on four occasions in 1531. After his fourth vision, Mary's likeness was imprinted onto his cloak. It is the well-known image of La Virgen de Guadalupe.

In the image, Mary has darker skin than most of her other portrayals in paintings and films. She looks like she could have been Nahua herself. This image, and the story, which says she spoke to Juan Diego in his native Nahuatl language, was pivotal in the conversion of so many Mexican Natives into Mexican Catholics. It surely played a role in making Mexico a country with one of the highest numbers of Catholics in the world.

• • •

Mom worked on a large banner with the image of La Virgencita for La Sociedad de la Virgen de Guadalupe. She used lots of glitter and sequins on a white satin cloth to adorn Her image. Last year, there was a schism within La Sociedad, and the previous banner went to the other faction. It is a great honor for Mom to have created this new banner for La Sociedad.

"It's so beautiful," Daniel declares. "I wanna touch it."

"Don't!" Pedro warns. "She'll sting you like a hornet!"

Daniel's large eyes expand then contract. Then he gives a sheepish grin, which Pedro returns.

"You mean Mom, *not* La Virgencita."

The boys giggle.

The glitter on the large banner was hard to apply. It didn't want to adhere. Even the slightest movement of the hanging banner produces a shower of tiny reflective colors raining down from the cloth. Then, the loose glitter clings to the static white fabric where there should be no color at all.

It would be easy to see if it had been disturbed.

"I like it too," Pedro says as his eyes roam around the banner. "It's so colorful and sparkly."

"Yeah."

"Mary is so beautiful," Pedro adds, "but I wonder how come her skin looks more like mine, not like all the other Marys we see."

Daniel looks at him with a closed-mouth, chipmunk smile, and shrugs.

There is a gold rope loop fringe along the bottom and large gold tassels on the top, falling on each side of the banner from the golden rod.

• • •

"¡Cuando vienen todos, los quiero bien portados!" Mom declares, expecting good behavior when everyone arrives tonight.

"¡Los niños deben ser vistos y no escuchados!" she adds.

Children should be seen, but not heard.

"¡Mejor no salgan de su cuarto!" she concludes.

Better yet, don't leave your room!

The children disperse to their bedrooms. Juan is sledding with friends, so Pedro and Daniel have their room to themselves without the worry of ropa tendida listening to their conversation. The boys sit on the floor with the crayons and coloring books they got at the Santa's Workshop on the courthouse lawn.

"I'm glad we have to stay in our room," Pedro states. "Those comadres always look for everythin' wrong with us."

"I know," Daniel agrees. "Someone should remind 'em:

'La mejor palabra es la que no se dice.'"
The best word is the one left unsaid.

"How do you remember so many dichos?" Pedro asks. "It's like . . . you never forget any of them!"

"I could *never* forget any of my dichos. They're a part of me!"

"I don't usually understand 'em, 'cause they're like riddles, but in Spanish."

"Dichos are like fables, but a lot shorter," Daniel notes, nodding his head in agreement with himself.

"That's true."

"Like 'The Tortoise and the Hare' is just, 'Más vale paso que dure, no trote que canse.'"

Better a pace that lasts, and not a trot that tires.

"That *is* a lot shorter than the whole story!" Pedro laughs.

• • •

The comadres of La Sociedad are dropped off in the late afternoon to prepare for the December 12 commemoration of La Virgen de Guadalupe. It's already dark outside.

51

"Do you think they brought any cookies?" Daniel asks, peering down the hallway from a slight opening of the bedroom door. "I'm so hungry."

"Me too. We only had eggs and beans today," whispers Pedro.

After a little chitchat and chisme, the women kneel in front of La Virgen to start their recitation of the rosary.

Pedro and Daniel don't know the prayers of the rosary, in English or in Spanish. Pedro has learned the basics of the Hail Mary and the Lord's Prayer in his three months of parochial school, but he believes he's mispronouncing words, and he doesn't understand others. There's a line about the "fruit of thy loom Jesus," which doesn't sound right; Pedro doubts it means Jesus' chonies.

• • •

Daniel pestered Mom when they were in Mexico last year until she finally bought him a small statue of La Virgen de Guadalupe. It usually sits on the little table next to the bed the boys share.

"She really is beautiful," Pedro murmurs to himself.

He stares at the statue in his hands as he caresses it softly.

"I know. She's like all the beautiful Mexican actresses rolled into one!"

Daniel is coloring the ornaments on a tree. Despite Pedro's efforts to show Daniel how to hold a crayon, a small yellow tip protrudes from a tight fist just below his pinkie.

"Daniel," Pedro says quietly, "do you remember that time we saw those animals on Sara's wall?"

"Yeah. I'll never forget it."

Daniel puts down his crayon, and looks at his brother.

Pedro still holds the statue. His now blurred vision sees two beautiful Mary faces.

"Do you think it was like when Juan Diego saw Mary?" Pedro asks.

The boys lock eyes for a moment.

"Kinda," Daniel replies. "I think God sent 'em to comfort us 'cause Mom 'n Pop were fightin' so bad."

Daniel's large brown eyes shift slightly; then they dart back and forth, then they stare at a spot on the wall.

"Why do you think He sent us cartoon animals . . . not Mary?"

Pedro's eyes have rimmed, and a tear escapes the dam. He hopes that Daniel has the answer. He *always* has the answers.

"I don't know. Maybe we wouldn't've gotten the same effect. Those animals made us feel good, and we forgot about Mom 'n Pop fightin'." Daniel thinks for a moment, then adds, "How do you think we would've felt if Mary, Mother of God, La Virgencita, showed up in the middle of the fight?"

A question is unexpected, unwelcome. Pedro has many questions already. He desperately wants answers, not more questions.

"I think a beautiful, carin' woman would've been wonderful," Pedro declares, perhaps a little louder than his usual soft voice.

"Don't forget, even Mary was afraid when angel Gabriel showed up at her house!"

Daniel moves in closer and puts his arm around Pedro.

"I guess you're right. . . . Still, I just wish I really knew what they were. . . . And I wish God didn't forget about us ever since then."

"Algo es algo, menos es nada," Daniel says. *'Somethin' is better than nothin'.'*

And he pulls Pedro in for a hug.

Aunque la jaula sea de oro, no deja de ser prisión.
Prefiero libertad con pobreza, que prisión con riqueza.
La libertad es un tesoro que no se compra ni con oro.

JANUARY 1969

A gilded cage of solid gold,
The jailbird's life is in its hold.

If there's a choice, then hear this plea,
Live unconstrained, content, and free!

9

WORDS IN HIS HEAD

PEDRO AND DANIEL love tortillas. They are made of either corn-meal or wheat flour, with distinctly different tastes and uses in Mexican cuisine. Sometimes they are integral for holding the meal together, as in tacos, burritos, and fajitas. Other times, they are served with meals where the tortillas are used as a sort of bread to make bite-size morsels, or to mop up the savory sauces.

Arroz con pollo, beans, and mole are common Mexican dishes. These meals — and the senses — are enhanced with the visual, tactile, olfactory, and gustatory characteristics of warm, browned tortillas served alongside. When corn tortillas are fully toasted on a griddle or fried with oil, they also add the sensation and sound of crunching to the experience.

• • •

Mom says, "Necesito huevos y tortillas."

I need eggs and tortillas.

She makes delicious flour tortillas, but she always buys corn tortillas. She's tried making them, but they don't come out right, and it's not worth the trouble. Sadly, store-bought packages of tortillas in Ohio are not like the fresh ones off the conveyor belt at the tortillerías of Mexico.

Scattered houses, fields, and woods surround Pedro and Daniel's house, located five miles from the center of their small town on Lake Erie. There is a cluster of Mexican American families in this sparse rural neighborhood. Most families speak Spanish at home, and they have a steady diet of traditional Mexican cuisine.

The Garza family runs a small store from their home. It is a relief for those who can't get to the grocery store for a convenience item.

Mom gives Pedro money and instructs, "¡Habla claro y con fuerza!"

Speak clearly and loudly!

She knows he can do neither.

"¡Yo quiero ir!" Daniel cries out.

"¡No, que vaya solo!"

Daniel frowns. He likes adventures. And he knows Pedro will struggle without his help.

Pedro repeats the words in his head so he won't forget them, and the practice helps him pronounce them better:

webos y toh-tillas
WEBOS y toh-TILLAS
¡WEBOS Y TOH-TILLAS!

Pedro walks down the road a little and takes a right after Don Roberto and Doña Hilda's house. After passing two houses, he takes a left onto the big road where cars and trucks usually race by. He is thankful he won't need to cross this road today. The Garza's house is next to the one on the corner.

Ramón Garza helps when he sees Pedro struggle with the door.

"¡Buenos días señorito! ¿Qué le puedo ofrecer este día tan hermoso?" Ramón Garza speaks clearly, and nicely. His unruly, black-and-gray eyebrows have a slightly bigger sibling sitting below his nose. The folded apron tied around his ample belly is a circus tent held up by two poles with feet.

"webos y toh-tillas," Pedro whispers, and his blurred vision searches for a spot on which to focus.

"Huevos y tortillas. Muy bien patroncito. ¿Y cuántas tortillas quisieras?"

Oh no! Did she say how many?

"uno?" Pedro asks, and he regrets it immediately.

Should I say dos?

Ramón Garza goes to the back room to retrieve the items. Pedro is left to wonder what will happen if he arrives home with the wrong quantity.

"Aquí tienes tus huevos y tortillas. Y tu cambio, señorito." Ramon Garza gives Pedro the items and his change. "¡Saludos a tu mamá!"

It is a much longer, more anxious walk home for Pedro.

Pedro thinks: *I don't know if she said how many tortillas! I kept saying those words in my head! I always have words in my head! They don't come out right, she gets mad! I don't hear everything, she gets mad! Whatever I do, she gets mad!*

Mom's watching from the doorway as Pedro approaches.

"¡¡¡¿Dónde están las otras tortillas?!!!"

Oh no! SHE DID WANT TWO!

"no tenen," he whispers, and he immediately regrets it. He wanted to say, "No tenían más"—they didn't have more—which he does not know is true. Pedro can't explain anything when Mom is yelling at him, so frantic sounds and words and phrases spill out.

And he doesn't like to lie.

Whoever said, "Honesty is the best policy," never saw Mom being Mom.

Daniel frowns. He knows Pedro's words come out funny, or in the wrong order, but he doesn't laugh at Pedro or make fun of him.

People laugh when Daniel talks, because he's funny and clever, but he knows Pedro is different.

Mom calls Ramón Garza on the telephone and says all kinds of things about Pedro. He tries not to listen to the mean words she is sharing with Ramón Garza. There is no room for those words in his head.

His head—which has two, new, throbbing lumps on the top.

Pedro's red ears burn and his full eyes spill, but Mom shoves him out the door, back to see Ramón Garza, who just got an earful of complaints about Pedro and his uselessness.

Ramón Garza greets Pedro with an open door and a big smile. He gives Pedro the tortillas, a lollipop, and a wink. "¡Que tengas un buen día, hijo!"

Have a nice day, son!

Then he playfully tousles Pedro's hair, and the tender lumps underneath don't even notice.

With eyes on the treat, and those beautiful words in his ears, Pedro blurts out, "¡Gathas!"

Pedro is mortified! He meant to say, "¡Gracias!"

This is why Pedro doesn't like to speak!

Why was he given a mouth and tongue that betray and humiliate him whenever possible?

Why can't he just be La Momia Muda all the time?

He runs out of Ramón Garza's store before the tears start.

Una onza de alegría vale más que una onza de oro.
Más vale un presente que dos después.

FEBRUARY 1969

Happiness surpasses gold,
A greater truth cannot be told!

You may observe, it might just seem,
A happy life would be my dream!

IO

PAST, PRESENT, AND FUTURE

THERE AREN'T MANY celebrations in Pedro and Daniel's house, or in their community. Though they usually allow their children to play with their neighbors, the adults try to avoid conflicts and generally keep to themselves, except when huddled around a clothesline, tending to ropa tendida, while remaining vigilant for ropa tendida.

Occasionally, someone will have a small fiesta for a baptism, a communion, a graduation. These can be understandably limited to family, padrinos, classmates. Few would question the guest list.

Larger fiestas with an exclusive guest list are generally a risky business, with long term ramifications for the host, the invited, and the delicate balance of the neighborhood. Estrella Mendoza lost her Señora status when she thought she could have a gathering with only a select few comadres, without consequences.

Estrella's husband, Señor Emiliano Mendoza, still goes drinking with the men who go out drinking. The social rules and their punishments don't apply to the men in the community.

So it is a surprise to the neighborhood when Mom announces she is having a birthday party for Pedro and that *all* the families are invited. Pedro has never had a birthday party. Everyone knows *about*

Pedro, but few have ever *met* him. To give him a first birthday party at age seven is too delicious to ignore.

The chisme starts. . . .

And it is chisme caliente. . . .

"¿Por qué invita a los gringos?"	"Why is she inviting gringos?"
"¿Por qué invita esos gringos?"	"Why is she inviting *those* gringos?"
"¿Por qué invita las sin niños?"	"Why is she inviting comadres without children?"
"¿Por qué invita a esa?"	"Why is she inviting THAT one?"
"¿O esa?"	"Or *that* one?"
"¿Sólo quiere muchos regalos?"	"Does she just want a lot of presents?"
"Y, ¿el Pedro? ¿Quiere fiesta?"	"Does Pedro even *want* a birthday party?"
"¿Conoces al Pedro?"	"Have you ever met Pedro?"
"¿Cómo es?"	"What's he like?"
"Es pequeño y delgado."	"He seems small and skinny."
"No le gustan los deportes."	"He doesn't like sports."
"Dicen que es listo."	"They say he's smart."
"Nunca lo he oído hablar."	"I've never heard him talk."
"Se habla a él mismo."	"He seems to talk to himself."
"Es reservado."	"He seems to keep to himself."
"Parece un poco raro."	"He seems odd."
"Parece un poco triste."	"He seems sad."

The comadres know there is no explaining Mom. Her capricious manner of liking or disliking something — or someone — defies explanation. They all remember the "handsome husband" incident that consumed the neighborhood for months. They've seen and heard the middle-of-the-night dramas at 1238 Dirella Street, which usually result in a visit from the authorities, or a broken windshield, as gears grind in the getaway.

But the comadres must wait, because only time will reveal Mom's true objectives in this suspicious scheme.

No one knows why Mom is having a birthday party for Pedro.

Least of all, Pedro.

"Why does she even wanna have a party for me?" Pedro asks.

"I don' know, but I kinda wanna find out," Daniel says.

"I don't! 'Cause it's weird. Somethin'll go wrong, she'll get mad, n' she'll blame me."

"Try not to worrya 'bout it Pedro. Maybe we'll have fun!"

But they both think it's unlikely.

The days leading up to Pedro's birthday are fairly uneventful.

"Siempre tranquilo antes de la tormenta," Daniel warns. "*It's always calm before the storm.*"

Pedro knows that expression; he has lived it. "Ugh, I know," he says. There are usually clues about an impending storm, but he hasn't seen any, despite his hypervigilance.

The morning of Pedro's birthday, February 14, is like most other days, but with happy birthday wishes from his siblings. Mom even gets out of bed and greets him with "Feliz cumpleaños" before the kids leave for the bus stop.

School today revolves around the festivities of the holiday. Pedro feels less conspicuous about his birthday because everyone brings in Valentine's Day cards and candy. Everyone is giving and receiving. It's an unusual occasion. Pedro feels special, but almost anonymous, at the same time. It's the epitome of a perfect birthday for Pedro.

Pedro pays close attention to the cards he gets from some of the boys in his class. Do any say, "BE MINE," "I'M YOURS," or "KISS ME"?

• • •

Pedro's birthday party will be held at his padrinos' house. His godparents have a big family room in between an open kitchen and a two-car garage, perfect for large gatherings, and for folks to avoid others when necessary. They have decorated with many-colored papel picado, and there is a donkey piñata in the garage. Mariachi and ranchera music play on the record player.

Pedro loves Mexican food, but a potluck meal, with all kinds of food at the same time, is a special treat. There is a chocolate sheet cake with pink frosting and red lettering that Doña Ignacia Perez brought; she is the go-to baker for any celebration.

Food and cake, and still nothing has happened.

What is she waitin' for? Pedro wonders, and worries.

Now it's time for presents. Pedro has never seen so many presents! And they are all for him! The attention is unusual and uncomfortable. He feels the glances and whispers all at once, and individually.

After he opens each present, he must approach each giver, thank them clearly in English or Spanish, and give them a hug . . . a hug!

"¡Recuerda dar las gracias y un abrazo a todos los que te den un regalo!"

This combination of unpleasant duties is possibly his worst nightmare.

Pedro's hands pop out and away from people at the wrists as he robotically wraps his arms around them. His hands always avoid touching others as he offers himself up for these dreadful rituals. The kissed wet lips left on his cheeks will taunt, tease, and torment him until he can scrub his face clean.

If Daniel were closer, he'd remind Pedro to take deep breaths.

At last, he has opened all the presents, and nothing bad has happened.

Pedro closes his eyes and takes a deep breath.

Then, Mom announces she has another present.

Daniel's trained ears hear faint gasps in the crowd.

If Pedro hears them, he makes a valiant effort to hide his reaction, although the right light angle might show a sudden glisten in his slightly larger eyes.

Mom's dramatic presentation of the last gift is met with stunned silence in the room. It seems even the babies know to hold their breath.

With shaking hands and trembling fingers he can't hide, Pedro opens Mom's present very carefully.

He once saw a movie with a party scene in which the gifts had to be buried in a tub full of water, just in case they had a bomb inside.

Pedro really shouldn't watch any more war movies.

But Mom's present isn't a trick, or a ticking time bomb. It's a beautiful sweater. A dark maroon cardigan with white, purple, and violet stripes, one of each color, on either side of basket-weave leather-knot buttons.

There is a collective sigh—of awe, relief, disappointment?—from the partygoers.

Later, the children hit the piñata and collect the candy.

Eventually, comadres gather their children and dishes and give their farewells. Each comadre, and an occasional compadre, glances at Pedro with difficult-to-discern expressions as they leave.

Pedro's family is last to leave, after they help his padrinos clean up and reset their home to normal.

"I can't believe nothin' happened at the party," Daniel grumbles with palms high on his hips. They're getting ready for bed. "De músico, poeta y loco, todos tenemos un poco."

We all have a bit of musician, poet, and crazy.

"I know. Isn't it wonderful!" Pedro marvels, holding his beloved new sweater. "El que mucho mal padece, con poco bien se consuela... or somethin' like that."

He who suffers much evil is comforted with just a little good.

"Wow, I'm impressed!" Daniel cheers. "And there's also, 'Cuando hay hambre, no hay pan duro.'"

When one is hungry, everything tastes good!

"Is there a dicho about being quiet you two?" Juan mumbles from under his covers.

Todo por servir se acaba.

MARCH 1969

Useful things will wear away,
Fall apart or tear and fray.

Your daily shoes will bear some holes,
Right on the bottom, on their soles!

I I

A SMORGASBORD
OF DELIGHTS

EVERYONE IN THE neighborhood, at the schools, and in the parish knows that Pedro and Daniel's family is poor. Most folks are kind, or at the very least don't have bad things to say. The family's children always appear to be bathed, wearing clean clothes, and exhibit remarkably good manners.

Some question the parents' choice to have so many children: it's an overabundance, an overindulgence.

The government sends the family cheese, butter, and dried milk in waxed brown boxes. The chunks of cheese and blocks of butter taste different than store-bought cheese slices and margarine, but the kids know better than to say anything. The reconstituted powdered milk is sour with a gritty texture; Mom mixes it with regular milk to help with the taste, but it only prolongs their exposure to this displeasure.

The Immaculate Conception School holds an Annual Smorgasbord Fundraiser in the high school cafeteria. Patrons pay a fee to attend a cafeteria-style dinner with many types of foods and some light entertainment. They bid on a silent auction, and a city councilor who serves as emcee hounds the wealthy patrons and business owners to donate to the parish and parochial school.

Today, nuns from the school have surprised the family with trays of food left over from last night's event.

There's a mixture of aromas emanating from the covered dishes in the kitchen: savory meats and sauces, buttered noodles, chocolate, vanilla, new spices the boys have not smelled before.

Mom and Pop talk with the nuns in the living room. Sister Diana is Pedro's teacher and Sister Francisca is Sara's teacher. Mom wears a happy face as they discuss Father Ambrose — the handsome new assistant priest — who is expected to join them soon!

Dr. Fritz and Father Ambrose are Mom's favorite people in the world.

She believes doctors and priests are the best people in the world.

Daniel pulls Pedro into the kitchen and whispers into his ear, "I'm so hungry. I wanna try some!" He lifts foil off trays before Pedro even replies.

"No! We have to wait till Mom says!" Pedro warns.

Daniel repeatedly bites a cookie, then a brownie, until they're gone.

"Jello!" he exclaims, and grabs a spoon. "Come on, Pedro, just have some! Aren't you hungry too?"

"Yeah. We didn't even eat today."

Pedro takes a Swedish meatball, then a spoonful of beef stroganoff. "It's so good! I wonder if we'll ever have this kind'a food again."

"La vida no es un ensayo, Pedro. You gotta enjoy life while you live it!"

There's a loud commotion in the living room when Father Ambrose appears. Mom beams, and hopes the nosy neighbors noticed his arrival. Having an unexpected honored guest must be heralded.

Pedro knows Father Durbin's young assistant priest. They alternate saying mass in the morning before the children's classes begin. They occasionally visit the classrooms. Pedro is afraid of them both because they talk with God. He would rather not come up in one of their conversations. Since Mom is always mad at Pedro, maybe God doesn't like Pedro either. He'd rather not know.

Daniel spies on Father Ambrose from the kitchen doorway. He has only seen him a few times at church. Here, in their house, Father Ambrose is wearing a black shirt, black pants, and a white collar. To some, he might look like a regular man, but of course, he's not!

"He looks so different!" Daniel says. "I didn't know they could drive cars!"

"¡Daniel! ¡Daniel, ven pa'ca!" Mom says. She has already introduced their other siblings to the priest.

"Faller Ahmbrosh, Danyel wanno be prees' when he beeg 'n growin' up," she announces.

Daniel's large eyes focus on Father Ambrose's kind, attractive face when he takes his hand.

"It is an honor to meet you, Daniel."

A few moments later, Father Ambrose spots Pedro's bodiless, floating head peering in at an angle from the kitchen doorway.

"And, I know Pedro!" Father Ambrose declares with enthusiasm.

Pedro quickly looks at Mom, ready for a reprimand.

"¡Ven y saluda!" Mom commands.

Pedro knows he must shake his hand and say, "Hello, Father Ambrose, nice to see you, sir." Mom has paid close attention to the formalities of greetings in her TV shows, and Pedro is expected to be courteous and respectful. She is *not* raising maleducados.

"I hear Pedro is a good student," Father Ambrose glances at Sister Diana. "I hope you will be a good student as well, Daniel! We're looking forward to having you at our school next year. Remember, you have to study a lot to be a doctor, and to be a priest!"

Daniel thinks, *How many times has Mom said,* "Para tonto no se estudia!"?

You don't need to study to become a fool.

El que ansioso escoge lo mejor, suele quedarse con lo peor.
Anda tu camino sin ayuda de vecino.
Más vale dar que recibir.

APRIL 1969

When it's your goal to have the best,
What might remain is all the rest.

Within your means, is what they say,
Is the best way to live each day!

I2

APRIL SHOWER
MAY FLOWER

LYING IN THE grass outside his house, Pedro is motionless, with eyes unfocused and mouth agape. The sky is perfection, a sophistication of blues, pinks, lavenders, and their complementary colors. Wisps of clouds flutter by in the afternoon breeze, bringing life to the vast impressionistic landscape painting. The clouds themselves appear to have dozens of colors and their shades, tints, and tones.

The recent rains have awakened the trees and plants. Spring has taken hold after an oppressive gray winter. Birds and insects trill, chirp, and buzz — and fly, flit, and jump in a symphony of sounds and a ballet of movements.

Pop took Mom on compras. Sara is taking care of the babies inside, Juan is out with friends, and Daniel is probably in Sara's room playing with her dolls and the pretend oven.

This bucolic setting has never been so peaceful. Pedro is always alone in a crowd. Now, he is truly alone: by himself in his own world.

Pedro's peripheral vision is on alert for any movement, vigilant for any potentially approaching car. He is ready to get up quickly and run inside if necessary.

Pedro is breaking many rules right now. Mom does *not* want her children to go outside when she's not home. Ever. She does *not* want a comadre to mention in an off-hand way that one of her children was outside ... or without shoes ... or with their hair uncombed ... or with dirt on their face ... or otherwise looking like a huérfano.

Mom would not be expected to control her rage or her actions resulting from these infractions. The consequences of her fury would not be her fault in the least. Instead, the responsibility would rest solely and unquestionably on the child who disobeyed her edicts.

This is all of it obvious to anyone who has paid attention in her household.

• • •

It's a good day to fly a kite, Pedro thinks, still lying in the grass. *If I had a kite. . . .*

The bright sunshine triggers his sneeze reflex, resulting in three forceful sneezes.

It would be nice to read under a tree, . . . if I had my book with me, and if we had a tree.

He makes grass angels.

Even if I could ride a bike, it would take me too far from the front door.

He adjusts his shirt so the sharp crab grass won't lance his tender back.

But still, it's so calm and peaceful and beautiful.

He takes a couple deeply satisfying breaths.

I don't really need anythin' else right now. . . .

His eyes close unexpectedly — for a single scary second.

He forces them open, and blinks repeatedly to sweep the sleep away.

This is wonderful. . . .

He yawns.

And peaceful. . . .

He blinks.

I could just . . .

• • •

"¡¿Y qué haces tú allí?!"

Oh no! Pedro gasps as he suddenly sits straight up. *I fell asleep!*

"¡¡¡Vente pa'ca!!!"

In a befuddled bewilderment, Pedro reluctantly wobbles toward Mom, who is coming around the car at a fast and furious pace, her face contorting between evil sneering, smirking, and demonic delight. Her familiar stance approaches with one hand reaching, the other stretching toward his beautiful sky.

She meets him with the crack of a coscorrón that stings the top of his head, sending electrical waves down the side of his face, ending in a sharp stab inside his ear.

Few people know that a quick clap on the cranium with a single knuckle affects a complex nervous system, one that serves the scalp and skull, resulting in a sudden, searing sting. The pain is a useful, natural defense mechanism that alerts its human of danger to the vital tissues just below the skull. The brain must be protected!

"¡¡¡¿Por qué estás aquí afuera, en las nubes de mierda como un malDITO MARICÓN?!!!"

She grabs him in a deliberate death grip and drags him by the elbow into the house, his little feet struggling to keep up, his toes combing the grass.

• • •

Pedro knew the risks in defying the rules — in going outside without a clear and immediate purpose. He knew there would be consequences if he were discovered. Doesn't he deserve to be punished and humiliated?

Maybe Mom was just worried someone might come and kidnap him and take him far, far away?

But wouldn't that make them *both* happy?

Maybe I shouldn't wish it so much.

Maybe that's why it hasn't come true.

• • •

"¡Dale una nalgada para que aprenda!" Mom yells at Pop, demanding he spank Pedro so he can learn his lesson.

"Eso no lo voy a hacer," Pop responds calmly, and firmly.

But nor does he defend Pedro from her.

"¡¡¡Yo siempre soy la que tiene que sufrir con este RENEGRIDO PENDEJO Y MALDITO MARICÓN!!!" she screams, reaching to take off her shoe, spit showering down on Pedro as each hateful word grows louder. The other kids flee to their rooms. Each must defend themselves as best as possible. Mom's crazed mind will soon decipher they had all been complicit in Pedro's delinquency. They must all be punished for their role, either direct or indirect.

All of her rage is now in her shoe, which has gone from her foot toward the ceiling, and in a perfect arc is now traveling swiftly downward till the tip of the stiletto finds its mark.

Few people know that scalp wounds bleed profusely because of a convoluted network of blood vessels close to the surface of the scalp's skin. Perhaps if Mom knew this amount of blood would seep out continuously, for such a long time, she would have aimed elsewhere. She should not be blamed for her ignorance of this deceitful web, invisible to her eyesight. She is not, after all, a physician.

Once the bleeding stops, Mom hands Pedro an old towel so he can clean up the mess he has made, the repulsive metallic smell of his blood threatening to add vomit to the obscenity before him.

"¡Y si alguien te pregunta, dile que te pegaste con una puerta, como el pendejo que eres!"

If someone asks, tell them you ran into a door, like the fool that you are.

Pedro has painfully learned the lesson he has heard before:

'Camarón que se duerme, se lo lleva la corriente.'
The sleepy shrimp will be swept away by the current.

So, don't fall asleep at the wheel, or in the grass.

**Contestación sin pregunta, señal de culpa.
No pidas perdón antes de ser acusado.
Excusa no pedida, la culpa manifiesta.**

MAY 1969

An answer given, before a question,
Denotes your guilt, without a question!

So hold your tongue so it won't say
Words for which your neck will pay!

13

SADNESS IN THE WOODS

PEDRO AND DANIEL noticed an imbalance in the neighborhood last night, but they couldn't go out to investigate. Kids were running from one house to the next in a reenactment of the telephone game they play at school. Each new child hearing the chisme squealed in delight, or quite possibly disgust. It was impossible to tell from Sara's bedroom window.

Now, Pedro chews his cheek, and he can't stand still when other kids arrive at the school bus stop. He wants to know what's happening!

A group of children chitchat excitedly nearby. They're talking about the woods, or touching, or fingers, or crosses.

"What are you talking about?" someone finally asks.

"THE WOODS!" the cluster calls back.

"What about the woods?" Pedro asks.

"The Woods family moved into the tiny trailer across from the Garzas!" shouts Sharon. "Those boys will be on our bus!"

The chitter-chatter resumes, but Pedro still can't comprehend the commotion. He moves in closer to get more details.

"When those boys board the bus, cross your fingers!" Steve states.

"Don't let them look at you!" David declares.

"Don't let them touch you!" Sam says.

"What happens if they touch you?" Pedro asks.

"YOU'LL CATCH COOTIES!" the crowd cries.

Pedro has heard of cooties. The teachers at school say cooties aren't real, but someone usually has cooties at recess, and you're supposed to avoid them. Pedro always reads a classroom picture book at recess, so he hasn't paid attention to this make-believe bother.

The school bus arrives. Pedro, Juan, Sara, and the other kids climb aboard. They plant themselves in their previously planned places throughout the bus.

At the next stop, two boys get on, and the other kids snicker.

Matt Woods is in third grade. Mark Woods is in fourth grade. Pedro has seen kids pointing at them in the playground at school. They look a lot like Pedro's cousins—on Pop's side.

The Woods family is Native American, or American Indian. They have lived in this town for a few years. Their only known history is that no one has bothered to talk with them, to be kind to them, to welcome them.

Pedro isn't fully aware that his relatives here and in Mexico are descended from the Indigenous Peoples of Mexico, but he's always been drawn to them. They have darker skin, like Pedro and Pop. They have a similar brow, eyes, nose, mouth, hair, . . . all of it.

Pedro is an Indigenous Mexican American.

And few have bothered to care about Pedro either.

Pedro's chest pounds with pride. His head, in which he lives, speaks to him now in a loud and clear voice:

> *They may be blood brothers. But,*
> *We are each a son to one Mother, Earth.*
> *We are fractions of a familiar family.*
> *Of Father Sun, and Sister Moon.*
> *Why must new, or different, cause chaos?*
> *Matt and Mark don't speak, don't smile, don't play, don't laugh.*
> *They are sad. . . .*

They are kids. . . .
Like me!

If only the voice in his head were the voice in his mouth. . . .

• • •

Pedro always sits in the front seat of the bus, so he can look out the big front window. The other kids say it's strange to sit in the front seat where the bus driver can keep his eyes on you. Pedro doesn't care what others think; he gets enough of that at home.

Now, Matt and Mark stand at the front of the bus, with bare benches further back. They are aware they are unwelcome. This kind of cold reception on a bus, or at a school, is all they have known.

Pedro grabs the safety bar in front of him, his hands now visible to everyone behind him.

"Pedro, cross your fingers!" Yolanda yells from behind him.

"No!" Pedro cries back. "I don't *need* to!"

Mark's eyebrows twitch, his eyes glancing at Pedro's hands.

Pedro looks at these two boys. They're wearing familiar, ill-fitting, gray clothes. Their hair looks like Mom had them squirming under her buzzer, with nick marks on their necks like those on his. In a group photo, they could be his brothers or cousins.

"Do you wanna sit down?" Pedro asks.

"Um . . . okay, thanks," Matt replies softly, looking unsure. Then he adds, as he sits next to Pedro, "Yeah, thanks a lot!"

Mark's eyes dart back and forth between Pedro and the empty space on the bench. He chews the side of his bottom lip.

"Yes, thanks," Mark says, and Pedro is almost sure he sees Mark smile as he sits in his seat.

There is space to spare for three boys on the bench.

Hay que aprender a perder antes de saber jugar.
Nada arriesgado, nada ganado.
No da el que puede, sino el que quiere.

JUNE 1969

Learn how to lose, then learn to play.
Put on display a sportsman's way.

No fortune if you have not trained.
Nothing ventured, nothing gained.

14

OUT OF THE SHADOWS

PEDRO AND DANIEL hide in their room as much as possible.

When Mom naps in the next room, they have to be particularly quiet. Why did fate place their bed against the common wall?

"Would it be worse," Pedro whispers, "if we woke Mom, or one of the babies?"

"When one of the babies wakes up, Mom will too, and that would be the worst-case scenario!"

"You're right. . . . If we play on the bed, we might hit the wall. Let's play on the floor."

"Fuera de vista, fuera de mente," Daniel grumbles.

Out of sight, out of mind.

Pedro brings books home from the school library. They read them quietly; they sound out words they don't know yet, and whisper them into each other's ears.

"I'm hungry," Pedro says after a while.

"I'm always hungry. We didn't eat since this mornin'."

The boys use their own sign language and code words so their siblings won't know what they're talking about. Although tattling on your sibling isn't nice, there are rewards. A tattling tattler with chisme caliente will become Mom's favorite child. At least for a little while, they can breathe freely and relaxed.

"'Hay ropa tendida,'" Daniel notes, "means the walls have ears, which means we have to be careful with what we're sayin'."

"But if we say, 'hay ropa tendida,'" Pedro responds, "won't they know we know they're listenin', so they can run to Mom with their chisme?"

"Yeah. Maybe if we just say 'ropa' to each other, we'll know we need to talka 'bout somethin' else. Just change the topic."

"Okay. And don't forget to use Mom's codename when we're talkin' 'bout her!"

When Juan comes back from the bathroom, Daniel mouths the word *ropa*. Pedro smiles inwardly.

After a while, the boys hear Mom get up and turn on the TV.

"I'm hungry, and I wanna watch TV," Daniel moans into Pedro's ear.

"I know, me too. What do you wanna watch first?" Pedro asks, to distract him.

"I wanna watch cartoons. Prob'ly Bugs Bunny or Tom and Jerry."

Bugs Bunny has a rapid-fire and sarcastic wit. He has a propensity for mischief. He enjoys dressing in women's clothes.

"I love when Bugs Bunny dresses like a girl," Pedro says. "And Elmer always falls in love with him."

"I know! His red lipstick and big chichis are funny," Daniel chuckles. "Even Fred and Barney sometimes dress like girls!"

"And Bob Hope and Milton Berle," Pedro adds. "The best is when they have beards 'n mustaches 'n makeup. They look like they're havin' so much fun!"

Daniel quickly turns to look at his brother and gives a wide, missing-teeth smile.

Every afternoon, the family watches *Dark Shadows*, which starts soon after the kids arrive from school. It's a soap opera unlike any other: a gothic story with witches, warlocks, werewolves, and vampires. It is both terrific and inappropriate for young children.

"I really like *Dark Shadows*," Pedro says. "I feel sorry for Barnabas Collins, even though he's scary when he's a vampire."

"Angelique is my favorite," Daniel notes. "Don't mess with that gorgeous witch!"

'No hay furia como la de una mujer despreciada.'
There is no fury like a woman scorned.

"That's for sure! I feel sorry for Quentin the most," Pedro adds.

Barnabas Collins is an odd, brooding gentleman, when he's not in vampire mode. Angelique is a beauty with a remarkable fury, who cursed Barnabas because her love for him was unrequited. Quentin Collins has handsome facial features like those of the blue-eyed boyfriend in Sara's room, but he has an unfortunate werewolf curse.

"I like the props they use, like the voodoo dolls, the crystal ball, and the ring that flips open to unload its poison in a cuppa' wine," Daniel says.

It is the comeuppance and the immurement of Reverend Trask that has the most immediate and chilling effect on Pedro. Buried alive behind a brick wall in the cellar of the old mansion, he is consigned to eternal darkness.

"I've had so many bad dreams about Reverend Trask," Pedro murmurs.

"I know," Daniel agrees. "But I think he got what he deserved. Can you imagine being buried alive?"

"Kinda," Pedro notes quietly. "That's why I keep havin' bad dreams."

Barnabas Collins, with his Benito Juárez hair, is a tortured and tormented anti-hero, hiding a secret—a great shame—in plain sight. He is cursed to never be loved, for those who would love him have been destined to die. He will never come out of the shadows that oppress him.

These themes, day after day . . . for weeks, months and years . . . are what plague Pedro's sleep.

Las deudas viejas no se pagan, y las nuevas se dejan envejecer.
Gasta con tu dinero, no con el del banquero.
Más lejos ven los sesos que los ojos.

JULY 1969

It is a fool whose debts aren't paid,
And, to the wise, new debts are made.

Spend only funds that are your own,
And not the cash a bank would loan.

15

LESSONS IN THE FIELDS

FOR WEEKS, PEDRO and Daniel's family has been picking tomatoes in the fields of neighboring Ohio towns.

Pop gently rubs the boys' chests every morning until the aroma of freshly made flour tortillas tickles their noses and flutters their eyelids. They must be on the field when the sun is rising. They will stay until after sunset. It is essential to take advantage of all sunlight, to pick as many tomatoes as possible. Even dawn-light and dusk-light are precious moments.

> 'El que madruga coge la oruga.'
> *The early bird catches the worm.*

A neighbor takes the babies while the family is working in the fields.

Pop leaves Mom and his children next to a group of workers standing around a big tractor on a large tomato field. There are no visible buildings anywhere.

Then, Pop drives to his factory job.

Red dots ornament the green field under the blue sky.

El Patrón gives them baskets — or canastas — at the start of each day, then he leaves. Pedro already yearns for his return, which will signal the end of the day, when they can stop picking tomatoes and go home.

Pedro always wishes the days away, hoping for a better tomorrow.

He hopes someday he will be happy, and he won't want to wish his days away, and he'll want time to stand still so he can savor every moment.

Mom wants everyone to carry canastas to the field so they won't waste time coming back for more.

"Pedro, can you help me?" Daniel pleads, but his brother is struggling with his own canastas.

Mom is always watching them. . . .

"¡Ese no! ¡Es muy verde!"	*Not that one, it's too green!*
"¡Ese no! ¡Es muy chiquito!"	*Not that one, it's too small!*
"¡Los grandes para llenar la canasta rápido!"	*The bigger ones, to fill the basket faster!*

Mom will be paid for each canasta llena con tomates.

Tractors bring empty canastas, then take others away, llenas con tomates.

"¡Ya deja esa canasta! ¡Está llena!"	*Leave that basket, it's full!*
"¡Comienza otra!"	*Start another!*

Pedro savors the salty sweat dripping into his open mouth. It's perfect for the sweet cherry tomato he secretly pops in.

He imagines his classmates on summer vacation, playing on columpios, having una fiesta with ice cream and pastel, or reading un libro under un árbol.

He imagines he is a piston on a train as he bobs up and down, arriba y abajo, to pick cada tomate.

He imagines a day when he won't need to pick tantos tomates.

In the humid heat, Pedro and Daniel swat las moscas. They won't stop buzzing!

"¡Ya deja!"   *Stop!*

Sara and Juan are focused on their work. Mom doesn't have to yell at them.

At lunchtime, Pedro's family huddles together to eat tortillas con papas con blanquillos. It's cold in the foil, but still un favorito! The only thing missing is ketchup. It might sound odd, but the combination of flavors is delicious.

The agua they brought in mason jars is warm in the sun and doesn't quench their thirst.

· · ·

Las otras familias working the fields live in their cars. Many don't have a home anywhere. They travel all over the country, throughout the year, to pick fruits and vegetables. They have been in Ohio a few semanas. Mom has talked with them, but mostly she wants everyone to keep to themselves, to pick tomatoes. There is no time for lazy loitering or chitchatting.

Pedro thinks of his cama.

He shares it with Daniel, but it's comfortable!

Where do those families sleep?

Pedro thinks of his baño.

In the field, they walk past the plants to pee, but there is nowhere to hide!

Where do they poop?
Where do they bathe?

Pedro thinks of his cocina.

Mom makes tamales, mole, and arroz con pollo.

Where is their food?
How do they cook?
What do they eat?

It's not unusual for Pedro to have so many questions, or for him to get no answers. These questions are about people who have so much less than he. Pedro has never felt fortunate, and he doesn't know how to process this new sensation, these new emotions.

. . .

Pedro has met some of these families. There are boys and girls his age. He wonders if they go to school, but he's afraid to ask.

Pedro notices these families *seem* happy. They talk and laugh all day—even the boys that look a lot like him!

Sometimes he wishes he lived with them, in their cars—with no beds, no bathroom, no kitchen.

He thinks Mom would be happy if he stayed to live with them. But he doesn't think Mom would let Daniel stay with him too.

. . .

Pedro and Daniel were recently careless around treacherous ropa tendida, and suffered painful reminders to be secretive and protective at all times. Now, they talk about running away in whispered conversations.

They think they should run away after Mom brings home a lot of food she bought on sale. They have memorized their lists and plans; nothing can be in writing. They would take a bag of bread, some bologna, and corn chips. Sometimes Mom buys the small pies Daniel loves so much. Clothes and other supplies would be minimal.

They know hitchhiking is hazardous, but sometimes, in the movies, a nice man and woman stop and take the kids to their home and adopt them and send them to a nice school.

Couldn't it happen to Pedro and Daniel?

Pedro wants to keep going to school. He wants to learn everything in the world. He doesn't want to stay with anyone if he can't go to school.

. . .

There's no time to rest or daydream, after eating. They all need to get back to llenando canastas.

"¡Comienza otra!"   *Start another!*
"¡Ándale, con energía!"   *Come on, with energy!*

The ripe tomatoes Pedro picks are sweet and juicy, and a deep red unlike those at the store. The peppery perfume of plantas de tomate tickles his nostrils.

¡Yay, Pop está aquí!   *Yay, Pop is here!*

Pop gets to work without delay. He takes Mom's focus away from Pedro and Daniel.

In the dank dusk, Pedro and Daniel swat los mosquitos. They won't stop biting!

"¡Ya deja!"   *Stop!*

There is an excitement, a rush, an anticipation, in the air.

¡Yay, El Patrón está aquí!   *Yay, the boss is here!*

With the boss back, it's time to go home!
Almost.
Mom has them urgently filling más canastas.
It is the sprint after a marathon!
Mom has brought a flashlight so they can work in the dark, pero El Patrón wants to pay her so he can go back to his casa.

"Donde hay patrón, no manda otro," Daniel says quietly to Pedro.

Where there's a boss, no one else commands.

"Nadie puede servir a dos," Pedro responds.

No one can serve two masters.

There will be little rest before they return for another full day in the fields.

El pendejo no tiene dudas ni temores.
Sabe el precio de todo y el valor de nada.
Mal piensa el que piensa que otro no piensa.

AUGUST 1969

Fools who do not know a thing
Will neither doubt, nor fear a thing.

They know the price of everything,
And, the value of not one thing.

16

FISH IN THE RIVER

PEDRO AND DANIEL'S small town has a public park where the river feeds into Lake Erie. Large granite blocks are unevenly placed along the edge of the river and lake. After a heavy storm, the water rises and the entire park becomes an extension of the lake. At those times, there is no distinction between lake, river, or land: trees, street lights, basketball hoops, trash cans, and picnic tables jut up out of the water in odd arrangements.

It's a treat for Pop when Mom agrees to fill the station wagon with kids and tackle. It's not often he gets to go fishing. For her part, Mom looks forward to catfish, lightly breaded and fried.

Pedro and Daniel don't like fishing, but they don't have a choice. It's what boys are expected to do under Mom's roof.

From the back seat, all Pedro can see is water as his family drives toward the parking area. There are no barriers along the river's edge. He holds his breath, knowing they could easily swerve and plunge into the deep river.

No one knows how to swim, so a sudden plummet would be their certain death.

The worst part of fishing is definitely the bugs. During the day, flies are everywhere, and on everything.

At dusk, mosquitoes are all over them, especially Pedro and Daniel.

Tonight, mosquitoes are out in mesmerizing, murmuring clouds, swarming around one boy, then the other, then back to the first. Daniel has a bad reaction to mosquito bites. On this sweltering evening, a loose tank top offers no protection. He scratches until he is covered in open sores.

"Stop, before she sees you!" Pedro whispers in a rush.

"I can't help it! They itch so much Pedro!"

Pop and Juan are already fishing.

Mom holds the baby, and fans herself with a Mexican hand fan that has the depiction of Juan Diego kneeling before La Virgencita.

Their sisters play nearby.

"Pop, ¿pon el lumbri?" Pedro quietly asks Pop. He means la lombriz.

Mom yells, "¡¡¡Deja que lo hagan ellos mismos!!! ¡¡¡Esos dos nunca aprenderán!!!"

Let them do it themselves! Those two will never learn!

But Pop hooks the worm, gives Pedro his pole with a smile and a wink, and for that split second, Pedro wishes he liked fishing. A friendly smile is the key to his heart.

When they've been caught and reeled in, Pedro and Daniel fear the flopping fish. Pedro wants to grab them and toss them back into the river—if he only had the nerve to touch them. The boys hate what happens next even more. It's barbaric, but Mom makes them watch. They fight back tears. They feel an unexplainable connection with these defenseless, dying fish from the river.

Mom says boys are supposed to be strong. They're supposed to like fishing, and sports! She spits out:

"¡Pero estos dos son distintos!"
But these two are different!

Pedro sits with his pole as far as he can from the river's edge. He prays for a magical tug on his bobber which will announce he has finally caught a fish for her. He prays that the fish will get loose before it's hauled out of the water, even if he'd be blamed for his weakness and incompetence.

Daniel has long abandoned his pole. He sings to himself, absent-mindedly swatting mosquitoes along the river's edge.

And, in an instant, he is gone.

There is screaming and chaos and confusion.

It happens so fast.

And

so

slow.

Pedro knows something is wrong.

He starts to cry.

Panic sets in.

His vision blurs.

Nausea arrives.

Suddenly, Daniel is lying at the river's edge, drenched, coughing, spurting water from his spout. Juan was able to grab Daniel when he miraculously came to the surface for air, and Pop pulled him out of the river.

Daniel stands, still drenched and dripping. He shakes and coughs. His hoarse voice cries out in panic before his imminent, inexorable, ironic reprimand.

"¡¡¡Estaba mirando peces en el río!!!"

I was looking at fish in the river!

There is:

Delirium and disbelief,

Reality and relief,

Exhilaration and exhaustion.

Without respite, Mom scolds everyone in an irregular, syncopated rant of words and breaths and gasps.

They pack up in sullen silence.

• • •

All are saturnine in the station wagon.

Pedro holds Daniel's hand in the back seat. Pedro can't clearly comprehend that he almost lost him; that Pedro would have been alone in this world, if Daniel had not been safely returned.

Daniel's large eyes stare forward, unblinking. His lower lip twitches, slightly, slowly, like a fish in its final moments out of the river.

They are in their bed that night when Mom comes in with blessed palms from church.

She whispers prayers, and uses the palms to sweep away los malos espíritus. Pedro has seen Mom's aunts do this in Mexico. The people there say her aunts are brujas, practicing their craft, but Pedro wonders why they pray to God and Jesus Christ and Mother Mary if they are brujas. Maybe he doesn't know what bruja really means. Maybe it's not the same as a witch in Ohio, America.

Mom starts at their chests, and sweeps down their arms toward their fingers, and down their legs toward their toes. Her eyes aren't closed in prayer, but rather stare at a button on Daniel's pajamas. The incantations escaping her lips are barely perceptible.

Her entire being is different from the Mom that Pedro and Daniel have always known.

Who is this kind, gentle, and loving Mom?

For a brief moment, Pedro feels safe from all the evils in the world.

He wonders if it's true that,

'El tiempo lo cura todo.'
Time heals everything.

Part 2

1969–1974

17

HOME
Daniel – 5

WHEN PEDRO COMES home from kindergarten, the first thing I wanna know is what he had for snacks and for lunch, and did he bring me anythin' 'cause I'm always so hungry.

Mom said to be quiet 'cause Lola and the baby are asleep. Now Mom is sleeping too. She always sleeps most of the day, and I get so bored. She says, "Eres como un elefante en una cacharrería,"'cause I can't sit still or be quiet.

I'm in here with Juan's cars and trucks you're supposed to crash into each other. His toy soldiers don't have arms or legs that move; I can't put clothes on 'em; they don't have hair to brush; I can't pretend to put lipstick on them.

Or can I?

Mom says it's a good thing she can't hear when I roll my eyes, when I have somethin' naughty to say—somethin' I have to hold in—and the words slip out of my eyes instead.

• • •

Here in Ohio, America, kids hear about Snow White and Cinderella. When we go to Mexico, we hear about La Lechuza, a witch that turns into an owl, or La Llorona, a lady who's lookin' for her dead children, but she'll take you instead if she finds you first, so go to sleep.

You don't get kids to fall asleep by tellin' 'em some scary ghost lady or witch owl is comin' to get you.

· · ·

Sara says I'm sarcastic. But who asked her? She's learnin' big words in fourth grade. She says I'm precocious, but I think she means I'm precious, and I agree!

Three rooms for Mom, Pop, Sara, Juan, Pedro, me, Lola, and the baby. Juan says, "Do the math." I think I know what it means, but I won't be in kindergarten 'til next year and I can't do the math yet. I wonder why Pedro hasn't taught me the math. He's teaching me everything else.

Mom finally got up 'cause the baby is cryin'. She smells so good. The baby, not Mom.

Mom smells nice when she puts on perfume for a baile with Pop. She gets in a good mood when she's goin' out to dance. I love to watch her put on makeup, especially lipstick. She bites on tissue with her lips, and leaves a buncha kiss marks that smell so good when I take 'em out of the trash can when she leaves.

If I kiss the tissue the exact same way, I can get some lipstick on my lips.

Pop uses Brilliantine in his hair. I love the smell. When I use it, Mom says I look like Benito Juárez. He was a president in Mexico. He looks like a vampire on the peso dollar bill, so I don't like when she says I look like Benito Juárez.

· · ·

Pedro got stuck on the bus today! The bus driver finished his route and went to drop off his bus. He was real mad 'cause Pedro was still on the bus. When he got home, Mom said, "¡¿Cómo puedes ser tan pendejo?!" and gave him a coscorrón on the top of his head. She used the spoon she was using to cook.

"Mom told me not to get off at the bus stop. She told me to wait 'til he makes a loop and comes closer to the house," Pedro says between hiccups. He always gets hiccups when he's been cryin' a lot.

"Today," Pedro continues, "the bus driver said, 'Everybody who lives nearby should get out here, 'cause I'm not gonna make the loop.' I didn't know what to do. If Mom saw me comin' from the bus stop, she'd get so mad. You know I can't esplain anythin' to her."

"I know."

"The bus driver even looked at me and said, 'Shouldn't you be gettin' off here?' And, I said, 'No sir.'"

"You're always so polite."

"So I stayed on the bus. All the way to the big garage where they put the buses. I was so scared. I had to tell the big boss where I live so he could bring me home. Now everybody's mad at me!"

Poor Pedro!

I say to him, "Pedro,

'A palabras necias, oídos sordos.'"
Let foolish words fall on deaf ears.

And he smiles a little through his tears.

18

CHONIES
Pedro – 6

"I NEVER LIKE how Santa treats Rudolph," I whisper into Daniel's ear. "Right up 'til Santa knows he can use Rudolph, 'specially his nose, Santa is mean to Rudolph."

"Santa wants Rudolph to hide his nose, so it's not blinkin' and makin' noises," Daniel whispers back.

"But why does it bother Santa? It's not something Rudolph can help. It's not something Rudolph should hide."

"Who knows, but I think Santa's more naughty than nice."

We both giggle, and Sara shushes us.

I'm so glad Mom and Pop went to a Sociedad de la Virgen meeting. Sara and Juan are on the couch with the babies. Me and Daniel are on the floor, on our sides, so we can look at the TV and each other at the same time.

• • •

Christmas is in two days, and Daniel is lookin' for our presents. I'm sittin' on our bed coloring on a paper bag.

Daniel runs in, and he almost hits the bed!

"Come on Pedro! Mom and Pop went on compras with the babies," he urges, almost out of breath. He has the crazy look of a travieso.

"No, I don' wanna get in trouble. . . . Mom always yells at me, not you." This is the real truth. Mom says she yells at me 'cause I'm older, and I should know better.

I do know better, but it's not 'cause I'm older.

"Just come on! Sara is in her room, and Juan is outside. . . . No one will ever know! ¡Con la honra no se pone la olla!"

"Daniel, what does that even mean?"

He moves my crayons and drawin' away. He takes me by the hand and drags me into Mom and Pop's room.

I have to be careful not to step on somethin' that'll break.

"I found a bag under the crib!" Daniel exclaims. He's so excited as he starts to dig through, then he's not. "But it looks like we're all getting chonies," he grumbles.

Kids only talk about chonies to laugh at somebody. They say they're dirty or yellow or smelly. I won't tell anyone at kinnergarden I got chonies for Christmas.

Daniel tosses them aside. He takes out some dresses for the girls and puts them aside too.

There are three things left in the bag, and he takes them out one at a time.

A transistor radio, a Jesus-on-the-cross, a baseball glove.
A transistor radio, a Jesus-on-the-cross, a baseball glove.
A transistor radio, a Jesus-on-the-cross, a baseball glove.

Juan loves baseball. He knows all the teams. He knows the players, and their stats: he says it's importan' information that tells you how good they are.

Juan already has a new baseball glove. Me and Daniel laughed so hard when Juan got the funny chonies with no cloth for his butt — just two strings! I couldn't figure them out, but Daniel knew what they were right away.

Then Daniel put them on his head, like the bonnets we saw in *Oklahoma!* with the strings coming down on each side, and Juan got so mad. I think he was embarrassed. Good thing they were still new! Why don' they wanna cover their nalgies with those chonies? I don' get it.

Daniel has been begging for a Jesus-on-the-cross. He wants to put it on the little table in our room, next to his Virgen de Guadalupe, and the saint that loves all the animals.

This only means one thing about those presents in the bag on the floor under the crib.

My eyes sting and water.

I feel like the heat is on real high.

Drums are beatin' in my ears.

I thinka 'bout Christmas mornin'. I 'magine myself, and Mom looking right at me the whole time, when I open my present. I'm gonna have to lie. I'm gonna have to pretend I like my new baseball glove. And my chonies.

Daniel is holding his Jesus-on-the-cross. He's touchin' Jesus' head, his belly, his hands, and his feet: everywhere He's bleedin' from the thorns on his head, the nails, and the hole the soldiers made with the spear 'cause he wasn' dyin' quick enough.

Daniel is coverin' Jesus' chonies with his thumb, so Jesus almost looks naked.

I'm glad Daniel is gonna get what he wants.

● ● ●

We're watching a scary movie at the Mexican cinema about mummies that came back from the dead, and a man behind us just yelled out: "¡Mordí mis chones!"

"What does that mean?" I ask Daniel, who is laughing with everyone else.

"It means he bit his chonies with his nalgies 'cause he was scared!" he says. Then he suddenly stands up and squeezes his butt cheeks together.

Now I know why everybody laughed so hard, and I wanna laugh too . . . but Mom shushes us to be quiet.

19

CHISME
Daniel – 6

MRS. WALKER REMEMBERS WHEN I came to school with Pedro last year for show and tell. On my first day, she said, "How could I ever forget you and Pedro!" Now she keeps sayin' things like, "Daniel, can you be a little quieter? . . . You know, like Pedro?"

She just said to me: "How is my Pedro? I miss him."

I don't think she would like it if I said:

> 'La ausencia hace crecer el cariño.'
> *Absence makes the heart grow fonder.*

I love Pedro, but I can't be quiet like him. Even if I really try — which I don't even wanna try — I can't be quiet like him.

I've got big eyes and big ears, and I guess I have a big mouth.

It reminds me of:

> 'Dos oídos, pero una boca. Escucha más y habla menos.'
> *Two ears, but one mouth. Listen more and talk less.*

Then, I think: *I have two ears and TWO LIPS!*

I like Mrs. Walker. She's nice, and she's pretty. I would help her with her outfits if she would only ask me. I would suggest a little makeup sometimes. And definitely dangly earrings. Until then,

'Guardo la ayuda para quien me lo pida.'
I'll keep my advice for those who ask.

I don't like playin' with the boys. They wanna crash everythin' into each other at high speeds so they can yell out "Kapow!" or "Kaboom!" or some other words they saw on the Saturday mornin' cartoons. Or they wanna throw balls at you so you can catch 'em, and throw 'em back. Back and forth. It's hard to believe they really like doin' that.

I don't like playin' with the girls either. Some of them want to kiss me or hold my hand. I don't even know why. Mary Beth cried when I said, "I don't even like you!" What I really meant was "I don't even like you 'like that,'" but it's too late to say anythin'.

Why did *I* get in trouble 'cause I didn't want Mary Beth to kiss me?

I like to play with the pretend kitchen that has a fridgerator, stove, sink, and cabinets for the food and dishes. I'm making dinner for my guests, like Samantha Stephens on *Bewitched* or Laura Petrie on the *Dick Van Dyke Show*.

"I know they're not real dinner guests," I say to the crowd around me. "I'm just pretendin' to have a dinner party."

"Why would you *pretend* to make dinner for *pretend people*?" one boy asks, and the rest agree. They're hopeless.

I know Mrs. Torres's gold rimmed teeth will tell Mom what I do here. I don't think she knows,

'En bocas cerradas no entran moscas.'
Flies can't enter a closed mouth.

Mom will get mad at me. She'll be embarrassed 'cause one of her comadres saw me doin' girly stuff. Then Mrs. Torres's gold-rimmed teeth will mention it to all the other comadres in the world.

'No hay fuego más ardiente que la lengua del maldiciente.'
There is no hotter flame than the tongue of a gossip.

I think that's where "chisme caliente" came from.

Mom knows beatin' me again won't be worth the effort 'cause I'll keep doing it anyway.

'Quien comenta, inventa.'
Where there is gossip, there are lies.

I guess I like chisme, when it's about other people.

Why does talkin' about other people feel good, but in a bad way?

It's like chocolate, when you know you shouldn't have another, and another, and another, 'til there's no more, and all you want is more chocolate. What you had wasn't enough. You want more and more. But I don't think chisme can make you grow a big fat belly and then give your big fat belly a bellyache like chocolate can.

. . .

Last year, when Pedro took food home to me, he was always nervous and afraid that he would get caught, and get in trouble, because all the walls have eyes *and* ears.

Our mean tío in Mexico calls Pedro the "paniquito chiquito gatito blaquito," which sounds funny, but it's not. It means something like *little black scaredy cat*. He made up blaquito just for Pedro. Tío calls Pedro *blaqui* in a mean way, 'cause he's darker, and Pedro cries so much in a corner so no one can see him. Mean Tío just laughs and laughs.

. . .

Next year, I'll finally be in the same school as Pedro.

When Mrs. Walker asks me to skip to see if I'm ready for first grade, I'll skip around the whole school! I'll even skip all the way home! 'Cause nothin's gonna keep me from goin' to Immaculate Conception next year!

20

COLUMPIOS
Pedro – 7

ME AND DANIEL have been hanging from the columpios in our backyard for a long time. Mom says it will make us grow. My hands get sweaty, and I keep falling down.

"El que se fue a Sevilla perdió su silla," Daniel chants, still hanging on.

"El que se fue a Torreón perdió su sillón," I respond. It's a silly dicho about losing your place, or your seat.

I think we should hang from our feet to make our legs longer. But I won't tell Mom. I won't tell Daniel either, 'cause he'll prob'ly tell her accidentally.

Daniel sometimes tells Mom stuff 'cause he just can't help it. Then she gets crazy new ideas, or she gets mad at me. So, I have to be careful not to tell Daniel everythin' I keep in my head.

But sometimes I forget 'cause he's the only one I really talk to.

"It's the comadres' fault we're hangin' from columpios," Daniel grumbles. "They're always tellin' Mom we're skinny and small."

"They're not really lyin'," I think aloud.

"Those comadres 'les gusta lo ajeno más por ajeno que por bueno,'" Daniel continues.

"What? Say it slower!"

"Basically, the grass is always greener. They want Mom to want what she doesn't have 'cause Mom doesn't have what she wants."

"Which is what? Wait. . . . You're makin' me dizzy with your words."

"Mom wants tall, muscular sons."

"Yeah, I don't think that's ever gonna happen."

"Mom wants us to play sports so the comadres can stop asking why we don't play sports," Daniel adds. "And she wants us to be the star quarterback or the star pitcher so she can really 'show those comadres' a thing or two."

I think I'm gonna have long columpio arms. It won't make me taller or stronger, but I will reach things on the top shelves. Maybe that will make Mom happy.

• • •

I wish I was a superhero. I would fly away.

Or, I wish a superhero liked me. Then I would have a friend. They could take me far, far away. And Daniel, too. I wish my wishes would come true. Like in all those books and movies. Cinderella and Snow White and Sleeping Beauty have handsome princes that rescue 'em. And all the superheroes always save their girlfriends.

Can boys get handsome princes and superheroes to rescue 'em, too?

• • •

Mom gives us medicine to make us grow. It tastes like fish and liver and boiled cabbage all at the same time!

The comadres told Mom we prob'ly don't grow 'cause we got worms. So Mom gives us gross medicine for worms too. One of her comadres makes an awful syrup from a recipe she got from a curandera in Mexico. I think she uses dirty socks in her recipe. Maybe even dirty chonies, but I don't wanna thinka 'bout it.

"Consejo no pedido da el entrometido," Daniel says. "*The busybody gives unrequested advice.* And this advice tastes gross."

Mom also gives us iron so we don't get anemia 'cause the comadres told her worms cause anemia. That medicine tastes like somebody scraped a buncha rust off an old bike, put it in water with a tiny bit of sugar, then boiled it all together for ten hours.

I'm not sure how I know the taste of rust, but I think of well water in a clay cup sitting in Mamá's magical maze.

"Lo que no mata, engorda," Mom claims.

What doesn't kill you makes you fatter.

I don't like that killing us is one of only two choices.

"'De mal el menos,' and 'El mejor no vale nada,'" Daniel whispers into my ear.

The lesser of two evils.
The best choice isn't good.

"I don't even know what that means," I respond quietly.

Auntie Em told the Scarecrow or the Tin Man—or was it the Cowardly Lion?—to feed the pigs before they worried themselves into anemia.

If I get anemia, it's prob'ly 'cause I worry a lot.

• • •

"Please try to be a Catholic," I tell our friend Oscar who lives around the corner on the main road. His parents are my padrinos. I don't know how they can be my godparents if they aren't Catholic.

Sister Josephine said everyone who isn't Catholic won't go to heaven when they die. I don't like that *H - E - double hockey sticks* is the only other choice.

"Oscar, I don't want you to go to that other place!"

Oscar and his parents are taking me and Daniel to the drive-in to watch the new Disney movie. My padrinos ask if we wanna play on the columpios under the screen 'til the movie starts. Daniel and I politely say, "No, gracias," at the same time. Jinx!

Instead, they take us to the confession stan' and buy us ice cream samwiches, and now I have a new favorite thing in the world.

113

21

DULCE
Daniel – 7

JESUS ON THE cross over Father Durbin's head looks so sad. And, so handsome. I don't know if I can think he's handsome, 'cause I'm a boy and boys aren't supposed to say other boys are handsome. I'm not allowed to say it, but can I think it?

Jesus is almost naked, except for the funny chonies they used back then. They look uncomfortable and complicated to put on and take off.

I don't think Jesus peed and pooped, 'cause he was God too. I think God prob'ly used magic so Jesus didn't have to pee and poop.

I can't wait to talk to Jesus when I'm a priest. We'll probably talk about world peace. The Miss America girls always talk about world peace in their speeches.

I really like coming to church. I just don't know what Father Durbin is saying. I like his outfits with all the colors and patterns and layers. It's almost like he's wearing a dress for a man, but nobody yells at him for wearing it. I've seen pictures of the Pope wearing red shoes with red outfits. They sure make some funny fashion statements.

· · ·

First grade is better than kindergarten 'cause I see Pedro in the halls. A couple times when Sister Rose took me to the principal's office 'cause

I talk too much in class, I saw Pedro sitting in the front row, paying attention to his teacher.

I don't know how he does it, but I won't even try.

'El que quiere algo, algo le cuesta.'
If you want something, it'll cost you something.

• • •

When Pedro told me last night that Mom and Pop were going to have a fight in the middle of the night, I didn't want to believe him e v e n though he can usually tell — because last night, I thought Mom was in a really good mood.

It doesn't make any sense.

And then the police took Pop away, like they always do, even though he didn't do anything wrong.

I think that's why he tries to drive away before Mom calls the police, but she usually breaks his window before he can escape.

• • •

"I like everything sweet," I say. "It's funny, *dulce* means sweet, and it means candy too. I like dulce dulce!"

"Sometimes a person can be dulce 'cause they're sweet," Pedro says.

"Sometimes I can be dulce. But no one has ever said it."

'El que es puro dulce, se lo comen las hormigas.'
If you're very sweet, the ants will eat you!

"There's a girl named Dulce at school, but they just call her Candy instead," Pedro says.

"I guess it makes sense. Like Truly Scrumptious in *Chitty Chitty Bang Bang.*"

"Truly is so nice and pretty. I wish we could live with her."

• • •

I didn't know there are different kinds of pinching.

Mom has figured out a way to put slapping, coscorrones, and spanking into a quiet pinch that she can give you in a church pew if she wants you to know she's mad at you. She takes a little bit of skin between two fingernails and she squeezes with all her might, until you're quietly sobbing because you can't make any noise when you cry, especially not in a church.

I wish I could talk with Jesus hanging on the cross above Father Durbin, and ask him, *"Why is Mom so mean?"*

She usually says, "No hay que ahogarse en un vaso de agua," which literally means, *No need to drown in a glass of water,* but really means, *Don't make a big deal about it.*

It's easy for her to say.

• • •

One of the girls that used to babysit us when Mom was in the hospital got married today. We know her boyfriend, Arturo, and we think they're gonna be happy.

"She's so pretty in her white dress, her white veil, and her white shoes," I say.

"And he's handsome in his dark suit and tie," Pedro responds. "He sure used a lot of Brilliantine."

They have these little bags of nuts — with a dulce white coating — all over the table for everybody to take.

"They're supposed to be boys' balls in a bag," Juan mutters under his breath.

"Why are there five, not two?" Pedro wonders.

"And why would they want us to eat boys' balls?" I ask.

Before they cut the wedding cake, they already have a lotta little round cookies covered in powdered sugar that are so good. Mom says they always have 'em at weddings. Now I can't wait 'til somebody else gets married.

"Pedro, who do we know who should get married soon?"

"I don't know anybody else."

"It doesn't matter. ¡Mientras dura, vida y dulzura!" I chant.

Enjoy the sweetness in life while it lasts.

"I wish it would last a long time," Pedro mumbles with a full mouth. "Especially these cookies!"

22

FAIR
Pedro – 8

THE OTTAWA COUNTY Fair mostly has a buncha animals. They have some rides, but nothing like Cedar Point 'musement Park. There are lots of games with guns you shoot and balls you throw to win a prize, but you have to pay cash money, so we don't play 'em.

When we were walking around today, we saw a guy who shaved his legs! They were so smooth! He was wearing small, tight, cutoff jeans—right here in Ohio, America! His legs were big and muscular, and you could tell he used oil because his skin was shiny in the sun. Maybe he was a bodybuilder because he had big muscles everywhere; he had a dark tan, long, light brown hair almost like a girl, and big movie-star sunglasses. I felt embarrassed, but I couldn't stop looking at his legs. If they were on a girl, men would definitely say they were sexy. Can men have sexy legs? Can men be sexy?

I'm feeling funny in my belly.

I might throw up.

Daniel just looked at me with his big eyes, his mouth wide open. Then he let out a long, loud cackle. You could tell he couldn't help it 'cause we've never seen anything like it before. It's like there was a flashing neon arrow pointing right at 'em saying, "Come look at these shiny muscular sexy legs on a man! They're *not* on a woman! You've got to see it to believe it!"

I couldn't laugh with Daniel 'cause Mom's head turned around real quick, and you could tell she wasn't happy. She had seen the guy's legs, with the flashing neon arrow and the sexy words. And, she knew what we were thinking.

"'Más sabe el diablo por viejo que por diablo,'" Daniel whispers in my ear.

"Are you comparing Mom to the devil?"

"If the shoe fits," he says with a grin. "But really, the dicho says, 'The devil knows more because he's old than because he's the devil.'"

"I'm just glad she didn't come over and give us a coscorrón."

"She usually won't in front of other people. Hopefully, she'll just forget."

The fair has a concert every night with someone who's *almost* famous — maybe a sister or a cousin of somebody *already* famous.

"That's Marcy Williams!" Daniel exclaims loudly, and she turns around and waves at us. "I love all the sparkles in her dress."

"She sounds just like her sister," I say. "The famous one."

"I hope she gets famous soon."

After the concert, everybody runs to their cars so they can get out before the traffic gets bad. Tonight, there's a really long line of cars trying to get out of the parking area in the fields of the fairgrounds. We can hear people talking about an accident on the road. Maybe somebody got hit and they called the police or the ambulance.

It's gonna take 'em a long time to get all the way out here.

When we finally get off the fields and onto the road, we see there's a truck with a horse trailer that's not moving. The road is raised above the fields, so the road won't get flooded when it rains a lot. There's barely enough room for two-way traffic, with a small shoulder and then some ditches on both sides.

It looks like somebody with a flashlight is trying to get cars through — one side at a time. Then they have to make that side stop so cars going the other way can get through. But people aren't cooperating; everybody's always in a hurry.

There's a lot of beeping, and, sometimes, you hear a lot of screaming. It's mostly women, but sometimes men start screaming too. It's like they're at a scary movie or something. Why do they have to scream like that? It sounds like there's an ax murderer murdering everybody, and I don't like it. I'm getting pimply bumps and my hands are sweaty. I think my eyes are as big as Daniel's right now.

When it's our time to move, our side goes real slow, because everybody wants to get a good look at what's going on. That always happens when there's an accident.

The screaming is louder because it's the people in the cars in front of us.

We're really close to the trailer, and Mom starts screaming too all of a sudden. It makes me jump. She's screaming a lot, really loud, and I don't like it. I wish she would stop. She yells at us to close our eyes, duck down, not look out the window. We all start crying.

It really is the ax murderer murdering everybody right here at the Ottawa County Fair in Ohio, America.

There's a drum hitting the sides of my head; I can feel it inside my ears. I'm squeezing my eyes tight, and I see light blue stars like fireworks under my eyelids. I'm gonna throw up, but I don't want to.

Mom is still screaming, but mostly into her scarf. She keeps trying to get a better look, then she screams louder and covers the babies in the front seat so they can't see. But they're really crying too. Mom keeps doing this over and over and over.

Sara and Juan lay face down in the back seat. Me and Daniel huddle together in the back of the station wagon. Sometimes he steals a look, but he can't see what's happening.

Now we're next to the horse trailer, and Pop's trying to get by quick. The whole car rocks back and forth because he gives gas, then hits the brakes. It's like he's hurrying to slow down, over and over, back and forth, gas and brakes, hurry and slow. The station wagon swings like a boat in a storm, and my nausea gets worse.

Everyone everywhere is screaming.

It's really scary.

There are too many people for the ax murderer to kill everyone at the same time!

I'm glad he doesn't have machine guns.

Pop starts yelling some pretty bad words in Spanish we're not allowed to ever say. He sounds really worried and I think he's even scared he's about to get ax murdered. Mom's still screaming, and Pop's yelling and sucking in his breath, like he's biting his chonies.

We're all in trouble, and we're all gonna die.

I don't want it to hurt.

I just hope he kills us real quick. . . .

Then I look up, and see it. . . .

I instantly know he was once very beautiful.

He's so big, next to our car. His eyes are almost popping out. You can tell he's scared. He's snorting and baring his big teeth. He's trying to get up, but he keeps falling. There's a big space of missing hair and skin under his mane on one side, and you can see ribs and lots of blood. I want to help him. Oh God, I really want to help him. But what can I do? Now I'm crying because I feel sorry for him, not because I'm scared anymore.

23

HOMER
Daniel – 8

ME AND PEDRO are outside playing sports. I'd like to say to Mom, "Dios te bendiga," or *God bless you* for trying, but it's me and Pedro doing the work. We think it's funny she keeps pouring water on a couple of stones, hoping they'll grow into mountains. At some point, we're gonna drown.

'No se puede sacar sangre de una piedra.'
You can't get blood out of a stone.

Pop installed a basketball hoop above the garage door. Juan tries to teach us how to throw, dribble, layup.

High expectations.

Good intentions.

Poor compensations.

All those times me and Pedro hung off the columpios, we didn't get taller. We didn't get stronger either. When I throw the ball, it doesn't even touch the bottom of the net. In my defense, the driveway is on an incline, so I'm farther from the net down here.

The basketball hits the garage door straight ahead with a loud bang and rattle.

"¡¡¡No golpeen la puerta con esa pelota!!!"

It's a nobody wins situation.

I'm playing tee ball this year. I don't want to, but my opinion doesn't matter. I really wish Mom would find herself a new batch of comadres, ones that mind their own beeswax and stop suggesting things me and Pedro should do.

"They are like 'hierbas malas que nunca mueren,'" I mutter.

Bad weeds that never die.

"It's so true about weeds," Pedro responds. "We can't get flowers to grow anywhere, but weeds grow in a sidewalk crack, in the bright hot sun, with no water."

Poor Pedro never got to play tee ball. He went right into regular little league with a pitcher. He gets hit by the baseball *so many times.* He says it hurts a bunch, and I believe him. He comes home with all kinds of bruises.

Sometimes it's hard to tell which bruises he got at home from Mom and which he got from a baseball.

At some point, someone should surmise that sports are a menace to our health.

. . .

Pedro laughed when I burned my neck while ironing my baseball uniform. I know I should've taken it off and used an ironing board, but it seemed like a good idea at the time. I guess it *is* funny, but he should've waited to laugh *with* me, not *at* me.

Okay, I get it. I would have laughed too. It *was* kinda pendejo to iron a shirt while you're wearing it.

My teammates always laugh at my stain-free, starched, ironed uniform.

When I'm standing in right field, the coaches yell all kinds of encouragement:

"Heads up Dan!"

"Get ready Daniel!"

"Eye on the ball Danny!"

Me and Pedro don't like "eye on the ball." They're always yelling it at us. What does it mean? How do you put your eye on the ball? It doesn't make any sense. What am I missing? I'm out in right field, nowhere near the ball!

And, apparently "heads up!" doesn't mean "look up!" because if I look up, they yell, "look down!" which usually gets us back to "heads up!"

Every time I've stood in front of the tee, I hit the tee, and not the ball. I really should get credit for hitting the tee, even if the ball plops over and rolls a few inches away. Maybe they could put marks on the tee, like on a dartboard. I'm pretty sure they get points based on how close the dart is to the bullseye.

I haven't learned all the rules because I don't have that kind of interest, but depending where the ball lands when it plops off the tee, someone may yell, "RUN!"

We apparently have a good team. We've won most of our games, and the dads in the crowd get very loud and animated. When Coach told me I may play tonight, he just looked at me for a while. I finally figured out he was waiting for a response. I forget they don't know I have no interest in playing.

"Yay Coach!" I exclaimed in his kind face. I surprised myself with the level of excitement I made.

Maybe I should be an actor.

At the bottom or the top of some inning, Coach says, "Okay, Dan, you're up!"

For the record, I don't like "Dan," but Coach says it with such enthusiasm, I never say anything to him. I guess I like "Dan" when he says it, but I'm not going to encourage anyone else.

I hadn't been paying attention. I should've been swinging the bat with a weighted donut to strengthen my arms.

"What arms?" a teammate once asked. "With all due respect," he added.

Anytime someone says "with all due respect," you know they really mean they're saying it with no respect at all. It's Irony 101. That's why I kinda like it when I get to say it. "With all due respect . . . insult . . . insult . . . insult. Con todo respeto . . . insult . . . insult . . . insult." It's like a magic wand that absolves you of the consequences of your statements.

It reminds me of people who start a sentence with "I'm not complaining, but . . ."

There is no greater advertisement you're about to complain than to start a comment with "I'm not complaining, but."

Or, "I don't mean to brag . . ."

The other thing that annoys me is when someone sighs nearby, and you don't want to, but you feel you don't have a choice, and you have to ask, "What?!" and they answer with, "Nothing." And it's not because I say, "What?!" with total exasperation and irritation, which is completely appropriate under the circumstances.

Coach always says, "Think of the ball as someone you really want to hit!" It's a bit aggressive, and definitely violent, but again you gotta love the enthusiasm!

Today the ball is Dylan, the twerp who calls me a sissy. I know I should *turn the other cheek*, like it says in the Bible, but I've decided some religious teachings need a good review. I have never seen *anyone* turn the other cheek.

"Batter up!" the ump yells. He gives me a sarcastic side-eye look, and I'd like to say something, but you've got to pick your battles. He puts Dylan on the tee. The dirt and grass stains on the ball even look like Dylan's mouth with the missing front teeth.

With all my might, I lift the aluminum bat — it's supposed to be lighter than wood — take a swing, and aim right for the gap in Dylan's teeth.

I hit the tee right below him, and Dylan plops over.

Thwummpfff Flittll Mmisshh

"Run! . . .

Dan, run! . . .

Run!"

What?

What's happening?

I see Coach jumping up and down. He's stabbing the air with his index finger toward first base. I know about first base. I've never had to run to first base, but I run toward first base.

I'm not much of a runner.

But I keep running.

Coach's cheers are registering somewhere in my head. I'm kinda panicking. I don't understand what's going on.

I hear screams . . . shrieking sounds . . . screeches.

Oh . . .

They're coming from me.

The first baseman approaches me, but he's looking up at the sky. I have to run around him because he's in my way. Is that allowed?

"Run Daniel! Keep running!"

Bill, the assistant coach standing near first base, is cheering me on as well.

"Touch the base! Touch the base! Touch the base Daniel! . . .

Oh my God, oh my God, oh my God, Daniel!"

I stand on top of first base and take a breath.

Then I hear Bill command, "Go to second! . . .

Daniel, go to second! Go to second! Go to second, Daniel!"

I start running again.

The opposing team are keystone cops with the ball. It's total chaos.

"Keep running, Danny! Keep it up buddy! Keep running, Danny! . . .

Touch the base, Danny! Touch the base! Touch the base!"

That's Joe, the coach at third base.

Honestly, . . . I know I have to touch each base before I can go to the next one. I do know *some* of the rules.

There's growing commotion and enthusiasm.

"Danny, come to third! Come to third! Come to third!"

"Dan! Run to third! Dan! Run to third! Dan! Run to third!"

"Daniel, go to third! Go! Go! Go! Daniel, go!"

Something happened behind me, but I don't have time to look at the mayhem on the field.

I'm having trouble running because I'm having trouble breathing because I'm laughing so hard.

I'm having trouble seeing because it's sunny, and there's so much water in my eyes.

"Keep it up, Danny! Come right toward me!"

"Dan the Man! Keep it up, Dan the Man!"

"Go Daniel, go! Go! Go! Go!"

I see and feel and hear an opposing player also running toward third base, looking back as he runs.

I see a boy who's probably the third baseman licking his lips, looking up, shifting his weight between his legs, and reaching up with his free hand to cradle his gloved hand.

In slow motion, I see the ball fall from the sky, hit the tip of his glove, then bounce away toward the left field. That's the area behind the third base.

Oh, yeah, I'm learning the lingo.

"Touch the base! Touch the base! . . .

Run home Danny! Oh my god, run home! Run home!"

The noise and cheers are deafening.

I'm still laughing and crying and wheezing—I've never run this much—when I see my new goal, and keep running.

Coach, Bill, and Joe are in my side views, cheering and jumping with arms and legs flailing in all directions.

The catcher is standing in front of home plate, his arms crossed in front of him, his glove just sitting on top of his head. He and the ump behind him are looking somewhere behind me, both with their mouths open wide.

A while after I touched home—yes, I had to run around the catcher boy who was standing in my way—the catcher actually catches Dylan in his glove. By some odd reflex, he moves to touch me with the ball, even though he knows it's way too late.

Because, news flash, I hit a homer!

Dylan tried and tried. He chased me around the baseball diamond, but he couldn't catch up with this sissy. I now realize the other team made a bunch of errors that let me advance one base at a time, but a homer is a homer.

They say, "El éxito llama el éxito."

Success beckons success.

Could this happen again?

24

FANTASY
Pedro – 9

WHEN WE MOVED closer to town, Juan got a paper route because he thought he could save money and buy neat stuff. But as soon as Mom saw his money, she took it all away. She said she would save it for him, and he could get it all back when he went to college, or when he wanted to get married. Daniel and I felt bad for him, but we kinda knew this was gonna happen.

She is Mom after all.

It didn't take long for Mom to say I needed to get a paper route. It was another chore to add to the growing list. And I get the benefit of riding my bike in the rain, the humid heat, the freezing cold, the impenetrable snow.

The worst part of delivering papers is collecting. Collecting money that reluctant customers owe for a product and a service. Occasionally, I have to knock on doors and ring doorbells on Saturday and Sunday mornings to collect.

It's very weird when someone answers the door in their chonies and they just stand there.

I was uncomfortable when Doug Jensen's dad answered the door, and his pajama hole was open, and he didn't have chonies underneath. A big scrub brush of hair just stuck out, and the root of his polla was there, framed in the opening. I was on the porch, and he was a step higher inside his house, so it was all there right in front of my face, just inches away.

Mr. Daly always answers the door in boxer shorts. He wears weird sock suspenders, which I've seen in movies but not in real life. Mr. Daly is very nice and polite. He seems lonely, so I feel bad for him. But I think he's a maldito maricón, and I have to remember not to be like him too much.

• • •

Mom said I have to collect from everyone today because she needs money.

I don't think she's saving my money for when I go to college.

Mr. Harris, the guy at the newsstand where we get our papers, gave me a long banker's bag with a purse string to collect my money. It has the local bank's name printed on it. I like that it's new and different, but sometimes when I dig in to get coin change at the bottom of the bag, a bunch of dollar bills fall out. It really needs separate compartments.

I'm about half done with my route when I get to Mrs. Knudsen's house. I always put my kickstand down, then wait to see if my bike will fall over, because of the heavy bag on the handlebars. The last time it fell, all the newspapers flew in the breeze like radio waves broadcasting the news. Now I know it's worth the extra few seconds to make sure the bike is stable.

Mrs. Knudsen is one of my favorite customers. We always chat and she gives me a snack so I can stay longer. I think she's lonely because she quit her job last year, and her husband died recently.

I saw this boy watching me on the street as I went from house to house today. I've seen him before, riding his beat-up, rusty bike with playing cards, attached with clothespins, strumming the spokes.

He must go to one of the public elementary schools.

He finally rides his bike over to me at Mrs. Knudsen's when I'm ready to leave her house.

Mom would give this poor boy so many coscorrones, because he looks like a real huérfano. He's got sleep in his eyes; I don't think he washes his face, or his hands. His clothes look worse than the used clothes we get at church. I wonder if he could get clothes there. I don't think you need to be Catholic, because they're supposed to help all the poor people, not just Catholics, but I don't know for sure.

I probably won't say anything because I don't want him to feel bad.

"Hey," he says.

"Hey," I respond.

"Watcha doin'?"

"I'm collecting for my paper route."

"What's that mean?"

"It's when customers pay for their newspapers."

Funny, I didn't know what "collecting" meant either when I first got my paper route.

"Oh," he says. "You make lotsa money?"

"Sometimes."

"Lemme see."

I put my bag out in front of me, but I instantly regret it. I don't know if he noticed my knuckles turn white. I feel bad that I feel nervous when he's just a boy . . . and, I want a friend.

The kid pushes up on the bag to weigh it. I just let him. I don't want him to know I have doubts.

"Don' feel like much in there, ya ask me."

I bring the bag back to my side. "That's because it's mostly dollar bills," I mutter, and instantly regret that too. What is wrong with me? Do I really want a friend that much?

"Gimme some?"

"No . . ."

I try not to sound mean, or mad. I get pressure around my chest, and a slight bit of nausea. My doubts were right! I can't trust anyone! I can't ever have friends!

"Com' on, lemme have some," he begs earnestly. "My momma's sick. I jus' wanna buy 'er somethin'!"

"Then get your own paper route!" I yell, now angry at my own betrayal of myself. Slow motion and clumsiness take control, like when I try to get onto an escalator, and I keep trying, but it keeps moving so I'm not able to get both feet on.

I'm a clumsy fool.

I can't get my kickstand up or climb onto my bike before the boy dives for the bag in my hand. It reminds me of Gollum lunging to get the ring back from Frodo, right before he bites off Frodo's finger. I yell and pull the bag in close, losing my balance and falling over, pulling my bike on top of me. The newspapers fly out of the bag and become radio waves in the wind. The boy gets scared, kicks me in the side, then rides away fast.

I disentangle myself and run up to Mrs. Knudsen, who heard the commotion, and is opening her door.

I'm gathering my newspapers when the police arrive. A big, mean-looking man with a military manner and a much smaller mouse of a man listen to what I say. I mention the playing cards on the bike. Then they listen to what Mrs. Knudsen has to say.

Then they leave.

Mrs. Knudsen makes hot chocolate and gives me cookies. "You've had quite a fright!" she says before I leave to finish my route.

When I get home, all the kids run to the door to look at me.

"Are you okay?" Sara asks. "The police were here!"

"What?"

"They said you told them someone tried to rob you!"

"He *did* try to rob me, but I didn't let him!"

"Que bueno que no soltaste la bolsa!" Mom announces from her chair in the living room, then returns her attention to her soap opera. She didn't even get up to look at me. She just blurted out her singular interest, her only concern: I hadn't released the bag of money.

"Then," Sara continues, "the police asked if you have a tendency to fantasize."

• • •

Does he have a tendency to fantasize?

Sara did most of the talking with the police.

Apparently, mom only asked if they took my money.

I'm afraid to ask if anyone asked if I was okay.

• • •

Does he have a tendency to fantasize?

A Brown boy accused a White boy of something.

A Brown boy accused a White boy of something White boys aren't generally known to do.

A Brown boy accused a White boy of something Brown boys are *sometimes* known to do.

• • •

Does he have a tendency to fantasize?

Do Brown boys have a tendency to fantasize?

Do Brown boys have a tendency to fantasize about being believed?

Do Brown boys have a tendency to fantasize about not needing to fantasize?

• • •

Does he have a tendency to fantasize?

I think of it every time I see a policeman, a kid on a bike, Mrs. Knudsen, or when I collect for my paper route.

The next time I see her, Mrs. Knudsen tells me the police went back to her house after I left. They told her they found the boy, but he denied trying to steal my money. She said the boy told them I *wanted* to give him my money.

I wanted to give him my money?

And the police believed him.

Does he, the White boy, have a tendency to fantasize?

It doesn't matter that he didn't get any money from me. And it makes no sense that I would want to give a random stranger my money.

I didn't have to tell Mrs. Knudsen the police asked my family if I have a tendency to fantasize. It was clear the police put that doubt in her head, and afterwards, she could not resist the temptation to attach a label on me. She would never look at me or talk to me in the same manner again. She had been the closest thing to a witness, and still, she believed I made it up.

The irony, of course, is I do have a tendency to fantasize.

When you imagine every day, multiple times a day, that someone will help you — *that* is a tendency to fantasize.

When you imagine every day that every superhero, every fairy godmother, every witch and wizard will form an alliance on your behalf, and rescue you — *that* is a tendency to fantasize.

When you imagine every day that it was all a terrible mistake — an accidental switch at the hospital! — and I need to go live with my real, loving family, and somehow, the same thing happened to Daniel, and he's still my real brother, and we're both going to go live with our real, loving family far, far away — *that* is a tendency to fantasize.

• • •

Daniel comes home later. By the time he enters our room, he has heard what happened. He is cautious, and surveys me with his big eyes open wide.

"Are you okay?" he asks.

"My pride and my side hurt. But I'm okay."

I'm sitting on my bed, looking at my hands on my lap.

"I'm so glad you're not hurt!" he exclaims. "Maldito pendejo who thought he could rob you."

He sits next to me and takes my hand.

"He was just a kid. I kinda feel sorry for him. . . . What the heck is wrong with me? Why can't I be mad at him?"

"El hombre que se levanta es más fuerte que el que no ha caído," Daniel notes.

The man who rises is stronger than he who has not fallen.

25

KENNY'S
Daniel – 9

I HAD TO get a paper route like Juan and Pedro. Pedro usually finishes his route, then he'll pick me up here at Kenny's Market, and he helps me finish mine.

They really like me here. I make them laugh, and I buy a fruit pie, a soda, and a candy bar . . . or two. I can look at the magazines or just chitchat 'til Pedro gets here.

• • •

"¡Hijos, hora de levantarse!" Pop whispers from the doorway, then he turns to return to the kitchen for his second cup of coffee. It's his Sunday morning routine before he takes us to deliver our papers.

"Okay, Pop," Pedro says as he gets up quickly. It takes me longer to wake up, get up, each day. I think I hear Juan brushing his teeth.

"Daniel, don't forget we get donuts when we're done!" Pedro whispers in my ear.

I'm up, and I'm ready, before Pedro has tied his shoes.

Pedro laughs quietly because everyone upstairs is still asleep, and we need to keep it that way.

We drive to the newsstand where Mr. Harris has stacked the correct number of newspapers for each paper boy. The Sunday paper has many more sections than the dailies, and we have to stuff a dense bundle of advertiser flyers inside them. Each newspaper is so thick, the back of the station wagon is overflowing with newspapers for our three combined routes.

"Thanks for helping us Pop," Juan says from the front seat. "It's so hard to do this on our bikes."

"You're welcome, hijo."

"Thanks Pop!" we yell from the back seat, and Pop looks up and winks at us in his little mirror.

Our three paper routes are pretty close to each other. Pop stops at one end of a block where we get off to deliver to those customers, then he drives to the next where we'll get the papers we need for that block. He reads the sports section as he waits for us.

Pedro usually looks at me when we drive by Kenny's Market, and I'll give him the gigantic grin he's looking for.

Our big secret from Mom is that Pop takes us to Matthew's Donuts when we're done. They're the best, cakey donuts we've ever had, and they're in our little hometown.

We hardly see Pop during the week, so spending time with him *and* eating donuts is two-treats-in-one. But sometimes we don't know what to talk about while he's drinking his coffee and we're eating our donuts with a glass of milk. Sometimes he asks about school. Usually, he just smiles at us as we talk to each other. When he and Juan talk about sports, my heart aches a little; I wish *I* could talk with Pop about something.

Later, Pedro asks, "Where do you think Pop gets money to buy us donuts?"

Pedro looks, and sounds, sad. Sometimes he wants me to reassure him about things. He usually thinks I know what I'm talking about.

"I don't know," I say slowly.

Now, *I* feel sad.

"But just remember," I advise. 'Lo que no sabe Mom no le hace daño.'"

What Mom doesn't know won't hurt her.

"But if she finds out, *she'll hurt all of us*," Pedro notes with his pinched eyebrows almost touching.

• • •

Mom did not look up from her knitting when she demanded her weekly payment from my paper route. Then I told her I didn't have any money. Now she's looking straight at me, and all her facial muscles are competing for dominance.

I am Bob Cratchit, just after he asked for a day off, waiting for . . .

"¡¡¡Dónde está todo tu dinero!!!" Mom screams, in an impressive crescendo.

"¡¡¡Yo no sé!!!" I screech as my mouth fills with saliva.

It's hard to tell if she's *more* mad that I don't have any of my paper route money, or because she has to get up to give me a proper coscorrón. Usually, she just pulls me in from her chair, but that approach hampers her swing, so it doesn't hurt me enough.

"¡¡¡Pendejo!!!" she shrieks, then calls for a belt. She'll grab a broom or a rolling pin if they catch her eye, but one of my siblings usually has a belt handy to prove their usefulness. Their short-lived reward of breathing freely for a few moments outweighs the label of "cabrón" or "cabrona" fired from the angry eyes of the betrayed.

• • •

"I know Mom knows the money went to Kenny's Market because Juan has told her, more than once," I sputter, between sobs. "Why does she pretend she doesn't know?"

"Who knows," Pedro says.

He's got his arm around my shoulder as we sit on my bed.

My butt and legs hurt from all the lashes of the belt.

"I don't even have enough to pay Mr. Harris at the newsstand."

"Oh no! What happened to the tip money I gave you?"

"Kenny's," I answer quietly.

"Daniel, . . . I can't keep giving you money. She hits *me* even harder when I don't make enough tips."

"I know. . . . You're right."

"Like your dichos, I'm always right," Pedro replies, and we both smile.

"Of course, now I can think of some dichos perfect for the moment:

> 'A los tontos no les dura el dinero.'"
> *A fool and his money are soon parted.*

"Pedro, you've got a fool for a brother!" I add.

Pedro snorts, then slaps his hands over his mouth. Mom's fire is still lit, and he needs to avoid her crosshairs.

"There's also:

> 'Quien poco tiene pronto lo gasta.'"
> *The poor man spends his money quickly.*

Then I add, "I wonder if there's a dicho with pronto and tonto."

"That would be funny!" Pedro hoots.

"I don't like:

> 'Quien mal anda mal acaba.'"
> *Your bad ways will end badly.*

"Yeah, that's too serious," Pedro says. "But I've got a good one:

> 'Más vale lo que aprendí que lo que perdí.'"
> *What I learned is worth more than what I lost.*

"Hmmm, that implies I learned my lesson today, and I won't go back into Kenny's Market tomorrow," I tell him tentatively.

"Daniel, you've *got* to stop going to Kenny's!"

But, I think to myself:

'El que jugó, jugará.'
Once a Kenny's Marketer, always a Kenny's Marketer.

• • •

"How many pies have you had?" Pedro asks with a half-smile, shaking his head in disbelief. "We just talked about this *yesterday*!"

I glance over at Kenny who's laughing at the register. "I started with the lemon, and I saved this one for you," I mutter, reluctantly handing Pedro my French apple pie. He rarely takes my pies, but this is his favorite.

I'll have to explain that I've spent the money I collected from the Petersons today.

"That's okay, you can keep it. Let's get going, I have lots of home-work to do again."

"But you're the only person I know who *loves* doing homework."

"I *do* love having homework, but I need time to do it!"

He holds the door open for me, and that's when I see Mom and Pop in the parked car straight ahead, with the car window open.

"¿Ya mero acaban? Vamos a compras. ¡Dales de comer cuando lleguen!"

And with that, Mom and Pop drive off.

"What just happened?!" Pedro asks as we walk quickly to the bicy-cles that had disclosed our clandestine location.

"Mom wants us to feed the kids when we get home."

"I know that! I heard her. But why did she ignore the fact we were in Kenny's Market and *you're* holding a fruit pie?"

"Add it to the growing list of head-scratchers known as Mom."

"Unbelievable!" Pedro exclaims. "If *I* had been holding the pie, she would have beaten me right here on the sidewalk."

And I know he's probably right.

"Dame pan y dime tonto," I quip.

Give me bread and call me a fool.

"I dare you to say that to Mom!"

"Wow, I just had a great idea. I'm gonna change it to 'Dame pan *pronto* y dime el *tonto*!'"

"I can't believe you just improved a dicho with a rhyme!"

"You've got to respect and honor the dicho, but no one said they can't be improved."

"That's true."

"It was a close call with Mom, but 'De casi, no se muere nadie.'"

Nobody dies from almost.

26

BEST
Pedro – 10

I LOVE THE back-to-school smells from books, pencil shavings, eraser nubs, and especially the aroma of new clothes.

Unlike Daniel and me, Juan grows every year, which means he gets new clothes, and I get all his hand-me-downs. It would be nice to have clothes that fit so I wouldn't always look like a huérfano from Oliver Twist. I usually get one new pair of pants and a shirt that I'll wear on the first day of school. I inhale the new-clothes-smell for weeks, until it sadly fades with the thievery of washings.

I suppose it's similar to new car smell for some people. New clothes smell means I will return to school, where I'm happy and safe, at least while I'm there. Mom never comes to the school; she just waits for me at home.

I believe fourth grade will be my best year, until next year when it will be even better. I absorb information easily even though I still have trouble saying words and sentences.

I don't have to talk much to show my teacher I want to be her best student.

I call myself a Broom Sweeping Reader. I collect the big stuff in my brain with my first reading—or sweep—then I continue to grab more of the smaller bits every time I reread something. Eventually, I collect all the remaining dust with each additional sweep. Somehow my dustbin brain sorts it all out eventually.

Unfortunately, it takes me a really long time to read something. And any type of noise, like talking or music, moistens the dust, making it hard to sweep up.

"I feel some relief being able to describe it," I say, "though I realize detailing my problem doesn't help me at all."

"El saber es fuerza," Daniel responds. *"Knowledge is strength.* It always has been."

"I guess you're right," I answer.

"Los dichos no mienten," he retorts with a grin, palms high on his waist, thumbs pointing forward.

• • •

We moved to a split-level house over the summer. Now we live across the street from the high school. If we walk across the high school field, it takes about thirty minutes to get to our school. Across the street from Immaculate Conception is the junior high school I'll attend in a few years.

Our new house is much bigger than the old one. Its six bedrooms are almost enough for Mom and Pop, my three brothers, four sisters, the baby that's coming, and me. Mom and Pop have their room upstairs where Sara has her own room, the younger girls have a room, and our younger brother shares a room with the crib. Downstairs, Juan has his own room, and Daniel and I share the other. There's a family room with a TV downstairs that can't be loud enough to disturb Mom from watching her shows while she knits in her chair in the living room a few stairs away. I don't like the split-level design.

But having a separate room with Daniel means we can talk freely without having to say "ropa" and change the subject.

It's not that we don't *like* our siblings; we just don't *trust* them with information that might get us in trouble, . . . and pretty much *any* information could get us in trouble.

Honestly, I still don't trust Daniel with my big secrets. The risk that he might accidentally tell someone something is too great.

Sometimes my stress reminds me of Daniel underwater at the river, and I gasp to breathe until I calm down. I wish I could make it all stop.

Everything.

Completely.

• • •

When you're not like other boys, and you don't have friends, or even toys, like other boys, you've got to use your imagination in your little bedroom in the far corner of the house.

When the unusual captures my attention, my imagination is set free.

So, Daniel and I play different kinds of word games we make up, like rhyming, or thinking of synonyms, antonyms, homonyms, and contronyms. We like experimenting with alliteration and onomatopoeia the most.

Sometimes we use flash cards, one of my favorite ways to learn.

And we've noticed that our grammar is better than our classmates', and our vocabulary has grown significantly.

• • •

In the last days of fourth grade, I'm feeling really nervous. I think Sister Denise might fail me, even though I got really good grades on everything.

All year, I sat next to Stevie Perkins. I was kinda his only friend. Stevie got in trouble pretty much every day, and he got paddled by the principal all the time. I thought I might end up failing fourth grade because they already told Stevie he failed. But, they passed me, and it is the end of my friendship with Stevie Perkins.

27

ALTAR
Daniel – 10

I LOVE BEING in church all by myself. Most of the lights are off. The red sanctuary candle is always burning to confirm that Jesus Christ is present in His house at all times, which I find comforting. I know He is here. I can feel Him. I just wish I could see Him, and talk with Him, like the priests do.

I can't wait to be a priest!

I wish they would tell me what it's actually like to talk with God and Jesus. I haven't heard anything about priests talking with the Holy Spirit, who is an enigma to me; I don't understand what He does, or if He's a He. Sister Piety referred to the Holy Spirit as an It, like a third person, which was kinda fun, then confusing.

Somehow the sanctuary candle never runs out of candle wax; I've been keeping an eye on it for weeks, even months. It's one of the great mysteries of this church. Like when the fish and loaves of bread never ran out when Jesus was handing them out to the poor.

I wish there was a way to feed all the poor and hungry people in the world.

'Pero, con esperanza no se come.'
With hope, one does not eat.

It seems Jesus could make that miracle happen again. Most people in the world would probably be happy with some fresh fish and bread. When we were kids, we were hungry all the time. It's not something you forget, and I wouldn't want people to be hungry.

One of the reasons I don't like fishing or eating fish is the idea of choking on a fish bone, a fear that was probably hatched by the annual "blessing of the throats" ritual, in honor of St. Blaise, who saved a boy who was choking on a fish bone.

I've often wondered why that is an important blessing to do every year. Do a lot of people choke on fish bones? It may be a chicken-or-the-egg type of thing. Maybe it will become a problem again if they stop the annual blessings.

People pay for votive candles under the large statue of Mary on the left side of the altar near the side door. She is Our Lady of the Immaculate Conception, the name of this church, parish, and school.

Most people think Mary is the Immaculate Conception because she was a virgin when she got pregnant with Jesus through the grace of God, via the Holy Spirit—*that's* what the Holy Spirit does!

The truth is, Mary is the Immaculate Conception because she was born without Original Sin when she was conceived in her mother's womb.

That's why we say Mary is full of grace. . . . She is full of God, without any sin, including Original Sin.

• • •

Now that I'm in fourth grade, I've completed my training, and today I'll be a real altar boy, with one other boy, for Father Donovan.

"Are you boys ready?" Father Donovan asks from the doorway to the room where we put on our black cassocks and white surplices.

"Yes, Father," we reply, in unison.

On any normal day, I'd say, "Jinx!"

We follow him into the vestry to help him put on his vestments. I still haven't gone through the door on the far wall to enter the sacristy.

That's where they store the chalices and all the other important things they use during mass services. Someday, I'll be able to go in and see all the gold, silver, and precious stones.

Father Donovan doesn't talk much. He's kinda old, and a little grumpy. We're supposed to know what to do so we won't get in trouble.

But we got in trouble when we put his chasuble on backwards. With all the embroidery, it was an honest mistake.

"No, no, no! . . . Who gave you your training?"

Eventually we got him dressed right, then he ran a comb through the hair he has left.

'Casi, pero no.'
Almost, but not quite.

I don't think I will *ever* understand the comb-over. All it does is make you look like you have a comb-over. I prefer bald men who embrace their bald heads, because being bald is better than a comb-over.

I miss Papá.

• • •

A priest serves *in persona Christi*. It means he becomes Jesus Christ himself during mass. I can tell when this happens because they become like a different person. It's like they're actors. Or, like they're hypnotized. Or, I guess, like they're God. It's a little scary, but you just have to stay out of their way and do everything you're supposed to do at *exactly* the right moment.

• • •

I like lighting candles. I like flames and fire. I don't think I'm a pyromaniac though. I heard about one in the news who kept lighting fires and burning things down. I just like lighting candles.

Sometimes the really tall candles are hard to light because you can't see their wicks. You have to bend the taper on the candle lighter before you light it. A large taper will cause a large flame and more soot. I keep the flame in the metal follower — the metal "collar" at the top of the candle — until I can tell the candle is lit.

It's really embarrassing when you need to attempt this more than once. There are always early birds in the church, way before mass is gonna start. I think they come to watch us grapple with the tall candles. My eyes always zigzag around to see who's looking at me struggle.

One of the reasons we want to minimize soot is because it's our responsibility to clean the wax-covered followers. Wax and soot are hard to remove without chemicals and without scratching the metal. It seems to me the nuns get a special delight when they declare it's time for the altar boys to clean all the candle collars in the church.

But as the saying goes, "El que la hace, la paga."

Actions have consequences.

And I would add, "El empezar es el comienzo del acabar."

The start is the beginning of the ending.

So, the sooner we start, the quicker we'll finish!

• • •

There are so many things an altar boy does, which is why it takes so long to train us. I don't know what my favorite part is, but my least favorite part is holding the paten under people's chins when they receive communion. Our church has a huge arc in front of the altar where people kneel to receive communion. When they get up, a conveyor belt of Catholics take their place. The priests race from one person to the next, and I'm supposed to keep up with them, which means I hit a bunch of people in the neck with the paten, and they usually give me a mad look.

147

I don't blame them, because it would hurt to be hit in the neck with a sharp metal object.

I'm mostly scared a host will fall on the floor because the paten wasn't in place under someone's chin. Allowing the blessed Eucharist—which has transubstantiated into the body of Jesus Christ—to fall onto the floor where shoes have trampled in billions of bacteria is a serious sacrilege.

There are rumors about the last time it happened. . . .

I know the boys are probably exaggerating, but they say the last altar boy that let a host fall onto the floor, well, he just sorta disappeared, and no one was allowed to ask what happened to him, not even his parents.

There's an elderly couple that comes to mass most days. The woman always wears a black veil, and the man always wears a frown visible from their back row in the church. Neither ever comes up for communion. The boys say they're the parents of the missing altar boy, and they come in hoping he'll show up again.

I feel so sad and sorry for them.

28

FRIENDS
Pedro – 11

ALL MY CLASSMATES seem to have friends. I think it's hard to have friends if you can't talk with them outside of school, you can't go to their house, and they can't come to yours. Daniel is my best and only friend, but he's my brother, so it doesn't really count.

I appreciate when school *requires* us to work together outside of school on an assignment. I wish they would do it more often. Mike Mason and I are in his basement making a telegraph machine for a science project.

A full circuit with a 6V battery turns a wire-wrapped nail into a magnet, which attracts a piece of metal close to it. The metal "taps" and holds on to the magnetized nail.

Releasing a lever within the circuit releases the metal from the nail. Repeating this process causes tapping sounds that can be used in code.

"That's so cool!" I say enthusiastically.

"Now, imagine if that nail were in a different building, or in a different town, and we had the lever here," Mike tells me. "When we tap on the lever, the people in the other building would hear the metal tapping the magnetized nail head!"

"*That's* how they can communicate with Morse code!" I exclaim. "I wonder how someone figured it out."

"Probably just a couple guys tinkering in a basement," Mike muses with a grin.

"*Now* I want to figure out how a radio and a television work!"

Mike laughs as he says, "I think we're gonna need a lot more parts!" He notes, "Hey, did you ever think about joining the Boy Scouts? We do all kinds of cool things in the scouts, including science stuff."

"I would *love* to be a Boy Scout."

It's true, I would love it.

Mom wanted Juan to be a scout, but he wasn't interested. Now, she won't let me be one. It was so cool when I saw a Boy Scout wrap a long rope around his cupped hand and his elbow. This long rope was wrapped into a nice coil, quickly and easily. I don't know if I would have thought of that on my own. I saw him make a bunch of knots as well. I don't know why anyone would need so many types of knots, but they looked pretty cool to make. I want to learn to do things with my hands. It's not just book-learning I like!

And it would be a great way to have friends.

"My mom won't let me join," I grumble.

"That's too bad. . . . We have to perform different types of tasks to get each new badge, so we learn something new each time. . . . We have meetings and meals, and we go camping together. It's so much fun!"

"It does sound like fun!" I say.

"But first you have to go through the initiation and you have to do it completely naked!" Mike laughs, and he slaps his knee.

"What?" I ask, unsure if he's kidding, or if he's testing me for some reason.

"Yeah, you have to climb a pole and do a bunch of exercises completely naked. It's so funny! But it's no big deal because afterwards we all go skinny dipping together. It helps build camaraderie."

"That sounds kinda weird," I mutter.

"It is kinda weird, . . . but we become more than friends. It's like we're brothers, because we're in this special club."

"Hmm. . . ."

"I have a really great troop of fellow scouts. Most of them don't go to our school; they go to one of the public schools."

I'm not sure what Mike means about all of this, but I guess for once I'm glad Mom didn't let me do something I wanted to do. I don't think I could ever do that kind of initiation, even if *everybody* ends up naked.

Especially if everyone ends up naked.

• • •

My cousin Graciela is in my class, but I'm not allowed to talk with her. It's another Mom rule. None of us are allowed to talk with our cousins even though they are in our classrooms. She has ways to find out if we disobey, so I don't let Graciela catch me looking at her. I wish I could talk with her, like I see cousins talking on TV shows or in movies. . . .

My abuelita lives with Graciela's family. Her dad is Pop's brother.

I know Pop would love to see his mother, not just at church or at weddings. I can tell he really loves her.

I wonder what that feels like.

We could be at Graciela's house in ten minutes, but we've only been there a few times. Abuelita is so cute with her wrinkled, brown skin, her hair in a tight bun, wearing a large, pocketed apron over a floral house dress, white ankle socks, and black, clunky, men's shoes.

• • •

Ben Milner moved here last year. He has dirty blond hair and greenish-blue eyes. He's a bit of a travieso in class. The nun yells at him all the time, but the additional attention adds fuel to his fire.

Ben sits next to me on one side. One day he reached over and grabbed me between my legs and squeezed. Then he laughed and pretended nothing happened. What did that *mean*?

Now, Ben calls me Taco, like I'm his sidekick or something. I don't like it, but he says it with a big grin, those eyes, and he has nice dimples, which always get me. Now others call me Taco. Mom says I should call them potato.

"What does that even mean?" I ask. "We eat potatoes all the time."

"It's not really the best advice to give a child," Daniel notes.

"I'm not sure if Ben is really my friend. I think he may not be right in la cabeza."

"Borra con el codo lo que escribe con la mano. Ben erases the nice things he does with the bad things he does. He's not really a good friend."

"I think you're right."

"Pedro, we'll never have the kind of friends we see on TV."

"I know, but wouldn't it be nice . . . to have *some* friends?"

"Regular, imperfect friends with flaws? . . . Yeah, that would be nice, and more likely. Cada quien con su cada cual. Just give it time. Maybe your Quien will meet your Cual."

"You're funny. . . . Thanks for knowing what to say."

"Dime con quién andas y te diré quién eres," Daniel adds.

Tell me who your friends are, and I'll tell you who you are.

• • •

"Do you ever lose hope?" I ask, through soft sobs, after a sudden onslaught of callous cruelty, because we hadn't done our chores to Mom's exact standards.

"About what?" Daniel replies.

We're each in a fetal position on our beds, facing each other. It's the least painful position. The welts on my butt and legs are too tender to touch.

"That we'll make it out alive."

"Yeah. Sometimes."

I wish I could make it all stop.

I don't know how I would do it.

And I don't want to leave Daniel here all alone. . . .

I'm scared God knows I have these thoughts that would get me in worse trouble if anyone ever found out.

• • •

"There are a lot of songs playing on the radio that tell stories," Daniel says, "like 'The Night the Lights Went Out in Georgia,' 'Tie a Yellow Ribbon,' and 'You're So Vain.'"

"Those are good ones," I respond. "But you gotta love 'Daniel, My Brother.'"

"Well, I would hope you love that song, Pedro! Only I don't like that Daniel dies in the song."

"I used to think that, but I don't think he actually dies. I think he just went to Spain. The guy misses Daniel because he went to Spain on a plane, . . . In the rain," I say with a grin.

"Oh, that's better. I guess I don't really know what it's about."

Daniel almost died, . . . right in front of me, . . . in the river, . . . a few years ago. I would miss him so much if he ever really died.

29

¡BAILE!
Daniel – 11

THE AM RADIO STATION out of Toledo has a Mexican program every Saturday afternoon that Mom listens to religiously. It's her most obvious connection to Mexico. The announcer sounds like those on the radio in Mexico: he has a bravado voice when he reads the news, sells a product, relays sports highlights, or introduces Mexican music.

He just reminded us, his listeners, about the *¡Baile Mexicano!* happening tonight in a neighboring town.

A few times a year, Mexican bands perform at regional dance halls, attracting families from several northeast Ohio counties.

"I can't wait for the baile tonight!" I declare.

"Bailes are so boring," Pedro grumbles. "There's nothing for us to do until a drunk comadre makes us dance with them."

"That's usually when it gets interesting! Literally *and* sarcastically. . . . It'll be fun! Literally *and* sarcastically."

• • •

When we enter the VFW dance hall, it's almost full. The band is already performing, and the dance floor is quite active. I wave at a few kids who will be my fifth-grade classmates in the fall.

"There are so many people here," Pedro groans.

"Some are here to drink *or* dance, some to drink *and* dance, and some will have an itch they'll need to scratch by the end of the night.

'Al que le pique, que se rasque.'"
If you've got an itch, you should scratch it.

"That sounds ominous . . . and funny!" Pedro laughs. "But I know what you mean, based on past 'bailes with a bunch of borrachos.' I hope there won't be any arguments or fist fights tonight. *Those* can get messy."

Mom never drinks alcohol. Pop will drink if he gets Mom's okay to grasp the beer bottle kissing his face, held there by a daring compadre desperate for a drinking buddy.

There is a cash bar, but most people lug in their own styrofoam coolers with ice, beer, rum, vodka, soda, and OJ.

The band plays Tex-Mex conjunto music. There are drums and guitars, but it's the accordion that gives it a polka sound similar to the music on the *Lawrence Welk Show*.

"I love conjunto music," Pedro murmurs, swaying along, just outside of Mom's gaze. "Even *I* can dance to it . . . not that I want to."

"Look at Hilda and Isidro Morales," I point. "They must have invented how they dance with each other."

Isidro towers over Hilda, who is shy of five feet in high heels. His left arm squeezes her against him; her nose sniffs his shirt pocket. Their feet seem tied together the way they move in a mesmerizing unison.

"They must have practiced a lot," Pedro muses. "It looks like tango dancing."

"I like how each couple has their own dance style," I stare in amusement.

The couples dance their version—their combination—of waltz, polka, tango, salsa, the cha-cha, and who knows what else.

"Why do they always dance in a moving mass around the dance floor, like at a roller rink?" Pedro wonders.

"Good question. Not-Mexicans seem to stay in the same single spot when they dance. Not here!"

"Look at Irma and Morelio Fuentes," Pedro directs. "He looks funny with that Cheshire Cat smile and his sleepy head laying on her bosomy bosoms."

"They're like big bottles for a baby boy in need of a burp," I quip, and we laugh like a couple of maleducados.

"Sometimes, we have a way with words."

"I love our alliterative games!"

We watch the dance floor for a while.

"I like how Mom and Pop dance," Pedro says quietly, almost sad. "They look happy together."

Mom is smiling, looking around the hall as they move. Pop has his head on Mom's shoulder. He's got a large, closed-mouth smile. He's looking up, as if he's thanking God for something.

"They're pretty good dancers. They *do* look happy, don't they? I hope it lasts."

"Pop kinda looks like he's in love."

"Yeah, I think he *does* love Mom."

"Do you think *she* loves *him*?"

"I hope so, Pedro. I really do."

We watch Mom and Pop for a while, in silence. I glance at Pedro, and I see his eyes have welled. I move in closer and put my arm around him. His only movement is a weak smile.

"Did you ever notice Yolanda and Arturo Romero dance like they're in a race?" I wisecrack. "They have a double beat to their steps, and they keep passing the other couples on the dance floor."

"Yeah. I'm not sure where they're heading in such a hurry."

That seems to lift Pedro's spirits a little.

When the men get tired or tipsy, women — and even girls — pair up and dance alongside each other, carried by the current of circling couples.

"It's always funny when two comadres dance face to face, like one of them is the man," Pedro notes. "Doña Inés and Carmen López sure look like they're having a good time."

"Actually, their husbands look like they're enjoying themselves, too."

I motion towards Don Diego and Camilo López deep in conversation at their table.

"Huh. From a different angle, it would look like those guys are kissing!" Pedro exclaims.

The men are sitting side-by-side but facing in opposite directions, as if sitting on a Victorian tête-à-tête chair. I've always loved that design.

"It must be really noisy where they're sitting."

Women in need of a partner look around and spot a bunch of bored boys in a corner in need of distraction, or amusement. Juan and his experienced friends knew the risk of appearing available to dance; they left the hall a while ago. . . . They're probably hiding out in a car.

Eager eyes suddenly focus on me and Pedro.

"Oh no!" Pedro moans under his breath.

"¡Ándale mijito, anímate!" Doña Josefa chortles as she grabs Pedro's hand and hauls him away.

Poor Pedro's face is buried between Doña Josefa's large chichis swaddled together in her low-cut dress, then she rests her head on top of his. I know he'll want to scrub himself clean when he's done. He struggles on his tiptoes to keep this tipsy woman upright. It's a gravitational marvel.

My eyes are fixed on Pedro's misfortune when a rose-scented cloud of Bonita Jiménez engulfs me from behind, followed by Bonita's hand on my shoulder. I look up at her seductive smile and her wicked, María Félix–arched eyebrow as she asks, "¿Me acompañas?"

How can such a simple sentence suddenly sound so naughty?

She places my right hand on her lower back, on the shelf her nalgies make as they protrude past her. My right cheek rests against her soft pillow belly. She holds my left hand high above her shoulder. Her left arm has me pinned against her as she grasps my belt, so she can rock and spin me around the dance floor in a wedgie. I hold on for my dear little life as she hoots and hollers along with the singers.

. . .

The sleepy men wake when the life of the party arrives in the form of a couple curvy women in shrink-wrapped dresses, sauntering into the hall on spiked stilettos to a cacophony of catcalls and wet-fingered whistles.

Several men suffer slaps to the scruff of their necks for their enthusiasm. Their wives are not amused.

"Hold on to your seat, Pedro," I smirk. "This is gonna get good."

"I remember those girls! . . . How do they squeeze into those dresses? They're one sneeze from an explosion!"

"I hope they don't look into a bright light!" I jest, and we laugh.

Maybe Mom *is* raising a couple of maleducados and delincuentes.

"I kinda feel sorry for them," Pedro murmurs. "I think they're lonely and want to have fun like everyone else. They're not even old. . . . Wasn't one our babysitter when we were little?"

"Look at Mariana Castro. She looks ready for a fight. Remember when the girl in blue sat on Roberto Castro's lap at the last dance?"

"Oh yeah. They do sometimes cause trouble."

"Como dos y dos son cuatro."

I feel sorry for Mariana. Roberto looks like a young Pedro Infante, and he sure knows it, with his slick black hair, dark eyes, pencil-thin mustache, the corner of his mouth raised just enough to complete the look.

These women flirt with young men in a corner of the hall before they spend the rest of the night on the dance floor, each young man jockeying for their attention. The married women sigh in relief; the married men sulk in disappointment.

. . .

Mom enjoys chisme caliente with Rosa Álvarez and Valeria Ortiz, stopping occasionally for the release of whole-hearted laughter. Pop is huddled across the table with Rogelio Álvarez and José Ortiz.

"I wonder what they're talking about," Pedro motions to the women. "Pop and his compadres are definitely talking about baseball."

"What else would married men talk about, when their wives are sitting across the table?"

· · ·

Pedro and I sure laughed a lot tonight. He enjoyed himself more than he had expected. We each danced with several comadres under varying degrees of inebriation.

"My neck and back hurt," Pedro says. "I had to hold up Señora Valencia the whole time!"

"Rosario Sánchez sweated all over me. God love her. Somebody's got to!"

The drunk people are sleepy, sloppy, or sappy. Comadres and compadres haphazardly hold each other, shedding tears of joy and affection as they clear the air of make-believe slights, ill-conceived rivalries, and a mishmash of other misunderstandings.

When the band takes a break, so do the dancers. The band manager plays Tex-Mex records no one dances to, and folks go to the bathroom, get drinks, go out for a smoke. *This* break, some teenagers begged the band manager to play the record singles they brought in from home.

I will always remember these men, women, and children from our community dancing to Cher, Elton John, Steely Dan, Little River Band, and other Top-40 music.

30

SCHISM
Pedro – 12

"SISTER FRANCISCA, *BOTH* boys are crying," says Sister Jude, the principal of the Immaculate Conception Elementary School. "I can't tell who *won*, or what's *happening*."

"Pedro won with *DIOCESE*, Sister Jude. I don't know why either of them is crying." Sister Francisca does a military worthy about-face and leaves the principal's office to return to her classroom. It seems she's had enough of us.

I just won the spelling bee for fifth and sixth graders combined. It was held in the auditorium in front of the whole school. I hadn't *tried* to win; I just knew how to spell the words we were told to memorize. Now I'm in the principal's office for the first time ever.

Why am I crying?

Am I scared?

Am I happy?

What is wrong *with me?*

I don't know why Héctor Ramírez is crying either. He came in second out of a hundred students, which is still good. Maybe he thinks his sixth-grade classmates will make fun of him because he lost to me. I want to comfort him, but he's not really my friend, and I don't want him to hit me.

"Pedro, you must be pleased, *and proud*. You're a fifth grader, and you won! That's quite an accomplishment!" exclaims Sister Jude. "I'm sure your mother will be pleased and proud as well. I'll call her now to let her know."

Oh no! I forgot I have to tell Mom! Will she be happy? What if Sister Jude wakes Mom, or the babies?

I can't tell what Mom is saying, but Sister Jude keeps repeating herself, "No, no, this is not bad, it's *good*. . . . Yes, it's *bueno*, not malo. . . . No, *Pedro's* not malo. . . . He's . . . bueno. . . . He's bueno. . . . You should be very happy. . . . Feliz cumple. . . . Feliz! . . . . You should be very feliz and proud. . . ."

"Pedro, how do you say *proud* in Spanish?" Sister Jude asks, with a hint of exasperation and the beginning of an eye roll. She's holding the phone against her ample bosom, just below her silver crucifix necklace. If she has hair under her headpiece, she'll want to pull it out soon.

I shrug.

"I'm sorry, Sister Jude, I don't know."

I don't know the word for proud in Spanish. I don't think Mom has ever used the word. Wouldn't I know if she had?

"No, Pedro really *is* a good boy. . . . You seem surprised. . . . No. . . . No, Pedro never gets into trouble. . . . No. . . . No, Pedro is actually very *smart*. . . . He's intelligent-tico. . . . He just won the spelling bee . . . spelling bee-o, with words, word-os. . . . You must be. . . . you should be very proud . . . proud-o? . . . Yes, happy! . . . Feliz bueno!"

When I get home, I can hear Mom on the phone with one of her comadres saying I beat María Ramírez's son in a test at school. She doesn't seem to know more than that, and she never asks me about it.

• • •

Now that I'm in sixth grade, I dread having to defend my win at the annual spelling bee. Daniel has to do the bee as well, so we practice with flashcards.

I wish I didn't have to speak in public, on a stage, in front of the whole school.

It's a nightmare.

Unless I don't make mistakes.

Which means, I have to win again.

No pressure. . . .

No problem. . . .

I'm picking up Daniel's sarcasm, and it suits me.

Spelling is an enigma for a dyslexic like me. I seem to spell very well when I'm writing. Spelling out loud, with no words or paper and pencil, without making mistakes, should be impossible, but I can *see* the words spelled out in my head if the other images flashing in my mind quiet down. If I can memorize the correct sequence of sounds of saying the letters that spell the words, I should be okay, because my main problem with spelling and reading *out loud* is *saying* what I *see*.

Letters and words get jumbled, eliminated, or replaced.

I still mix up *c, s,* and *z,* or *g, j,* and *z.* Then there are the risky mirror images of *b* and *d.*

I also have problems with numbers. If I see *five* or *5,* I just say *f* until my brain unfreezes. Another example of my speech challenges: if I see *chicken,* I might say, *kitchen.*

It all makes me look kinda dumb, so I avoid talking, which kinda makes me look more dumb.

Which makes me think that lots of dumb kids aren't dumb at all, so maybe we should all stop using the word.

• • •

Sister Francisca is administering the spelling bee again this year. She reads each word slowly. Mrs. Curtis starts the timer as soon as the word has been repeated once.

We were given a list of five hundred words to memorize for this spelling bee. They are words we might use in everyday life, but mostly, they're words we learned in catechism. That's why I won last year with DIOCESE.

All the kids are sitting on the floor in the auditorium, unless they're in the group called to form a line on the stage. One by one, each student is eliminated or sent to the next round.

Joe Morass whispers—not so quietly—to the boys around him, "You're a pussy if you don't get eliminated!" Joe Morass was born for his last name. He got eliminated in the first round, and he wants everyone else to join him and the intellectually uninspired.

I think to myself,

'No es lo mismo hablar de toros que estar en el redondel.'
Talking about bulls is not the same as facing them in the ring.

In other words, Joe Morass, *talk is cheap.*
Daniel will be so proud I remembered that one.
Now it's clear I not only *need* to win, I *want* to win.

• • •

I'm one of a mix of fifth and sixth grade students in the final ten. I can feel everyone's eyes on me, even when I'm not spelling. Probably no one is *actually* looking at me; it just feels like they are. It's a pressure I feel in my head, in my chest, in my clenched fists lightly tapping my thighs.

Now, there are only two of us left on stage with Sister Francisca and Mrs. Curtis when Sally misspells her word. I have to spell my word correctly to win. Otherwise, she and I go into another round.

Sister Francisca says, "Pedro, your word is *schism*. Schism." She says it with the *sk* pronunciation. I know it can be pronounced a couple ways. And I definitely know how to spell it.

I say, schism, *S-C-H-I-S-M*, schism, without hesitation.

Schism is one of my favorite words. I like both pronunciations. It's spelled like a three-lettered prefix stuck to a three-lettered suffix without a root word. And I like that it means a "great religious split," like when parts of Christianity broke away from Catholicism because they didn't believe the Pope was infallible.

I believe the Pope is *not* infallible, something I could never say without getting into serious trouble, but I won the spelling bee with *schism*, and I know I will *always* remember that word.

• • •

It's the last day of sixth grade, and I'm the last student out of class. The little hairs on the back of my neck tingle. Mrs. Davidson watches me over her half-glasses miraculously clinging to the tip of her nose.

Last week, she pulled me aside and said, "Pedro, I want you to know I recognize all your efforts this past year. You have *earned* your good grades. You work *hard* for your successes. I am very proud of you."

I remember I felt a little dizzy, and I struggled against tears, but I managed to say, "Thank you Mrs. Davidson."

I was surprised she had noticed *me*, had been watching *me*. *Me* — not just my homework or my test papers or my grades.

Lots of my classmates don't like Mrs. Davidson because she's strict and assigns a lot of homework. Sometimes I wish I could say what's in my head so they would know she's the best teacher we've ever had.

Now, I want to tell her I love her.

It's my best understanding of love, of the word and the feeling, which I've only felt for Daniel, Mamá, and Papá.

Tears are welling, and willing to betray me. I want to be strong. To show her I'll be okay next year, across the street, in the unfamiliar. I'm close to mustering the courage to give her a hug. Would she mind?

"Goodbye, Mrs. Davidson. . . . Thank you."

"Goodbye Pedro," she replies, with her friendly smile and a glimmer in her eyes. "I am so very proud of you. It's been an honor to be your teacher."

My mouth seizes — no actual words *could* come out, even if I had the courage to speak them.

Will I forever regret that I didn't give her a hug?

Part 3
1974–1980

31

CHAOS
Daniel – 12

I MISS SEEING Pedro at school. Junior high sounds like a wild jungle. I don't think I'm going to like it at all.

"I don't think you're going to like it at all," Pedro says as we walk home from school. "Everything is so different. The kids seem to be crawling out of their skins, wanting to conform *and* rebel. I sure don't fit in anywhere."

"Maybe you can try out for a sport or something," I tell him.

Why do I have this scalding, sarcastic streak, even with Pedro? "I'm just kidding!" I add, before his contorting face can respond.

"They would need to be pretty desperate for me to make a team. Por el amor, Daniel, *please* don't say anything to Mom!"

"Are you kidding?! If I suggest it, I'll have to play sports when I get there next year! I'm still living off my historic home run at tee ball."

"Haha!"

"Hombre precavido vale dos," I assert.

The cautious man is worth two.

And I need to be cautious for the two of us: if I *accidentally* plant an idea in Mom's head, it could be bad for Pedro *and* me.

• • •

At this point, I serve mass as much as I want since I'm in sixth grade and I'm going to be a priest. No one else wants to become a priest, so I've got that corner of the market all to myself.

School is going all right. It feels like I should be in a grade or two higher, around kids with a more advanced vocabulary and inquisitiveness. I can't find a classmate who is interested in my word games or in learning outside of the curriculum.

I just get bored of the same old, mismo viejo.

I didn't like when the nuns gave me an eye roll or sent me to the principal's office, so I'm quieter than I used to be. It's not that I was a class clown. Although I did make the kids laugh a lot. Maybe I was a bit of a clown. . . . But it wasn't my intention! I was born hyperactive, with the gifts of gab, wit, and sarcasm. I *do* wish I were more puntastic though.

* * *

"*All* of you, DON'T WORRY! Your dad is *okay*. He was just in an accident," Irma Mendoza tells us when we walk through the door. "*My* mom took *your* mom to the hospital to see him."

Irma seems to brace for the mayhem before we deliver our verbal assault.

"What?!"

"What happened?!"

"What kind of accident?!"

"Where is he?!"

"She already said he's in a hospital!"

"I know, I was just asking where!"

"Is he going to die?"

"Can we see him?"

"Did he have a heart attack?!"

"She said it was an accident, not a heart attack!"

"I know, I was just asking!"

"You two stop fighting!"

"She started it!"

"Nah-ah, he did!"

"They fight like Mom and Pop."

"What?!"

We bombard poor Irma with more questions through sobs and general hysteria. Pablo and Rosa continue to bicker and pinch each other in a corner.

"He's fine, he's fine. His hand got stuck in a machine at work. . . . They said he might come home tomorrow, or maybe the next day."

Irma is a short and stout young woman who graduated from high school a few years ago. She works at Kroger as an assistant manager. She isn't married, so she still lives with Doña Cata, la viuda.

"Are you going to stay with us tonight?" Pedro asks Irma through sniffles.

"We'll see. Your mom will stay with your dad tonight, or until he's better. Right now, I'm making your dinner, and you all need to do your homework or whatever you do when you get home."

We're used to Pop's absence on weekdays, so it doesn't seem strange that he's not home. What is most unusual is *Mom's* absence. She *does* end up staying with Pop at the hospital. It kinda seems like she really cares about him. Her absence, along with the knowledge that Pop is okay after having had hand surgery, means we have some relatively stress-free days; all mayhem and madness have ceased.

On the last day, there is no bickering at all.

Pop finally comes home after three days.

• • •

"Buenos días hijo. ¿Cómo amaneciste?" Pop asks as I enter the kitchen. He's having a quiet cup of coffee at the kitchen table. I'm sure Pedro will remark about how early I got up today.

I want to spend some time alone with Pop. . . .

"Hi Pop."

Now that I'm here with him, I'm at a loss for words. The *only* times I don't know what to say are when I'm alone with Pop.

Why can't I think of something to say?

I should have brought Pedro.

"¿Quieres comer algo?" he asks.

His hand and forearm have been mummified with a cast and bandages. It makes me think of Halloween. And Halloween candy.

"I'll just have some cereal, Pop."

I get a bowl, spoon, sugar bowl, and cereal and put them on the table in front of me. Pop watches me silently. It's odd to have an audience for such a routine effort. I realize he's looking at my bowl, which is more of a mixing bowl than a cereal bowl. I feel my ears warm, and my invisible arm hairs stand. No matter; I continue. I pour cereal into my bowl and lift the sugar bowl to pour sugar. . . .

"¡¿Tanta azúcar, Daniel?!"

Pop's eyebrows are in the middle of his forehead, and his mouth is open in a perfect circle. It reminds me of something, someone. . . . I forget people use a spoon to sprinkle just a little sugar on their cereal.

Pop doesn't have a sweet tooth. He wouldn't even eat donuts with his coffee if there were ten trays of Matthew's Donuts right there in front of him.

"You love your chiles calientes," I retort with a growing grin. "And I love my azúcar!"

Then Pop and I laugh silently. He reminds me of Pedro, holding in his laugh to avoid waking Mom, his shoulders shaking slightly. I guess I have this effect on everyone.

I want to keep this special moment a secret between us, at least until I tell Pedro about it later.

When I see Pop's misty eyes, I notice my vision is blurring slowly through happy tears of my own.

I found something to say to Pop.

• • •

"There is so much static energy at school right now!" Pedro exclaims as we wait for our siblings to exit their classrooms. "The slightest spark will lead to an explosion."

"What do you mean?" I ask.

"The kids want some sort of release. They're trying to get the two jock factions to fight each other, like the rumble in *West Side Story* . . . except everyone's White."

"Do you think they'll do any Jerome Robbins–inspired choreographed dancing?" I wisecrack, because the set up was too easy, and sometimes I can't help myself.

"What?" Pedro responds, clearly distracted. "I think the two leaders are gonna have to fight each other soon to avoid a full-on brawl."

"That's barbaric!"

"I know. But they somehow don't have a choice anymore. It's gotten out of control."

"Why is it always the jocks fighting?" I ask. "Can't they release their aggression in their sports?"

"I think coaches don't want any injuries, when they practice. They're supposed to save hostility and aggression for teams from other schools. . . . Of course, it's just my guess. I don't really understand boys who play sports."

"La suerte está echada," I note. "*Their die has been cast.* Those boys don't have a choice anymore. Poor things."

I don't tell Pedro I hope they don't hurt each other's handsome faces. Those boys are so cute! I won't like junior high, but I will like seeing all the new boys from the public schools mixed in with the ones from my school.

• • •

"Pedro, what's it like in your head?" I ask.

I can tell the heat and humidity have kept him awake as well.

"What?"

"What's it like in your head, with all your words and thoughts and everything going on in your . . ."

"Controlled Chaos," he interrupts, almost involuntarily, like the words are a hot potato he needs to toss hastily.

"Um, okay, . . . but what does it mean? . . . I mean, I think I know what it means, just from the words. That, 'cada cabeza es un mundo.' That every mind is its own universe."

"Yeah, believe me, I've thought about it a lot. Controlled Chaos is the simplest, most visual description I have for it. I've always got so many words and phrases and music bouncing around in my mind. I spend so much energy trying to organize things, trying to quiet things, trying to control my nonstop inner monologue. I'm always practicing what I'm going to say so I won't make as many mistakes when I speak."

"It's funny you have a name for it."

"You remember KAOS on *Get Smart*?" Pedro asks. "It was the first time I heard the word, even though it's spelled differently. Once I knew what chaos really meant, it kinda just clicked. I only say 'Controlled Chaos' because I work hard at keeping it under control. But I'll be honest, 'controlled' chaos is a lost cause."

"Does anything make it better, . . . or worse?"

I saw a doctor on TV ask that once. It seems like a good question.

"Good question," he says.

"Jinx! I thought it was a good question right when you said it was a good question! '¡Los genios pensamos igual!'"

"Well, I can tell you Mom makes it worse. She makes me nervous, and everything in my head gets worse. Remember 'La Momia Muda'? It's me freezing up. I can't talk when she's yelling and screaming. I *become* La Momia Muda. My vision blurs, I'll scratch the bottom of my shoes with my toes, my hands contort. . . ."

"I've seen you do that!" I pause a little. "Pedro, I can't imagine what it's like having all that nonstop chaos."

"I know. . . . It took me a while to figure out my brain is different. Even just knowing it helped me a little."

"Your stutter is a lot better now."

"Thanks, I know. . . . I can control it better . . ."

He seems to appreciate it. I can't see his face in the darkness, but I can hear his emotions in his words.

". . . but I still have trouble saying some words."

"You never have a problem when you talk with me. . . ."

"Do you really think you're *anything* like Mom?" Pedro asks, kinda surprised, kinda sarcastically.

"No, I see your point. . . . But how did you win the school spelling bee? Twice?"

"Another good question. And I'm not really sure. . . . I guess, you know, I'm a little obsessive about learning. . . ."

"A little?" I interrupt, and we both laugh. "I'd say you're a philomath."

"A what?"

"A philomath. You're curious about everything, and you have an insatiable desire to learn."

"Of course there's a word for it. . . ."

"Don't forget, I like to learn new stuff too! If I weren't so bored at school, I think I'd get better grades. I really think I'd do better too if I were in your grade, with you, since we used to study together all the time."

"I don't doubt that. . . . Have you ever noticed I'll blurt out an odd word when I start talking?"

"No. . . . What do you mean?"

"If I'm obsessing about something in my inner monologue, and somebody asks me a question, I'll say a word associated with what I was thinking about. It's so embarrassing. It's one of the reasons I avoid talking."

"I can't say I've ever noticed."

I honestly haven't.

"I thought it was part of my stutter, but it's something different," Pedro mutters. "For a while, I thought I had Tourette's, like that guy we used to see on our paper route."

"I remember him."

"And I've got signs and symptoms of anxiety, depression, dyslexia, and a bunch of other disorders. . . . I keep looking things up, and I see myself in all the descriptions."

"You sure love your encyclopedias! I've wondered if I have something that makes me so antsy and unfocused."

"Hmmm. . . . You might. . . . I just wish I could get all of the noise in my head to shut up!"

"¡¡¿QUIÉN ESTÁ HABLANDO?!!!" Mom yells from the living room.

I don't know if it's a rhetorical question, and she just wants us to shut up so she can pretend we don't exist, or if she really wants us to tell her who's talking.

"Good night Daniel."

"Good night Pedro."

32

SKINS
Pedro – 13

I'VE BEEN TELLING Daniel how different seventh grade is from Immaculate Conception.

Students from all the elementary schools in town come to this *one* junior high school. Here, most of the kids wear jeans and T-shirts and jewelry and makeup. A lot of them smoke. They even smoke marijuana pot cigarettes in the parking lot.

Many of my classmates from parochial school wouldn't be allowed back at the school where they went just a few months ago, right across the street.

Mom says I can't be friends with *any* of them, even if we were friends before. I still don't have outside-of-school friends, so I'm gonna try to keep the school friends I have, at least the ones who still talk to me. The ones that are trying on new antisocial personalities don't want to be reminded of their recent previous lives as Catholic school students. It's okay, I don't mind.

I still can't wear jeans because only bad kids wear jeans, in the world according to Mom. I stick out with my rayon-polyester-blend trousers and shirts with odd fabric motifs. I have a long-sleeve shirt with mallard ducks going in every direction. Talk about having a bullseye on my chest and back.

My newest friend Lori loves to answer my questions about the new kinds of music on my classmates' radios.

"You're just used to AM stations that play Top-40," she says. She's wearing her Pink Floyd *Dark Side of the Moon* black T-shirt, with the iconic light beam distorting into a rainbow as it passes through a prism. "FM plays more of the album music you hear around here."

Lori says I'm "kinda cool," which is one of the nicest things anyone has ever said to me. It seems more sincere to say I'm "kinda cool" before stamping me with the garden variety "cool."

I like the word *kinda*, because it really means "kind of."

But the word *of* still gives me sweaty palms. There are certain words that make my brain freeze, and *of* is on the top of the list. This little two-lettered word is pronounced "uhv" for some reason. When I look at it, I think it should be pronounced "off," then I can't remember how to pronounce it.

I need to get my mind off of pronouncing *of* like *off*.

I don't think I could speak that last sentence clearly if I were trying to read it out loud.

• • •

"It's called *jamais vu*," Daniel says.

He's on his bed reading my library copy of *Breakfast of Champions*. Mom will let me "waste time" with books when I tell her I need to read them for class. What she doesn't know won't hurt her, right?

Daniel doesn't look up when he adds, "It's kinda the opposite of déjà vu."

"There's a word for what I feel?" I ask.

"Yeah. . . . *Jamais vu* basically means you feel as though you've never seen something before, like a word, even though *you know* you've seen it a million times already," he says, then flips a page. "*Déjà vu* means you feel as though you've already seen or experienced something."

"I've heard of déjà vu. And, I have them all the time."

"There's also *presque vu*, which I know you also get a lot," Daniel muses, and he finally looks at me. "It means you're almost about to remember something, like when something is on the 'tip of your tongue.'"

"Seriously Daniel, how do you know *everything*?"

I don't even *try* to hide my envy or exasperation.

"Sister Angélique loves to throw in French words when she's teaching, and I, politely, as is often my nature, request a full explanation." He gives me a devilish smirk as his index finger skates through the page looking for his place in the book. "*Déjà/jamais/presque vu* means already/never/almost seen. It helps make the class go by quicker. I've told you how bored I get."

. . .

Phys ed is the worst. I think kids who don't like regular classes probably feel the way I feel about phys ed. The school has a small, paved, outdoor area, so most of the time we're in the gym, throwing balls at each other until we're out. Some of the boys seem to enjoy throwing the ball hard, making the smaller boys hurt. I've been hit by baseballs *by accident*. Why do I need to be bombarded by balls in gym class *on purpose*?

And why do I always end up a skin in "shirts and skins?"

And why do boys laugh every time someone tells me not to stand sideways, because I'll disappear — as if it's the first time they've heard this stupid slight about being skinny?

. . .

This month, we lost our Abuelita and our Papá.

"I feel bad for Pop," I say. "I know he loved his mom. I wish he could have seen her when he wanted."

"I wish we *all* could have known her better," Daniel grumbles. "I don't know what the problem was, but it's not right that we never saw her."

We did see her occasionally: at church, weddings, and even once at a *¡Baile Mexicano!*, but I know what Daniel means.

"I can't imagine what Pop's feeling. . . . It's all so sad."

"And there will never be another man like Papá," Daniel adds. "I feel bad for Mom, but I feel bad for all of us too."

"Yeah. He was the definition of a gentleman . . . and a gentle man," I confirm.

Visiting Mexico will *not* be the same without Papá.

It's so sad.

• • •

"¡¡¡AY!!!" Mom shrieks loudly.

Daniel and I quickly look at each other.

In the next seconds, the next sounds will determine our fates.

She might exclaim how cute the baby is, or she might . . .

"¡¡¡PEDRO VEN PA'CA!!!" Mom screech-screams.

My spine tingles.

I fight back tears.

I know that voice, that intonation.

So do the neighbors, who will vicariously experience my imminent assault.

Daniel looks at me with "I know that voice, too" eyes, puts his book down, and gets up from his bed.

"¡¡¡PEDROOO!!!"

Although she is seething, she won't make the effort to come down—not right away—but the longer I wait, the worse it will be. Daniel touches my shoulder, and follows me down the hall.

Mom is standing at the top of the stairs holding the extension pole for the vacuum cleaner. Her face is twisting and contorting as she figures out what expression she wants to wear. Her chest heaves violently. Spit is dripping from her slightly open mouth.

She lifts then points the pole at my face.

"¡¡¡RENEGRIDO RETARDO!!!"

It's remarkable how clearly the words, drenched in spit, emerge through her clenched teeth.

Before I can climb the few stairs, she reaches with her free hand, grabs my hair, and pulls me down toward her foot so she can kick me in the face. I see stars as the searing pain in my eye grows exponentially. I'm momentarily blinded with both eyes squeezed shut in agony.

"¡¡¡Dejaste este palo tirado en el piso, y me golpeé EL PIE!!!"

For a moment, I wonder if it's the same toe that pummeled my eye.

She beats me with the metal pole that stubbed her toe.

I can hear Daniel and others pleading for Mom to stop.

But she will only stop when her demon has had its fix.

33
CIRCUMSPECTION
Daniel – 13

SOMETIMES LIFE IS a one-sentence thought.

Sometimes I like to think of dramatic statements, especially if I'm bored, and have to be quiet because Mom is taking a nap. I'll write them down and give them to Pedro, to make him laugh silently. He'll get mad because it hurts to keep your laughing bottled up while your body is spasming.

I tell him, "La risa es el mejor remedio."

Laughter is the best medicine.

"I agree," Pedro responds, "but don't they also say, 'everything in moderation,' because too much can be too much?"

"Ah, yes. 'Todo con moderación, incluso la moderación,'" I muse. "*Everything in moderation, including moderation!* . . . I never liked that dicho."

"What?!"

• • •

Sometimes I think I should study philosophy so I can ponder, examine, and analyze questions and situations, then come up with vexed questions, vain comments, and vague answers without making a clear decision about what the right answer or solution might be.

But then I think it would get boring.

I suppose I'll need to study philosophy when I become a priest. Sermons *are* philosophical. Although they are just words, not actions.

'Las palabras se las lleva el viento.'
Actions speak louder than words.

I miss going to church every morning. I often wonder if my home-room teacher would mind if I came in late so I could attend church.

It's right across the street!

I doubt you would even notice I'm gone!

• • •

With all due respect to Dorothy, "*My. . . . priests come and go so quickly here!*"

Father Richter is the newest priest in our parish. He always uses a *Peanuts* comic strip to help explain his sermon. He describes the characters, and reads the words in each panel of the comic strip. Then he spends about fifteen minutes tying the characters, their words, and their actions to the scriptures that had been read during mass. It's really rather clever and impressive.

I hope I can give sermons like that someday. It's my goal to help people better understand the scriptures and the teachings of Jesus Christ and his disciples.

• • •

Dr. Fritz says I should get a circumcision because I'm having problems down there. Usually, they do it when you're a newborn baby boy, when you don't know what's happening. Most parents don't know they can say, "With all due respect, no thank you."

I want to say, "With all due respect, no thank you."

At least let me think about it.

Yeah, the answer is still no.

I've heard kids talk about a movement to stop circumcisions at birth that aren't part of a religious ritual. I guess lots of men, and probably some of my classmates, are angry they were circumcised without regard to how they might feel about it when they became adults.

Boys sure talk about penises a lot.

Then there are parents who say they want their sons to look like their fathers, as if fathers and sons compare those things. Maybe they do in less repressed homes, I don't know. The point is, I don't need much time, I've thought about it, and I prefer to remain intact, please and thank you.

I think to myself,

'Los mirones son de piedra.'
Onlookers should remain silent.

And, I've got a couple of onlookers in front of me that really should remain silent about this matter.

Mom just asked Dr. Fritz if Pedro and I are the way we are because they didn't circumcise us when we were babies. She asked him right here in front of me. Sometimes she has no filter, no awareness of her surroundings. Maybe she just doesn't care. That's probably it.

'La cabra siempre tira al monte.'
A leopard cannot change its spots.

"I'm not sure what you mean, Mom," Dr. Fritz responds, and I want to say, *neither do I*! He always calls her "Mom" when the appointment is for one of the kids. We think it's kinda funny. I really do like him.

"Que, they no likey beisbol o fuhbol no notheen," she says. "An they likey dolls y dresses. Ahl the theen fo girls to likey."

"Oh, I see." He pauses a moment. "No, Mom, circumcision has nothing to do with any of that."

Okay, rude. They're talking about me like I'm not even here. Sitting right in front of them, . . . wearing a sadist's interpretation of a gown. And for Pete's sake, really? You think I like what I like and do what I do because I have foreskin? For the love of God and all that is good. Por el amor, people. Por el amor.

'Mala piensa la que piensa que otro no piensa.'
She thinks wrong if she thinks that another doesn't think.

And I think this should be my decision, which is still no, and I should just get a cream or a pill to help with the problem.

In her defense — though I'm *definitely* not defending her — Juan was circumcised, and he's totally the type of son she wants. At least in the athletics and non-doll-and-dress-liking sort of way.

I don't mean to be talking about everybody's penis, but it *is* kinda what we're talking about.

Wait a minute. . . .
I don't even like dolls and dresses anymore!
At least, . . . I don't like Mom's clothes. . . .
A glamorous red carpet ensemble may attract my attention. . . .

I don't doubt Mom got this crazy notion from one of her trusty comadres. I *do* believe more than one of them has been confronted by similar queries — pun clearly intended — with their own sons. Let's just say I never expected there would be others in this little town of ours, but there are. Call it intuition or a sixth sense. . . . When everyone else is busy not seeing what is right in front of them, I can see the faint glance or gesture or expression, and then the boy and I lock eyes and it's confirmed. I don't know if they're always aware of it themselves. Sometimes you can't know the truth when you're living smack dab in the middle of it. You need to see it from an eagle's eye view.

Now that I think about it, Mom *has* remarked about my eagle's eye for discerning details from a distance.

• • •

I'd like to approach this cautiously, and make a decision after circumspection, and careful consideration of my options other than circumcision.

Any way you look at it, the answer will still be a very polite, but clear: "No thank you, Dr. Fritz." I might add, "Say hello to Mrs. Fritz for me," so he knows I'm not blaming him for any of this.

I just don't like the idea of them cutting me down there of all places.

What are my other choices?

There must be other choices, right?

• • •

I guess I didn't have a say; the decision was made *for* me. They actually never asked me if I had any thoughts, comments, questions, concerns, suggestions. I'm having a circumcision. At my age. And I *know* what they're going to do.

It makes me think of Zipporah, the wife of Moses, beautifully portrayed by Miss Yvonne De Carlo—yes, Lily Munster—in *The Ten Commandments*.

LET MY PEOPLE GO!

Anyway, Zipporah hacks off her son's foreskin with a rock—yeah, the Bible says she did it with a rock—musta left a nasty scar—because God was angry with Moses, possibly because he never got around to circumcising his son, and she's afraid God is going to kill Moses.

God sure punished a lot of people with murder back then.

Why am I thinking about this?

Oh, circumcision.

• • •

"Wait, what? . . . Why? . . . When?" Pedro asks.

His eyebrows are doing push-ups as his eyes dart side-to-side.

I hadn't even told him about this until now. . . .

"Doesn't yours get inflamed and red anymore?"

"No. Not since I was little."

"Well, mine does, . . . and when I get a boner, it really hurts because it can't push through the tight foreskin."

"Okay, wow. More information than I was expecting, but that's okay. So what do you think about it?"

"I think I don't have a choice. Both because Mom already decided after Dr. Fritz said it should be done, and because it's a problem that won't go away on its own. Although, Dr. Fritz didn't really use those words."

"Then I guess you don't have a choice. I assume Dr. Fritz thought this through carefully, and decided it was the right thing to do for you."

I kinda wish Pedro was already a doctor so he could say more, and maybe even talk with Dr. Fritz. Maybe that's unfair. No, it's totally unfair since he has at least twelve years before he'll be a practicing doctor.

I just need somebody on my side.

. . .

Let's face it, dicks aren't attractive. Well, . . . most boys' dicks I've seen in gym class aren't attractive. I've only seen a few men's dicks. In *Playgirl*. At the newsstand, when Mr. Harris was busy.

Okay, . . . if I'm being honest, I look at *Playgirl* at least once a week. I've seen a lot of men's dicks. They intrigue me. Everything about men's attractive, muscular bodies that look nothing like mine intrigues me. I can't imagine my skinny little boy body ever looking like that. It *does* seem most men, at least the ones in *Playgirl*, are circumcised. I think it became a standard of practice for boys in America, and only a few of us managed to escape the horrid contraption in the hospital.

Now my dick has an ugly scar all the way around. And the head is really sensitive, . . . and not in a good way. It had been completely covered for thirteen years, and now it's out in the open: unprotected, angry, and inflamed. Did I mention sensitive? And not in a good way?

And the first few times I got a boner, the incision bled. It bled a lot. Mom helped the first time, then I asked Pedro to help me, since he's going to be a doctor.

I'm going to go out on a limb right now and say *nobody* wants to bleed from their dick. Never. No way. Not even the sadists. Or the other ones in the S&M thing.

At least I get to skip phys ed for a few weeks because of the surgery. I really hope no one notices or says anything the first time I have to shower with those bozos.

34

MISFITS
Pedro – 14

I'M A MISFIT.

I'm a Misfit.

We're a group of boys that defy categorization. We're not jocks, or nerds, or cool, or rich, or smokers, or stoners. We're four boys drawn to each other because we're what's left over. Misfits. Like the toys in the Santa cartoon.

If I had to guess, I'm the choo-choo with square wheels on its caboose.

Ron is methodical and analytical, with a Beatles obsession. He can dissect with forensic precision the theoretical subject matter in every song and album. I'm not a Beatles fan, but I don't think I should mention this. . . . ever.

Craig is endearingly odd. He is a bit of a philosopher and he's a bleeding-heart liberal like no other. I think he'll make a difference in the world, and I will look in awe from the sideline.

Mike's allowed to watch R-rated movies, and he's the only one of us who watches *Saturday Night Live*. Every Monday he regurgitates all the punchlines and highlights to his knowledge-starved companions.

The rest of us wish we had cool parents like Mike's. We make do with living vicariously through his freedoms.

I round out this quartet as a smart but painfully naive and quiet introvert.

We are all socially awkward misfits.

• • •

Wishing to disappear into the wall does not make you invisible, or invincible. I keep my head down and avoid eye contact to remain anonymous in the junior high school hallways for as long as possible.

But even within the Misfits, I stand out as completely ignorant of all things adolescent. . . .

"Hey Pedro," Mike says with a smirk, so I already know he is about to be a travieso. "Do you know what a uvula is?"

"Yeah," I half-whisper, dreading the obvious next question.

"What is it?"

"I'm not going to say!" I blurt out, knowing the other foot hasn't dropped. There's more to this joke, and I'm about to be its butt. I know what he wants me to say, that it has something to do with a girl's front area anatomy, but honestly I have no way of explaining it since it's all a mystery. And, I don't know why he's asking. Why would he ask me about it?

"It's the little thing that hangs in the back of your throat," he smirks and laughs. "What did you think it was?" The others laugh as well.

I suppose I should be glad I didn't rush in with an erroneous, "It's the external female genitalia at the entrance of the vagina that consist of the labia majora, the labia minora, the clitoris, and other tissues."

Of course, if I *knew* all this, I would also know *those* are the vulva, *not* the uvula. Hence the reason the joke would work for 95–99 percent of the boys in this junior high school.

I wish my brain could memorize these encyclopedia passages, and my mouth and tongue could recite them at will.

I envy Daniel, the walking, talking encyclopedia.

• • •

"Hey Pedro, how do you know if you're coming or going?" Mike asks.

"I don't know," I sputter.

Should I know? What is he talking about? Of course I would know if I'm coming from somewhere, or if I'm going to another place. My brain can't work this fast, plus I know it's a riddle, so I'm doomed.

"One's white and one's yellow!" he exclaims.

The rest of the Misfits laugh.

I don't get it, but I won't admit it.

Wait, . . . what's the answer?

Is this something about sex?

Damn, . . . of course it's something about sex.

• • •

"Hey Pedro, how did they know the girl from *Jaws* had dandruff?"

"I don't know," I respond.

I saw *Jaws* with my brothers. I hated it. I was so tense and anxious and afraid. And how could there possibly be a funny riddle about *Jaws*?

"They found her Head and Shoulders on the beach!"

Ugh.

No explanation needed.

• • •

I'm pretty sure Craig said something, so Mike doesn't ask me those embarrassing riddles anymore.

Now we all laugh at the same things at the same time.

• • •

The eighth graders get a special health retreat as part of catechism; one for boys and one for girls, separately. A priest or a nun talks about health, and human bodies. They avoid the word sex completely: "The married man places his penis into his loving wife and releases his seed."

Not only does it not explain *anything* to me, I now have more questions than I had yesterday.

Many of the boys have older brothers who have already gone through the retreat. I guess Juan did as well, but he and I would *never* talk about this kind of stuff. Some of the boys in my class have even had sex, or so they say. I rely on crumbs of information the Misfits, or other boys, may carelessly sprinkle drop here and there, since I won't come out and ask questions.

In this health retreat, we see cartoon diagrams of naked middle areas of boys and girls. Actually, I think they are diagrams of full-grown men and women from the size of everything. The bodies are cut down the middle so you can see what's inside as well. The girl cartoons make no sense; I try to orient myself, but it's so confusing.

The boy cartoons are also confusing even though I am a boy. In the side view, there is a big penis — cut down the middle! — and there is one big testicle, also cut down the middle. The big half-penis juts out from the body, and entirely overhangs the big half-testicle. It looks like it ends halfway down to the guy's knee.

Those *do not* look like mine.

There are all kinds of squiggles and lumps labeled as different organs inside the body. I wonder if I really have all those inside me, since I'm still small and skinny and can't seem to grow taller or grow muscles. Maybe I'm not a full real boy? Maybe that's the problem? Am I missing some of those squiggles and swirls inside me?

• • •

In middle school, the boys shower together after phys ed.

I don't understand why the humiliation of complete incompetence in sports has to be followed by the humiliation of being naked with your classmates. Boys' naked bodies are so varied at this age. Lots of jocks have sprouted pubic hair. Their penises and testicles look almost full-sized.

But most of us are the same as always.

I'm relieved I'm not the only one who hasn't developed any signs of puberty.

Nudity does seem to get less humiliating over time. You see the same boys naked every day, the shock and embarrassment lessen. But if I'm really being honest, I still hate taking my clothes off in front of anyone, especially in front of those I know who can easily wound with a few choice words released in the hallways: word-balloons floating in the air as the gentle whispers push them down the hallway, until everyone in the school has heard the words, and everyone, including the teachers, janitors and cooks, are aware of the betrayal of the unspoken commandment that the contents of the boys' locker room must stay within.

"Do you know what I mean about this?" I ask. "I feel exposed and vulnerable in the locker room."

"Yeah, I get it. 'Qué bonito es ver la lluvia y no mojarse,'" Daniel replies. *"It's nice to see the rain and not get wet."*

"What does that mean?"

"Some boys criticize without fear of negative reciprocity because they were blessed with certain genes. They can't be hurt by words. I know *exactly* how you feel."

• • •

I hate having heavy dreams. No surprise, most of them are about Mom being Mom at her worst. I wake up sensing someone watching me. I already know spirits, or angels, can get into our bedrooms. I won't open my eyes when I roll over onto my belly to protect it from the ax. It's rare for me to have two nightmares in one night, so I should be okay.

Lately, I wake with my face, neck, and pillow wet because I was weeping in my dream, and my whole body is actually really crying. I wake up and my life is as bad as it was in my nightmare. *Is there anything sadder?*

I keep having thoughts of making it all stop, which I guess *is* even sadder. I contemplate ways I'd do it, and I'm consumed with guilt for even thinking about this mortal sin.

35

HOPE
Daniel – 14

THE FIRST TIME I went to a Catholic mass, I saw theatrical magic under candlelight, and I sensed the mysterious aromas and effects of incense. I was entranced by the statues of Jesus Christ and Mother Mary, and the stations of the cross on the side walls of the church. The ringing of the bells at the moments of transubstantiation of bread and wine into the body and blood of Jesus Christ captured my attention. Then, of course, there were colors, fabrics, grandeur, chimes, and pomp and circumstance, all in a one-hour extravaganza.

But the most bewitching moment was when the priest said during his sermon that he speaks with God. I was hooked. This is my calling, my desire.

After that service, I declared my wish to be a priest.

Mom was thrilled: it is a great honor for a Mexican woman to have a son become a priest. She beamed the news to anyone who would listen. The priests and nuns in the parish took note, and they have actively nurtured my interest throughout my time in parochial school, and in junior high.

Now in eighth grade, it seems many are invested in my successful entry into the priesthood. It's becoming very clear how unusual it is for a boy to want to become a priest.

• • •

"Daniel, I know your heart has told you to become a priest," Father Randolph says. "You must know the path to priesthood is long and difficult. There are many years of study and you'll need to make some serious sacrifices."

Father Randolph asked to speak with me after I served mass with him today. We're sitting in a pew in the church.

"I know, Father."

But I don't *really* know. What sacrifices? It almost sounds like I'll need to give up chocolate, candy, and pies, like I'm supposed to at Lent, but I never make it past a day or two; last year, I only lasted a few hours.

"I think you should consider going to the high school seminary next year. I'm aware of your family's financial footing, but I think I can help get you grants and scholarships. What do you think?"

"Father, it would be terrific! I hadn't thought it was possible," I reply, then pause. "But I don't know what my mom would say."

"Don't worry about her, Daniel. It will bring her *great joy* when you are ordained. This would be the beginning of the journey to becoming a priest. . . . I'll explain all this to your parents, if you really are interested."

"Yes, Father, I am! Thank you for all your help! I really appreciate it!" I can't hide my enthusiasm, and my hope.

"I'll call your parents and see if I can stop by to chat with them this weekend."

• • •

The Holy Cross Seminary in Toledo is about an hour from home. If I go there next year, I would live on campus, and I'd only come home every other weekend. It would advance my ability to leave home, somewhat, by four years! I know the weekends home would be brutal, but I'll finally get out and experience the world.

• • •

Father Randolph and Mom talked this morning. Pop was there, but he just listened. He wants whatever will make me happy, . . . as long as

Mom says yes. For her part, Mom seems excited about this opportunity; I'd be going to an expensive seminary on a full scholarship — which she can announce to all her comadres — I'd get an outstanding education, and I would start my journey to becoming a priest, something she desperately wants.

But now her doubts have surfaced.

"Sólo quieres irte para dejarme aquí," she complains. "Y allí estarás de paseo."

As with every major decision, Mom struggles with this one. I can't understand any possible downside to my going to the seminary, except her perception of feeling abandoned, and the misconception that I will be there purely enjoying myself.

How many times have I thought of this dicho for Mom,

'No hay más que temer que una mujer enfadada.'
There is nothing as fearsome as an angry woman.

But in this case, I would replace angry with abandoned, or misperceivedly — is that a word? — abandoned.

I admit I would enjoy being away from home, but it would still be school. Like any other school, I would need to study, do homework, and take tests. It would *not* be a total joyride.

• • •

"What do you think, Pedro?" I ask.

I know he's sad. He's heard all the commotion about this unexpected opportunity that threatens to break us apart, at least physically.

I think about all the times we talked about running away together. We never even tried once. The fear of being caught was just too great. In movies, we saw how slaves in various cultures were treated when they were captured and returned to those people — I hate the word *master.*

Pedro and I have talked about the multimillennial history of human slavery throughout the world. There have always been humans who treated others as less-than-human, as property, as a commodity of economic value, nothing more. We've talked about how Mom has always treated us like slaves: she's terrorized us, abused us in unspeakable ways, and I know Pedro feels hated because of his skin color.

I'm now aware of the ingrained racist views of some lighter-skinned Latinos against those with darker tones. It doesn't make sense, except that humans tend to enjoy subjugating others. Even those that know better, that say they're Christians.

"You're going to leave me here . . . with her . . . alone," he mutters.

I think his face is flushed. He won't look at me, and I won't force him.

"You won't be alone," I retort half-heartedly.

But I know what he means.

"You know what I mean."

He slowly looks up, with moist eyes and a pinched chin.

I don't understand why Mom is so hard on Pedro. Is it really because he looks so much like Pop? Because he's darker, a prieto? Because he doesn't like sports? Because she thinks he's a maricón?

It's hard to understand how a mom could dislike a son like that, with all he has to offer.

Not that she's particularly fond of me! I'm aware of my own proclivities that meet with her deep derision and disappointment. I'm definitely a maricón — I've gotten a better idea of what it means from locker room talk and childish drawings from schoolmates — but she doesn't seem to care anymore. Wanting to be a priest is my only redeeming quality. It probably makes sense to her that I wouldn't be interested in girls since I won't be able to get married anyway.

Mom's prone to rudimentary, or concrete — rather than abstract — thinking. She had thought it all had to do with foreskin. Now that I don't have it, she probably thinks I've been cured.

For the love of . . .

I hope she won't get Pedro circumcised!

"What are you thinking about?" Pedro asks.

"Nothing," I lie.

My face must have given me away as I thought of Mom having Pedro circumcised to "cure him" . . . to "cut the gay off," like they used lobotomy or sterilization in the past as barbaric remedies for who knows what. I would *not* put it past her.

She thinks she *owns* us, and our bodies.

"I'd be back every other weekend," I say. "I'm sure I'll pay for having been away."

"Daniel, I know you want to be a priest." Now, he looks me in the eyes. I know the look. He's acknowledged and accepted what's coming. He's at peace with it. "I don't understand it . . . at all, . . . but if you can get out of here, and follow your dream, you need to go. 'Deja de mirar atrás, si no nunca llegarás.'"

Stop looking behind, otherwise you'll never arrive.

"That's a good one! . . . I'll miss you Pedro."

My eyes get misting, and my throat is full.

"You still have to get in!" he quips with a grin. "And you still have to wait until next September!"

"Ugh, that's true. You know . . . I wish you could go to a medical school high school somewhere far away too!"

"Are you kidding me?" His face contorts. After a pause, he adds, "She won't let her best slave go *that* easily."

I hate that I see pain, grief, and fear in his eyes.

• • •

It's been a couple months since Father Randolph spoke with Mom. On any given day, she will say yes I can go, then no I can't go to the seminary. I pray to Jesus, but mostly to La Virgencita, because Mom is more likely to listen to her.

• • •

Father Randolph is driving me to Holy Cross for a weekend open house. It's meant to persuade students to enroll next fall.

I don't need any convincing.

Where do I sign?

36

DOT
Pedro – 15

I STARTED GROWING pubic hair. I hadn't even noticed until one day I got a sharp pain down there, ran to the bathroom, saw a hair stuck in my foreskin. This single hair in that sensitive area was getting pulled when I moved or walked. And the hair was tearing into my foreskin, like a wire garrote digging into a neck. It was an odd two-for-one pain sensation, but I was happy puberty let me know it had finally arrived.

'Todo llega a su tiempo.'
Things happen when they're supposed to.

• • •

I discovered a jobs program for high school students from low-income families. Daniel and I are working in the Department of Transportation for the summer.

Juan drops us off at the huge industrial garage building before he drives to his own job nearby. All of the county's DOT trucks park in this garage. Daniel and I scrub and wash them, put sand over oil puddles, and sweep the entire garage every day. We also mow the lawn around the building. Later in the summer, we'll have to paint the outside of the building.

The first weeks here, we chip off all the rust from the large snow-plows so that Stan the Man can give them a new coat of bright yellow paint. It's boring work, using chisels then sandpaper. In effect, we have to remove all the old paint and rust so the new paint can stick to the clean metal below.

. . .

When you walk in the front door of the DOT, there is a large room with three picnic tables where the workers congregate in the morning to have their coffee, where they take their breaks, if they're onsite at those times. There is a fridge, a water cooler, and lots of cabinets with supplies. There are doors to the manager's office, a bathroom, and double doors to the large garage with all the trucks and machinery in the back. The trucks come in from huge garage doors in the back of the building.

There are candy bars, sodas, and other snacks in the fridge, along with a plastic container for the change you are supposed to add for the purchase of those snacks. It's on the honor system.

"Let's get a Choco-Nutty Bar!" Daniel says at least once a day, every day. Although he will be going to seminary school in a few months, he doesn't seem to know about the "honor system." It makes me think of his wayward will at Kenny's Market.

"We need to put in the twenty-five cents Daniel!" I say with increasing exasperation. Invariably, he'll get a chocolate bar—or two. How does he *not* have a mouth full of cavities? The jack-o'-lantern smile of his youth is now an attractive weapon he uses to distract and disarm others.

. . .

If it's raining, we'll have our lunch on the picnic tables in the front room. Otherwise, we sit out back under a tree where the men can't see us.

After we eat our lunch, we open up the girlie magazines we borrowed from the boxes in the manager's office. There are hundreds of magazines in those boxes. The magazine titles and the front covers usually advertise what's inside, like big chichis or girl–girl or whatever you might want. I guess you can judge a magazine by its cover. I can't imagine why they're there for anyone to see, and borrow.

"Open it up!" Daniel blurts out, eager to see today's pictures, and to read the funny stories inside.

"Why do they always wear spiky high heels?" I ask.

"And why do they wear chonies that don't cover their front? And bras that don't cover the chichis? I don't get lingerie. Do women really wear this stuff? I know Mom doesn't."

"No! . . . Daniel, please don't put images in my head!" I slap my hands against my eyes, as if that would magically prevent the images already forming in my mind from entering through my pupils.

"And, . . . why do they always have long, red fingernails? Don't things get stabbed or scratched that probably shouldn't get stabbed or scratched?"

Boy, Daniel's got a lot of questions today. I look at the woman's front area on this page, and I can't figure *anything* out. Then I have my own question: "Where does the pee come out?"

Daniel giggles. "I don't know either."

The pictures in the magazines rarely have a man. If there is a man, you only see his nalgies and his muscular arms and legs. His postman, fireman, or policeman uniform is usually bunched up at his ankles with his chonies.

The stories are funny, at least to us, and confusing. The man puts his penis inside the woman, but I'm not sure where it ends up. I don't think the whole thing fits inside. Although, a whole baby comes out, so maybe? Wait, . . . a whole baby comes out of *there*? How is that even possible?

I think I'm missing information. . . .

Then the man comes. Or cums. I think it's just another way to spell it. Why can't they be consistent, less confusing?

How is sucking the same as a blow job? Is it like sucking on a lolli-pop and blowing out a candle? Because those almost seem like the opposite direction of things.

Sometimes, the stories say the woman comes too. I want to ask Daniel if he knows what that means. He always seems to know *every-thing* about *everything* I can't find in a book.

"Why do you think they have all these magazines here?" I ask, too nervous to ask what I really want to ask.

"I don't know, but 'Donde fueres, haz lo que vieres,'" Daniel chants. "When in Rome, do as the Romans."

"I'm not sure I would compare the DOT to Rome."

"Or Stan the Man to a Roman," he smirks, and we both laugh.

• • •

Okay, now I know the difference between coming and going. From last year with the Misfits! One's white and one's yellow! This magazine today is more graphic, with plenty of penises. But how did that white stuff come out? Did they push it out somehow?

How can two completely different fluids come out of the same place?

You can eat and breathe through your mouth, but I don't really understand how air and food know which way to go.

It must be like a railroad track switch.

I don't know anyone I could ask, other than Daniel. I don't go to camp or Boy Scouts. The encyclopedia wasn't helpful. Could I ask Dr. Fritz? Would he tell Mom? Either way, it's way too risky.

• • •

This new guy, Keith, just started working here. He's more beautiful than handsome. He has Doobie Brothers bright blue eyes with little gold flecks, and really large, straight, blindingly white teeth. His neatly trimmed beard accents his square jaw. His loosely curled light brown hair sits on his shoulders.

Keith looks like Jesus in the movies and paintings we've seen of Him.

"Jesus was a Jewish, Middle Eastern man who lived two thousand years ago," I contemplate. "Wouldn't he have had dark hair, dark eyes, and dark skin?"

"Maybe," Daniel replies. "The Shroud of Turin is the only known image of Jesus. Although, I heard some altar boys say it's fake — then the priest who overheard them blew a gasket."

Daniel places his fingers on his temples and fans them out like fireworks as he makes his eyes pinwheel around in circles. We both laugh.

"I've noticed priests don't like it when you ask questions they can't answer," I observe.

"Not at all."

Daniel's leaning on his broom, looking through a large window in the garage up at the sky.

The DOT manager is on the road, so Stan the Man is spending the day in the manager's office. He keeps taking long bathroom breaks, but he could check in on us at any moment, so I start sweeping.

"I read they tested the Shroud, and it's not old enough to have an authentic image of Jesus." I say. "It's just interesting he always looks White with blue eyes and curly, light brown hair."

Not that there's anything wrong with blue eyes and curly, light brown hair, I think to myself. It's always good to clarify things in case the karma gods are listening to my thoughts.

Keith probably thinks I'm weird because I won't look him in the eyes. I'm afraid they see the truth hidden within me.

I can tell Daniel is also attracted to Keith.

This may be the first time Daniel and I want the same thing.

But what do we want exactly? . . .

I'd like to look at Keith's eyes for as long as I want, without anyone saying anything.

• • •

Once a week, the DOT manager sends us out with Bill to clean the trash cans at the public parks around the lake. The lake motto is

Vacationland USA, and people come from all over to fish and go to the state beaches.

Bill is goofy, but nice. He won't smoke when we're in the truck with him. "Don' wanna poison yer lungs." I don't think he's that old, maybe twenty-six or twenty-seven. He has a thick beard he never trims, and stringy, dirty brown hair, so it's hard to tell what's underneath. It's as if he wore diver's goggles when the rest of his face decided to grow out hair, so that's all I can see clearly. His crooked teeth are stained from tobacco, but he could be good-looking, if he had a makeover of some kind. Yeah, I'm imagining Bill with a neatly trimmed beard and mustache and a much-needed haircut, and he is kinda handsome under there.

He's got nice eyes.

• • •

It's the first week in August and the humidity has been unbearable. Daniel and I wear loose tank tops, and we're still soaking wet in the cab with Bill.

When we see household trash, we're supposed to open the bags and look for names and addresses so the culprits can get a letter warning them it's against the law to dump trash in public parks.

Bill empties heavy metal garbage cans into the back of the truck while Daniel and I go through bags of household trash. When I pull out a single page of porn with two guys, I take in a loud and sudden deep breath. I frantically keep rummaging. My chest is pounding, my head is throbbing; I may be panicking with building anticipation. There's other household trash in the bag, but just this one page of porn.

It's odd, . . . and sad.

I suppose it's better than nothing.

"Let me see!" Daniel shouts. His eyes are open wide. His mouth seems uncertain if it will remain open, partially close, or perhaps settle into his signature grin.

I hand him the single page, pretending I'm not interested in it.

Daniel giggles. "I didn't know they *made* these kinds of magazines."

"I didn't either, . . . It's weird someone tore this one page out and put it in this bag of trash."

"I know. Are you sure there isn't more? Mejor que nada. Here, you can hide it for us."

The words "for us" ring in my ears.

I'd like to say, "Daniel, I know you know I'm gay, and I know you're gay too. Can we talk about it?"

But, as much as I think about dying, . . . I don't want Mom to kill me. It's not worth it. *She's* not worth it, and I don't want to give her any excuse.

I'd rather do it on my own terms, when I can't go on anymore.

Later, when I'm alone in our bathroom at home, I examine the single sheet of guy–guy porn. The same two boys are in each of three pictures. They're probably in their late twenties, so I guess they're men, not boys. There are a few paragraphs on the first page that detail Lyle and Kurt's attraction to each other, how they start to undress, and start to kiss. The second page continues the story a little, but the sex of the story is probably on the next pages I don't have.

The pictures aren't really risqué. In the first one, they have one arm around the other and they don't even have erections as they look at the camera. The smaller photos on the second page show each of them looking at the other guy's penis, a few inches away, with their mouths slightly open. It looks staged, and not really sexy.

I can't use the money hole under my mattress to hide this. I still keep some money there, but if anyone found this page, I really don't think anything or anyone would stop Mom from beating me to death for bringing this "filth" into her house.

But I can't throw it away. It is my first sign, first proof, first physical evidence of the existence of this outside world, which has previously existed on innuendo and murmurs. It is my only connection to that outside world. I wouldn't cut the tether between an astronaut and his ship and relegate him to be forever lost in space. I have been lost and ignorant for far too long.

I found a good hiding place in the bathroom cabinetry. There is a space behind the dummy drawers under the sink where I put the folded page for safe keeping. I hit the sink counter a few times just to make sure it won't accidentally fall out, but it's nicely wedged between two pieces of wood.

. . .

The marching band starts practicing in early August, right across the street on the high school field. Some evenings are chilly enough for a sweatshirt.

Lots of neighbors listen to the music on their front lawns, watch fireflies, and swat mosquitoes. When the crickets really start going, they're as loud as the band.

It's almost back-to-school time.

And it's almost time for Daniel to leave for the seminary.

I am dreading it.

What will I do without him here?

He was my first friend.
He is my only friend.
He was my first love.
He is my only love.
I will be lost without him.

My moods are more and more sullen. It's becoming unbearable.

I know what I could do, if I wanted to.

. . .

"Pedro, I'm going to miss you."

"I'm going to miss you too."

Daniel's leaving me later today.

I've got to get out of here. I can't do this right now. I'm bound so tight, if I even look at him, we'll both get caught up in the aftermath of my unreeling. I'm not sure what that would look like, but Mom can never pass up a chance to unreel herself on me.

And I know what that looks like.

Please God, don't let me be like her.

"I'll be back in twelve days."

I still can't look at him. . . .

"I know. I've got to go to work now."

We hug.

He gives me a long, wet, noisy kiss on my cheek.

And I smile.

He knows how to bore through my protective layers.

I manage to maintain control.

But I'll have to scrub my face before I leave for work.

37

SEMINARY
Daniel – 15

IT WAS A long summer.

Pedro and I worked at the Department of Transportation, which had many memorable moments. I wonder what stories Pedro would tell about his experiences, and his exposure to new and unusual things.

He'd certainly never seen a colossal collection of pervy pornography like the one we saw at the DOT.

Years ago, there were times I'd drag him to the corner of the newsstand when Mr. Harris was attending a customer, and I'd open up a *Playgirl* magazine. Pedro's eyes would get so big, . . . then he'd run out and leave me there alone with my vice.

Things were different at the DOT.

• • •

Mom was classic Mom all summer. She kept threatening to pull me out of the seminary before I even started. She savors dangling those carrots over us. It made for a lot of eye-rolling moments. Do this, or do that, or you won't go to any damn seminary!

Well, I'm at the damn seminary now, and I couldn't be happier. And, I didn't have to use reverse psychology, which is Pedro's lifeline.

Speaking of Pedro, it was hard to say goodbye to him. He started working at a nursing home the day after we left the DOT, and he plans to keep working once school starts for him.

I couldn't get him to look at me when we said goodbye, alone, away from eyes and ears, down in our room, before he went to work. He's in a lot of pain. I don't know how to help him, especially since my leaving is contributing to his despair.

Although I will miss him terribly, I am starting a new life, with new experiences and opportunities. I know he doesn't resent my good fortune. I only wish I could share some with him.

• • •

Someone thought it was a good idea to design our rooms with only three walls, no doors, no privacy. From the hallway, my twin bed is against the wall on the left; there's a window on the facing wall; and on the right there's a built-in desk, shelving, cabinetry, and a small closet. The fourth wall is literally missing. Anyone can stand in the hallway and see everything inside each room.

"I guess we left our privacy at the door when we entered the building," another newbie comments.

"No kidding," I respond. "I saw these dorms before, but now that I'm supposed to live here, I feel totally exposed."

"I'm Harry," he says. "I'm across the hall from you, so I guess we're each other's front row seats."

"I'm Daniel. I have a feeling we'll get to know each other very quickly."

The bathrooms are down the hall. There are open shower rooms, which I guess is standard in schools; the junior and senior high school showers at home were open shower rooms.

There will be no privacy here at the seminary, except for the toilet stalls. I appreciate being able to do that alone.

• • •

My teachers are primarily priests. Some are young, still in their twenties. At the other end of the spectrum are old, arthritic men. Contrary to how it sounds, their personalities vary greatly, and I often prefer the nice, grandfatherly teacher.

It's a pretty regimented life here. We get up early, make our beds, have breakfast, and attend mass. There's a short break, then we start classes: philosophy, theology, math, English, Spanish, science. We have a short lunch break. After classes, we enjoy an hour of free time before prayer service, then dinner.

• • •

It took me a while to get used to boys walking around naked. Most of them have been to summer camps, or they were in the Scouts, or they came from less repressed homes, and they are used to nudity. It almost seems natural to them, which when I think about it, makes sense: nudity is about as natural as we can be. It only *feels* unnatural, *to me*.

It reminds me of the whole circumcision debate. How some families want their boys to "look like their dads" down there. I've never seen Pop's penis, but I hadn't realized how different it is in other families.

When we were little, Pedro opened the bathroom door and saw Pop taking a bath. He was kneeling with his head under the spout, washing the shampoo away; we didn't have showers back then. Pedro saw Pop's butt and was so traumatized about invading Pop's privacy, he couldn't sleep for days afterwards. Poor Pedro gets into some sticky situations.

We're not separated by class year, so there are boys who are thirteen to seventeen years old on my floor, all going through various stages of puberty. The older boys have full bushes, and their dicks and balls are basically adult-sized. I started the process earlier this year, so at least I'm not the last to blossom.

These guys have learned about sex from their brothers, cousins, friends, campmates. Some have experimented with guys along the way; they don't seem to have hang-ups about it, even the ones who say they aren't gay.

So, I'm learning about masturbation and sex. I'm experimenting, and having sex with my schoolmates.

I feel guilt and shame every time.

The church has very strict rules about sex. It comes down to marital sex—which is okay, if the purpose is procreation—and premarital sex, which is every type of sex before you're married, which is never okay.

What we're doing is worse because it's gay sex. Now I can definitively confirm I'm a maldito maricón. I'm a damned fag. Emphasis on damned, as in damned to hell.

Then there's masturbation, which isn't technically sex, but there are passages in the Bible about spilling your seed. When boys jerk off, they "spill" their semen, with millions and millions of sperm in the fluid. I recently learned that sperm are considered "seeds," at least biblically.

In the eyes of the church, those spilled seeds could have been perfect for the moment when you and your lawfully married wife coupled for the purpose of a miraculous conception.

But come on—millions of sperms, on the off chance one conception will occur?

The moral of the story is when you spill your seed, you're kinda killing *the potential of a child.*

In the Bible, God slew Onan's brother because he was "wicked." I wish they would define wicked.

Then God forced Onan to marry his widowed sister-in-law so his dead brother—killed by God—could have an heir. With this arrangement, Onan's son would not be considered Onan's heir, which Onan did not appreciate.

So Onan would have sex with his widowed sister-in-law—who was now his wife, because he was forced to marry her because God killed her husband, his brother—but he would withdraw before he ejaculated, and he "spilled his seed" rather than get her pregnant with a child who would not be his heir.

I'd say Onan: 1, God: 0, but the story doesn't end there.

Apparently, God was angry at Onan for disobeying him, and He slew Onan for spilling his seed. Essentially, God killed Onan for coitus interruptus, also known as withdrawal, but ultimately Onanism is known as masturbation. And it's considered a crime.

At least, in the Bible.

That's why masturbation is a no-no.

Although, if I can be picky, there is a technical difference between withdrawal and masturbation since they can occur independently.

God slew Onan's brother, then He slew Onan himself. God took time out of His busy schedule to take a look at what these two were doing, and then He killed them on the spot.

And, Zipporah worried God would kill Moses because he hadn't circumcised his son.

Leviticus 5:17 says, "If a person sins and does any of the things which the LORD has commanded not to be done, though he was unaware, he is still guilty and shall bear his punishment."

In other words: "Ignorance of the law is no excuse."

Ignorance would have been my excuse until Father McCarthy mentioned Leviticus and the sins of onanism in one of his fire and brimstone sermons.

Basically, I'm screwed.

And I might get slain any day now.

• • •

For most of my early childhood, I didn't think priests were real men. I didn't think they had full bodily functions. Actually, I didn't think they had dicks and buttholes, or that they went to the bathroom. I'd never seen them eat, except for the body of Christ during mass, so they were mysteries to me.

I can't imagine Jesus was a regular, normal man: that Jesus peed and pooped. But the scriptures say He was truly God and He was truly man. He was the incarnation, "made flesh."

Some people argue whether Jesus ever laughed or owned property. I wonder if He peed and pooped, if He got erections, if He had orgasms or wet dreams or sex. I don't think I can ask anyone those questions.

Someday, when I'm a priest and I can talk with Jesus, I wonder if I'll ask Him these questions directly.

Some people might think it's sacrilegious to even *think* these things, but honestly, doesn't everyone wonder about Jesus as a boy, an adolescent, a man? Should it be shameful if Jesus' body functioned the same as other men's bodies?

Are we all shameful in the eyes of God?

I know priests talk to God, and serve *in persona Christi*—they become God during certain rites. I'm still not sure how they "talk to God," or if God talks back somehow. Do He and Jesus whisper in their ears? Do They show up as a hologram like Princess Leia? When I saw *Star Wars*, that scene reminded me of the animals we saw in Sara's room when we were kids.

Talking with God is what drew me to the priesthood in the first place.

I think I can help people, if I can just get answers to some burning questions. People want answers to questions, not more questions as answers to questions.

I wonder if the Pope and the archbishops have a more direct line of communication with the Trinity. It seems to me they aren't asking the right questions, or they're not getting detailed answers, or they're not sharing the answers with the rest of us.

It reminds me of a quote attributed to Saint Bernard:

> There are those who seek knowledge for the sake of knowledge; that is curiosity.
> There are those who seek knowledge to be known by others; that is vanity.
> There are those who seek knowledge in order to serve; that is charity/love.

I sometimes wonder *why* God lets some of these questions enter my mind. I don't want to be disrespectful in wondering what I wonder.

I'm definitely not doing it on purpose. I can't seem to "cleanse them" from my thoughts, like the priests say I should. I know it's their way of telling me to stop questioning how things have always been.

Maybe it's the messaging: *Follow the Ten Commandments* and *Treat Others as You Would Like Others to Treat You* don't seem to be working with people.

I think we all need updated directives from more recent conversations with God.

• • •

I now know my early childhood ideas about priests were misperceptions, based on the little information I had at the time. Now I know priests are just men like other men, with real bodies, vices, and flaws; men who have studied to become priests, but who remain men in all other ways. They preach: don't have sex, unless you're married, and only if you're having sex for the purpose of having children.

But now I know some of them have sex. Some have sex with each other. And some have sex with us, their students. They don't seem to have a problem with it while they're doing it, then later they feel guilt and shame—until the next time they come into our doorless hallways.

> 'El hábito no hace al monje.'
> *The habit does not make the monk.*

Guilt and shame have been lurking behind every thought and action all my life. I tell my sins at confession every week, and I feel a momentary reprieve, but my subsequent thoughts and actions only bring more guilt and shame. I wonder if I'll ever break this cycle. Not likely when those who are meant to guide us down a righteous path prefer to mislead us in a different direction.

We are all maldito maricones, . . . damned fags.

Of course, not *all* gay men are damned. Just those of us who can't practice what we preach.

'Haz lo que bien digo, no lo que mal hago.'
Do as I say, not as I do.

• • •

Homosexuality was known in ancient civilizations before and during Jesus' time on earth. It makes me wonder why He didn't say anything about homosexuality. . . . or masturbation.

More food for fun thoughts.

• • •

"It's not the same, Pedro!" I cry out, irritably, and definitely defensively.

"It's not the *exact* same, but there are significant similarities! You've *got* to see that!"

"Okay, explain it again. But I think you're enjoying this much more than me."

"There is *nothing* to enjoy about any of this!" Pedro exclaims as he throws his arms up in the air, then waves them around. I wonder if he's adding our sad situation to the mix. "Those people devoted themselves to their beliefs."

"Okay, so far," I snarl through my teeth. He's working my last nerve, and testing my faith in my church. Yes, I'm definitely defensive.

"These people did what they were told to do," he replies sternly, and perhaps, sadly. "They didn't question it, despite the severity of the order."

"Some of them."

"Most of them, Daniel. . . . You've seen the same reports."

"Okay, most of them followed orders. . . . Blindly," I say, knowing I'm not going to win this argument. Though. . . . I should not even try.

"They committed mass murder and suicide," he chokes out, and his voice breaks.

"Yes, it's true. But other religions don't do that!"

"Daniel, . . . the colonization of the world? The Crusades? Okay, they didn't commit mass suicide, in general, but they killed countless Indigenous Peoples, Muslims, and Jews — and they even killed Christians who didn't follow papal rule! In the name of what?"

"Some were sanctioned by the Pope at the time, but not always! And there were other religions that did the same, in their own ways. There have been *many* types of holy wars."

"Exactly Daniel! I'm not singling out Christianity. There are *many* examples of holy wars involving most known religions."

"Yeah. I can't argue with that."

"Religion is the opium of *some* people, the Kool-Aid of others, and who knows what to who knows who," Pedro says. "Religious leaders and their followers don't generally follow their own basic tenets of compassion and care for others. Okay, to be fair, I'll reword it: 'many' religious leaders, and 'many' of their followers."

I can tell Pedro is sad, and exasperated. These news reports, and the graphic images coming out of Guyana, are devastating. He will have to ponder this in his head, full of pain, grief, suffering, and so much else.

I really can't explain how this could have happened in this day and age.

38

BLT
Pedro – 16

THE COMADRES KEPT asking why I don't play sports, so I had to join cross-country. It was the lesser of all evils. I'll have to run track in the spring. I'm hoping to avoid winter sports, with the worst uniforms: the singlet and the Speedo. The least amount of fabric during the winter is a special sort of head-scratcher.

The comadres keep asking why I don't have a girlfriend.

But I'm only fifteen, going on sixteen, and I'd prefer a Rolf over a Liesl.

Mom explains I don't have time for girls—I'm going to be a doctor!—but *still* she flounders, and the circling sharks smell the bloody scent of vulnerability.

If Mom knew I don't want to date girls, there'd be a long line of comadres and their daughters at our door. Thankfully, I've discovered reverse psychology works wonders with Mom, but it must be used sparingly so it doesn't lose its effect. You have to choose your battles to win the wars.

So, I occasionally drop a girl's name into a conversation. . . .

"¿Quién es esta Carolina? ¡Nunca quiero verte hablando con ella! ¡No tienes tiempo para estar persiguiendo faldas!"

Jackpot!

Now I can't talk with Caroline, or "chase her skirt." I certainly couldn't date her either. Mom can tell her comadres how "una Carolina" pursued me, *and I wanted to date her,* but she (Mom) told me I don't have time to date girls because I'm studying to be a doctor.

Which, I'm not.

Not really.

Not yet.

I'm only a sophomore in *high school.* I've got *six more years* before I start medical school, *ten* more years before I'll *be* a doctor.

I can't explain why some people think I've got medical knowledge or training already.

I would feel bad for Caroline, and her bad reputation I am helping create, if she actually existed! Caroline is just a name I used in a fabricated story.

Of course I don't want to lie about a Caroline who doesn't exist. But what's the harm? At the end of the day, I pretend-to-like a make-believe girl, Mom won't let me date her, and I have to spend more time with my studies.

I'd say everyone, including Caroline, is getting what they want.

I wonder what will happen when Mom realizes I've been duping her for years. I haven't mentioned reverse psychology to anyone, other than Daniel. He's much better at keeping my secrets now that he's older, and *his* stakes are higher.

But there are some secrets I still won't share with Daniel. The risk for me is just too great. I'm a mistreated, indentured servant without a contract or an escape plan.

It would be catastrophic if Mom heard my confession second hand. No one could understand this threat. . . . not even Daniel. No one sees the hate I see in her eyes.

• • •

It's hugely embarrassing that I get free lunch at the cafeteria. Most of the kids know, and most are kind enough to keep it to themselves. But there are always a few kids who forget their Christian values.

To be clear, I don't know of a single family that isn't Catholic or Protestant. There are no temples, mosques, or other non-Christian houses of worship in our little town.

"You wouldn't need to get free lunch if your parents would stop having kids, Pedro. They're like fucking rabbits!" Larry Sommers chuckles as laughter grows around me. "They *fuck* like fucking rabbits! Have they heard of contraception . . . or self-control?"

"Leave him alone Larry. They're just Catholics. . . . They don't believe in contraception," Molly Greene states. "Still, Pedro, how many brothers and sisters *do* you have?"

"Maybe they should just go back to Mexico instead of mooching off the government," Larry adds. His many minions mutter agreement.

Even with my complexion, my ears must be red to match the heat they're producing. My blurred vision stares into a corner.

I would like to say, "*I was born down the street at the same hospital you were born in!*"

The familiar sand-and-cotton concoction sits at the back of my throat. I avoid ejecting garbled and useless letters and punctuation marks.

• • •

My secret stash of money in my box spring buys me an extra carton of milk each day. The usual lunch lady is sweet, and seems to understand my attempt to hide my shame. The best trick is giving her a dime instead of a nickel for the extra milk so she has to give me change. Then kids can clearly see the monetary exchange.

But when she's gone for any reason, the substitute lady is heartless, almost sadistic.

"Sixty-five cents," she squeaks with her eyes, nose, and mouth pinched together, as if she just smelled the fart that pinched face squeezed out.

"I get free lunch," I whisper. I offer my five cents for the extra milk.

"What? Speak up!"

"I get free lunch," I say, a little louder.

"What's your name? I'll check it on the FREE LUNCH LIST," she screeches with increasing volume. "EVERYONE JUST HOLD UP WHILE I LOOK AT THE FREE LUNCH LIST OF PEOPLE WHO CAN'T AFFORD TO PAY FOR THEIR LUNCH BUT CONTINUE TO HAVE MORE AND MORE MEXICAN CHILDREN ANYWAY."

I might be showing some artistic license.

• • •

Last year, there was a significant fear of a new flu strain called Swine Flu. At first, it was thought to be related to the virus that caused the 1918 flu pandemic that killed millions worldwide. The federal government initiated a fast-track effort to vaccinate every American this past fall. As vice president of the Future Professionals in Medicine, I volunteered to help with the vaccination efforts, and I encouraged many folks to get vaccinated.

There were politics involved, but it otherwise seemed to be a well-intentioned public health measure against a pandemic that never actually materialized.

Unfortunately, the whole affair was a debacle, with inferior science behind the initiative. I feel some responsibility for those I recruited, although I'm relieved no one in our community suffered the serious vaccine side effects reported in the news. Now, vaccines are getting a bad rap even though they were previously considered safe, and were very effective at preventing debilitating, deadly diseases around the world.

• • •

"It was really hard to watch *Roots* when it showed graphic violence," I remark. "I couldn't look at Mom. The scenes felt too close to home."

"I know what you mean," Daniel notes. "I wondered what was going on in her head."

"Every one of the Black actors was terrific. I really felt their pain and anguish. But I think it was a particularly poignant portrayal of the atrocities committed against Black people because of the specific White actors they used."

"What do you mean?"

"In general, those men and women were acting contrary to their usual casting. They've portrayed funny and lovable characters in movies and other TV shows. Seeing them play vile, violent people made me wonder if *anyone* is capable of such hate."

"Hmm. . . . You're right. Most of those slave owners were 'God-fearing Christians' committing cruelty and dreadful deeds. . . . It reminds me of *Lord of the Flies.* That story was so disturbing, I only finished it because I had to write a report. Obviously, I felt so bad for Piggy."

• • •

Brian Lawrence Taylor is like few other boys in our class. He is a god among us, which sounds like hyperbole, but it's not. He's got a square jaw, a butt-cheeks chin, distinct dimples, light brown, slightly curly hair, a narrow nose, perfect puckers, and hazel-blue eyes.

And his body matches his face.

He looks like the drawings of Greek gods in our history books, painted on old vases and plates, or sculpted into stone. Michelangelo's *David* comes to mind, with his perfect face, body, nalgies, and well, everything else.

Boys want to *be* Brian; girls want to *date* him. Oh, some boys want to date him as well.

Okay, *I* may be the only boy who wants to date him.

Brian is a jock. He's the celebrated quarterback, the wrestling captain, the all-star pitcher.

It's like every other story of unrequited love, except it's about two boys, with very different physical appearances, race, socioeconomics, athletic abilities, and inclinations. He's always had a girlfriend.

He is *nothing* like me.

Is *that* why I like him so much?

• • •

I always have thoughts bouncing around in my head.

Does he have a tendency to fantasize?

I wish we could replace the words penis and testicles with other, easier to say, easier to hear words. One-syllable words that don't make me feel self-conscious about my own body, that don't broadcast that I'm interested in them: penis and testicles.

What if . . .

ONE could replace penis, dick, cock, Johnson, manhood, etc.

TWO could replace testicles, balls, nuts, nads, etc.

THREE could mean all of the above.

It's almost too simple.

For example: "My one hangs over my two, and my three are snug in my chonies."

There's nothing embarrassing about saying that sentence, even though I'm talking about my penis and testicles. My dick and my balls. My cock and my nuts. . . .

• • •

I just ran twenty laps around the athletic field for track practice. I'm always the last to finish running practice. Mom watches from home, across the street from the high school fields. I know she doesn't like that I'm always last. But I think she secretly admires my determination to finish. Sometimes when I get home, she instructs, "¡Toma agua!"

That's the best "good job!" she can muster.

Everyone thinks I come in last because I'm a lazy Mexican. I know this because the boys say I'm always last because I'm "a lazy Mexican." The truth is, I'm an adolescent boy going through the worst part of puberty—the instant erection of my *one*, and the constant achiness of my *two*.

I'm working on a replacement word for erection.

And if *ever* there were a word that needed an immediate replacement, it is scrotum.

I come in last every day because I want to "hit the showers" last, preferably by myself. Mom won't let me waste water at home because I can shower in the gym at school. So, I wear my best Benito Juárez combed hair when I get home, as proof I have saved her money.

• • •

The baseball boys encourage me to put my arm up inside the soda machine in the locker room before I go warm up for track. I know it's stupid, and potentially dangerous, but I can't say no to Brian. My arm is barely small enough to get past the machine's inner curves to release its sodas, one after another. I always give Brian the first.

Sometimes I feel bad, because it's not right to steal, but then the team tousles my hair and cheers me on:

"Pedro! Pedro! Pedro!"

It's nice to have someone touch me without hurting me. . . .

The baseball boys are so handsome. It feels incredible to *not* be invisible. The scrapes on my arm, the trickles of blood, don't seem to bother them. For me, they're a badge of loyalty.

Or of servitude?

· · ·

There's a pair of white shorts on the floor by my locker, which is always in the corner, where I can hide myself between the wall and the open locker door when I change.

No one is here, so I throw the white shorts into my locker before anyone comes in. I hate wearing cut off pants for running. It will be nice to have normal gym shorts.

Damn, someone is in the shower.

Please don't let it be Brian.

Please don't let it be Brian.

Wait, what am I thinking?

Please let it be Brian.

Please let it be Brian.

The boys' shower room is an open room with twelve showerheads. It's a torture chamber. A wet and slippery torture chamber. Boys don't just shower quietly or privately. They yell and scream, and touch and slap, and joke and insult. They pour shampoo on you when you're trying to rinse off. Sometimes, they grab your one, or put a finger in your crack, you know, as a joke.

Usually, no one notices me—they're too busy with their shenanigans—so I shampoo, soap up, rinse off, get out fast.

It's Mr. Miller, the shop teacher, in the shower. He swims after school for exercise. Mr. Miller has so much hair: everything from the bald spot on top of his head, all the way down to his ankles, is covered in thick hair. When he turns around and faces me to wash between his nalgies, it's hard to see his three because of all the hair. But, they still look bigger than mine.

When you're a "grower, not a shower," the last person you want washing near you is a "shower shower."

That is a fact.

At least I've started puberty, and things have started to grow, but I wish they would hurry up and get to full growth already.

I've heard Mom say, "Todo llega a su tiempo," which means *things happen when they're supposed to*, but sometimes I'd like to push on the gas pedal and accelerate.

'Mejor antes que después.'
Sooner rather than later.

Mr. Miller's eyes are closed, and he's humming to himself. He doesn't know, or care, that I'm here. I've got to hurry up before my three wake up. I don't think Mr. Miller is remotely handsome, but he does have a nice body—all his swimming pays off. Maybe if he shaved . . . anywhere? No, . . . still not likely. But I can't trust my one not to stand at attention. . . .

Oh, . . . I forgot about the white shorts in my locker.

I dry off quickly so I can put on my chonies before anyone walks in, even though my back is still dripping. Now, I want to hurry home and try on my new white gym shorts.

• • •

I can't even believe it.

Right there, inside the waistband.

BLT.

They're a little big for me, but I'm still so excited to have them. I don't know if they fell out of his bag, or if he just discarded them like regular people tossing out clothes they don't need. They're not ripped or even stained. They're just ordinary boys' gym shorts that BLT has worn.

Oh, wow, . . . BLT has worn these shorts.

These shorts have touched him . . . *there*.

And now they're touching *me* . . . there.

Needless to say, I've got an erection.

I can't let Mom see them. I take them off quickly, and stuff them in the money hole in the box spring. I had to rip the opening bigger. No one can see them. No one can know I have them.

I start my homework. . . .

Geometry.

I can't concentrate. . . .

American history.

No luck.

I take the BLTs out and put them on again. I put pants on over them to help hide my erection. Darn, I really need a new word for it.

Maybe, to hide my "one-plus"?

I'm too distracted when Mom yells, "¡Ven a comer!"

I have to admit, Mom is a good cook. I love everything she makes except boiled menudo, boiled cabbage, and boiled zucchini. Some people actually *love* those flavors, but their textures are unmistakable and unpleasant to me. I won't even say what's in menudo in case yours is full, because you might vomit just thinking about it.

"¿Y por qué tienes pantalones puestos? ¿No tienes calor?"

"No," I murmur quietly, without emotion, even though it *is* too hot to be wearing pants.

Frijoles refritos, fresh flour tortillas, and arroz con pollo. Everyone should experience home-cooked Mexican food. Most people haven't enjoyed the aromas of peppercorns, cumin seeds, garlic, tomato, and jalapeño being mashed in a molcajete con un tejolote—a mortar and pestle made of volcanic rock. The savory scents that make it to my bedroom downstairs always make my mouth water.

After a few hours of my continued one-plus inside my BLTs, there's an achiness of my two. I've managed to finish my homework, and I'm trying to reread *The Hobbit*. . . .

I decide to wear my BLTs over my chonies tonight. I can't stop obsessing about them, or Brian.

• • •

Brian is my best friend, and I'm his!

I'm like his sidekick!

He tousles my hair,

and gives me a slight squeeze with his athletic,

muscular arm around my shoulders.

He gives me a side-eye, and a sly smirk smile.

There's pounding in my ears.

Rhythmic pulsing beats . . .

Brian and I are walking together.

The whole student body suddenly surrounds us.

He's so considerate.

He had hoped to hold my hand,

but he doesn't want me to feel uncomfortable

in front of everyone.

Everyone wants to be me.

Stuttering, sputtering speech and sounds.

Pounding, pandemonium, palpitations . . .

Brian looks up at me in the stands when he throws the football.

I think he winked at me!

Yes, his handsome, dimpled face definitely winked at me!

Pounding, rhythmic pounding.

Pulsing, beating pulses . . .

Brian is wearing his wrestling singlet.

He's walking toward me.

His eyes are firmly focused on my face.

I'm laying on the wrestling mat feeling exposed and exhilarated.

His lips part as he kneels down to touch my . . .

Ummffuh - uhhssssshhh - uhhh

Hmmm?

Oh no!

I peed my chonies!

I wake up in a panic.

Oh no!

I peed my chonies, and my BLTs!

I have to be quiet. I don't want to wake Mom. My younger brother doesn't stir when I get out of bed. The sheets aren't wet though. I just peed all over the front of my chonies.

That's weird.

It's like that night I was dreaming about Ryan O'Neal, after I watched *What's Up, Doc?*

· · ·

"We haven't been consistent with our annual year-in-review, but this year will be known for the great blizzard of 1978," I announce.

"And the Susan B. Anthony dollar!" Daniel shouts out. "I love that we'll finally have a woman on our currency, and people will need to get used to saying, 'the dollar coin.'"

"I want to add the movie *Grease*, and Louise Brown, the first test tube baby."

"Olivia Newton John, both before and after bright red lipstick, tight leather pants, high heels, and cigarettes," Daniel says with a grin.

"Gosh, she was great in *Grease*. And I *love* her velvety voice."

"And, we can't forget it was the Year of Three Popes!" Daniel proclaims.

"If I could roll my eyes, I would definitely roll my eyes right now."

I will also remember *Superman*, with Christopher Reeve. He is every bit my fantasy of a superhero.

39

CONFESSIONS
Daniel – 16

MISS SAMSON WAKES up half the class when she knocks on Father Orlando's classroom door. I'm glad for the distraction. Ancient civilization is boring old news. It's so *last millenium*.

Hmm, I'll have to use that line.

"Daniel, you have a call in the principal's office," she announces to the class.

I imagine—for my own amusement—that her name is Edna, or Enid, or Eunice. Or, Eugenia. I love pronouncing Eugenia in Spanish: *Eh-oo-heh-nya*.

Miss Eugenia Samson.

She's an upper-middle-aged woman with glasses of a cat woman, both the persona and the comics heroine. I have been asked, "Who was better, Julie Newmar or Eartha Kitt?" This is a debate with one clear answer. They were *each* perfection.

Mom keeps calling me to talk. Now that I'm at the seminary, it's like I'm one of her comadres. She'll call to gossip, or to complain about Pop, Pedro, or a comadre. At times, she complains about me—how I didn't do something she wanted me to do over the weekend when I was there, or to accuse me of enjoying myself, "revolcándote con puros muchachos."

I don't know what she's heard, but *"rolling around with just a bunch of boys"* seems pretty specific.

Sara is in college and Juan is in the Army now, so Pedro is the oldest at home. And Mom is pregnant again. Honestly, I would not trade in any of my siblings for anything, but "contraception?" "The rhythm method?" "Abstinence?"

Knock, knock, knock. . . .

Hello, . . . is anyone listening?

'Es como hablar a la pared.'
It's like talking to a wall.

Since Pop leaves home for work before school ends, and he comes home after everyone is in bed, Pedro has become a father figure to those kids. When Mom goes into one of her phases and she doesn't get out of bed, or she just rants and rages, Pedro assumes full responsibility for them.

Mom just drones on and on on the phone. It never occurs to her that I'm at school, and I'm supposed to be in a classroom.

• • •

I . . .

I think . . . ?

I think Mom thinks I'm a priest already.

Our phone calls sound like she's in the confessional. She keeps confessing her sins to me, but she prefers to explain why her actions were necessary. She craves validation. She's not *really* understanding how confessing your sins is supposed to work.

In a confessional, you disclose your sins freely to expunge them from your soul, and then you're supposed to repent for those sins so you can be absolved when you do your penance.

She's missing the "repenting for your sins" step. The part where she acknowledges they are sins, and she feels sorry that she committed them.

I don't think she wants me to know some of this stuff, and I try to tell her, but she just rambles, and rumbles on. These are things she should keep to herself or share in an actual confessional with her priest, *not* with her son.

I wouldn't trust a comadre with this stuff.

I don't want to disturb her racing train of thoughts because a derailment would be disastrous for her, for me, for so many.

So, I just listen.

Once, she talked for over thirty minutes before she asked if I was still listening. I had to pick up the phone receiver quickly to respond:

"¡¡¡Sí!!!"

• • •

¡¡¡No!!!

NO! NO! NO! NO! NO!

I don't want to know about your sex life Mom!

Por el amor de Dios, people, I really don't want to know any of this! This falls somewhere under

'Consejo no pedido, consejo mal oído!'
Unrequested advice is unappreciated advice.

Whatever I say will not be what she hears. She's in a hypnotic trance, and I'm afraid I'll accidentally snap my fingers, she'll wake up, and all hell will break loose.

• • •

Mom gets mad when Pedro doesn't know the answer to a medical question. I think she thinks he's already a doctor, *just because he wants to be a doctor.*

"¡¡¡Ya sé que no eres un médico, pendejo!!!"

I know you're not a doctor, you fool! sounds more like an accusation than an affirmation of the fact.

It's really weird how she sees us as a priest and a doctor already, when neither of us has started our actual studies for these professions. Those will start in medical school or seminary college, years from now.

She has lived with our career goals for a decade. Does she wonder what we've been doing all this time? I guess now is not the time to tell her it's going to take another decade before she gets her desired results.

'No hay peor sordo que el que no quiere oír.'
There is no person more deaf than she who does not wish to listen.

This reminds me of Hermey, the Misfit Elf, giving Rudolph and Yukon Cornelius dental advice, when his only expertise was saying he wanted to be a dentist. Lucy charges Charlie Brown five cents to administer psychological advice, and she's obviously a child with no training in psychology, although common sense can go a long way. And Dr. Smith in *Lost in Space,* what kind of doctor could that ninny have been?

I'm sure there are other examples in TV and movies that may have confused Mom about all of this. Her nature is to be impatient. Having to wait for what one wants is antithetical to her core.

• • •

"¡¡¡Y QUÍTATE ESA CARA!!!" Mom screams as she slaps me once more.

My face stings and my ear rings from the multiple impacts. Still, I won't give her the satisfaction of crying like I once did.

I finish the chore I hadn't done to her *exacting* satisfaction, then go down to our room where Pedro is clearly waiting for me.

"Sorry," he mumbles, looking ready to cry.

"For what? You didn't make *that woman* our mother!" I look back to confirm I had closed our door.

"Did you take your face off?" he asks.

Sometimes Pedro knows *exactly* what to say.

"I *hate* when she says that. It reminds me of 'eye on the ball Danny!'"
We both laugh.

But I don't think the demon has had its full fix, so Pedro needs to be careful, be quiet.

"Have you noticed she's getting more dependent on objects to beat us?" Pedro says.

"What do you mean?"

I'm intrigued. Pedro notices subtle things about Mom, as if he studies her. He's always been able to predict when Mom and Pop are going to have an awful fight, based on his observations of her moods. It's funny how we each have distinct strengths and weaknesses in life.

"She needs metal poles or brooms to inflict more pain since she requires a certain response to feel satisfaction."

"Pedro, that's creepy, and sadistic, if it's true."

"Sadism is the enjoyment of inflicting pain and humiliation."

"Oh. . . . I never thought about it like that."

"I've thought about it . . . for many years."

• • •

"Mom and Pop are on the phone!" Pedro yells from upstairs. I grab the downstairs telephone. All the kids run in from every direction and crowd around the two phones to try to hear.

It's been three weeks since we've heard from them. They drove down to Mexico without any of the kids. I understand Mom wanted Pedro and me to stay home so we could work our summer jobs and make money for her. We stopped going to Mexico every year when we got old enough to work summer jobs.

Poor Pedro works full-time at the nursing home during the summer, and he takes on extra jobs as well. If it were up to him, he'd only come home to sleep. Actually, for two years he tried to get a job at Cedar Point Amusement Park where he would have lived in their employee campus. It was a long shot, but ultimately, Mom thought he would enjoy himself too much there and said no.

We think it was irresponsible for Mom and Pop to leave all the kids with us when we're not even home most of the day. But these details don't register in Mom's head.

"¡Hola hijos! ¿Cómo están?" Mom asks. "Los extrañamos tanto."

Okay, hold on. . . .

I don't know who this person is. . . .

She *sounds* like Mom, but this person does *not* sound like Mom. Those words aren't words Mom uses. *How are we? She misses us—a lot?*

Something is up.

I wish I were upstairs with Pedro.

"Queríamos decirles que estamos aquí con mi papá."

For the love of god, something is not right, and an eye roll will not suffice. . . .

Papá died *years* ago. How can Mom be with him?

What's going on?

Who *is* this *Mom*?

"Quiero contarles una historia. . . ."

Mom—this person . . . this "different Mom"—starts to tell us an odd and complicated story. Each snippet is part of a larger puzzle:

It appears Mamá got pregnant with Mom when she was very young, and unwed.

In 1930s rural Mexico, this was scandalous.

To address the shame brought to his sister and family, Mamá's brother challenged the scoundrel—Jorge—to a duel.

In the duel, Jorge shot and killed Mamá's brother.

Although challenging someone to a duel to reclaim a family's honor was not uncommon, and Jorge had not made the challenge—he had only accepted it—duels were by this time illegal in Mexico.

Jorge had committed murder in the eyes of the law.

He had to flee and go into hiding.

Even all these decades later, he had not seen his daughter or his childhood lover, Mamá.

When Mamá was pregnant, she was sent to live with family in a different village until Mom was born.

At some point, Papá—*our* Papá—entered the picture.

Having known this lovely man, it is not surprising that he married Mamá and raised Mom as his own.

Years later, they had a child of their own — Mean Tío, also known as Tío Bigote — who is now Mom's half-brother with this news.

Mom relays there is much more to the story, but she wanted us to know she finally met her father, her half-sister, and her half-brothers in a small village not too far from Mamá's distant relatives in Rancho San Miguel.

What is going on?!

• • •

Once Mom and Pop return from Mexico, more details emerge about this unsettling situation.

The chisme of the pregnancy and the scandal of the duel and murder spread through the small villages of the region when they happened years ago. Chisme caliente never really dies. Families talked and whispered for years. Their children heard the murmurs, and then a new chisme cycle commenced.

It was only a matter of time when whispers wound their way to Mom's awareness when she was only a child.

Things are starting to make sense:

'Lo que se mama de niña, dura toda la vida.'
A woman is the product of her upbringing.

40

SHAME
Pedro – 17

MOM JUST ASSAULTED a woman in the parking lot of Pop's factory.

Her interactions with people have been increasingly inappropriate, but this insanity is belfry batty, even for Mom.

I'll go back a few hours:

I only have my learner's permit, but Mom insisted I drive her across the bay bridge. My neck is fully extended, so my face sits above my bloodless knuckles squeezing the steering wheel at ten-and-two positions, my elbows sticking out as if on a cross, a shower of cold sweat dripping from my pits, the perspiration pouring onto my startled flanks.

Unpleasant and forceful palpitations worsen my sense of panic.

It is an unpleasant sensation meeting an unpleasant situation.

When I was little, I feared this big bridge being built over the bay. I had dreamt we rammed right through the guardrail and barreled into the greenish-brown bay waters. I've hated going over it ever since.

Now, the first time I'm *driving* over this bridge under an unrelated emotional duress, I'm going way too slow, and everyone around us is flipping their fingers and honking their horns to encourage me to get out of their way.

I realize Mr. Turner, my driving instructor, would have advised me long ago to get into the right lane so that faster drivers can pass me on my left. But the right lane is next to that sinister guardrail.

I trust that guardrail like I trust someone who drives left of center.

Once we get to the other side, and my fear of drowning-in-my-teens abates, we have to stop a few times to ask for directions. There has never been a need for us to come to Pop's factory. For reasons of safety, liability, and intellectual property concerns, we could never enter the facility, so why would we come here?

Now that I think about it, I'm surprised Pop has kept this job. For as long as I can remember, Mom calls him every day, and keeps him on the phone for long periods. I can tell when he says he needs to get back to work: "¡Sí, lo sé! ¡Pero déjame contarte otra cosa!" After the umpteenth time, she'll let him go, . . . then she'll call him back later.

I don't know why we're waiting in the parking lot where Pop works. Mom keeps grimacing and murmuring to herself, reminding me of Eunice in *What's Up, Doc?* after her last nerve had been worked over and she was certifiably committable.

I know whatever this is, it can only end badly, and I don't like having been lassoed into this whole affair. Mom always manages to wiggle herself out of culpability in bad situations, but I have a big fat bullseye on my forehead. I can feel it throbbing; I see the accompanying scotomas in my vision. I'm regressing into the black hole of my chittering and uncontrolled chaos.

I am startled out of my busy work of compartmentalizing the thoughts and words in my head when Mom yells, "¡¡¡ES ELLA!!!"

I wonder how she knows who her target is, . . . then it registers. There is only one woman leaving the building with a group of men.

In an instant, Mom is out of the van, running toward the woman whose car must be in our direction because they meet just past the car parked in front of me in the parking lot. I have a front row seat to the pandemonium that plays out. Mom is screaming and scratching and slapping. She grabs and pulls at the woman's blouse until it is shredded material, and the battered, stuporous woman is left standing in her bra.

Quite satisfied, Mom hurries back to the van, and commands me to leave while the door is still wide open, before she's even seated. She sighs and holds up her cherished prize: the woman's torn, tattered blouse. . . .

I'm the antithesis of a getaway driver. . . .

I carefully back out of the parking space using a painfully slow, socially awkward, three-point maneuver, . . . then I click on my directionals to advise the shell-shocked onlookers that I intend to turn right to leave the parking lot, with the deranged assailant posing as a qualified, mature, adult, driving supervisor.

My blurred vision reminds me that my eyes have *not* been dilated with eye drops; I'm just entering one of my panic attacks.

For the love of God, I don't know what the fuck is going on.

• • •

Mom and Pop went on their ritual weekend shopping excursion. Daniel and I have a little time alone before we need to perform our list of chores, including supervising the kids and their own chores. We're in a corner of the downstairs family room where we could safely react if Mom made one of her infamous *surprise* early returns to check up on us.

He and I are eager to discuss the latest installment of trickling details emerging from their visit to Mexico.

It's as if Mom is writing a new capítulo in her telenovela every day, and she's using us as sounding boards until she gets it "just right." There's so much to process.

"What's most remarkable is that Mom knew about this since she was a little girl, but she never told anyone, including Pop," I remark.

"I know. I can't imagine what Pop thought."

"Mom loved Papá, and he treated her so well. . . . like a loving father. He really was a wonderful man. On the other hand, Mom frequently argued with Mamá, which usually ended with Mamá crying. . . . That always broke my heart."

"This might explain why Mom resents Mamá so much," Daniel considers.

Our eyes meet, then dart away, then meet, then dart away . . .

"Another layer is Papá was of mostly Spanish origin. Papá, Mamá, and Mom are lighter-skinned. But her biological father, our biological abuelo, is of Mexican Indian heritage. . . . He is darker-skinned," I pronounce. I take a moment before adding. "Although I am a spitting image of Pop, . . . Mom carries Native Mexican ancestry in her blood as well, even if it's not evident."

"I hadn't thought of that," Daniel murmurs. He ponders this a moment before he adds, "I wonder if Tío Bigote knew about Mom, and tormented her about it."

"When I came out 'prieto,' she couldn't *really* blame Pop completely. I bet I'm the embodiment of her shame."

"For the love of—*please* don't think of it that way Pedro!"

Daniel's mouth is wide open, and his now larger eyes are rapid reading the words he sees in his head: the hidden message behind my words.

"Daniel, think about Mom's psychological state throughout her childhood. She was a bastard child with a Native Mexican father surrounded by bigots who value light skin and denigrate those with darker skin. Mamá's family hated him for what he did to her, . . . and her brother. Abuelo's skin color was the easily identifiable culprit, or scapegoat, of it all."

"Hmmm. . . ."

"Mom learned the word *renegrido* from *someone*, and I suspect she learned it early. Imagine her constant battle between attraction and aversion to prietos like Pop. It's as if we were handed the secret cipher to help us decode her."

• • •

My science fair project is about in-vitro fertilization. The first "test tube baby" was born last year. The process through which the baby was conceived has garnered the full spectrum of reactions between condemnation and high praise.

When the unusual captures my attention, my imagination is set free.

Over the last year, I obsessively read all the newspaper and magazine articles I could find at the public library. The ramifications for families who have not been able to have children, as well as the medical breakthrough in and of itself, are significant.

I don't entirely understand how natural or in-vitro fertilization works, which makes my project more challenging, but I have found the discourse fascinating. I'm especially interested in the way religious leaders and politicians are addressing it. I'm looking for similarities, differences, inconsistencies with regard to their positions on birth control, abortion, premarital sex, homosexuality, even the death penalty.

Fairly consistently, anger seems directed at the medical profession—for playing God—not the married couple that just wanted to have a child. At least until the talk turns to the details, and the possibility that unmarried couples or single women could take advantage of the science without getting married. That's when it starts to get personal, and inflammatory.

As an unexpected side note to this story, Mom gave me a book she had hidden in her underwear drawer about sex and conception. She advised me it was for my project, and only because I'm going to be a doctor. A few days later, she called me a pervert, pig, and degenerate, in Spanish, and demanded the return of her book.

Honestly, the book was about as helpful as our eighth-grade retreat with its confusing anatomical posters and the nervous priest's verbal innuendos.

It was an entire book about sex and conception, and it still wasn't helpful.

What is *wrong* with me?

And why does *Mom—of all people*—need a book about conception?

• • •

I have three judges in front of me for the science fair: Ms. Steinway, the girls' sports coach; Mr. Driscoll, a community leader; and Mr. Tyson, a math teacher.

They all look more nervous than I feel. Their eyes keep roaming around my large, three-panel poster board with schematics of men's and women's bodies similar to those I saw at the eighth-grade health retreat. Mr. Merle, my chemistry teacher, gave me a large test tube, and at the bottom, I placed a tiny baby doll I had serendipitously found at the thrift shop a few weeks ago. I thought it was quite clever. It is literally *a test tube baby*.

I have memorized my speech in which I detail the basics of in-vitro fertilization. It's going fairly well, and then I say, "Sperm was collected from the father by masturbation. . . ."

It looks like Ms. Steinway is going to be sick. Mr. Driscoll and Mr. Tyson are a couple of slapstick comedians trying to escape through the single classroom door at the same time. Needless to say, I don't finish my presentation.

I know white liquid with sperm comes out when men masturbate; I just haven't figured out how it gets out. Even after all those magazines at the DOT. The stories in the magazines didn't give me clues since they were always about sex, not masturbation.

Somehow, a second person doesn't seem necessary to get it out.

And apparently, it's not something that should come up at a high school science fair. After scrotum, I think masturbation comes next as a word that *immediately* needs a better replacement.

. . .

Mom has been sued by the woman she assaulted. Since I'm her only witness, Mom wants me to lie to the judge and say the other woman assaulted her first. I have repeatedly told her I will not lie to the judge, and I've told her my continued beatings won't change that. She is so angry, and I can tell she's scared, but I don't give a shit. I really don't. This isn't the first time she assaulted someone other than her husband or her kids.

I'd love to say, "A lo hecho, pecho, Mom, because it's finally time for you to face the consequences. Or better yet,

'A cada cerdo le llega su San Martín.'
Every pig has its day."

Unfortunately, it is a reference to Saint Martin of Tours, not San Martín de Porres, the patron saint of mixed-race people, my patron saint. And he's my look alike, according to Mom.

• • •

"How are things going at school, Pedro?" Dr. Fritz asks.

I'm here for my annual sports physical for cross-country.

If I don't get this done now, the athletic director will take me out of class, along with every other boy who hasn't gotten his sports physical. He'll take us to a clinic where we'll all undress in front of each other, the athletic director, the doctors, and the nurses at the clinic, and then we'll have a communal physical examination, like they do in military movies. I can never cough the way they want—I'd like to suggest they shine a bright light at my eyes to trigger three loud and forceful sneezes—so I have to cough repeatedly, all while they're poking and prodding me down there, and everyone's eyes are roaming all over the room.

I endured this public humiliation twice. This year, I take care of the requirement ahead of the deadline.

"Things are going well. I'm looking forward to taking some advanced placement classes this year."

"That's terrific," he replies. "Still determined to study medicine?"

"Yes, it's my goal! Ever since I was a little kid."

"I know Mom will be very proud of you."

After an odd pause, I realize he is waiting for me to respond. "Oh, yes, she's very happy she'll have a doctor and a priest in the family."

I still don't know the Spanish word for proud. I once asked Mom, "How do you say *deserve* in Spanish?" but it was hard to think of synonyms in Spanish, and she was getting irritated with me, so I just gave up. I'm convinced she thought I didn't deserve to know the word *deserve* in Spanish.

"So, Pedro, it looks like you've gone through the physical changes of puberty. You could even start shaving!"

We both laugh. And with each moment, I'm building confidence and courage to tell him my secret, get some answers, and maybe some reassurance.

'Al médico, confesor, y letrado, no le hayas engañado.'
Don't deceive your doctor, priest, or lawyer.

Other than a priest, a doctor is the only other person with whom you can talk about yourself, your body, your inclinations. They are supposed to keep these confidences completely. I don't have a relationship with any of the priests, and honestly, I don't like any of them, so it has to be Dr. Fritz who can tell me everything's fine, that I'll be okay, that things will get better.

"Do you have any questions about anything Pedro?" he asks.

I look him in the face, take a deep breath, and start to say, "I think I'm . . ."

But Dr. Fritz has started to ask, "Do you have a girlfriend yet?"

And in an instant, my confidence is deflated, sucked back into the black hole in my head with its tail between its legs.

If he hadn't asked that last question, Dr. Fritz would still be my hero, my mentor, my friend.

And I promise myself I will never make that sort of an assumption when I'm talking with a patient.

• • •

The assaulted woman has dropped her suit against Mom, so she's going to get away with it, again. There's more to the story, but it's not worth repeating here. Suffice it to say,

'La hierba mala nunca muere.'
Only the good die young.

. . . I just thought of my own version of this dicho:

'El malo no muere porque tiene buena suerte.'
The bad guy won't die because he's got good luck.

And, as for me,

If it weren't for bad luck, I'd have no luck at all.

• • •

I'm losing the little hope I'd kept secreted in the recesses of my chaos.

I'm thinking more about ending this helplessness and hopelessness.

• • •

"Daniel, when did you start talking with her?" I ask in a loud whisper, down in our room. He's home from the seminary for the holiday weekend. It's Thanksgiving night and I've been dying to question him about the call he got this morning.

Our family was having breakfast around the large kitchen table. Pop was sitting between us, Mom was across from us, and the other kids were everywhere in between. The phone rang and Pop answered it.

"Daniel, es para ti," he said, and handed the phone to Daniel at the table. It has an extra long cord so Mom can talk with her comadres from just about anywhere.

It is highly unusual for any of the kids to get a call from anyone.

"Hello?" Daniel said, then his furrowed brows relaxed and released his eyes so wide there was white surrounding his irises. "Oh, hi! . . . I'm well, thank you, how are you? . . . Yes, Happy Thanksgiving to you, and to all your family. . . . Yes. . . . Yes, thank you. . . . I'm so glad you called. . . . Yes, you too. . . . Okay, I will. . . ." For a split second, Daniel's eyes purposefully met mine. "Thank you so much for calling. Bye bye."

His voice sounded unusually high and squeaky. . . .

"¿Y quién era?" Mom asked. She hadn't taken her eyes off Daniel during the entire call. My eyes had table-tennised back and forth between the two of them.

"Una amiga que trabaja en la escuela," Daniel replied, then he shot me a quick glance, sending a shockwave right through me. Thankfully, Mom didn't notice. Or at least, she didn't comment.

Who could have called him?

"¿Una amiga? ¿Y por qué te está llamando una cualquiera? ¡Ya sabes que no puedes tener novias!"

I've decided Mom's picture should be in the dictionary under this entry:

irony NOUN i•ro•ny /ˈīrənē/
The use of words in a way that's opposite of what's expected,
resulting in a humorous effect.

She had asked Daniel why some "anybody" was calling him, then she reminded him he can't have girlfriends.

After some chores, Daniel tugged on my arm when Mom wasn't looking, and we separately disappeared ourselves from the kitchen.

"That was Graciela!" Daniel said as soon as we got to our bedroom.

"What? . . . Our cousin?"

"Yes!"

"¡¡¡DÓNDE ESTÁN!!! ¡¡¡QUE LOS NECESITO!!!" Mom yelled from the kitchen, summoning us back for more chores before I could extract further information.

We hadn't had a free moment since this morning. . . .

"I saw her at the Kroger over the summer, and we started talking," Daniel says. "I really like her! She's a firecracker. When I went back to the seminary, she'd call me there, and we'd gab and gab for a while. It's like she's a comadre, now that I think about it. I was kinda surprised, but I'm really glad she called today!"

"It's unbelievable! I wish I could talk with her! I *still* can't, even though I see her every day at school."

"I know. She knows it's beyond our control. I told her you would love to be her friend someday. . . . And by the way, she said to say hi to you when she called this morning."

"Daniel, you're amazing! And Mom thought she was 'just any girl' on the phone . . . that she might be your 'girlfriend' calling you on a holiday. I sometimes wonder if Mom hears what she says," I say, and we both laugh.

41

JESÚS
Daniel – 17

PARENTS HAVE NO clue how names can affect kids. Do they forget childhood antics, like name calling? Kids can find a rhyme for pretty much any name: Scary Mary, Hairy Harry, Luke Puke, NoWay José, Ready Freddy. Or they'll purposely mispronounce a name, like Luke-ass, Angle instead of Angel, or OleNic for Nicole.

Then there are the names with one particular double meaning: Dick, John, Willy, Jack, Rod, Peter, Roger, Mickey, Jimmy, Johnson.

Which is why I admire Willy Dick Johnson, who is a year ahead of me in seminary. He could go by William or Bill or Billy. Or, he could go by Richard or Rich or Richie. But no.... He *owns* his name. His *triple dick* name. Willy Dick Johnson. You've got to have *big balls* to go by Willy Dick Johnson.

Actually, no privacy here at the seminary means I've seen his big balls.

I do believe he's meant for great things.

A friend claims he knows a guy named Paul Ennis who always writes his name as p ennis. Supposedly, he wants to star in one of e e cummings's autobiographical plays, and he wants large billboards to say: p ennis is cummings.

This silly story seems like an adolescent prank, like the missing altar boy back home, which I'm starting to believe wasn't true.

My name is Jesús Daniel.

Jesús is supposed to be pronounced *heh-SOOS*, but you've got to pick your battles. I don't mind Daniel, but I *definitely* prefer it to *HAY-SOOZ*.

My official school records show me as Jesus Daniel, without the accent.

I like the name Jesus, but not for myself, just for Jesus. It's a bit of a burden to have His name. Kids look at you for a split second to see if there's something special about you, something that would explain your having His name. I can't live up to it. Who could?

The only times someone has called me Jesus out loud has been a new teacher on the first days of school. The kids always laughed when the teacher would ask, "Do you want us to call you Jesus, or just Daniel?"

Hidden message: "Because what boy would want to be called Jesus?"

Is it too much to ask that someone acknowledge my real name periodically, without laughing?

For a while, I used J. Daniel, but no one picked up on the hint.

I can't walk on water. I still can't even swim all these years after falling into the river. So, until it changes, I'll stick with Daniel.

Please, and thank you.

• • •

Every Christian knows Jesus at both extremes of his life: sweet little baby Jesus in a manger at Christmas, and poor, suffering Jesus on the cross, who rose from the dead at Easter. Right from the beginning, you get to know Him at opposite ends of his short existence. It's not possible to see Him as one without the other.

How could I *not* fall in love with Him, my namesake?

Unlike most people, I've spent a lot of time imagining Jesus as a child, and as an adolescent. I can see him as a young man, a preacher, a philosopher. We definitely have images of Him later in life, in the months before his death, still young at thirty-three.

But I haven't heard what he was like as a kid.

I think he was precocious and inquisitive, not just because I'm a Jesus, and I was precocious and inquisitive. His mind had to have been going nonstop. Maybe like Pedro, who has so much going on in his head!

Jesus was talking with God, and figuring out how he was going to convince a bunch of different kinds of people there was a different, one true God, a different kind of life, a different kind of purpose.

• • •

There are interesting controversies about Jesus Christ. . . .

Few question his existence two thousand years ago, but why have scholars argued for centuries whether Jesus ever laughed? Nowhere in the Bible does it say Jesus laughed, as if the Bible chronicles every moment of his thirty-three years. Why is it important to maintain an image of Jesus as serious and sorrowful? What's the matter with laughing? He loved people and He especially loved children. Is it possible He never laughed around them? What child would want to be around a man who never laughed?

I've actually heard theologians say Jesus never lost his temper. That He had "righteous and controlled anger" when He overturned tables in the temple and used a whip to drive away men and animals.

Did Jesus ever own property? Why would it be bad if He owned property?

Did Jesus ever marry? I know I'm walking on thin ice for even thinking about it, and one of my classmates will never wonder again, after the tongue-lashing he received for asking it in Father Bernardino's theology class. Ugh, I'm aware of the double entendre, so I'll say it was a scalding hot scolding instead.

I don't know a lot about Jewish people. It seems, though, that marriage and having children was an important part of Jewish life, and every other culture, two thousand years ago. Unless Jesus was gay — I can't imagine saying that out loud — why wouldn't He have married, if He had been a man in every other way?

And then there's the question of Jesus' presumed appearance as a light-skinned, light-haired, blue-eyed, Middle Eastern man.

These are questions that will never be conclusively answered to the approval of all. If the answers exist, they are in texts written two thousand years ago, in ancient languages, on ancient documents with ancient materials, hidden away in some vault, cave, or tomb.

I fear arthritic doctrine will never bend the rigid minds of the resolute who strive to maintain the status quo. Unanswerable questions have *always* been the foundational strength of the churches. Years of theology have taught me much.

I'm going to make it my mission to find out what I can about Jesus as a human, to help me better understand Him as the son of God. I'll probably ruffle feathers along the way. But:

'Nunca es tarde para aprender.'
It's never too late to learn.

42

IMPOSTER
Pedro – 18

HIGH SCHOOL SENIOR year is a dream come true. Only one more year of this miserable life, then I can get away. The clock has changed from measuring my incarceration in years, to months. The next milestone will be the change to weeks. The countdown starting with a single-digit number of weeks will change my blood chemistry toward normalcy.

Mom's beatings still hurt, but I don't cry like before. My tears are increasingly of anger and hate. Mom is more violent as she struggles to get her required response. Her traitorous stamina sputters, and then she stubbornly surrenders, incensed and unsatisfied.

My fear of fear has finally found relief.

> 'El valiente vive hasta que el cobarde quiere.'
> *The brave man lives until the coward wants.*

Mom fears I am losing my fear of her.

Gloria Gaynor's glorious voice is blasting my eardrums right now with, *I Will Survive!*

• • •

Oh my god.

Don't speak.

Don't move.

Don't breathe.

Just wait.

Maybe she didn't. . . .

"¿Qué fue? No comprendo. ¿Qué pasó?" Mom asks. She is confused about the movie's ending.

Pop explains that Billy Joe had sex with a man when he was drunk, but Billy Joe admitted that the sex was *not* a drunken accident or a mistake. He says Billy Joe told his friend—the girl we assumed was his girlfriend—that he really *did* want to have sex with that man. And then Pop says, Billy Joe jumped off the Tallahatchie Bridge and killed himself.

"¿Qué? No comprendo. ¿Cómo es eso?"

Then, a bright light turns on over Mom's head.

I want to say I actually see it—the light—like in the cartoons, but it's a look on her face that clearly screams out, "A bright light just turned on over my head!"

She comes out of her trance, then quickly turns to me and yells, "¡Tú ya vete a la cama!"

I will gladly go to bed, but first I have to perform my repulsive kiss ritual with her, then with Pop.

"Buenas noches," I say to each with their kiss. Mom rarely responds, la maleducada.

"Buenas noches, hijo," Pop replies.

We never add, "Te amo," but I believe he does.

The movie was loosely based on a popular song that was on top of the charts a few years ago. I can't believe a popular teen actor, a teen idol on the cover of many teen magazines, played a role in which he confessed he wanted to have sex with a man. It was sad the character felt he had to kill himself because of it.

It does make me wonder if there are regular guys who don't want to kill themselves after they have sex with another man. Will I want to kill myself if I someday have sex with a guy? Will I ever know love? Acceptance?

. . .

I'm at the end-of-the-year awards ceremony for the senior class. The high school staff, the school board, and local groups, clubs, and organizations will recognize student achievements with awards and scholarships.

Between my GPA and my extensive extracurricular activities—taking part in blood drives and vaccine clinics; volunteering then working at the nursing home; National Honor Society, Future Professionals in Medicine, and other clubs; the three sports teams I graced with my presence—the awards and scholarships I receive tonight are not entirely surprising.

I should be happy, and proud.

Instead, I'm questioning my worth because:

I appreciate *pats on the back*.
But,
I abhor *pats on the head*.

Eric Jones announced to those at our table, "Fer all intensive purposes, Pedro got all them awards n' money cuz they feel sorry cuz he's a poor Mexican. Tha'sall. Ain' right . . . ain' fair, . . . ya ask me."

I almost believe him.

I've been an imposter all my life, *haven't I*?

Miserable, passing as *happy*.

Panic-stricken introvert, passing as *just a regular guy*.

Gay, passing as *straight*.

Agnostic, passing as *devout Catholic*.

Loathing, passing as *loving*, son.

Smart?

Yes . . .

Hardworking?

Hell yes.

Determined, competitive, resilient?

Yes, yes, and yes, goddammit.

Did I get my good grades over the last twelve years because I'm a Mexican American—yes, *American*—or because I *worked* for them? Did I get my regional and state test scores because I'm a Mexican American, or because I *worked* for them?

Wait a goddamn minute. . . .

When the *fuck* did any Mexican American get an award just because they are Mexican American?

So yes, Eric *"fucking"* Jones, I *will* "use a wheelbarrow," as you put it, to carry out all my awards and scholarship money. And I'll place my Outstanding Senior Boy Award on the very top, like a cherry on a fucking sundae.

Please do not excuse my French, with no due respect, and thank you for nothing.

"I wish I could have said all that in a cohesive, coherent speech at our table," I say, "instead of keeping it all in my head."

"'Sólo se tiran piedras al árbol cargado de fruto,'" Daniel remarks.

People only throw stones at trees full of fruit.

"What does that mean?"

"Basically, people criticize those doing well," Daniel explains. "I suppose it's related to "misery loves company," and how the miserable want to make others miserable."

"That seems true."

"Congratulations, by the way. I'm very proud of you, Pedro. You deserve all those awards, and more. Don't forget:

'A palabras necias, oídos sordos.'"
Let foolish words fall on deaf ears.

He gives me a hug, and my neck and back muscles relax.

• • •

Mom is unbearably bitter that I'll leave for college in late August. After eighteen years, I won't be under her control.

I anticipated the worst, so I lined up three summer jobs. I'll work full-time at the nursing home, part-time at a small, family-owned theme park, and I will be a handyman for a middle-aged woman.

Mom enjoys the added income, so she can't complain too much that I'm not home.

But her capricious nature can't help itself.

She pushes me to do more chores, to see how I'll react.

I am gasoline, kindling, and flint against Mom's jagged steel. We can barely stand to be in the same room together.

• • •

"¡¡¡RENEGRIDO CHINGADO!!! . . .

. . . ¡¡¡CÓMO . . . TE . . . ODIO!!! . . .

. . . ¡¡¡NO . . . TE . . . MEREZCO-O-O!!! . . .

. . . ¡¡¡MALDITO . . . MARICÓN . . . de mieRDA-A-A . . . !!!"

Mom collapses with that last strike on my face, but she knows I'm watching her, and she quickly gets up.

I've finally grown. Now I'm too tall for her favorite slanted stance approach. She can't get the momentum needed for a satisfyingly administered coscorrón.

She'd been slapping me for a while. She wanted to see me break—otherwise, she would have used the broom handle she had cut to her specifications, which always stands at the ready next to her chair.

I don't react or say anything. I just look at her with the hate that consumes me. I am La Momia Muda with a distinctly new, blatantly defiant mask of resistant resilience that rattles and enrages her.

I know she knows I know she's panicking, and it reinforces my resolve.

Frustrated with her disloyal exhaustion, she calls Pop at work and commands him to come home immediately. He knows he has no choice. She will call every few minutes until she is told he has left.

It takes Pop about forty minutes to get home. I haven't moved. I'm still standing in the same spot. Mom is fuming in her chair a few feet from me, pretending to watch TV.

"¡¡¡Pégalo!!!"

She screams at Pop to hit me.

He stands before me a battered and beaten man himself.

"Eso no lo voy a hacer," he tells her, reminiscent of another time, long ago. . . .

I don't waste a second.

"Why don't you leave her?" I demand of Pop, clearly and loudly, steadily stabbing my finger toward "her" — taking total control of the situation.

There is no turning back. . . .

"¿Qué dice? ¿Qué dijo?" Mom asks, betrayed by a panic she suddenly can't control, or hide. She feigns not understanding my words. Words for which I summoned a super strength to enunciate with perfection.

"Why don't you leave her, Pop? Tell me!" I pause. "You had a chance before. You can still leave her! Be happy with your life Pop! Before it's too late! Just leave her and start over, with someone who loves you, who deserves you."

"¿Qué dice? ¿Qué está diciendo?"	*What is he saying?*
"Quiere saber por qué no me he ido."	*He wants to know why I haven't left.*
"Y, ¿qué le dijiste?"	*And what did you tell him?*
"No le he contestado."	*I have not answered him.*

No, Pop, . . . you have *not* answered me. But I believe you have finally answered *yourself.* And, when I think about it, that's all I want right now.

I have won this battle, the first of many to come before I am emancipated.

My new motto is:

'Más vale morir parado que vivir de rodillas.'
I'd rather die standing, than live on my knees.

I have a new strength and determination.

And I will think of suicide no more. . . .

• • •

Pop has only hit me once in my entire life.

When we were little, Mom gave us huge pills to get us to grow, to get rid of worms we didn't have, to treat anemia we didn't have.

I've never been able to swallow pills. I don't know if it's related to my stutter, or my other speech conditions, but my pill-swallowing muscles and reflexes do not work. Pills just sit there, on the back of my tongue, slowly dissolving into a salty, bitter paste.

Desperate attempts to swallow only beat the batter into a lather. I'll start to gag, which is the logical last step before vomiting ensues.

Mom's screams, slaps, and swats have never helped.

That particular time, when I was little, she told Pop to hit me so I would *swallow the damned pill.*

By this time, I think *anyone* would have done *anything* to get her to stop screeching, to get her to shut the fuck up.

To be clear, this is an observation, not an endorsement of the situation or the actions that followed.

Pop got up, took my left arm near my shoulder, and gave me a swat on my butt. One whack was enough to convince me I was truly alone in this world. The belt barely registered on the pain scale compared to Mom's beatings. But that swat was a swing of a sword that cut the few feeble fibers that formed our fragile alliance.

It caused irrevocable and irreparable damage. I was devastated by the betrayal.

Then Mom's capricious and duplicitous nature surfaced without a whisper of paradox.

She yelled at Pop for having hit me, and she threw him out of the house.

Perhaps, after all these years, Pop still remembers that pivotal moment as clearly as I do.

Although he has only hit me the one time, he has never defended me.

I love Pop, . . . but I have never really respected him. I have always known he is aware of my simmering, disgraceful contempt despite his continual efforts to repair the damage. It is a deep shame that has gnawed at my insides to this day.

• • •

I have confirmed Mom's kryptonite is a fear of abandonment, of being left alone. There is a morose irony in her behavior that drives people away, beats people away, and culminates in her fears coming to reality.

I have to be careful though. A scared, injured, rabid animal should not be cornered and approached. It's best to leave them to battle their inner demons alone.

• • •

Mrs. Ludetsky is a mid-forties woman who drives a pristine 1958 Chevrolet Delray in baby blue and white, with only 1379 miles on it. I only know this because the car is so unusual, and beautiful, I had to ask her about it. She says she gets an oil change and service every three months. Her mechanic must love her.

After working for her last summer, Mrs. Ludetsky has rehired me to be her handyman. She picks me up at 8 a.m., then she drops me off in the evening on days I'm not working my other jobs. Her husband died a few years ago, and her house and garden show signs of neglect.

I do a lot of raking, pruning, mowing, and clearing of brush on her extensive property. Mrs. Ludetsky went in to change, and now she joins me wearing a large straw hat over a sheer scarf tied loosely under her jaw, Jackie O sunglasses, a loose floral-print blouse with wide lapels, and, of course, capri pants and sensible slip-on garden shoes.

I get an abrupt image of her friend, Mr. Martin, who hired me last summer for similar work. It's how I met Mrs. Ludetsky, although I can't remember how I met him.

When Mr. Martin came to my house to pick me up, wearing a leopard-print silk cravat, starched white shirt, sharply pleated nautical-themed pants, a light-blue blazer, a Panama hat, a large, jeweled, signet ring on each pinkie, and a slight lisp, I could tell he was a homosexual.

Even Sara could see that Mr. Martin was a sissy. She told Mom I shouldn't go with this man to his house, but she couldn't explain why — not in the vulgar Spanish words Mom would need to hear to understand the concern — but I knew what she meant. All Mom saw in this man was cash money at the end of the day, so I went along with him.

It was an uneventful summer day of yard work. He was just a man who needed help getting his summer home ready for summer entertaining. I returned to his house for one banal afternoon after another. Sara's concerns — that I would be corrupted? — were biased and unfounded.

One day, Mrs. Ludetsky waltzed onto his manicured lawn in a wispy, ankle-length caftan and matching head scarf straight off a Hollywood studio costume rack. Her sophisticated sunglasses and oversized costume jewelry were artistic accomplishments. Her lips were a luscious crimson. To my eye, she was only missing a glamorous pair of platform booties on her bare feet. And perhaps a Marlene Dietrich–style cigarette holder. The nail polish color on her toes and fingers matched that of her lipstick.

Daniel would have loved her.

She and I exchanged pleasantries, then I was contracted to start working for her as well the following week.

During my time with him, I had been afraid to ask Mr. Martin if he was a homosexual, and what does that mean, and can I ask you some questions? He might have told me we're not the only ones, and

I'll be okay, some day. Maybe he would have explained masturbation, though I never would have dared to ask.

I kept all my questions in my head.

• • •

It suddenly occurs to me that Mom *did* understand Sara. Of course she did. With an all-stops-pulled, towering maricón specimen standing in front of us, Sara's concern was a pestering annoyance Mom callously swatted away.

Although Mr. Martin was never a threat, Mom did not care who he was, what he might be, or what might happen to me when I left with him, . . . as long as I made money for her. . . . as long as I handed her the cash at the end of my shift.

All those *many years* of hateful, noxious vitriol against homosexuals vanished when she found she might benefit from one.

She knew what she would get for my time in service to Mr. Martin. She simply *didn't care* what that service might entail.

They had negotiated my price as I stood there in front of them.

I could have been standing on an auction block.

She had pimped me out, without a whisper of concern.

Mom truly believes she *owns* me, and my body.

That she can sell me. . . .

She can rent me. . . .

She can discard me. . . .

• • •

Mrs. Ludetsky and I burn the brush and leaves in a large fire in an isolated area over several hours. I both enjoy and dislike the smell and the heat of the fire.

I am enraptured when thick gray smoke engulfs me . . . consumes me:

Suddenly, voraciously, completely.

This controlled danger calls to the *newly uncontrolled* chaos in my head:

I stand mesmerized.

My eyes sting.

My eyes water.

Is it because of the smoke, or my immense sadness?

Chaos calls this coward.

My eyes fill.

My eyes spill.

Is it because of the smoke, or my immense sadness?

I yearn to dive in, to make it all stop.

A cough startles me out of my stupor.

My eyes overflow.

Is it because of the smoke, or my immense sadness?

• • •

Mrs. Ludetsky makes lunch at 11:30 a.m. We each have a sandwich of cured ham, Swiss cheese, and grainy German mustard on thin pumpernickel bread. Each component is a new, sharp, odd flavor. I'm unsure if I like *any* of it, but I'm not a maleducado, and I eat it all.

Mrs. Ludetsky raises her long sleeves to wash the dishes, and I immediately see the tattoo of numbers on her forearm. I've read about them, but I've never seen anyone with one of these tattoos. When my gaze leaves her forearm, I look up at Mrs. Ludetsky's kind, caring face. She gives me a smile, rolls down her sleeves, and we get back to work.

Part 4

1980–Diagnosis

43

LIFE
Daniel

I HAVE A BETTER understanding of the despair Pedro endured when I left for the seminary in ninth grade. The trivial time we had together on my weekends home, outside of Mom's scrutiny, were the last tendrils tying us together.

And now, *it is he* who has left *me*.

Pedro is living a new life at college. My weekends at home without him are dreadful. I still don't have a meaningful relationship with my other siblings. We are the glass bulbs in a Galilean thermometer to Mom's constant temperature changes.

My last year at Holy Cross Seminary isn't going well. I'm having my first real heartbreak. Thomas, my *almost* boyfriend, has decided he isn't gay anymore. Or rather, it's been brought to his attention that he best not be gay. His mother found out about us and threatened to pull him out of school and send him to a camp that specializes in extrication and expungement experiments worthy of a Mengele Star of Approval.

Instead, he will stay in school, but his parent's probationary plan requires his transfer to a different dormitory floor, and a rearrangement of his school schedule to minimize his exposure to the evidential evil incarnate I represent.

I am devastated by my loss. I am humiliated by the perversely public shaming of our affairs.

I watch Thomas from a distance. He cringes if I approach. He is growing gaunt and gloomy, as if the threats of torture are as terrible as the torture itself. It appears he is not eating, sleeping, bathing. I believe I'm his only hope for help, and, simultaneously, if I intervene, I would be the accelerant and propellant toward his condemnation, then damnation.

Thomas spent a couple days in the infirmary.

And now, *it is he* who has left me.

He left the seminary on a cold December morning. His mind, body, and spirit were wilted whispers of the happy, healthy, very handsome young man he had once been. It is an inauspicious baseline with which to face the persecution that awaits him at home, or at a conversion therapy camp.

'Las desgracias nunca vienen solas.'
Misfortunes never come one at a time.

There really isn't anyone to talk to about boy–boy relationship loss in a sexually repressed environment with rampant boy–boy sexual activity. My confessors aren't unbiased or unsullied in this subject matter. They are furtive foxes inside the henhouse. Keys are superfluous when locks are absent from missing doors.

I think about calling Pedro. I haven't officially come out to him, though he must know I'm gay. He is undeniably unaware of my sexual activity here over the years. I certainly could not have told him when we were home.

• • •

Every other weekend home meant Mom could demand to speak with the administrative staff or teachers when she picked me up on Fridays, or when she dropped me off on Sundays. After years of her metiche mischief, I hope no one believes I am bad-natured, lazy, disrespectful, spiteful, insolent, devious—or add any number of other adjectives she used as labels.

Mom, over time, you might find that the reputation you wished to build around another has surrounded and claimed you instead.

Next year, I'll attend St. Joseph's Seminary College in Columbus. I'll be further from her grasp.

'Mañana será otro día.'
Tomorrow will be another day.

• • •

I've taken up smoking. Add it to the list of vices laden with my constant companions: guilt and shame. I suck in the chemicals that anesthetize me as if I have already become an emphysemic gasping for oxygen.

It will be a definitive act of defiance when I slip into the restroom on my new dormitory floor, then return to breathe my unmistakably sour breath onto Mom's face as I lean in for her final kiss, when she and Pop prepare to leave me at seminary college.

• • •

Seminary college is mostly different from seminary high school in the age of its students. We have the same regimented routines of meals, masses, classes, cleaning. We are to keep our rooms and bathrooms clean and clutter-free—it's a metaphor for scrubbing our souls. For extra pocket money we help tend the gardens, make minor maintenance repairs, work in the kitchen.

Free-time entertainment is enhanced with easy access to alcohol, cigarettes, and pot. Sexual activity starts quickly, with no fanfare.

"Do you fool around?" Jason asks.

Jason is my second-year mentor who's been directed to show me the ropes. I guess fooling around is one of the ropes.

"Yeah," I respond.

"Cool. When you'd like company, just leave your door open a little. That's the sign."

"Oh, . . . okay."

"Obviously, you won't know who's going to join you until he's in your bed," he says, with a self-satisfied smirk. "Unless you arrange something with someone in advance, in which case you won't need to leave your door ajar."

"Oh, . . . okay."

"Any questions?"

"Do you?" I ask. "Fool around?"

I quickly find out "the sign" isn't just for boys on our floor. And, it isn't *just for boys* either. When Father Matthew cooed my name as he entered my room and closed the door behind him, I decided I needed to make prearrangements in the future. It seems surreal to have doors with locks that can keep out the unwanted.

44

FREEDOM
Pedro

"ARE YA GONNA miss me?" I ask with a grin I couldn't wipe off my face if my life depended on it.

"Yes, Pedro," Daniel replies. "Of course I will miss you . . . a lot."

No surprise, we're both crying downstairs in our room, with no extra eyes or ears to spoil these moments for us.

My day of emancipation has finally arrived. I am leaving for college today. Of course, I haven't left the house. I haven't arrived at college. Something could still go terribly wrong. I know better than to relax in the face of these uncertainties until she has left me there, and she is gone.

"I will miss you as well, Daniel. Only you."

I pull him in for a hug. He smells of the marigolds he'd been deadheading. He's the only one that could cajole a flower to grow in our nutrition-starved garden soil.

"I wish there were a way we could see each other regularly," he whispers in my ear.

"Could you come visit . . . somehow? Never mind. I know she'll never allow it."

We both sigh. Daniel's face is uncharacteristically blank. I can't read his thoughts. He seems thin for some reason. I had thought him carefree when we were kids, but the seminary seems to have given him an edge, an anxiety, I haven't really seen before.

I'm afraid to ask him if he's okay . . . if he's *going to be* okay. A "yes and yes" would be wonderful, but how could I possibly help, if either were a "no"?

"Thanksgiving is a long time away," he says.

"In some ways, . . . it's not long enough. Is it possible to dread returning before you've left? It will be like your weekends home from the seminary. I'm sure I will pay."

"No doubt. . . . By the way, did you know you have your own dicho?"

"What do you mean?"

"'Quien quiere a *Pedro*, quiere su *perro*.' In this case, I'm your dog. Whoever loves you, will need to love me as well," he says with a big grin. "We're a package deal."

A weight has left my shoulders, and I return his smile.

"Yes, we are," I agree, and we hug one last time.

• • •

A couple months into college freshman year, Mom calls the one phone for the twelve guys living on my floor to interrogate me. She asks if I have signed up for the military, because "you're the type of disgrace to get out of your dutiful service." Something about María Ramírez reminding her I should have signed up already, like her precious son who chose the military over college. All these years after Héctor Ramírez lost to me in a spelling bee, Maria Ramírez is still bitter, and Mom remains susceptible to these metiche chismosas.

I remind Mom I signed up with the Selective Service when I turned eighteen, like I was supposed to, while I was still living at home.

But she got me thinking. . . .

What if I *did* join the military? Mom did *not* save any of the money I made at all my jobs before college. Actually, let me rephrase: Mom hoards money like she hoards everything. She has not offered to return any money to help me with my college education. And, like the lost cause that I am, I am sending her money. I'm working my ass off with my pre-med studies and I'm sending her most of the money I make in work-study. I know it's fucked up, but it's the only way to keep her from calling me repeatedly at the dorm.

I'm buying her cooperation to leave me the fuck alone.

I have a good financial aid package, but I have to apply every year, which requires Mom's collaboration. And my work-study commitment is twenty hours a week, while I'm at the same time taking time-consuming pre-med classes, and I have to pay back all my loans when I get out of college.

Then, there's the cost of medical school to think about.

The military could help pay for most of my education. It might help me make a clean and complete break from Mom. It definitely helped Juan.

. . .

Senior Chief Petty Officer Andrews is a generically handsome man in his thirties who responded to my inquiry call about joining the Navy. For a moment, I wonder if a buzz cut and a uniform increase every man's attractiveness, at least a little. He drove down from Cleveland to interview me, and to administer the Armed Services Vocational Aptitude Battery Test (ASVAB). His face lights up when he gives me my score of 94. "You only needed an 18 to pass," he remarks, his eyebrows still high on his forehead.

"Really?" I'm confused, and concerned. An 18 is considered passing?

"Now, we just have to go through a few questions about your overall health, and other things."

"Okay."

He asks various questions about my physical fitness. He says they will be gathering my medical records, so I have to be accurate and forthcoming. I mention X-rays for some back problems I had when I was doing heavy lifting at the nursing home, but it was thought to be muscular. Otherwise, I am skinny, but healthy.

And then he asks, "Have you ever been attracted to members of your own sex?"

"What?" I cough out.

It takes me a moment to recover from the sudden frog in my throat.

I know you can't join the military if you're gay. I just didn't know they would come right out and ask.

"Sorry, we have to ask everyone. Don't worry, as long as you're not an active homosexual, we can answer it in the negative," he continues, and marks the question as "no."

He mistook my nervous surprise to his question as an offense — as in, "Why would you think I'm a homosexual?"

"Oh, okay. . . . No, I'm not an active homosexual." And I think I just lied to the United States military. Although that tricky little word *active* could come in handy.

It was a good learning experience, but when he calls to follow up on our meeting, I graciously decline Senior Chief Petty Officer Andrews's enthusiastic endorsement, and his request for me to join the US Navy. I feel bad for him in a complicated sort of way.

I enjoy telling Mom I took the test and the Navy wants me to join. I let her sweat it a little — she's actually upset about it, for selfish reasons of course. I tell her I could become a medical technologist while serving our country.

"No, I won't become a doctor if I enter the Navy," I tell her in Spanish. I let her think it is she who persuaded me to stay in college and go to medical school. Welcome back, reverse psychology, my old friend.

• • •

"Oh! . . .

Uh . . . uh . . . uh . . ."

I've made a pretend vagina with my hands folded together in prayer-mode, and I'm thrusting into the space between my hands at my wrists.

This feels good!
This feels really good!

272

I'm trying to focus.

I'm trying to ignore the nagging question in my head:

Why didn't you try this before, PENDEJO?!

"Mmmhhh ... mmmmmhhh ..."

I think I'm supposed to think of something, or someone.
Why can't I fantasize when I want to?
When I need to?

"Uunnnhhhh ..."

This is unbelievable!
This feels so good!
Why the fuck didn't I try this bef ...

"Oh ... oh ... uh ... uhh ... uhhhh! ... uhhhh! ... uhhhhhh!"

• • •

WHAT THE FUCK JUST HAPPENED?!

• • •

So, I finally figured out masturbation last night.

It's unbelievable it took me this long.

My roommate went home for the weekend, and I spent my first night alone ... quite possibly ever. I've thought about it a lot, and I can't think of a single night when I was alone, before last night, in my entire life.

In any case, I did what felt good, until I had my first actual orgasm.

It was a long overdue and startling surprise. I guess a lot of kids figure it out by accident. Except I'm not a kid anymore.

Funny how privacy is a commodity.

• • •

I'm angry at myself. I knew sperm and semen come out with masturbation, but why did I have no clue about *orgasms*?

273

About wow-was-I-so-clueless, I-didn't-know-this-was-possible, full-body-consuming, there-is-nothing-comparable, unbelievably-great-feeling, I-can't-wait-to-do-it-again, *orgasms*?

How can I be such a PENDEJO?

· · ·

My release that first night, and every subsequent time, is accompanied by guilt and shame. They say "everyone masturbates." They also say that those who don't masturbate, well, "they lie about it, because everyone masturbates."

It still doesn't rid me of the guilt and shame.

Why can't I just enjoy it?

Who am I hurting?

· · ·

I guess I'm not your garden variety pendejo.

I'm more of a pinche pendejo.

After the guys on my floor polished off a keg last night, talk naturally turned to sex. Christopher did a lewd gesture, as if he were "jerking off" his pool-noodle-sized penis, and Alex thrusted his pelvis into his "twisting hands holding an invisible traffic cone representing his massive dick."

Three lights turned on over my head:

First, I needed this discussion with friends/cousins/campmates/ *anyone*, maybe six to eight *years* ago.

Second, I may not need to make a pretend vagina with my hands for it to work; I can use my hands the way these guys mimicked their own self-pleasure.

Third, I may not need to thrust. . . . I could just use my hands . . . or maybe *just one* hand.

Thomas mentioned hand lotion and Larry mentioned hair conditioner for "lube."

It's clear, I have a lot of experimenting to do.

I need to get rid of my roommate more often.

The last pearl of information I procured at the party was particularly curious: the guys generally love fucking, because *of course* they've all had sex, but it was universally agreed that blow jobs are the "crème de la crème for cumming" — and I do believe they meant it as a pun in that delivery.

At least I know enough to say that blow jobs *do* require another person.

I *think* Jeremy was kidding when he said some guys can give themselves a blowjob.

How would that be possible?

They all must think I'll believe anything.

. . .

This cute guy started talking to me at the salad bar in the cafeteria. I don't know how it came up that I played tennis in high school, but the guy invited me to play tennis tomorrow, right there at the salad bar, five minutes after I met him. He's in his third year, majors in biology, and lives in one of the fraternities.

. . .

"No strings attached?" Chris asks as he's cupping my crotch like a crude codpiece. We just played tennis in a public park off campus, then he led me to an abandoned shack in the nearby woods. I think he's been here before.

I don't know what "no strings attached" means. It makes me think of contraception and condoms — things boys and girls talk about in movies before they have sex. *We* don't need those. None of the DOT magazines talked about two guys doing anything together, and there were no references to "no strings attached" in any of the stories. *Now* doesn't seem to be the right time to ask Chris about it.

"Okay," I say.

. . .

My first sexual experience today, with Chris, in the spring of my freshman year, was awkward for lots of reasons, but he was sweet and patient, and it was memorable. Chris is definitely a pro at this, and I learned a lot from him.

The shame on my face refused to let me risk running into friends at the cafeteria, so Chris and I eat dinner at a burger joint off campus. We get to know each other with twenty questions.

I didn't have to ask him directly, but "no strings attached" apparently means, "I'm not lookin' for a relationship, cuz I have a girlfriend. We're gettin' married next year!"

It becomes a bittersweet moment because Chris, who clearly has had sex with other guys, is not gay. Or rather, he doesn't identify as gay. I still haven't met another one hundred percent guaranteed gay guy.

I hope I won't find out Chris jumped off a Tallahatchie Bridge somewhere.

45

GERARD
Daniel

MY FIRST YEAR in college is a blur. I robotically did what was necessary to advance. It was often unpleasant. I vaguely remember attending classes and learning the basics in my studies. Booze and bongs numbed me when I was beckoned to a professor's private den of depravity. I hadn't expected to feel such despair. I evidently envied Thomas's early escape years ago. Dishonor devolves into disesteem rather rapidly when there is no remedy for the rot within me.

Now in my second year, I've apparently lost my alluring appeal to the newer, wide-eyed novices. I feel contrite contempt when I spy these young men en route to my recent past, without making any attempt to intervene on their behalf.

My respite is reviving a sense of hope in me, albeit at their expense.

• • •

Rumors are rising that church hierarchy is concerned about the pervasive press researching reports of sexual abuse by priests. The students have been told sexual activity will not be tolerated, and will be met with *Expeditious Expulsion.*

"Sounds like, 'Do what I say, not what I do,'" Michael muses.

"Yeah," Todd retorts. "Old Father Summons was content last night as usual."

"What?" I ask.

"Father Summons?" Sam says. "You know, Father Simon who *summons* a first or second year pretty much every night?"

"Ugh," I spit out. "I'm glad to be off his roll call."

"So, the rumor is," Michael reveals, "they're gonna keep the gay priests, and try to weed out the gay students before they become new priests."

"Won't they eventually run out of new priests?" Sam speculates.

"I'd laugh," I chuckle. "But I don't think you meant it as a joke."

• • •

"Hijo, I've left your mom."

"What?! . . . Pop, what happened?"

"Daniel, I wish I didn't have to tell you on the phone. I just couldn't . . . ya no la podía soportar."

"Are you okay? . . . Where are you?"

"I'm okay Daniel. She threw me out last night, and I just started driving. . . . I'm going to Florida. . . . I'll find a cousin. . . . He'll help me. . . . Para eso está la familia. . . ."

So, it finally happened. . . . She drove him away for the last time.

But. . . . I doubt she wants this result.

"Okay, Pop. I understand. I really do. I want you to be happy."

"Gracias, hijo."

"Call me when you get there. Let me know if you need anything. I'll help if I can."

"Gracias, hijo. I should go. I need to call the others."

"Okay, Pop. Drive safely, and take some breaks along the way. I love you Pop!"

"I love you too, hijo."

• • •

Father Gerard was ordained a few years ago. He joined the staff this year in the philosophy department. Gerry and I have had an on-again, off-again relationship the last few months. He is exceedingly anxious about his tenure, in light of his sexuality, and the edicts emanating from his superiors. I believe he would self-flagellate or use the cilice if those were allowed. After we have made love, he often warns me to never return, then calls me back before I even reach the door. I'm not entirely sure he's right in la cabeza, but he's kind to me *most of the time*, during our on-agains.

• • •

When a friend is expelled because of his mundanely salacious sexual activity, I get scared. There's a new, Gestapo-inspired group of staff and students tasked with rooting out rotten students. Father Gerard takes his work on the task force very seriously.

So, our relationship is off again.

• • •

It's my last definitive act of defiance when I decide to go to a gay club to meet up with friends from the outside world — guys I've met at gay clubs, who keep me grounded when life as a seminarian suffocates me.

"Did you ever wonder where the word seminarian came from?" Brad asks, chewing the straw in his drink. He's got a blond, post-perm Mike Brady hairstyle, a satin, psychedelic shirt open to his belly button, and French horn–flared, bell bottom jeans. He's evidently still in a 1970s disco.

"What do you mean?" asks Tony, the self-monikered Italian stallion.

And, judging from rumors, he's not far off the mark.

"It kinda sounds like seminal, as in seminal vesicle, doesn't it?" Brad concludes.

They both wait for my response with curious amusement. I'm waiting for the bartender to make my drink.

"Guys, don't hurt your brains," I retort with a laugh. "*Seminarian* and *seminal* share a common root with *semen*. And the word *seminary* kinda means 'breeding ground,' but *not* in the way you might think."

"Oh honey, that explains everything," Brad replies with a smirk and laugh.

"And then there's that odd connection between rector and rectum," Tony adds with a snicker. "Makes you wonder who decides to use these words, . . . and why."

We all laugh, then head to the dance floor.

I'm not surprised to see Gerry on the second-floor balcony, looking down at me on the dance floor. He's wearing a tight tank top, and—pardon the expression—painted-on jeans, showing bulges and curves unbecoming a priest. He must have worn priestly clothes over this gaudy gay uniform when he left to come here.

"Just ignore her," Brad says with a sneer, while looking up at my nemesis.

"Yeah, that bitch isn't worth the price of admission," Tony adds.

But I can't help myself. . . .

• • •

"You're not supposed to be here, Daniel," Gerry moans into my ear as I wait for my drink at the bar. I knew he'd follow me.

"Oh, that's priceless," I say.

I'm disgusted with myself, because I may be flirting.

"Seriously, you better leave," he demands.

"Or what, Sergeant Schultz?" I spit out. Flirting has been aborted. "Are you going to report me to Colonel Klink?"

"I suppose you're Colonel Hogan in this terribly tiresome Gestapo analogy?" he smirks.

"Gerry, you sold your sorry soul, and now you're in search of a purpose," I yell over the music and noise. And, accompanying some previously painstakingly practiced, perfectly performed finger snaps—four. . . . in his face. . . . mimicking the letter Z—I add, "You won't last long, so good riddance . . . and begone, bitch, . . . you have no power here!"

• • •

I was *not* surprised to be summoned Monday morning to the rector's office, not to his private quarters, where I was unceremoniously and expeditiously expelled from St. Joseph's Seminary College.

I hadn't finished my second year, but I have become disillusioned, dispassionate, and several other *dis*-words.

Of course, I have no Plan B, no exit strategy, no clue.

I called Brad, who was truly gracious in offering me a place to stay until I land from this skydive-without-a-parachute.

• • •

I see Gerry coming out a side entrance of the dormitory as I death-march away from my dreams, toward a waiting taxi. I had hoped to avoid all goodbyes by leaving now, during a classroom period.

He's always been a pain in the ass. But right now, I wish Gerry would leave me alone. I have nothing to say to him. There is nothing I need or want from him.

"It's for your own good, Daniel," Gerry says sheepishly as he approaches in pious priest regalia—clerical collar, cassock, and cruci-fix—hands tucked into their opposite sleeves like a Mother "fuckin'" Superior.

Is this motherfucking asshole flirting right now?

"A otro perro con ese hueso, pendejo!" I declare.

To another dog with that bone, you fool.

"What's that supposed to mean?"

"For you Gerry, I'll rephrase: Father Gerard, you're a cold, calculat-ing, catastrophe of a cleric, and karma is gonna be a bitch."

46

GRINCHLY
Pedro

I HAVEN'T TALKED with Daniel lately. Calling off campus is tricky. We can receive long distance calls, but we can't make them from our single dorm-floor phone.

I stopped going home for my six-week holiday breaks after a particularly bad beating I received on Thanksgiving morning my freshman year.

Everyone was still sound asleep when Mom grinchly tiptoed into my bedroom, then switched on her maximum maniacal madness on me.

Even in war, basic human rights are considered inviolable. Not under Mom's roof. My sleeping body could not expect leniency, sympathy, goodwill. Naturally, love, tenderness, and kindness were never options.

I ran out of the house barefoot in my underwear, with snow on the ground. I didn't return for the rest of the long holiday break.

'Vale más huir que morir.'
It's better to flee than to die.

Because if you flee, you may live to fight another day.

. . .

Folks have wondered why I never fought back. I sometimes wonder as well, but there are several reasons. First, I can't imagine hitting someone. It's repulsive, when you've seen it up close or experienced it yourself. I can't even watch films that show violence or cruelty to people or animals. Second—and it may sound chauvinistic—you can't hit a woman. Period. And, third, they say that those who are abused often become abusers, though I can't imagine I will ever get past my repulsion of physical violence.

As a child, I rarely saw Pop hit back. Only after he'd been pushed to the brink, when he was broken, bruised, battered, and bleeding, and he couldn't take it anymore.

We all have our breaking point.

When you're completely dependent on your abuser for shelter and food, neither fight or flight are obvious self-defense options. Before college, I was defenseless. Now, flight is an option, though I will *never* allow myself to be under Mom's control again.

I need to *expunge* Mom from my waking life—*unambiguously and completely.*

But I fear she will always be: *my worst nightmares.*

• • •

In the breaks between semesters, I've managed to stay with friends near campus. I spent a summer at Harvard in a program for pre-med students of color. It was the first time I left Ohio on my own. My eyes took in so much newness. I have much to learn about life outside of small Midwestern towns.

• • •

I am running.

I am always running.

I am running for my life.

I am naked.

Of course I'm naked.

Veritably vulnerable. Vincible. Vilified.

I am shaking, shivering, shriveled.

The umbilical bullseye of my round ripe belly beckons the ax,

For evisceration.

My exposed genitalia beckon the ax,

For emasculation.

There is blue-eyed-boyfriend-doll emptiness,

Between my legs.

I am running.

I am Kunta Kinte.

I am running for my life.

It is she.

Of course it is she.

Mom is approaching.

She is reaching,

For me.

She is reaching,

For the sky.

Always the same slanted stance.

I am lost.

I've been found.

I have lost.

Soldiers in gas masks, boots, and bayonets hunt my brethren.

Los Prietos. Los Morenos. Los Renegridos.

The Indigenous. Los Indígenas.

When I wake, I am empty, empoisoned, empapado.

Drenching, torrential tears flow from

dreary darkened damned dreams,

into my

weary worthless waking world.

Medical school has been challenging. There's never enough time. My waking life is marred by the odd combination of sleep deprivation — due to lack of time for sleep — and garden-variety insomnia.

The last two years will be hospital-based clinical rotations, with on-call schedules, meaning I'll stay, and work, overnight, then continue to work through the following day. If I weren't so tired, I'd try to imagine a sarcastic comment Daniel might say, in the vein of, "What could go wrong?"

* * *

So, the answer to the question, "What could go wrong?" is that I can't really remember much of my clinical rotations in the last two years of medical school.

Outside of the hospital, I suppose I could mention my world travels.

Or the times I couldn't live in-the-moment, while sitting in the Broadway seat I had bought months before, for which my intensifying anticipation fizzled as I walked under the marquee toward the theater entry doors.

Or my various attempts at a relationship.

Those are stories, perhaps, for another time. . . .

Suffice it to say, I'm now a medical doctor en route to a year of internship, followed by two years of residency.

* * *

My first night in the VA Hospital intern's room, I awake to the pitter-patter sensations of a mouse crawling on my belly, my chest, and then my neck. I'm yelling and thrashing when I fall out of bed; the nurses run in to find me wrestling with the sheets, blankets, and myself, on the floor.

"The exterminators sprayed the kitchens tonight," they announce. "The mice had to go *somewhere*. Just go back to sleep."

I don't see, but I *hear* their eye-rolls.

* * *

Being on call in the ICU is very much like waiting for bombs to explode at any moment. The tension is amplified by the years of insomnia, and staying inside the unit every three nights. At any moment, the nurse will wake you with lab results, the beeper will go off to announce a new admission, the alarms will go off to declare someone is coding.

My body is not equipped for this.

But I don't have a Plan B.

• • •

When you're a kid, you're told it's a lot of work to become a doctor.

But you can't possibly know, understand, imagine the physical and mental toll it takes to survive medical training.

Your brain, your grades, your enthusiasm can't preimagine the unrelenting traumas of insatiable stress and sleep depriva-tion—especially when your baseline includes uncontrolled anxiety and post-traumatic stress disorders.

• • •

When you walk on an eggshell minefield every day of your childhood, you develop a sensitive startle reflex, which becomes your first line of defense for the rest of your life.

Life as a medical student, intern, and now resident on the wards of several hospitals has taken my startle reflex to another level. I can eas-ily start a startle chain reaction when folks see me startle. It's quite funny, if not tragic.

Traumatic nightmares come regularly now, worsened by my lack of sleep, and exacerbated by my nights on the wards. These night-mares consist of a mixture of Mom being Mom, war scenes, drowning, and valiant efforts to resuscitate patients who have coded.

I don't see the ax man anymore, but I know he lurks in the shadows.

• • •

In my final year of residency, I'm enjoying my elective months in vari-ous subspecialties.

My psychiatry rotation is particularly fascinating. I'm assessing a middle-aged man well into his first manic episode. His wife is quietly sobbing into one hand, their adolescent son holds her other hand and looks at his shoes, while the man flatly pronounces his personal prow-ess in counterespionage, high-stakes gambling, liquor consumption, and sexual seduction, all worthy of the James Bond persona his mania has awakened. A few days ago, he was a quiet and humble sports-shoe salesman at the local mall, who doted on his wife and son.

I wonder if Mom might be manic-depressive, or bipolar. This man's case is extreme, but seems familiar.

. . .

"This isn't working," I say — or he says — depending on which "attempt at a relationship" is ending right now.

"Yeah, I know," he — or I — say.

"Can we still be friends?" I — or he — asks.

"Yes, I'd like that," he — or I — say.

"One more time, for old times' sake?" I — or he — asks.

"Absolutely!" he — or I — say.

"Waiter!" we call out together.

Jinx!

. . .

Mom is maniacally pulling all the lines out of my patients'
arms and throats!
She's unplugging their life support machines!
The nurses are struggling to wake me in the resident's room.
I am so tired.
Please let me sleep!
I can't open my eyes, but *I can see* everything in the entire ICU clearly.
The nurses are slapping and beating me.
I can't hear their muffled voices, but their lips are saying,
"Wake up! Code Blue! Wake up!"
I am so tired.
Just let me sleep!
I can't even speak! No words come out.
Mom is pointing and laughing at me.
She doesn't have to come toward me in the same
slanted stance she's perfected.
Her surrogates are beating me.

My patients have turned into ax-wielding zombie momias!
They're coming after *me*, not Mom.
It was Mom who did this to them, not me!
Mom did it! I want to scream.
I can't even speak! No words come out.
She's getting away with it!
She's getting away with it, again!
I am so tired.
Please let me sleep!

I awake in a startled panic, quickly assessing the situation to determine the cause, casualties, collateral damage.

But I'm in my bed at home, far from the chaos of the hospital units, from the physical threat known as Mom.

• • •

A potentially long story made short, I have completed my residency and medical training, and I've decided against further training in a subspecialty. I'm content to be a general internist. I'll partner with patients to manage their health, then refer them to specialists when we need their help.

My ultimate goal is to learn as much as I can about HIV, the viral infection that's been devastating the gay community for years. Caseloads are too great for infectious disease specialists to assume their care. And, there is a worrisome trend of some doctors refusing to care for folks with HIV. Some have referenced that the patient's lifestyles are offensive to their faiths. Others fear for their safety in a regressive ignorance of the known HIV transmission routes.

Primary care providers and community health centers are stepping forward to uphold our Hippocratic oaths for the care of all people, without prejudice.

• • •

"Hi Pop," I say.

"¡Hola Pedro! ¿Cómo estás hijo?"

"I'm well. How are you, Gloria, and the kids?"

"We're all fine, gracias a Dios."

Pop moved to Florida when he left Mom, met a lovely woman, and now they have a couple kids. He's a previously bound, but now freed man, living life to the fullest.

I'm reminded of the night I challenged him to leave Mom. . . .

Pop calls me regularly. He's also punctual with holiday and birthday cards. I'm less disciplined in my commitment to rekindle relationships.

I'm just so tired all the time.

Sleep does not lead to rest.

Rest will not lead to peace.

Of mind.

Or body.

"I'm so glad you're happy, Pop," I say. "*Are* you happy?"

"Sí, hijo," he replies. "We're not rich, but we're happy, and healthy. And we eat good food. Have you ever eaten alligator?"

"Does it taste like chicken?" I ask facetiously.

"When it's grilled, it's a little like chicken, and a little like steak."

"Really? Actually, a thick piece of swordfish smothered in mayonnaise, grilled to perfection, also tastes like steak!"

"We will have to try it, hijo."

"Yes, next time I see you in Florida we'll get some."

There aren't many topics in which we share a common interest, so I make it a point to know some basics about the Cleveland Indians, the Cleveland Browns, the weather conditions in Ohio, Florida, and New England, and anything related to Mexico.

"I'll let you go Pop, it sounds like Gloria has dinner ready."

"Yes. She says to say '¡Hola!'"

"¡Hola, Gloria, and Francisco and Sonia!"

"I love you, hijo."

"I love you too, Pop."

And I hope he knows it.

47

OUT
Daniel

"I'M GAY TOO, Daniel," Pedro confirms.

He's visiting for a family reunion, and we're *finally* having this conversation.

"What?! Really?!"

"Yes! I thought you knew. I've always known about *you*."

"I was always a tad more obvious."

We laugh. This is not as awkward as I had feared. Why was I worried?

"When you left for the seminary, it was hard to share what was going on. But honestly, it was never safe to come out under that roof."

That is so true.

"But you're such a jock, . . . and you've had girlfriends!"

"First of all, *wow*, I'm a jock? Are you hearing yourself? Besides, some gay guys *actually like sports*. Second, there are girlfriends, and then there are 'girl-friends,'" he retorts, demonstrating big "air quotes." "I love women, but not love-love."

I guess I'm the same.

"But . . . didn't Sara see you with your arm around a girl in Boston? Weren't you kissing?"

"Julie is a woman, a girl-friend in air quotes. . . . We were in a large group outside the gay bar we had just left, near the Boston Public Library."

"Oh. False reporting from Sara, I guess."

"I had put my arm around Julie just as Sara and her friends were walking by. We were definitely not kissing; I would never kiss anyone in public."

"You're such a prude," I laugh.

"Imagine if I had had my arm around my boyfriend-at-the-time?"

"Meanwhile, my friends are going to be so happy! They've been in love with you since they met you at St. Joseph's."

"I'm glad you still talk with them, Daniel. . . . But what happened to the priest who reported you? Why was it okay that *he* was at the gay bar when he saw you, before he reported you?"

"Oh nothing happened to *her*. She said it was *her job* to report me. Funny how she didn't report that she had slept with me for months . . ."

"I don't get it, . . . He's a gay priest having sex with men, as well as his own students, but that's all okay?"

"It's not that it's okay, *per se*. She's already a priest, so they'd rather not get rid of her. She's a young investment. They want to get their money's worth out of her."

"That is both cynical and reprehensible."

That stings. It's a valid point, but it opens my wounds and pours salt into them.

"There's pressure from the diocese to prevent gay guys from becoming new priests. They want to keep their problems off the front page. . . . What would happen if I were to 'drop a dime'?"

"Maybe you'd expose the hypocrisy of the whole church. Imagine if the church weren't so repressed with regard to sexuality? It seems lots of priests remain sexual even when they commit to celibacy."

"Oh, you don't even know."

"I just realized that commit is a word that means 'to pledge,' but it can also mean 'to break that pledge.' You can commit to celibacy, then commit adultery."

"You're right, . . . but I don't think it's a true contronym like 'bill, bolt, or bomb.'"

"My *new* favorite contronym is *critical*. 'Mom's critical nature is critical to her nature.'"

What fun! I've missed my wordsmithing sparring partner!

"Gosh, I *love* our word games! My favorite contronym is *out*. The stars are *out* because the lights are *out*. And, *I* am out."

"You are *very* out!"

We laugh for a while, then sit quietly. We're both looking off to a distant place and time.

"Would you still want to go back, if they invited you to return?" he asks.

"Yes, without a doubt. The Catholic Church is so important to me."

"Why? If you don't mind me asking."

"Well, it's all I've ever known, all I've ever striven to attain. I had no alternate plan. . . . I have no idea what I'm going to do now."

"Are you *okay* with that?"

"It'll have to be okay."

"Are *you* okay, Daniel?"

"I'll have to be okay."

Pedro watches me for a second too long. I get self-conscious and look away.

"More wine?" I ask as I reach for the bottle.

"But of course," he replies with a grin. "Meanwhile, seriously . . . *why on earth* would you call me a jock?"

"I don't know. You're so different from me. You seem together. All buttoned-up."

"You mean repressed," he retorts, but at least he's smiling. "Like the Catholic priesthood."

• • •

I'm working at a pizza parlor. It pays the bills — most of the time — but it's not my dream come true. After leaving the seminary last year, with no hope of ever returning, I've been having trouble focusing on new goals. It's really rather depressing. What am I going to do with my life? Is this *it* for me?

It seems I grew up too fast, so I never grew up.

Ugh. It sounds like the Peter Pan syndrome.

I'm meeting guys, but haven't really dated anyone for a long period. I've never had an actual boyfriend. Pedro says I should leave Ohio, which makes sense. The gays tend to move to the coasts or the bigger cities in between. I'd probably have more opportunities to meet a guy in a big city.

But, start over, from scratch? How would I even do that?

• • •

Mom's angry that I've started inviting our various cousins to family gatherings.

Connecting with Graciela, years ago, was the catalyst to my rocking the absurd boat that prevented cousins from talking and having meaningful relationships.

Aggressive passive-aggression was a hallmark of *Dynasty*'s Alexis-Krystle feud. For the uninitiated, that's classy-but-bitchy first wife vs. slowly-learning-to-fight-back second wife. I use what these characters taught me to see my plan through: to integrate this fractured family.

I have no regrets. And, quite possibly for the first time, Mom won't win this argument. If she wants to see me at family events, she'll have to shut up *and* put up.

Has Pedro had an effect on me?

• • •

"Daniel, you know I love you, but you have *got* to get your ass out of this house," my roommate Brad says. He's wearing a *Wonder Woman* outfit for a costume party at Tony's house. I was invited, but never RSVPed.

I'll respond to Brad in a second, but first I just have to take in his hairy chest above his laughable foam basketballs — posing as breasts in *WW*'s brassiere cups — and his blatant disregard for the age-old custom of hiding your personals when wearing her outfit. Let's just say, I can tell he's not Jewish.

"First, I have to acknowledge your choice of orange-red lipstick, a *generous* amount of azul-celeste eyeshadow, Tammy Faye eyelashes, and a Loretta Lynn *blonde* wig."

"And?"

"That's it."

"Bitch."

"Bradley James Harrison, do you *eat* with that mouth?" I counter with a grin, but then more seriously, "I just don't have the drive to go out. It's too much work. It's not worth it. Sorry."

"Girlfriend, your man-dream isn't going to walk in that door if you haven't met him somewhere else first."

"I know."

"Oh, I know you know. I'm as right as those fuckin' dichos you keep reciting."

· · ·

The truth is, I walk the long route home every day, after an insufferable amount of regurgitating, in a high-pitched chirpy voice, "Would you like to upgrade your Pizza Combo with a Warm Apple Pie Pocket for an additional forty-nine cents?"

At that hour, the woods off of Emerald Avenue are full of ripe-for-the-picking diversions that mask the need to find a long-term or steady relationship.

· · ·

Pedro is visiting for a family wedding. We're both nurturing relationships with our siblings now that we're older, away from home, and there's no conveyor-belt, hurdled race to win Mom's fickle affection. Now, we can all talk and get to know each other as we slowly shed the layers of secrecy and defense.

It's been two years since I left the seminary, when my hopes and dreams dismorphed into obsessive, pathetic walks in the woods in search of a hurried oxytocin release.

I've stopped watching nightly news, reading magazines, listening to talk radio, all to avoid the jackhammering thoughts about the risks I incur with my liaisons.

"Have you gotten tested?" I ask Pedro. "I haven't had the nerve to do it."

"I haven't, but I'm pretty careful. I live with the assumption every-one has it."

"That makes sense."

"Our main focus in the hospital is prevention. That's how we're gonna get this under control.

"You mean condoms?"

"Yeah, they can decrease the spread of other infections as well, so we have an aggressive media campaign about it."

"Ugh. I forgot about all the other infections out there."

"It would be great to get them *all* under control."

Damn. . . . They make you focus on one thing, when there's so much else to fear as well.

"Can you tell me about HIV?" I ask. "Like . . . what is it *really*? I don't know what to believe."

"Unfortunately, we still have so much to learn about it. . . . Basically, viruses are tiny, dormant robots that require living cells to replicate."

"I've never heard it explained like that."

Pedro's face lights up, as if he appreciates this recognition.

"My brain does that—cuts out all the extraneous stuff to look at the simplest way to view things," he says.

"I know. You've always been that way."

He smiles.

It's so great to see him smile.

"When viruses take over the internal mechanisms of a cell in order to replicate, they often destroy the cell—maybe not immedi-ately, but eventually. . . . Our immune system kicks into gear to get rid of the infection. . . . Chemical reactions occur. . . . Depending on the virus, some people fully recover. With HIV, people eventually get symptoms or complications, . . . they can get very sick, . . . they often die."

I feel my eyebrows and ears shift. Pedro seems to notice.

"That's the scary part," I murmur. "Do we know where it came from? How it started infecting humans?"

"We may never know for sure. Viruses enter our bodies through our natural openings, and through artificial openings created by needles, bites, and scratches."

"Hmm."

He looks at me and holds my gaze when he says, "Some viruses *don't* infect humans. . . . They use other animals, or even bacteria, to replicate."

"Really? I didn't know *viruses* use *bacteria*."

"Yeah, . . . but at some point, these viruses *can* be introduced into humans."

"I get it now. It makes more sense."

· · ·

Brad got us a shower curtain of a life-sized, life-like cowboy wearing nothing but his hat, and a bandana around his neck. I guess it's the only clue he's a cowboy. The curtain is otherwise see-through, so it feels like you and Buck Nekkid are showering together.

"I love it!" Pedro exclaims as he enters the bathroom. "Will he be joining us for dinner? Is this the new meaning of casual dress?"

"Ha! I wish!" I reply.

I've made spaghetti and meatballs, one of a few dishes I've mastered. I'll make a salad and put some garlic bread in the oven.

"Are you dating anyone?" Pedro asks when he returns.

"No, not really. Are you?"

"No, I don't have time. . . . Or, the energy. Even in a big city, it's not easy to meet guys. I hate going to bars."

Pedro's eyes wander slightly over my shoulder, and his lips part like a ziplock in reverse. Sometimes I can tell when he's lost focus and left the conversation.

Then his eyes suddenly alight and zoom in on me.

"Daniel, do you think we'll ever find love?"

"Is it even possible?"

"Gosh, I hope so. I really hope so. I just don't know how it would look. What kind of guy can love damaged goods like us . . . and I mean it 'con todo respecto.'"

"And todo cariño! Although, humbly speaking, I have so much to offer, any guy should grovel for my hand."

"Haha! You are the most humble person I know!"

"It's a burden I carry."

Our whole-hearted laughter eventually dies down.

"I'm looking forward to seeing everyone tomorrow, especially all our cousins!"

"Everyone?" I ask.

"You know what I mean. I'm so impressed you've been able to integrate them into family events. I never thought it would be possible."

"They're all lovely people, and they've always wanted us in their lives."

"I hope they know it's mutual. At least for me."

I don't want to change the mood, but I'm curious. "What will you do when you see Mom tomorrow?"

"I'm not sure. I'll say hello, of course — I'm not a maleducado."

"I don't want you to have regrets, Pedro. 'Cuando puedo, no quiero; cuando quiero, no puedo.'"

"*When I can, I don't want to; when I want to, I can't.* Hmm. No, Daniel, I honestly believe I won't regret not having a *pretend relationship* with the person who physically and emotionally tortured me for two decades, and continues to terrorize me in my dreams."

"You don't think you could move on?"

"Move on? From what? Move on *for* what? Who would benefit from my forgiving someone who has never asked for forgiveness?"

'Ojos que no ven, corazón que no siente.'
What the eyes don't see, the heart doesn't grieve.

"She's lonely, Pedro. Since Pop left her, she calls me *a lot*. . . . I know she calls the girls as well."

"We each should decide what kind of relationship we want to have with Mom. . . . I prefer to live without her in my life. It's that simple.

298

And I'm glad Pop left. He's with a woman who loves him the way he *should* be loved."

"I'm glad he's happy too. I really am. But doesn't Mom deserve to be happy?"

"*Everyone* deserves to be happy. Funny, for most of my childhood I tried to figure out the Spanish words for *proud* and *deserve*. I doubt I could have pronounced *orgulloso* and *merezco*. But imagine if we had heard 'I'm proud of you' or 'you deserve love and happiness' when we were kids?"

"Things would probably be different for us."

"I can't even imagine it," he whispers.

"Well, there's the saying, 'El tiempo cura y nos mata.' *Time heals, and it kills us.*"

"Geez, Daniel, that's comforting," Pedro says, sarcastically. "But it is kinda funny, in a macabre, Morticia Addams sort of way."

"I'm more of a Lily Munster," I reply, and we laugh. "It's all about the hair."

48

MEDICINE
Pedro

THE PROBLEM WITH having thick black hair is my scalp is really white. Like, Ultra White, because no sunlight gets through. Actually, it looks very much like the cadaver skin we dissected in anatomy class my first year in medical school. The body was of a Caucasian man who had died in his late sixties of lymphoma.

There are bald men in Mexico with my complexion whose scalps match their skin color elsewhere, so I suspect my scalp skin cells have hibernating melanin waiting to be awoken.

"What happened here?" Jennie asks my reflection in the mirror, her comb and scissors in the same hand.

"Hmm? What? Where?" I ask, coming out of the reverie that always accompanies anyone touching my head with ticklish tenderness.

"Looks like a nasty scar," she says. "On the crown of your head."

And so, it turns out, a stiletto-shoe scar—seared onto my Ultra White scalp in a seaweed sea of solid black hair follicles—will scream out for attention even decades later.

"Oh that, . . . My mom says I ran into a door when I was a six-year-old fool."

"Musta hurt."

· · ·

When I wrote my Academy Award acceptance speech for the screenplay I haven't written yet, I made a point of thanking Mr. Merle, my high school chemistry teacher. I've loved so many of my teachers over the years, and I am humbly aware I was a teacher's pet more than once.

In many ways, Mr. Merle was like me. I won't say he was gay, because I don't know that, and I wouldn't want to give an Oscars speech with a mistaken-sexuality reference. Mr. Merle had a stutter. I won't say that either since it's not relevant in my speech. But it mattered to me. He endured so much ridicule, and yet he stood up there every day, talking to a bunch of knuckleheads about atoms and cations and anions.

I was a coward in high school. I spoke only when absolutely necessary. I couldn't handle the conjoined twins of speech impediment and ridicule. I knew I had dyslexia and a stutter. When I eventually got diagnostic testing years later, they added attention deficit disorder to the list of factors that affect my speech, my reading, my person.

I would not be surprised if Daniel has ADHD, *with the added dose of hyperactivity*, as he suspected years ago.

Although the specialists didn't test for the autism spectrum disorder, they did suggest I might have anxiety disorder and obsessive-compulsive disorder, almost as if those weren't self-evident. Under threat of abuse, Mom demanded timely, well-performed perfection in my chores and machismo manliness in all else. *Of course* I'm textbook anxiety, OCD, *and* PTSD.

I'm still surprised I haven't worried myself into anemia.

Chemistry was my path through college and into medical school. At Mr. Merle's encouragement, I placed out of first year chemistry in college and became a chemistry tutor and lab assistant my freshman year.

The chemistry credit allowed me to take a non-science class in women's studies my third year. I felt I needed to hone my feminist views since they are similar to an anti-homophobia and anti-racism approach to life.

I promptly got the first "Please see me" of my life, on the first class assignment.

Up until then, science and math homework required answering specific problems, equations, or questions with a formula, number, or a simple sentence. A paragraph was for novels.

The women's studies class assignment had been to write a paper on a book we had read and to answer five basic prompt questions the professor believed were at the core of the book's message.

This is a mock-up of my paper:

1. Blah, blah blah. (Answer to question 1.)
2. Blah, blah blah. (Answer to question 2.)
3. Blah, blah blah. (Answer to question 3.)
4. Blah, blah blah. (Answer to question 4.)
5. Blah, blah blah. (Answer to question 5.)

Yes, I even listed the corresponding numbers into my "paper."

I am mortified thinking about it all these years later.

And, then I learned how to write a paper. Thanks, Ms. Evans, for believing in me, and for giving me a second chance! I should mention you in my speech as well! Without the guidance and support you and Mr. Merle offered, I never would have learned how to write a paper, a thesis, a novel, or someday . . . a screenplay.

Yes, my brain still works in these circuitous and tangential meanderings.

• • •

Hunger is a weapon.

The physical and emotional sickness of hunger is unfathomable
to the fortunate.
I was not so fortunate.
Cafeteria Christians at their biblican buffet would deny children
meals in schools.
Others would use hunger to bend another to their will.

Hunger is a weapon.

The hunger for love is human,
The hunger for acceptance is human,
The hunger for community is human,
The hunger for meaning is human,
The hunger for power is human.

Hunger is a weapon.

Hunger for knowledge is formidable against other weapons.
It was my "ticket out of town."
Knowledge is mine,
Hidden,
Where no one can see it,
Where no one can find it,
Where no one can take it,
Where I can wield it.

"I got tested. . . . Pedro, I've got it, I have HIV."

Oh shit. . . . I'm glad we're doing this on the phone, so he can't see the hysteria in my eyes, the spasms in my body, the knot in my throat.

"Oh, Daniel." I clear my throat a couple times. "How are you?" I clear my throat again. "Do you have more information?"

I've got to take deep breaths! I can't let him hear my panic.

"My T cells are 483. My doctor says it's not too bad. She says it's almost normal. That the virus is probably hiding out in certain organs."

He sounds relatively calm. I may have heard a sniffle.

More deep breaths. But quickly. I can't allow an awkward pause.

"It isn't bad," I start to say, but I have to clear my throat yet again. "You're right. Normal levels are a little higher, but your present count isn't bad."

Why did I say, "present count"?

I'm buying time, creating a deflection.

These numbers can change, from hour to hour and day to day. Each level is a snapshot of a point in time. It's a clue, but not the full picture. We still don't have a good, clinically available test to measure viral activity or viral concentration. The T-cell count is our *poor*, but *only* marker for monitoring HIV disease.

Yikes, what should I say next?

My mind is blank . . . it's actually blank . . . at the wrong time.

"'La salud no es conocida hasta que es perdida,'" Daniel says.

Health is not valued until it's lost.

"That's so true!" I choke out. I'm so glad he's got his dichos to help us with this conversation. I've usually got a remarkable medical poker face, but I've been thrown off my game with this information. I would never say it out loud, but having HIV is still pretty much a death sentence. This is devastating news.

"You've got to take care of yourself, Daniel." Damn, this frog in my throat! "Get plenty of sleep. If you have trouble sleeping, get something to help you. We can talk about nutrition, exercise, alcohol, and everything else, now or later. But please get your rest."

"Oh honey, getting my beauty rest has always been my motto." Then he pauses. He clears his throat, and swallows the tears that have surely collected there. "But I know what you mean. I *have* had trouble sleeping because of the anxiety. I'll ask my doctor to give me something."

"And don't take no for an answer! Doctors get hung up on prescribing sleeping pills. They get stingy and militant about them. Right now, you need to take control of your health, and you need to get your rest. I will help in any way. Just let me know what you need."

I'm suddenly feeling optimistic. I don't think he noticed my inner roiling turmoil. We talk for a while, I answer his questions, we fall into a familiar rhythm.

"Thanks Pedro. I appreciate it. . . . When's the last time I said, 'I love you?'"

"You just did. And, I love you too, Daniel. . . . I'm going to help you beat this maldito virus."

For the love of god, I will help him beat this goddamn fucking thing.

Part 5

Diagnosis–1992

49

HIV
Daniel

I JUST TOLD Pedro I have HIV. I wish he were here with me.

I got the HIV-101 Talk, as Pedro calls it. It's the basics that will help me understand what's going on with my body. I really appreciate having him on my side.

But I feel so alone.

I *am* so alone.

I've got a small group of friends, centered around Brad, who's sort of our queen bee. . . . Or, Queen bee. I mostly work at the pizza parlor, then I come home. I no longer have my wayward walks in the woods.

On weekend days off, I visit my siblings and their families. I play with their children. . . . I kiss them. . . . They put their hands in my mouth, and they hook my cheek with their tiny fingers.

I don't know what will happen now. . . .

Although it was years ago, I still remember the controversy when Rock Hudson kissed Linda Evans on *Dynasty*. It was the most sterile, closed-mouth, passionless kiss imaginable, performed by a heart-throb from my youth. But he had not revealed his HIV diagnosis to Ms. Evans, or anyone else, and folks foamed as the venom spewed from their mouths.

I'll need to tell everyone.

I'll need to come out *again*.

First it was, "I'm gay."

Now it's, "I've got HIV."

It's terribly tiresome and demoralizing.

And now, with HIV, I've sealed my fate. No one will ever want me. No one will ever love me. I will die alone.

Ugh, self-pity does not look good on me.

. . .

HIV is a barbed hook. Once it gets its hold, it can't be extracted or eliminated.

I started off taking AZT every four hours around the clock, including a dose in the middle of the night. Needless to say, I missed that pill a lot. Now, they've reduced the dose, but I still hate it. The nausea and vomiting are brutal

"I think I'm going to stop taking it," I tell the phone receiver, which tells Pedro seven hundred miles away.

"Daniel, I wish AZT were helping and that you tolerated it. But if you're not taking it as prescribed, you should stop taking it completely. There are new drugs on the horizon, so don't lose hope."

"I know. . . . I do. . . . My doctor says the same thing. But I always feel like shit. I don't know if it's the medication or the disease. Honestly, I've taken some pill holidays, and I can tell you I feel *a little* better when I'm not taking it, but not *much* better. I'm going to stop it for good."

"Gosh Daniel, how are you otherwise? Are you sleeping? Are you eating? Are you keeping your food in?"

I know that last one is a euphemism for *are you having vomiting or diarrhea?* I'm grateful not to hear those words.

"Ugh, I hate talking about this."

"I can imagine. But those are so important. Especially getting good sleep and rest."

"I'm taking a sleeping pill, which seems to work. I guess it helps with anxiety as well? It's like a Valium, but not as addictive? I tried other things first, but they didn't work."

Even talking about this is exhausting.

"Don't worry about addiction for a medication that's helping you right now. Don't let a doctor shame you if you need something for sleep or anxiety."

"I'm glad I'm sleeping, but *'A swallow doesn't make a summer!'*" I say.

"What?!"

"It's a dicho. 'Una golondrina no hace verano.'"

"Oh. . . . Swallow . . . as in bird."

"What?!"

• • •

I haven't flown much, so I'm a little nervous about this flight to Boston. I asked for a window seat, and now I'm thinking an aisle seat would have been better, for quicker access to the bathroom. I've got two barf bags ready, just in case.

Pedro is waiting for me right at the gate when I get off the plane. His eyebrows have melded into a single, worried caterpillar.

"How was it?" he asks.

"Oh it was fine," I say. "I didn't barf."

"Gracias a Dios. Sometimes there's turbulence between Ohio and Massachusetts . . ." he trails off, then adds with a smirk, "and I don't mean politically."

We have a satisfying hug, then head for baggage claim. I'll be here for a week, so I was surprised I only brought one large suitcase and a carry-on. One never knows, so it's best to be prepared for all occasions. In a couple days, we're taking the train to New York City to see *Mexico: Splendors of Thirty Centuries* at the Metropolitan Museum of Art.

"Are you hungry?" Pedro asks. It's the first time we've seen each other since I stopped taking AZT a few months ago, and he looks antsy. Like he wants me to be happy, healthy, back-to-before. But he wouldn't say those things. Not in that way.

"Yeah, a little. I eat frequent, small meals now. It helps with nausea."

What I keep to myself is: *I'm still losing weight.*

"Well, we've got every type of restaurant, or I have arroz con pollo I made last night."

"Needless to say, arroz con pollo, please and thank you!"

Pedro has a sensible Honda Civic that fits into Boston parking spaces. He lives in a small one bedroom apartment in the South End, a congested but charming neighborhood. A couple Siamese cats greet us with odd cries when we open the door.

"Meet Héctor and Félix, or oftentimes called Hectorio y Feliciano," Pedro says.

"Of course, they have nicknames."

"How's little Sonia?"

"Oh she's a good pup. Brad will take care of her while I'm gone. He says hi by the way."

"Hi back, Brad. And, hello to Buck Nekkid, of course!" Pedro laughs. "How is he? I mean Brad, not Buck."

"Poor Brad fell for a queerdo, and got his heart broken, but he's recovering."

"Queerdo. . . . I learn new vocabulary every time I see you."

• • •

The next day, we go to my favorite museum here in Boston, then we walk the Freedom Trail. I'm an out-of-practice history buff. My presque vu was out in full force when the tour guide asked some very simple questions about Paul Revere and his contemporaries. It was quite embarrassing, though no one else knew the answers I could previously blurt out without a thought.

I sometimes wonder if HIV is affecting my memory.

I wonder if *every* new sign, symptom, or oddity is because of HIV.

It's the saturated rain cloud that follows my every movement.

• • •

On the third day, Pedro gives me a small duffle bag and tells me to choose outfits for two days in New York City. I pack for three days, just in case.

'Lo que es moda no incomoda.'
One must suffer for one's fashion.

We take a taxi to the train station.

"Ugh! That guy had a butt-ugly personality," I blurt out. "He could barely muster a nice word. He didn't deserve the tip you gave him."

I decided to go full *Harvard preppy* today, with a brand-name knock-off, pink Oxford shirt, khaki pants, and faux leather boat shoes, all courtesy of Filene's Basement. I feel particularly buoyant in my step.

"Butts get a bad rap," Pedro replies in a serious voice.

"What?"

"We say things are 'butt-ugly,' but some butts are far from ugly. Think Mel Gibson, Rob Lowe, Patrick Swayze. . . ."

"Ooh, I like this game! Let's see, . . . Christopher Reeve, Richard Gere, John Stamos, Kevin Costner, Harrison Ford, Tony Goldwyn. . . ."

"There are so many! Of course, we're *assuming* their butts look like our *fantasy* of their butts," Pedro confirms. "From now on we should say something is 'ugly-butt-ugly' to be more precise. Because there are *in fact* some poor butts that are ugly."

"You 'CRACK' me up," I say, with air quotes, of course. "You always feel sorry for the underdog, or the 'ugly-butt-ugly' butt."

"That is *so* true!"

"Not to be CHEEKY . . . BUTT . . . I've got a BOOTY of . . . BEHIND the scenes CRACKS about . . . DERRIERES. . . . We could take a SEAT in the CABOOSE . . . at the TAIL . . . END of the train . . . before the BOTTOM of my BUNS, I mean *puns* . . . REARS its ugly BACKSIDE . . . also known as KEISTER, . . . which would be a BUMmer."

"Are you done?" Pedro asks with one Ronald McDonald arched eyebrow.

"Ass, buttocks, and gluteus maximus."

I admit, I feel devilishly clever.

And relieved that I still have my wit.

"How do you do that?"

"I honestly can't tell you."

• • •

We laugh and move in search of the ticket booth. I've never taken a train before. I've never been to New York City. We're having a mini-adventure, before the big adventure. Pedro says trains are slower than flying, unless you count getting to the airport, waiting for the flight, taking the flight, then taking a taxi from the airport in Queens into the city.

"Door-to-door," Pedro says, "it's about the same amount of time, with less hassle."

"I'm happy to take a train. I'm far from fond of flying."

The train is on the track and ready for us to board. We find some seats in the middle of the car, not too far from the bathroom, which is always a priority.

• • •

"We've got a four-hour train ride to NYC," Pedro declares, "so, let's talk a little. How have you been feeling?"

We hadn't talked too much about my health, which is nice. Pedro usually gives me room to breathe, to pretend I'm healthy, at least for a little while.

"Oh, I have my good days. Which of course means I have my bad days. . . . I feel so much better off of AZT. My T cells are falling though."

"What have the numbers been?"

"The lowest was 280, but then it went up. They've been in the low 300s."

"Are there any studies you could enter? Maybe something through Ohio State?"

"I haven't qualified for new studies: my numbers are too high . . . or too low; my weight is too high . . . or too low. I'm too anemic, or this, or that. It's probably fine since my options seem to be 50 percent

314

chance of being on a placebo or 50 percent chance of having side effects."

Pedro's eyes zigzag and his eyebrows shift, but he decides not to share his thoughts.

"Well, I'm glad you're sleeping well, and small meals seem to work for you. . . . Have you tried meal supplements to help you gain weight?" he asks.

"You bitch! You want me to lose my trimmed physique?" I shoot back, with a fake laugh. I catch some nervous commuters snapping their eyes in our direction. My own eyes sting. "Yeah, I've tried them, but I don't like the taste. Unfortunately, ice cream and other dairy products disturb my *delicate digestive tract.*"

We chitchat about the usual: men, actors, athletes (but not sports), other men, chisme, Broadway, and a selection of glamorous women. I tell Pedro I found some VHS tapes of Cantinflas and old Mexican musicals we'd seen when we were kids. The quality is poor, but it was still fun to watch them.

. . .

After a while of contemplative silence, I say, "I guess we could talk about mutations and resistance since it's confusing, and my doctor keeps bringing it up."

"Good idea. So . . . you know the basics about HIV. It's a single-cell organism that requires a living host cell to replicate."

"Yep."

"Most living things have basic goals of staying alive, thriving, and reproducing."

"Are you still thinking of having kids?" I ask. "Sorry to interrupt, but you just made me think of it."

I seem to have derailed Pedro. His face almost winces. It was a sudden, personal question out of nowhere. Have I *always* blurted out questions like this?

"No," he says. "The older I get, the more I realize I don't have the energy to be a parent. It's definitely a lot of work. And, trying to figure out how to have a kid through a surrogate is too much for this head of mine." He pauses for a moment. "Adoption isn't a great option for a single gay man, even in Massachusetts."

He seems to relax, then he stifles a yawn. We *did* stay up gabbing late into the night.

"Yeah, I can't imagine being a father. But it's nice to have so many nieces and nephews to spoil. It's fun to feed them candy, cookies, and ice cream . . . then send them back to their parents!"

We both laugh.

"Anyway, where was I?"

"Live, thrive, reproduce."

"That's right! Your short-term memory is better than mine!" Pedro says with a grin. "I'll have to check your long-term memory later, . . . if I remember."

I hope we *do* remember to have him check my memory later. I really think I'm losing it. *Something*'s off.

"When any living thing reproduces," he continues, "there can be some 'blips' in the process."

"Blips. . . . Is that an official medical term?"

"It's a visual term for this explanation. Can I continue Mr. Smart Aleck?"

"Yes, doctor," I answer, thinking of Bill Murray in *Little Shop of Horrors.*

"When humans reproduce, there can be issues with the sperm, with the egg, both, or with the process after the two meet. That's how genetic illnesses start, or are passed on to another generation."

"Okay, that's easy to understand."

I think I'm starting to comprehend this.

"Viruses replicate in a different manner. They do it both quickly and repeatedly."

"I'm impressed, *and envious.*"

"It's not really sex though."

"I know. But it *is* intriguing."

"I suppose it is. . . . Anyway, rapid, repeated replication affects the reliability of making exact replicas of the parent virus. Even a minor change in the genetic code of a subsequent generation can have dramatic pros and cons for the virus, *and corresponding* cons and pros for the human."

"This makes sense so far. . . . It's not that the virus figures out how to mutate, it just happens accidentally as it replicates. And some of these mutations can modify the virus in a way that makes it resistant to medications."

"Exactly!" Pedro exclaims. "Mutations are just chance occurrences. Viruses replicate quickly, and in large numbers. Statistically, a chance mutation is probable."

"That also makes sense."

I'm vaguely remembering topics and details from my Statistics class: probability, chance, variables, the null hypothesis. . . .

"An example of a mutation that is better for the virus, and worse for the human, is when this new viral generation is resistant to the medications we have. Each new generation of that particular mutated virus replicates this *same, changed, mutated virus*, until a new mutation occurs in the future."

"Wow, okay, at least I can *visualize* what a mutation is now. That . . . it's not a coordinated effort by the virus, to become resistant to medications. In some way, it helps to know that mutations are accidental. It helps to know the virus is not *intentionally* trying to kill me. Do you know what I mean?"

"Absolutely, Daniel. When we look at viruses at their level of sophistication, and stop giving them human characteristics, it *is* less personal. It's not in the virus's best interest for its host to get sick, or to die."

• • •

New York City is incredible. I feel both alive, and smaller and more insignificant under its expanse. All my senses are taxed with constant movement, sounds, and smells. It may take me a while to find my land legs here.

We're staying at a gay bed and breakfast in the Village. There are men and women here from all over the world. What fun! I've always had a thing for accents.

Pedro takes me on a whirlwind tour of the major attractions. We see the Statue of Liberty from Battery Park. We walk around Times Square, including the seedier sections with all the establishments for adult entertainment, all out in the open with loud marquees to advertise their wares.

I'm happy for Pedro, but I'm a bit envious right now. He's seen lots of the Broadway shows we see advertised on theater marquees, with many of my favorite Broadway legends.

"This is how I escape reality," he says. "I come to Broadway and get transported to another place and time."

I feel as though I've squandered my time within my little five-mile radius since leaving the seminary, when I could have gone out and seen the world. But it's too late to cry over this spilt milk.

We walk around Central Park, which I had to physically experience to really appreciate. The movies I've seen don't give this marvelous gem justice. At least it seems New Yorkers are very proud of their park.

Then Pedro brings me to the Central Park Zoo. This lovely zoo is a welcome surprise and highlight.

50

MÉXICO
Pedro

"IT'S ONE OF my favorite things to do in New York," I say as we get our tickets to enter the Central Park Zoo.

The animal exhibits seem to have been built with the physical and mental health of the animals in mind. Every exhibit is terrific. I can tell Daniel doesn't want to leave, especially after I told him I've spotted many celebrities here with their children.

"I won't choose a favorite exhibit because I wouldn't want to detract from the others," he sighs as we exit, hours later.

"I wouldn't ask you to choose."

"Okay, the polar bears had me in a trance. . . . They actually looked like they were having fun."

They had been playing with watermelons and huge ice cubes with fish parts.

"You know, one of my earliest memories is of us at the zoo. I can't imagine how young we were. I remember feeling very sad while watching endless pacing back and forth, in one concrete jail cell after another."

I knew Daniel would love this zoo. We stayed so long, we had to skip the Empire State Building. Afterwards, we walked around various neighborhoods, ending up back in the Village, where we had a delicious dinner at a cute Italian restaurant, with a cute Italian waiter.

319

"What a wonderful day, Pedro!" Daniel exclaims, when we're in our hotel room, getting ready for bed. "Thank you for arranging it all."

"I'm so glad the trip worked out. I really want to see the Mexico exhibit with you!"

We get into bed—a queen for a couple of queens—instead of the twin bed we shared for so many years.

"Do you remember that time we drove through Mexico and saw the silhouette of a woman and a man in the mountain range?" I ask.

"I do. It was Iztaccihuatl, and Popocatepetl. That was a tragic love story if ever there were one."

"I know!"

I can't imagine a man honoring a promise and loving me like Popocatepetl loved Iztaccihuatl. Maybe we'll discover a Mesoamerican gay love story tomorrow.

"I love Mesoamerican stories," I whisper.

I'm aware my eyes have begun to mist.

"Me too. Each trip to Mexico opened my eyes to our history."

I turn on my side and rest my head on my hand above my shoulder.

"Did you know *Aztec* is an inaccurately used term?"

Daniel turns and mirrors me.

"No. What do you mean?"

"Its use started centuries after the deliberate genocide and enslavement of the Indigenous Peoples of Mexico, commonly known as the Conquest of Mexico."

"Don't *even* get me started," Daniel retorts. I see his eyebrows move toward the bridge of his nose as if cinched together by a corset. "Lo que mal empieza, mal termina."

"I know. I've practiced *that line* a lot. I love watching people's faces when I say it that way . . . when their confused *expression* slowly melts into *comprehension*. Especially if I can say it with a straight face."

"Your straight gay face is pretty convincing."

We both laugh, then let out a long sigh.

"You've always been punny funny."

Daniel reacts with an odd expression.

"Really? I've always thought my puns were my weakest link."

"Anyway, remember my trip to the Yucatán a few years ago?"

"Yeah."

"My gay tour guide shared some of his knowledge as we traveled from one archaeological site to another."

"Tell me more," he encourages. "Including juicy details about the guide."

He grins like only he can grin.

"Basically, there was a Triple Alliance of three Nahuatl-speaking tribe nations when Europeans arrived in central Mexico. Centuries later, the Triple Alliance was labeled the 'Aztec Empire,' and it caught on."

"Ugh, it's like they're erasing their existence," Daniel groans.

• • •

When Daniel returns from the bathroom, I continue, "My favorite new tidbit — and I can't believe we haven't talked about it — is that the 'Aztecs' and Maya have gods who are patrons of homosexuality."

"What?" he blurts out. "By the way, I *love* that you refer to them in the *present tense*." He shakes his arm, which must have fallen asleep.

"Yes! It's so important for them to be seen as cultures *that still exist*. And since they are our ancestors, and relatives, I'm including *us* in that sentiment."

That causes an unexpected frog in my throat.

"Sometimes I wish I had a bullhorn. . . . Or a pulpit." He shoots me a look, and I understand the reference. He continues, "I never agreed with the dicho 'Más vale saber que hablar.' *It's better to know than to speak*. Really? I think we should share knowledge."

I have to clear my throat before I can respond.

"I agree!"

He puts his hand up, and we perform what I believe is our first ever "high five."

"Thanks," I say to the room service attendant as I give her the signed slip and a tip. I decided to splurge on a bottle of Veuve for the occasion.

Pop!

I pour into each flute, stopping in time to let the bubbles rise and burst at the rim before adding more.

"Wow, you're pretty good at that," Daniel muses. "Not a drop wasted."

"To Mexico!"

"¡Mi México Lindo y Querido!"

We clink and drink in the cheer in the glass, and in the air.

"Anyway, I have more to share about Mesoamerican history," I say.

"Please, and thanks."

"The Mayan god of homosexuality is Chin or Chen. The 'Aztec' God is Xochipilli."

"I did not know *any* of this. Our people have been part of our people since . . . forever."

"You've always had a way with words."

"And you've always recognized my gifts."

We laugh, then stare off.

I'm in Mesoamerica, pretending I work in a temple dedicated to Xochipilli —
that I'm not a tradesman or a farmer —
that I'm not a human sacrifice . . .

Does he have a tendency to fantasize?

"The guide talked about the double-gender gods Xochipilli and Xochiquetzal who are twins, or two halves of a whole, or male and female aspects of the same god. The ancient people celebrated duality and opposing forces in their cultures. Like male vs. female, and chaos vs. order. It was too much for my brain to fully process, but I was fascinated by the opposing forces of chaos and order."

"Controlled Chaos!" Daniel exclaims.

"Exactly! Like in my head! The ancient people would have *loved* my mind!"

"But of course!"

"There is so much I want to learn about our culture," I finish. "I can't wait for tomorrow."

"Good night, Mary Ellen."

"Good night, Grandma!"

"You bitch!" Daniel retorts. "That was a good one."

• • •

We get to the Metropolitan Museum of Art the next morning after an early, and fabulous breakfast. I've been looking forward to this exhibition for months. Our connection with everything Mexico runs deep.

"I can't wait to see the Frida Kahlos," I say.

"And La Rana!" Daniel adds. "Those two were quite a pair."

"I've been a little obsessed with her."

"I know. La Sufrida suffered so much physically, emotionally, spiritually . . ."

"Sounds familiar."

Daniel turns to me, and his face relaxes. "It's one of the reasons I identify so much with Frida and her paintings. . . . I *understand* her suffering."

The exhibition halls are overwhelmingly crowded with people. On the one hand, I would *love* to see everything without crowds all around me. On the other hand, I'm pleased that so many people have an interest in the history of our people. I feel very proud to be Mexican American today — and every day.

We meander through the halls at our own paces, occasionally meeting to compare notes.

"Tanta gente," Daniel says to me when we're about halfway through.

"I know. I suppose it's good."

"I just wish I could get up to the little cards to read the information. I'm so glad we're doing the guided tour."

When we next meet, I tell Daniel, "There's one particular person of whom I knew nothing."

"Who?"

"Sor Juana Inés de la Cruz. She sounds like a fascinating woman." His face lights up.

"I know! I heard of her at the seminary. I believe she was a very 'out' lesbian nun. Her writing seems both outstanding and outlandish."

"My kind of writing," I say with a smile.

• • •

"He's cute," Daniel says as he approaches and stands next to me.

I'm looking at Emiliano Zapata in a painting by Diego Rivera. 'Cute' is *not* how I would describe him. Although, he looks like a cartoonish representation of Daniel, so maybe it was a tongue-in-cheek remark. I turn to comment, but see that he's been looking at a cute museum usher standing at the doorway leading to the next room.

• • •

"This exhibition did not disappoint," Daniel remarks as I approach him. We had agreed to meet at the coat check when he left me at the gift shop to go to the bathroom.

His face brightens when I hand him the huge book which accompanies the exhibition.

"I think there are photos of all the pieces in the exhibit, each with short descriptions," I say. "It's basically an encyclopedia of the artistic history of Mexico."

"Thank you so much Pedro! I will treasure this!"

Our eyes begin to fill.

"It's not surprising that my favorites were the Kahlo and Rivera paintings," he declares.

"I hope someday she has her own exhibition. She deserves it. *We* deserve it. I'd come back for that."

"I wish we could bottle her up and dab her behind the ears," he murmurs as we hug, then he leaves a kiss behind my ear.

"We're a couple of chillones," I say, wiping away my tears, watching as he does the same.

"They're tears of joy, and pride. Of solidarity with Frida and everything she went through. As well as Mexico, and everything she's suffered over the last five hundred years."

"Despite everything that's happened to her, Mexico is still rich in tradition, and I'm proud of her."

"¡¡¡Que viva México!!!" we say.

Jinx!

5I

MEN
Daniel

"PEDRO, A PERFECTLY performed eye roll takes practice."

"Practice makes perfect," he responds. His eyes are darting back and forth, right to left, side to side, like he's rapid reading.

"Por el amor, Pedro. How did you get so far in life without an effective eye roll?" I laugh. "You're gonna hurt yourself! So listen, it's like the 'ojo de gallo' side-eye—you have to keep your head still. At least until you've mastered it."

"Okay, head still," he murmurs, with his eyes bulging straight out. I have to suppress another laugh.

"Now, with your head still, look to your far left and gradually rotate your gay gaze up, then to the other side, until you're looking at your far right."

He's not getting it, so I suggest, "Pretend you're at the equator, and you're looking at the sun going up and down." Then I add, in a singsong voice, "Left to right. Up and down. Sunrise, sunset. . . . Or, you can pretend you're following a gay rainbow from one pot of gay gold to the other. . . . Whatever works for you."

Pedro attempts another eye roll. His eyes look like they're on a cog, or they're following the second hand on a wristwatch, one . . . second . . . at . . . a . . . time.

"Oh honey, you have *got* to keep practicing."

"Talk to the hand, 'cause you ain't right." His retort is equal parts serious, sarcastic, defeated.

"Sweetie, it's 'talk to the *LEFT*, 'cause you ain't *RIGHT*.' Honestly, Pedro, did you pay your dues to renew your 'gay card'? Those gays at Gay Headquarters USA are very strict about membership deadlines — *especially renewals!*"

"You're such a wiseacre."

"No, *SERIOUSLY* Pedro! *LISTEN* to me! You've got to Pay-the-Gay! You do *NOT* want to go into a probationary period because the readmittance process is a... PAIN... IN... THE... ASS! And *not* the good kind.... Pay your dues on time Pedro! I don't think I can help you if your membership lapses!"

He does a double take, then freezes.

"Are you serious?... I don't know anything about this!" His eyes are darting back and forth now, but this time, clearly in panic mode.

"Yikes Pedro!... I forget how gullible you are!"

I laugh, stifling a full on cackle.

He doesn't look amused.

"You can be such a pain in the ass," he spits out, then adds with a smirk, "and, *not* the good kind."

"Oh, a little *ass sass* in *gay class*. I love it!"

. . .

Pedro makes progress, but I doubt he'll be using an eye roll out in the wild, possibly ever. It's fun to be teaching him "gay stuff." He was always teaching me and helping me when we were kids.

It's been six months since our NYC excursion. Now, he's here for my birthday celebrations. Yes, there are *two* planned for family or friends, with some overlap.

Pedro and I are still close, but perhaps we don't know each other like we did when we were little.

Although when we were home, we didn't talk about being gay.

How well did we really know each other?

. . .

"Oh god, I hope you're not asking me to explain the mystery known as 'Men,'" Pedro moans.

"Well, you've had a better track record with men than I have."

"Perhaps I haven't told you about the bad, the worse, and the ugly!" he replies, laughing.

"Certainly, not ugly as in ugly-butt-ugly," I add with a chuckle. "All of your boyfriends have been quite handsome!"

We both laugh.

"I can't explain my luck," Pedro goes on. "I don't consider myself attractive; at least, I'm not physically attractive to myself—if *that* makes sense."

"I completely understand."

"The psychological damage from Mom's *repulsive racist rhetoric* has been hard to overcome."

"Yeah, I can imagine."

I pour him some wine.

"Para todo mal, mezcal," he toasts.

"Para todo bien, también," I reciprocate.

Some dichos are best when two are involved in the delivery.

"Getting back to men, they're needy, and so much work," he grumbles.

"Yeah, lesbians have it made. No men involved."

"And they can have a baby without a man involved! Remember my fiasco science project in high school?"

"That—and I say this in all sincerity—is the funniest story you have ever told! Everyone freaked out because you said the words *semen* and *masturbation* 'out loud' in a public school. . . . What I would have given to have been there! . . . And you still hadn't figured out masturbation! Gosh, I wish I had known, I would have spilled the beans. . . . Hmm, I didn't even mean it metaphorically, even though beans are basically a seed."

"Wow, your mind is fascinating."

"Oh! Oh! Wait a minute. . . . I've got a perfect dicho for this occasion! I learned it at seminary. . . . It's a little tricky, so you've got to get the words right:

Una vez al día, es manía.
Una vez por semana, es cosa sana.
Una vez por mes, es dejadez.
Una vez al año, se te oxida el caño."

"What?!" Pedro exclaims, "That is *hysterical*! And it *rhymes*!"

"It's about taking a bath, you filthy mind. What were you thinking of?"

"But of course! From the King of the Doble Sentido!"

"That's *Queen* to you, missy!"

"We're a couple delincuentes, maleducados, y sinvergüenzas, full of porquerías y pendejez!"

"Challenge and goal . . . accepted and fully met!"

"Mom would be so proud."

We laugh like a couple of torpe tontos.

Pedro asks me to repeat the dicho a few times so he can memorize it. I can't imagine when, and in what company, he would ever repeat it. It's a play on words about bathing—or much more likely—masturbation.

• • •

I went to my first AIDS-related funeral today . . . of someone I knew . . . of someone I loved.

Betty was my manager at the pizza parlor, years ago, right after I left St. Joseph's—when I had plunged into a deep and unrelenting depression. She was a combined Carol Brady *and* Shirley Partridge of a foster mother to strays like me.

She had taken Brad in when his parents kicked him out at fifteen. Then, in a truly remarkable act of benevolence, she nurtured Brad *and* his family until they were all much healthier individually, and as a family.

Betty may have saved *my* life.

She would call me every morning to encourage me to get out of bed, eat, shower, and come in to work, until it became a routine I could manage on my own. Her guidance led to my advancement up the pizza chain's corporate ladder. I became store manager fairly quickly under her tutelage. By then, she was my district manager.

Until that horrible day.

She was traveling between stores when a heart attack hit—she lost control of her sedan which engulfed a lamppost. The heart attack was minor, but she underwent emergency surgery for a leg fracture.

She required a transfusion.

I went to see her at the hospital, and a few times at the rehab facility. Then, we lost touch.

Why did I abandon such a lovely person?

When her husband called to tell me of her passing, my legs buckled.

Her long history of diabetes, and its effect on her kidneys, made it easier for HIV and those vile medications to ravage her weakened body. This delightful woman—and her goodwill—were no match for the insidiousness of this disease.

It was a devil vs. an angel.

"Oh Sam, I'm so sorry," I said. "I really loved her."

"I know Daniel. You were one of her favorites. She would recount your antics—and your dichos—and have us in hysterics."

"I'm so sorry I didn't keep in touch. I really am."

"Daniel, she was so happy you were thriving. That's what was most important to her. Honor her memory with continued success in your endeavors."

"I . . . I will, Sam. I'll see you tomorrow at the memorial," I replied.

And then I cried like I hadn't cried since I left the seminary.

• • •

Some people are born to serve others, either on their own, or in the name of Jesus Christ, or some other higher calling.

But I lost my way along the way.

I lost my commitment, and now I'm running out of time.

Sin propósito para servir, no sirves para ningún propósito.
If you have no purpose to serve, you serve no purpose.

52

PROVINCETOWN
Pedro

IT'S BEEN ALMOST a year since Daniel and I went to New York. We had a blast when I visited him in May for his birthday. He likes to remind everyone that it's also Cher's birthday. I hadn't seen him since, but we talk regularly on the phone.

Now, Daniel is visiting me in Boston for the weeks before and after Labor Day, which is a terrific time to be here. We're going to the Isabella Stewart Gardner Museum today. I've taken him before, but not surprisingly it's always on his list of things he wants to do when he returns.

The museum itself was the former home of Isabella Stewart Gardner. She had the home built in a Venetian palazzo style. From the street, the building isn't remarkable. But when you enter, you're transported to another place and time.

I don't know how often I've been here, but the empty frames placed where the stolen masterpieces once hung always give me a gut punch. How can anyone be so selfish, and corrupt, to acquire stolen art? I guess it's been happening since the beginning of humankind. How many pieces of art and other artifacts have been stolen by looters and robbers, and during wars, religious or otherwise? Every time I see ancient artifacts in a museum, I wonder how they came to be there. I often believe they would be better served in a display near where they originated.

"They still haven't found this artwork?" Daniel asks, pointing to the vacant frames.

"No," I reply, but I move toward Titian's *The Rape of Europa* nearby before he sees my bitter tears. The guided tour's description of Gardner's pairing — almost a hundred years ago — of her shimmering gold silk and satin dress with this masterpiece gives me goosebumps. She was a remarkable woman.

. . .

"WOW, that was John Waters on a bike!" Daniel cries. "¡El mundo es un pañuelo!"

"How did 'the world is a handkerchief' come to mean, *'It's a small world'*?"

"One must not question the dichos," he commands.

We're on our way to T-dance in Provincetown. I'd like Daniel to experience The Last Dance, with Donna Summer's 'Last Dance' blaring, and hundreds of gays and lesbians singing and dancing along as loud as they can. It's deafening and chaotic, with all the senses approaching overload at the same time. It can be heard quite a distance from the venue.

On Labor Day, The Last Dance moment signifies the symbolic end of the tourist season, the last T-dance until the following spring. It is dulce-amargo: *bittersweet.*

Daniel isn't keeping up with me this trip. Walking the lengthy jetty to Long Point, the very tip of Cape Cod, left him winded. Despite having taken antiviral therapy off and on for a few years, his T-cell count has dropped . . . *too much.* He's technically got AIDS now, but I don't think he knows.

And I don't want to tell him.

For medical providers, it's a complicated dance of caring for our patients without causing unnecessary stress or harm: primum non nocere. A T-cell count below 200 is a "semi-arbitrary" designation for the diagnostic transition from HIV infection to AIDS, or advanced HIV disease.

In reality, some can live for many years with a count below 200. Others have numbers that bounce around, above, below. Others succumb with counts higher than 200. This is an example of medicine being an art *and* a science.

Ultimately, having AIDS means Daniel is at *higher risk* for opportunistic *infections* and opportunistic *malignancies*. Those would definitely signify an AIDS diagnosis.

Fuck.

Fuck.

Fuck.

Daniel never tolerated HIV medications. I think he stopped taking them because they didn't help, or the side effects were rough. He enrolled in a clinical trial once, but he didn't improve, either because he was on the placebo or because it was an ineffective treatment.

I feel so useless. I'm a gay HIV provider, and I can't help my own brother with AIDS. This is a special sort of hell on earth.

"I can't believe how many gays there are here," Daniel remarks as we walk around Provincetown. "This place is magical . . . it's like no other place I've heard of."

We pass men and women of every flavor combination imaginable. . . . wearing colors and outfits they don't likely wear in their hometowns. Every summer, this sleepy little fishing village becomes a vacation destination for gays, lesbians, bisexuals, transgenders, and everyone else, including straights. Somehow it all works. The year-rounders depend on this influx of tourist dollars, and tourists anticipate their days or weeks here will be hassle free. Bigots won't enjoy this place, because their hate will be extinguished before anyone feels a burn.

Folks have written about the light here with regard to painting and artwork. You don't have to be an artist to notice how light reflects, interacts, dances, and moves around, between, and here and there. It is literally and figuratively breathtaking.

It occurs to me that Provincetown is in fact like no other place on earth. It's not surprising folks come from all over the world to this hard-to-reach spot at the end of Massachusetts. Aside from being naturally beautiful—with cascading dunes, beech and pitch pine forests, bike and walking paths, and stunning chromatic sunsets over the ocean—there is no tolerance for intolerance. It's the only place where I have walked down the street holding another man's hand. It's the only place where I have kissed a man, on the lips, out in broad daylight, without any concern for my life or safety.

"It's like this all summer. . . . I try to come as much as possible. I'm really lucky it's this close."

"Yes. . . . You are lucky," Daniel whispers.

He's looking off into the distance. His eyes have shifted almost imperceptibly towards each other, cross-eyed and unfocused. A shadow has fallen over him. There is writing on the wall.

"You're lucky you didn't get this shitty disease," he mutters as he comes out of his preoccupation, his eyes more focused, but welling. "I'm so glad you didn't—really I am, Pedro. But why did I have to get it? Couldn't we have some time together as happy, healthy adults?"

"Oh Daniel," I respond, and pull him in for a hug. We hold each other for a while.

"It's okay, I'm okay. . . . Pity? Pity-Party of one? Pick yourself up you pathetic piece of poo poo."

He mockingly slaps himself several times, with his head dramatically turning with each impact, mimicking a scene straight out of *Dynasty*. It's odd to see his signature grin paired with bloodshot, teary eyes, and a runny nose.

I put my hand on his shoulder, and we look at each other for a moment. Then we continue our walk down Commercial Street. "It's okay to be sad and angry," I say. "But we've got years to plan trips and get-togethers."

"Oh, Pedro. . . . I know you know I don't have years."

I draw a sudden breath. I pray it wasn't noticeable. I suppose I could protest. I could try to bend the truth. But he's right, and it's clear he knows something.

"I've got KS," he whispers, almost imperceptibly.

Kaposi's sarcoma, an opportunistic malignancy.

Fuck.

Fuck.

Fuck.

I've got to take control. . . . of myself. . . . of the situation.

"Look Daniel, it's not good news, but there are various treatments for KS. I'm sure your doctors are aware."

"I know, I know. But now I have AIDS. I have fucking AIDS, Pedro," he says, his eyes streaming tears again, mirroring my own.

53

RELIGION
Daniel

I DO BELIEVE in God.

I do believe in God.

I do, I do, I do, I do,

I do believe in God.

Though it is at times a cumbersome commitment to continue to carry. . . .

I understand skeptics like Pedro — he's more of an agnostic than an atheist — who wonder if there is a God. And I understand their go-to questions that start with "If there is a God, then why . . ."

Yes, why is there war, disease, famine, violence, and misery?

I'd also add, "Why did He make me gay?" Because, I am what I am because it's how God made me. I would not *choose* to suffer insults and other indignities all my life, since before I even knew what being a maldito maricón de mierda meant.

No chiquito, that's not how it works.

All those questions are valid, and without clear answers.

There are only philosophical expressions of possible explanations that *may* illustrate God's expectation that *man might* — out of the goodness He placed in their hearts — *change* . . . and love each other . . . and work together . . . to end all world suffering.

Blah, blah, blah. . . .

Ultimately, I'd say, without God . . . what *is* there?

Because after two thousand years of Jesus Christ's teachings, we don't seem to have evolved into better Christians.

I think it's too late to abandon our hope that He exists.

But I have no reason to query or question, no need to quell a quandary. I know God exists. He sent us angels when we were little and Mom and Pop were fighting. It is *proof* that He exists. And I have three witnesses who still remember, all these years later.

When I've told people about this significant childhood event, they always try to explain it away as magical realism from a child's mind:

Maybe it was shadows from the streetlights, or the trees!

There were no streetlights on our street or trees in our yard.
And, these images we saw were in three-dimensional color.
And, we could hear their music.

Maybe you forgot there were streetlights and trees!

There are pictures of Pedro and me on the front porch of our house at that time. The angle clearly shows our barren front yard, out in "remote and rural USA" where there were no street lights.
And, as I've said: three-dimensional color and sound.

You were so young! Maybe it was something else!

Sara was ten, Juan was nine, Pedro was six, and I was five.
AND WE ALL SAW THEM TOGETHER.

Who knows what they really were!

I don't know what they were for sure. I don't have a common-English-words-only explanation, but I can say with certainty:

WE ARE NOT ALONE IN THIS UNIVERSE.

• • •

I believe God prevented me from drowning when I was little; that He took Juan's hand and placed it where it needed to be, to find me in the waters of the river, to grab me so that Pop could pull me out. Why else did a scrawny little kid who can't swim survive a plunge into a deep river?

God probably saved me from countless other dangers over the years. I have vague recollections of saying, feeling, *Oh, my God, thank you for that.*

But God did not protect us from Mom.

And,

God did not protect me from AIDS.

• • •

Were You testing me? Trying to see if I could avoid this danger on my own? Checking if I'd learned *anything* from the many hurdles You purposefully placed in my poor pathetic path over and over and over?

Could You, I don't know, maybe have thrown some good opportunities my way? At least within my reach? Maybe occasionally? Or, I don't know, *ONCE?*

There was no single person I could love, who could love me in return? Out of billions and billions of humans on this earth?

Not one single man?

Really?!

Por el amor de Dios . . .

For the love of God . . .

And all that is good . . .

With all due respect . . .

Okay . . .
Deep breath . . .
I think I'm done . . .
Same time tomorrow?
I have to find solace in:

> 'Siempre se hizo lo que Dios quiso."
> *What was done was God's will.*

But his "will" has got some 'splainin' to do when I get to those pearly gates.

. . .

It's not lost on me that my life-long longing to talk with God was a purposefully fallacious metaphorical fallacy created by conspiratorial clerics to control their congregations, and that those who claim to truly speak with Him are in serious need of a psychological evaluation.

It took me too long to throw in the towel, but

> 'Más vale tarde que nunca.'
> *Better late than never.*

. . .

For many years, I looked for a reciprocal love. Don't I deserve it, like everyone else? Is it my destiny to be dejected and despondent until this fucking thing finally fucks me over?

This is more than self-pity.

I really want to know why I don't deserve to ever know love, to feel love.

> 'Más vale estar solo que estar mal acompañado.'
> *Better to be alone than with bad company.*

Why do these *fucking* dichos spring up in my head when I least expect them, or *want* them?

Ohio in the 1980s wasn't exactly crawling with easy-to-find, easy-to-meet, well-adjusted (loosely defined?), out-of-the-closet (at least to himself?), attractive (I'm not even saying handsome!), employed (at least employable?), not-too-old (under 35?), healthy men.

I'd love to see that in a personal ad, but I wouldn't give that sad sap a chance.

• • •

"Pedro, sometimes I wonder if Mom had taught me *how* to love — how to love myself and how to love others — if I still would have gone out looking for love in all the wrong places?"

Pedro looks up at me from across the dining table and robotically puts his fork down on his plate.

I continue, "It's a sad cliché and a total cop-out, and I'm mad at myself for even thinking it, I really am. . . . But I can't help wondering. . . . It weighs on my thoughts like a dark shadow clouding my vision, that smothers what little self-worth I've mustered in my measly life."

It takes no time for Pedro's eyes to fill, then spill. He's *looking* at me, but I don't think he's *focused* on me.

"Oh, Pedro, you're the only one who could know what I mean."

I get up and go around the table to hold him in his chair. He's still so quiet when he cries.

With such heartache and grief, he's so painfully quiet.

• • •

"They say, 'Es mejor haber amado y haber perdido que nunca haber amado,'" Pedro recites. "*It's better to have loved and lost, than to never have loved at all.* Sorry, I don't agree."

"Oh?"

We've both recovered from my previous comments about Mom not showing us how to love, and we're sitting on my couch with some wine.

"Although I've enjoyed my moments of feeling what I believed were love, the grief of losing a love outweighs it — without a doubt."

I've noticed he doesn't really look me in the face when he's talking about Mom or emotions. He may glance at me when he's done speaking.

"I think I know what you mean," I say. "I've never been *in love*, but I've been *infatuated*. When that's gone there's a suffocating despair, as if I'm drowning."

I wonder if having experienced near-drowning gives me a different perspective on the concept.

"Yeah. Sounds about right," Pedro says. "Certainly, with our past, doubt is front and center when guilt and shame aren't. You wonder if it was truly reciprocal love when it's gone."

"Hmm."

"I can honestly say losing a love, a *lover*, is the most hopeless, bottomless pit of anguish I have *ever* felt."

"Jesus, Pedro, it sounds really sad. Maybe it's best that I've never known love."

"Yeah, I don't like to talk about it," he responds. "Ironically, Mom helped spare us heartbreaks by preventing us from getting close to anyone, even friends. We have less to lose if we were never really close. Does that make sense?"

"Sadly, Pedro, it does."

"And we haven't dealt with much death. Papá and Abuelita were sad losses, but we didn't really know them, and we didn't feel their *physical* absence since we rarely saw them. I imagine some deaths would be worse than the loss of a lover."

Pedro did not glance at me this time.

I know he's talking about me.

He must be struggling, drowning in fear of my approaching death. I'm not in denial. I know it's coming.

"Someone once hit my shoulder when I hung up with my boyfriend without saying, 'I love you.' I told her, 'We don't *say* 'I love you,' . . . we prefer to *show* it.'"

"I bet that shut her up!" I mutter.

"It did. We never said 'I love you' at home, and Mom never showed love, but too many people say 'I love you' and don't actually mean it. They can be empty, useless, overused words."

"Las palabras se las lleva el viento," I remark.

"Exactly."

I have to wonder what still happens inside Pedro's head. The controlled chaos of his thoughts, demons, fears, desires. He has a fortress of a protective shell around him that admits no one. Inside, there must be the scared and abused little kid just trying to survive it all. Still, after all these years.

As for me, I went looking for a lover in the wrong places. And I was careless, I own it:

'Si te acuestas con perros, amaneces con pulgas.'
If you lie down with dogs, you get up with fleas.

Maybe I was just tired.

Maybe I'd given up.

Maybe I was looking for . . . it.

For it . . . to help me . . . end this misery I can't escape.

But I hadn't thought it through.

A slow distasteful death in this hate-filled world isn't a great way to go.

• • •

"Daniel, you've always been a pain in the ass," Tony spits out.

"And, *not* the good kind, as you often say," Brad adds.

"I like him," Aloysius chimes in.

"Of course *you* like him," Brad smirks. "*He* just said *you* have the single most perfect name ever."

Aloysius is Tony's newest boyfriend. His name has always hit all the right taste buds on my ear drums. It's musical, poetic, unusual, a spelling enigma.

We're sitting around Tony's table after dinner. Brad and I are their first dinner guests. Brad and I are *always* Tony's first dinner guests when he has a new boyfriend.

I may have made some heavy-handed cocktails before we polished off a couple bottles of wine.

I don't *think* I'm using that as an excuse.

"Guys, take a chillaxitive," I instruct. "I was just giving an honest opinion direct from Jesus himself."

"Girl, you are *not* playing the Jesus card right now!" Tony yells. "You said my name reminded you of the rotten-egg-smelling perm product your mom used."

"Well, now that he mentioned it," Brad smirks. "I *did* use Toni products for my Mike Brady perm years ago."

• • •

Of course, I knew Pedro was gay when we were kids, even if we didn't talk about it. My gaydar precision and accuracy are precise and accurate. Naturally, it's been of no use to me; it's just a feather in my cap.

Mom tried to beat the maricón out of me, but here I am, my true self. Love me or leave me.

I guess we all know how *that* turned out.

Mom tried to beat it out of Pedro, time and time again. I don't know what gave it away for him. He was never obvious, not like me. Maybe he was guilty by association. Mom's oppression made him so repressed, introverted, self-conscious, there was nothing for an untrained eye to see; there was nothing to suggest he is gay.

At least, it seems, he's coming out of the shadows now, albeit slowly. I actually wonder if he would have turned out gay if Mom hadn't suggested it since the day we were old enough to hold a doll. I wonder how much our environment played a role — with Pedro.

I know.

It also sounds like a cop-out.

Nature vs. Nurture is still a hot topic. I'm definitely Nature. But I wonder if Pedro was Nurture.

And what was it all for? Mom and Pedro haven't spoken in years, other than a brief "Hola" at a family gathering. When he visits, he won't go see her. When I tell him she *wants* to see him, he says, "It's unlikely," or, "That makes one of us," or, "So she can try to control me again? Mil gracias, pero no."

I wish he would see her, but I can't honestly tell him she's changed, that she's good to us, that she treats us well. She has a tunneled, paranoid view of everything, of everyone, still. Perhaps that will change in time.

But *my* time is running out.

I guess it makes sense for Pedro to stay out of Mom's grasp. Maybe he's healthier because he found a way to fully escape her.

The truth is, I'm sad for them. And, I'm sad for us as a family. Will we ever find peace and joy with each other?

It's a rhetorical question.

I know the answer.

54

AIDS
Pedro

"HOW ARE YOU feeling?" I ask, afraid to hear the answer through the impersonal telephone line.

"Oh, like butter," Daniel replies.

He seems healthier today. He bounced back after a week in hospice. Some big arm must have pulled him from the clenched clamp of death . . . again.

"Gracias a Dios," I say to fill the silence.

He's back home. He sounds tired, but I still hear his sense of humor.

"I'll miss Glenn, that's for sure," he moans. "He gave the nicest sponge baths."

Daniel laments he won't see his sweet, cute nurse anymore. Glenn was a comfort to him, to me, to everyone.

"I'm sure he was a consummate professional about it," I say.

"Sadly, he was," Daniel replies, with a giggle. "No hay miel sin hiel. *There's always a catch* with the cute ones."

Daniel will have a home health aide coming regularly, and the visiting nurses will help him with his IV medications. I pray he won't get another PICC-line infection.

● ● ●

"Pedro, Mrs. Langford's on the phone for you. You remember, Doug's mom?"

"Thanks Jeannette." It's been a long day at the clinic, but I'm still answering messages, taking phone calls.

"Hello, Mrs. Langford. How are you?"

"I'm well, Doctor. I'm well. . . ."

I give her a moment to collect her thoughts.

"I miss him, doctor. I miss him so much," she says, stifling a saturated sob.

I get an instant lump in my throat that I must clear before I can respond.

"I know Mrs. Langford. I miss him too. He was very special to us. We always enjoyed his office visits, and his one-of-a-kind humor."

. . .

Doug Langford was one of several patients on my team who died last month. Each painful loss was a sad reminder: we still don't have good treatments for this maldito virus.

I met Doug a few years ago at the opening night reception of *Little Shop of Horrors*. He was dating the director of a local theater company whose productions I enjoy. Doug was studying law here in Boston. A couple weeks later, he scheduled an appointment with me at the clinic.

At his first medical visit, Doug recounted that he had been living with HIV for years. Experimental and monotherapy hadn't worked for him.

I recall having asked an HIV mentor for his thoughts about combining HIV medications, like we do for tuberculosis and other infections.

"Pedro, as you know, experimental trials look promising, but the data are not conclusive at this time. I wish I could recommend it, but we're not even sure what dose would be appropriate for each medication. There are concerns about drug–drug interactions, and then there are the other medications a patient would likely be taking, with which there might be further interactions. We're just not there yet. We need more studies. We've got to let science guide us."

There is a tight network of mostly gay medical providers who spearhead treatment initiatives that often lead to clinical trials in the USA and around the world. Although our gut tells us to follow the science and the data, we sometimes seek out anecdotal stories that might help as well, to tide us over to the next breakthrough in the mysteries of this virus.

With no vaccine and no real treatment — one that works well and has few, preferably no, side effects — our hands are tied.

Monotherapy — just one drug at a time — isn't working because the virus often mutates when it replicates, and some of these new viral generations are resistant to the one drug treatment.

Over the last year, Doug's illness had progressed quickly, making him susceptible to opportunistic infections. Despite prophylactic measures, he had several hospital admissions for bacterial and fungal superinfections. His health deteriorated drastically.

Doug's eyes, and his sense of humor, were whispers of the attractive young man I met at the theater. They comforted me when I saw him at the hospital, and later when I would visit him at his mother's home where he was receiving care from visiting nurses.

Mrs. Langford had undergone a crash course in home health caregiving, and she took on the majority of Doug's home care.

Many parents throughout the world have suddenly become caregivers. Sadly, other parents have shunned their sons and daughters because of the HIV stigma. My patients come from the full spectrum of familial backgrounds and responses.

• • •

I have a couple medical students who shadow me Thursday afternoons. I scheduled one of my home visits with Doug on a Thursday so they could accompany me.

We greeted Mrs. Langford in her entryway. She gives the best ribsplitting bear hugs. They relieve the muscular tension that roots in my back and neck.

Doug was in the living room. It was the logical place for the hospital bed, which took up the space that would otherwise hold a sofa. Mrs. Langford had brought in folding chairs with cushions.

I took his hand and asked, "Doug, how are you, my friend?"

Through coughing and wheezing he replied, "Super duper. . . . Never better. . . . I'm gonna beat this 'maldito' virus."

His eyes had lost their shine. He closed them, and slept.

I caressed his hand and his hair as we talked with his mom.

Mrs. Langford appreciated my home visits. They calmed her worries. I reassured her that she was doing an extraordinary job.

At that time, Doug was receiving end-of-life care: the main focus was for his comfort. He got IV fluids, pain medications, and nutrition through a tube that pierced his belly and entered his stomach. He was not receiving actual HIV or other medical treatments.

Doug was sleeping when it was time to leave. I couldn't bring myself to wake him to say goodbye. I was very sure I would regret it.

But why should I wake someone who abhorred the waking world?

We each got an extra-long bear hug goodbye, then we left.

On the drive back to the clinic, I told my students it was likely the last time I would see Doug. None of us could help the sudden release of emotion. My steady stream of tears was easier to ignore than to keep stabbing my eyes with a tear-soaked tissue.

I gave out a chuckle when I looked over at the horror-struck passengers stopped at the traffic light next to us. Eventually, they seemed to register that I was actually okay. That I was not in a carjacking situation, or worse. Their faces subtly changed from looks of panic and fear to relief and embarrassment.

It was particularly cathartic to share these tears with students just starting their clinical careers. I hoped they would maintain their enthusiasm and compassion. We discussed the importance of self-care in this profession, especially during this maldita pandemic.

• • •

A couple weeks later, we attended Doug's funeral. I was touched that my students wanted to take part in this end-of-life event; that they wanted to share their condolences with Mrs. Langford, who had made such an impression on them.

Mrs. Langford and Doug had been devout Catholics, but his final wish was to refuse a Catholic mass and service, even if he were allowed to have one.

"As an exception to their rule? No thanks," he had stated.

Doug and I had talked about the lack of empathy from the Pope, and from the church in general, with regard to HIV and AIDS.

"Their focus on the 'sins of homosexuality' is a rigid defense of religious doctrine. It is a reprehensible dereliction of the basic tenets of Christianity." I was raw with disgust. These are sentiments I've shared with Daniel in the past, but have kept to myself recently.

Daniel is still very much in love with his church despite everything. The church means so much to him, even if *he* means little to his church.

Mrs. Langford accepted comfort from her priest in their home while Doug was dying, but had abandoned going to church for services — she suffered the sting of rejection of her beloved son.

They no longer felt welcome in their church.

• • •

"Doctor, I just worry you don't know how much Doug and I appreciated your care of him over the years. I know he was a smart aleck, with always something to say, no filter, a sharp tongue. Somehow you looked past it. . . . He was never good at exposing his vulnerabilities hidden deep inside his protective armor. I truly wish he had not suffered so much pain and conflict about himself, about who he was. . . . I hope he knows I loved him every day of his life. . . . I hope you know he loved *you* very much, Doctor."

I inhale an involuntary gasp.

"Thank you for saying it, Mrs. Langford. I loved him as well," I answer, choking back my emotions. "He taught me so much. . . . I will never forget him. . . . I don't want to lose any more friends, brothers, or sisters to this. . . ."

"Maldito virus?" she says, and we both laugh, my tissue drenched with tears and mucous.

"Yes, this maldito virus," I sputter, now laughing almost hysterically through the tears pouring down my face.

"Goodbye, Doctor," she almost whispers. "I hope you'll let me call you from time to time, to check up on you."

"Absolutely! . . . I would really love it. Take care, Mrs. Langford. Thank you so much for calling."

55

PERHAPS
Daniel

PEDRO USED TO get so mad at the Catholic Church, and the Pope. He'd recite "historical facts" he'd read that promoted his belief that the Pope is *not* infallible.

Now, he wants to present me with culled information he's discovered about the Popes in his extensive reading in books and encyclopedias.

"I want to share this with you so that you might understand my views. I don't *enjoy* knowing what I know. There's no *pleasure* in understanding how the Catholic Church, under the leadership *and direction* of the Popes, has caused centuries of atrocities, including its involvement in human slavery, and the physical, emotional, and sexual abuse of children."

"I understand Pedro. I want to hear what you have to say."

He's in my mid-century yard-sale-find armchair. I'm sitting on my couch with my hands under my legs. After years of theology classes and my own research, I don't think he'll tell me anything I don't know. I'm prepared to listen fully, carefully, without emotion.

"I'm reading this list because I want to correctly state the titles, dates, and the direct and indirect effects these edicts have had on humanity:

"The papal bull *Dum Diversas* of 1452 legitimized the slave trade.

"The papal bull *Romanus Pontifex* of 1455 sanctified the seizure of non-Christian lands and encouraged the enslavement of Indigenous, non-Christian people in Africa and the New World.

"The papal Bulls of Donation of 1493 divided the non-Christian world between Spain and Portugal.

"And the Requerimiento of 1513 required Indigenous Peoples to accept Spanish rule and allow Catholic missionaries on pain of war, slavery, or death."

Even with his complexion, Pedro's face and especially his ears are flushed. His voice keeps cracking.

He continues: "Hostility against the Spanish colonizers or missionaries was not allowed, and ignorance of these bulls was not a defense against subjugation. This 'Doctrine of Discovery' has been used for five hundred years to justify the thievery of lands and the enslavement of Indigenous Peoples all over the world. . . . Daniel, it all points to the Catholic Church, and specifically to the Pope."

His tears flow freely.

"I know Pedro. I read and studied all these bulls in theology classes. Imagine how I felt when I saw, 'to invade, search out, capture, vanquish, and subdue all . . . to reduce their persons to perpetual slavery. . . .' in a Catholic document."

"You've known all this?"

"Yes, Pedro."

"That these bulls are thought to have legitimized slavery and the slave trade."

"Yes, Pedro."

"And we've talked about Popes who had lovers — men and women. Some abused children. And others *fathered* children while they were Pope."

"These are all examples of a perverse corruption of *some* men within the church."

"So, we both have the same information, but have very different reactions to them."

"No, not really. I get it, Pedro. I really do."

"Oh?"

"I get it," I repeat. "The Pope—and all priests—are just humans. When you strip them away of the costumes and spectacle, they are just men. Most are trying to make a difference, to do good. But they are often flawed, and many break the rules about being good Catholics, and good Christians."

"Hmmph."

"I guess I'm saying the Pope is *not* infallible."

"Really?"

"Yes.

"Huh."

"I ought to kick the Pope right out of my life.... What an *odd thought* to burst into my mind."

"Haha! Good thing I wasn't drinking when you said it! I don't need an unexpected sinus lavage with a sparkling rosé!"

"I prefer a well-aimed, explosive spit take," I reply with a chuckle.

• • •

People have been excommunicated over the centuries for similar sentiments regarding the Pope. Religious splits—schisms, one of Pedro's favorite words!—have occurred over disagreements about infallibility. The way they choose a new Pope—through backroom wheeling and dealing, bribes, and back-stabbing—is also inconsistent with basic Christian teachings.

Of course I've known about all this. Perhaps there was an element of denial, of lazy lethargy, of a weak conviction to challenge the status quo.

But I love the Catholic Church despite doctrinal dissimilitudes and discrepancies. And, there is no Catholic Church without the Pope. I can't see myself in a different church or faith, so I'm stuck in this limbo for a church I love, that doesn't love me back. It's a three-decades-old story of unrequited love between us:

'Amor no correspondido es tiempo perdido.'
Unrequited love is time lost.

• • •

There are times I envy Pedro's view about religion. He still lives like a Christian, because he learned Christian values. In fact, he says, "I just embrace the teachings of Jesus Christ, nothing else."

It's so simple, it seems profound.

Without the layers of doctrine and pageantry, without the vast material wealth of the Christian churches, when you step back and take a good look at the Christian faiths, isn't it really about the teachings of Jesus Christ? Or rather, *shouldn't it be* about the teachings of Jesus Christ?

• • •

I've buried dozens by now.

Friends and coworkers. Former lovers. Former classmates. All of us with this damn thing wonder, every time we meet, who will be next? When will it be me?

Each day I awake is an exhilarating disappointment.

I don't *want* to die, and I don't know *how* I want to die, but . . .

'Es hora de cagar o salir de la olla.'
It's time to shit or get off the pot.

The services are starting to look and sound the same. There's a convenience and comfort in using the same funeral homes, function halls, and caterers that have shown a willingness to work with our communities. End-of-life event planning isn't the best time to have an argument with a bigoted business owner who doesn't want our "AIDS dollars."

I do want a Catholic Church service though. I'm not ready to say "adiós a Dios." I've arranged it with a friend who's a priest, who would be technically out of step with the Catholic Church. I want a full mass with readings, and I hope all my families will get together and work together to give me the celebration of life I deserve.

¡Qué yo merezco, gente!

• • •

"I don't like that I don't have any sort of legacy," I grumble. "Nothing that will remind people I was ever alive."

'La vida de los muertos está en la memoria de los vivos.'
The life of the dead is in the memories of the living.

We had a family reunion yesterday to celebrate my birthday. I knew there'd be a large sheet cake, so I kept the carrot cake Pedro brought me hidden in my apartment. He's been perfecting this recipe for years. It touches all the right tastebud buttons.

"Daniel, you're not dead," Pedro responds. "And if you die first, I will *never* forget you."

Pedro takes his slice of cake.

"What do you mean, 'if I die first?' What's going on?"

I may have raised my voice a little. And I may be pointing the knife at him. . . . I don't like nasty surprises.

"Nothing! You know how Lady Luck has been all our lives. 'Sólo se sabe que nunca se sabe.' *The only certainty is: you never know.*"

"I've never heard that one!"

"I kinda made it up."

"Pedro, I'm impressed! I love it, . . . and it's true. You just never know."

We enjoy our cake in silence for a while. But I can't let this nagging thought go. . . .

"I just wish I had kids, or that I had accomplished something important in my life. Anything that would keep my memory alive."

"Makes me think of Día de Muertos," Pedro says.

"Yes! I wish we celebrated the custom."

"Why didn't Mom and Pop grow up with it?" he wonders. "I've only become more interested because of Frida and other artists. It seems like a lovely tradition."

"Do you remember that dicho we made up about death?" I ask.

Pedro's eyebrows twitch, then relax, and I see recognition blossom over his face.

"That was probably our greatest poetic accomplishment, best when recited by dos borrachos pendejos," he smirks.

"Or sung by Vicente Fernández, borracho y despreciado."

"Can you imagine? Okay, you start it."

I clear my throat:

"Cuando la muerte te toca . . ."	*When it's your turn for death,*
"Todo se ve desenfoca . . ."	*Everything looks out of focus,*
"Tal vez te sientes desboca . . ."	*Maybe you feel out of control,*
"Mientras tu vida se choca . . ."	*As your life crashes,*
"Por tener suerte tan poca . . ."	*Because of your so little luck.*
"Hay que cerrar bien la boca . . ."	*It's best to keep your mouth shut,*
"No vale una provoca . . ."	*It's not worth a provocation,*
"Hasta el hombre que se ahorca . . ."	*Even the one who hangs himself,*
"Y el que brinca de roca . . ."	*And the one who jumps off a rock,*
"Sólo causan trastoca . . ."	*They only cause a distraction.*
"La Muerte no s'equivoca . . ."	*Because Death is not mistaken,*
"No miente cuando convoca . . ."	*She does not lie when she summons,*
"Ni si tendrás una roca . . ."	*It wouldn't matter if you had a diamond,*
"No vale una advoca . . ."	*It's not worth advocating,*
"Por tu vida tan loca."	*For your life that's so insane.*

We laugh like un par de rufianes.

• • •

'La Muerte:
Cuando te toca, aunque te quites.
Cuando no te toca, aunque te brinques.'
Death:
When it's your turn, even if you flee.
When it's not, even if you jump.

• • •

Pedro tells me he wants to tell our story in a book, a sort of bildungs-roman. He thinks it's an important tragicomedy to share with the world, for other boys like us to see that they're not alone, they're not throwaways, things can get better in time:

'Nunca es tarde si la dicha es buena.'
Better late than never.

"Más puede la pluma que la espada," I say.

The pen is mightier than the sword.

"Yes, that's true. . . . And I think it might be cathartic to tell our story, to expunge some of the anger, guilt, and shame I still feel. Maybe it will help me get rid of these fucking nightmares as well."

He's holding his fork like a club, ready to pummel his nightmares. As if it were that easy. Pedro and I believe that violence against violence only leads to more violence.

"Recordar es volver a vivir," I say.

"*To remember is to live again?* Did you make it up?"

"No, it's a dicho. Oh . . . oh . . . oh . . . I have the perfect ending for the book! I'll paraphrase. It's something like,

I have nothing,
I owe everyone,

358

I leave the rest,
to all the rest.

"That's terrifically sardonic!" Pedro exclaims. "I'll have to write it down, or I'll forget it."

"It was the one-line last will and testament of my dear friend and mentor François Rabelais, who lived in the 1500s. . . . And there's more! I want my tombstone to say:

I have gone in search of the great: 'PERHAPS?' "

"You are too much."

"I want people to scratch their heads . . . after I'm gone," I say with a self-satisfied smirk, "like they did . . . while I was here."

"You know people love you, right?" Pedro asks. "People have *always* loved you."

My face slowly blossoms into one of delighted glee.

"Feigned flattery will get you . . . far! Open up the faucet full force!"

"Family, friends, neighbors, classmates . . ."

"Perhaps not a teacher, or two, who may not have appreciated my too-numerous-to-list talents."

I put my index finger on my chin.

"Haha! You've been the wind beneath my wings," Pedro speak sings.

He's bent forward a little, bouncing his outstretched arms slightly, lost in his flight, far from the troubles of this world — a ridiculous, but loveable, grin on his face.

"Do you think you could maybe ask Bette to sing at my funeral?" I ask, almost wishing he could.

"Wouldn't that be nice?"

We get lost in thought for a moment. I get up to put the dishes in the sink.

"Just make sure you write how tall, muscular, and handsome I was. Don't let the truth ruin a good story."

I turn around and bat my eyes at him, giving my signature, full-sized grin.

"I thought you wanted people to remember *you*," he says sarcastically. "Don't forget, 'Al mentiroso le conviene ser memorioso.'"

"Ah yes, the liar should remember his lies. . . . But how else would you describe my enviably unique physique, my unparalleled intellect, wit, and charm, my inimitable style, and of course my exceptional modesty and humility? . . . Choose . . . your words . . . carefully . . . Mister."

I've got my palms firmly planted high on my waist, my menacing fingers point straight ahead at him. I might look like a lowercase *T*.

"Well, I would mention your dry wit and your dichos, which are always amusing, and informative."

"That sounded wholly half-hearted," I snort. "I'm going to *generously* presume there was a compliment buried in there somewhere. . . . Oh well, 'Hasta el mejor escribano echa un borrón.'"

Even the best writer makes mistakes.

"Hmmm. How about, 'A caballo regalado no le mires el diente,'" Pedro quips. *"Don't look a gift horse in the mouth.* Better known as, *beggars can't be choosers."*

He's now got his own letter *T* going.

"Oh yes, 'A quien dan, no escoge.' . . . I have taught you well my grasshopper. Go now, and prosper."

I steeple my hands and bow down slowly.

56

EULOGY
Pedro

"AND SO . . . I WANT to thank everyone for coming to celebrate Daniel's life.

"In particular, I'd like to thank his *LESBIAN SISTERS* and *GAY BROTHERS* who supported Daniel for years. Our chosen families complement, but they often surpass, our given families.

"Our gay and lesbian community has championed those living with HIV and AIDS, whereas our Pope, churches, government, and, in some cases, our families, have abandoned our siblings when they most needed our compassion and love.

"I also want to acknowledge our cousins and extended family, who are here because Daniel worked hard to bridge the unexplainable divide between us.

"I will end by saying . . . if there is a God . . . I believe *SHE* is welcoming Daniel home, so he may resume his faithful service to *HER*. . . .

"I hope *SHE* knows . . . that *SHE* doesn't deserve him."

And . . .

scene.

That'll get them! I think to myself.

Make sure you enunciate . . . and emphasize those fucking words.

Speak clearly and loudly.

There is an angry, bitter, manic man in the mirror before me. He seems to be going through a full-body catharsis.

I fantasize that Father Hopkins, or better still Sister DeStefano, will tackle me at the pulpit before I can utter those last words in my eulogy to Daniel, inside Our Lady of the Immaculate Conception Church . . . if they even *allow* Daniel's funeral to take place there.

Does he have a tendency to fantasize?

• • •

It's possibly malapropos, and probably premature, to work on my eulogy for Daniel before he dies.

Although, I believe Daniel would find it amusing.

Then he'd want to take out his red pen and go nuclear with the edits.

It helps me prepare for things by starting at the end, and working backwards. I often write the last sentence, the last chapter of a story first. Then, I can see the various paths to that ending. Of course, every writer knows there will be dozens of revisions, and the ending may change many times before the book is done. We all have our methods to set a goal and meet the challenge.

In theory, I should write the screenplay that will win the Academy Award before it can get nominated, so I'm many steps away from meeting my challenge and making that goal. In fairness to myself, my initial acceptance speech was for best supporting actor, but after I saw myself on a videotape recording, I knew *that* award is a real fantasy. I am, after all, grounded in reality . . . in *some* things.

My magical thinking tells me if I *imagine* Daniel's death, *it won't happen.* Having a fantastic fantasy world has its benefits. Magical thinking has been remarkably rarely reliable, so every day, I imagine Daniel's death. For added insurance, I imagine winning the lottery. I'll never win the lottery because I imagine winning the lottery, that much is obvious.

I wonder if it's possible to buy a lottery ticket without hoping to win. . . .

Shit, I won't win the Oscar if I *hope* I will. What the hell is wrong with me?

I guess I don't have to write the screenplay after all.

It reminds me of a dicho:

'El que no espera vencer, ya está vencido.'
He who does not expect to win is already defeated.

• • •

Unless I meet with a freak accident first—which let's face it, 'Sólo se sabe que nunca se sabe'—I'll need to talk at Daniel's funeral. We're a family of chillones, and the last thing I want to do is melt into a lachrymose spectacle sitting in a puddle of tears when I'm trying to, *not so subtly*, give the church, and *especially* the Pope, the finger. "With all due respect" should go without saying.

Hats off to my brand new hero, Sinéad O'Connor, who used an international soapbox opportunity to tear a photo of the Pope on live television to protest reports of sexual abuse of children at the hands of priests. In a way, she helped uncover the arrogant, bankrupt, corrupt, deceitful, evil, filthy, guilty, hateful, indecent, jaded, knavish, lecherous, malevolent, neglectful, obscene, perverse, quacky, repugnant, sanctimonious, tyrannical, ugly, villainous, wanton, xxx, and yellow-bellied zealotry that had seemed irreproachable.

So, I'm practicing in front of a full-length mirror, with stacked boxes in front of me for a makeshift podium. I've got a picture of the Pope taped to the front of the boxes so I can see this bald, baby-faced, fully fallible man in the mirror below my reflection.

• • •

I think about what we went through as kids, and the neighbors, comadres and compadres, priests, police, social workers, and guidance counselors who failed us as children. It's unclear how much Dr. Fritz knew.

But I believe many were complicit.

I wonder what would have been revealed if we had had parent-teacher conferences, which seem ubiquitous now. Would the nuns have intervened when the priests did not?

When I finally unloaded on Mr. Merle, my chemistry teacher, days after Mom attacked my sleeping body that Thanksgiving morning my college freshman year, he was in physical pain. I felt bad for him. I cherish his concern, which gave me strength, but it was too late; the two decades of damage had been done. There were other concerned adults as well. I remember and appreciate them.

I think about Daniel as a kid, at home with Mom, in high school seminary, at theology college, then his years adrift, and basically alone. He never got a break. The bony phalanxes of some evil always got a heinous hold of him. And this new evil has a grim, ghastly grasp around his neck. No Western remedy, santería, or brujería will help him now.

Daniel is convinced he will never know true love, comfort, and acceptance from a lover, his church, his country. My anemic conviction can't convince him otherwise.

Daniel has a close and courageous network of friends and family who help and support him as needed. I wish I lived closer . . . for both of us. Our siblings have matured into remarkable whirlwinds of energy, confidence, determination. Pop calls me often for information — then he calls Daniel to voice his love and support. He and Daniel seem to gab about everything nowadays. I often hear new information about each of them from the other.

Mom helps in her own way, though she wants her comadres chismosas to believe Daniel has cancer, not AIDS. And she does *not* want them to know he is gay. Although death should be about the deceased, the living often shifts the focus onto themselves, even before death has occurred.

I am thankful Daniel seems unaware of Mom's disgraceful shame and embarrassment. My eulogy will deal with it when the time comes.

* * *

I invited Daniel to meet me in Washington, DC, for the AIDS Memorial Quilt display on the National Mall. All 21,000 quilts — at least one from every state, and from twenty-eight countries — will be laid out. It will be the largest public art display that has ever occurred in the world.

It's both a comfort and a travesty.

I am aware this is a risky invitation given Daniel's deteriorating health. Perhaps it is willful ignorance and irresponsibility, but I want this memory for the rest of my life. And . . . I want Daniel to experience true love and acceptance from *many* segments of society during this solemn commemoration.

I'm in DC a day early. I have examined the public areas of the hotel and local restaurants. I am aware of the bathroom options in each. In my pocket, there is a list of ways to get to the National Mall on Saturday.

• • •

Tsking and throat-clearing coming from the frown of an uptight woman seated near me in the Washington National Airport are the snapping fingers that wake me from my peculiar hypnosis. I'm now aware I've been pacing between two structural pillars, my hands in knotted contortions swinging violently back and forth with each step.

I suppose I would have wondered about myself as well.

I see Daniel's plane pull up to the terminal. The accordioned walkway expands from the gate and engulfs the door on the side of the plane.

My involuntary gasp when I spot Daniel in the procession of passengers disembarking is thankfully out of his hearing range. In the months since I last saw him, his health has declined drastically. He is gaunt and emaciated. He is the standing figure looking upward, above St. Augustine who is holding Count Orgaz, in El Greco's painting. Unlike the standing figure, though, Daniel's gray complexion is that of the deceased count.

I quietly berate my stinging, welling eyes for betraying my wish to show no emotion, fear, panic. Tears flow, despite my fluttering eyelids trying to bat them away. It's no use.

"I'm a chillón," I cry, happy to have a familiar excuse for my tears.

"We both are!" he whispers in my ear as we hug and kiss.

Daniel has been nauseated for weeks, probably months. The Kaposi's affects his mouth, especially his gums. His fragile, frail frame is a shadow of Daniel, my brother.

We go to a quiet restaurant near the hotel. The menu includes some soups and pastas that might work, since he hasn't been eating solid, spicy, or chewy foods

I'm a pretzel of emotions.

I can barely stand myself.

I don't want Daniel to sense my sense of alarm at his rapid rate of decline.

Get a hold of yourself!

I find strength in denial.

I'm now annoyingly optimistic that he'll eat and gain weight.

"¡Comiendo entra la gana!" I urge.

Appetite comes with eating.

"A dicho for all occasions."

• • •

Unlike previous visits with Daniel, I've come prepared with lists of non-HIV-related topics we can chat about. It's similar to the sports-and-weather-research preps I do before I call Pop. There should be no need for awkward silences.

"What do you think is going to happen next month?" I ask.

"Ole Herb Bush will probably get reelected. Do you think Ole Barb will let him lose? I would *not* want to cross that lady on a good day, if she's ever had one."

We chuckle.

"I really hope Clinton will win. Eight years of Reagan and four years of Bush have sucked all joy and hope from the world."

"Speaking of Clinton and sucking," Daniel smirks.

"Ha! Yes, he's handsome, but Al Gore? That square jaw? That Tennessee drawl? Those broad shoulders?"

"That shoe size!" Daniel adds, then laughs until he coughs a few times. "I would not throw that guy out of bed for *any* reason."

We laugh some more.

The coughing seems to have caused him pain, but Daniel makes an effort to eat his bisque. I worry it's too rich for him. Later, he eats a couple pumpkin ravioli, which he loves, then he abandons the plate completely. He keeps eyeing the bathroom door in the hallway beside the open kitchen. I don't let him know I've noticed.

• • •

Daniel dashes for the bathroom when we get to our hotel room.

I'm channel surfing loudly so he can believe I can't hear him retch.

Then, the diarrhea starts. I've never felt so helpless, and useless. Exactly what *role* does all my training serve right now? Why can I offer him *nothing*? What is my *purpose*?

"Daniel, can I do anything for you?" I ask the bathroom door.

"Can you get me a soda?" he responds weakly.

"Absolutely! Anything else?"

"No, that's it."

I take my time down the hall, at the vending machines. I know he would appreciate some privacy to let his body do what it needs to do.

My emotions are in a swallow-regurgitate replay loop.

• • •

Daniel is unwell and weak when we wake up.

"I don't think I can make it today, Pedro."

"That's okay, Daniel. Really. It is. We can do whatever you'd like. . . . Would it help if I got a wheelchair?"

I will soon start to berate myself for failing to consider this potential need in advance. But I'm still hopeful we can see the quilt, experience the rally together.

"Probably. . . . Where would you get one?"

"I have no idea."

I call hospitals, ambulance companies, and pharmacies. . . . I can't rent—I can't even *buy*—a wheelchair. I'm ready to gift wrap my credit card for anyone who will take it.

After a while, Daniel seems to improve. His ashen skin starts to get some color.

"I think . . . I think I can do it. Let's go while I have the strength," he says.

We're near a subway stop, but we hail a taxi, just to be sure. We'll take our time today. There's no need to rush on such a beautiful sunny day.

• • •

Each quilt is a 3-foot by 6-foot panel. Eight quilts are sewed together into a 12-foot square. There are wide cloth runners around each square so people won't walk onto the quilts themselves. Experiencing the quilt requires lots of tissues, at least for us. Family and friends have created works of art using every type of material imaginable to celebrate their loved one's life. Some have three-dimensional objects sewn on. There's a rumor someone attached a bowling ball to a panel. Sometimes, I'm so proud of human ingenuity.

• • •

I can't describe the massive expanse of handmade quilts on display in front of us, as far as we can see. It reminds me of my—and later Daniel's—first impression of Central Park. All the movies, TV shows, written descriptions had failed to convey its immensity and beauty.

Feelings of exhilaration, sadness, hope, and despair are a lava lamp inside me. The organizers have a dedicated team of volunteers who ritually unfold and lay down each square of the quilt. We watch them in a trance, with tears streaming down our faces. It's futile to wipe them away anymore.

• • •

They say history is written by victors.

I've always been a cynic about "historical facts," as they're called, especially as it relates to the colonization of the Americas, and the rest of the world. In history, people, tribes, countries, regions have been thrown into conflicts and wars because of a maniacal quest for power, wealth, land, fame. The egocentric oppressors use a personal slight, a religion, or some other belief as a righteous cause. Then the losing sides in those battles are seen in a negative light for years, decades, even centuries.

I wonder how Reagan, Bush, legislators, Christian churches, and the Pope will be seen in history with regard to the HIV pandemic. Would they even *care* if their dyspathy were a footnote in their obituaries?

• • •

Daniel and I walk around the quilt squares, reading what folks have written about their loved ones. In some cases, strangers — volunteers — have paid tribute to a person who did not have a quilt made for them.

I see a quilt for J. Daniel Hernández, and it suddenly strikes me that Daniel is my brother's middle name. How cruel to have named him Jesús Daniel. We all of us ignored or were ignorant of his true name, which he tried to emulate his entire life. I have literally *never* called him by his first name. I wonder if this matters to him. I believe it is too late to ask him.

• • •

We stop in front of a panel with a fantastic artistic rendering of a bass guitar. There are loving words and many attached photos. On the bottom right, there is a photo of four boys in a garage band.

"Daniel, do you remember the time we saw those images on Sara's wall when Mom and Pop were fighting?"

He's concentrating on that photo. I'm not sure if it sparked the same memory for him.

"Of course, . . . I could never forget it. . . . I believe God sent them to comfort us. It's my proof He exists."

I sigh, as if I'm releasing some pent up pressure.

"It's what I would like to believe as well. But why do you think He never sent any *actual* help? Why do you think he let us suffer so much . . . for so long?"

"I don't know." He looks up, toward the Capitol Building. "But remember, Jesus had doubts after forty days and forty nights in the desert. Then he had doubts when he was dying on the cross. He said, 'My God, my God, why have you forsaken me?'"

"Why do you think God does that to people?"

He looks at me suddenly, as if in shock, then I see a flicker, then his light drains.

"Honestly Pedro, I have wondered, and I've asked myself that question more and more the last few years."

· · ·

We've only seen a fraction of the quilt when Daniel says, "Okay, I think I'm ready. I've seen enough." I'm not entirely sure what he means. Is he getting tired, and feels he's seen enough for him to say he's seen the AIDS quilt? Or, is it too emotionally draining, and he can't take it anymore?

I have a complicated mix of feelings when we stumble upon a panel for Rock Hudson. It's a chilling memorial to a childhood crush. I feel a magnificent obsession pulling me down, and pushing me under the quilt's immeasurable weight.

I suddenly realize the quilt is very much like a cemetery. The size and shape of each panel seems like an individual grave site. I not only see each person's life on display on the quilt, I now imagine their body beneath.

I wonder if this double meaning was part of the original vision in the creation of the quilt.

I think it is both genius and devastatingly poignant.

I am depleted as well.

We take our time getting out of the area, which is now packed with hundreds of thousands. There have been people talking on the main stage for a while: activists, politicians, and the occasional celebrity. We listened to their impassioned pleas for more funding, research, and compassion from our government, and the entire world.

I felt a fleeting flicker of hope before reality set in, once we were away from the unrealistic optimism at the National Mall.

Will people honestly care more tomorrow than they did yesterday?

• • •

Daniel rests a little. Then we go to the hotel restaurant downstairs for a light dinner. We're both emotionally and physically drained, so we don't talk much. Despite my prepared list, I'm having trouble thinking of topics, and Daniel seems content to have a meditative silence.

• • •

Daniel is leaving tomorrow on a plane.

It reminds me of the melancholic lyrics to "Daniel" by Bernie Taupin, hauntingly sung by Elton John.

Released when he was ten years old, I have always thought the song was written . . . for me, about Daniel . . . my brother. Though he is younger, not older than me, it speaks of pain, scars that won't heal, and Daniel's eyes.

Daniel's eyes.

When I first heard it, I thought Daniel died in the song, and I cried and cried. Daniel, my own brother, had almost died a few years before, and the emotional trauma was still a fresh wound — a scar that hadn't healed.

It seemed as if the songwriting duo knew about me and Daniel, about our shared histories, about our brotherly bond that won't be broken.

My eyes have cried.

Tears in my eyes have always come easy and quickly for me. It's been a great annoyance and embarrassment all my life. I've seen it as a sign of weakness, but I'm starting to believe they mean I care so much about Daniel, I just can't hold my tears in.

I know his journey will differ from that in the song.

Tears will cloud my eyes when I see Daniel waving goodbye tomorrow.

I will miss him very much.

I take Daniel to the airport the next morning. I want to make sure he gets onto the plane without a problem. His friends will pick him up in Columbus; they will make sure he gets home all right.

"Call me as soon as you get home."

"What do you want me to call you?" he says, with his unmistakable grin, his big brown eyes, and his dry wit.

It's odd, . . . I suddenly see some of Pop, some of Mom, and some of my siblings in his facial features.

I'd never noticed it before. . . .

Why had I never noticed?

I hadn't thought that he and I *looked* like brothers.

But it was there all along.

Why had I been blind to it?

We hug for a long time.

"I love you Jesús Daniel."

He gasps, then squeezes me tight.

We look at each other.

Our eyes overflow.

"We're a couple of chillones," he hiccups through short breaths.

I see Daniel through my murky tears. With each blink, I see new View-Master images of Daniel as my One True Treasure: in the tomato fields, buying dulces in Mexico, hanging from the columpios, running around the baseball diamond, at Kenny's Market, at the DOT, scratching his arms on the granite blocks next to the river . . .

These are how I want to remember Daniel, my brother.

I remember the assignment.
"Bring something special; your one true treasure."
Girls displayed dolls, dresses, diaries.
Boys brought baseball cards, cars, comics.
I'd been nervous on the bus.
How had I convinced Mom?
I remember the teacher's face, her open mouth.
Because my one true treasure was
Daniel, my brother.

ACKNOWLEDGMENTS

WHEN THE UNUSUAL captures my attention, my imagination is set free.

This book was written for my brother Daniel, and for children like Pedro and Daniel whose beauty, worth, and potential aren't appreciated or seen. I see you. It is my sincere wish for you to believe it will get better in time. Keep your hope hidden, if needed, but remember where it's kept, and nurture it regularly. You hold that key. What you learn, through teachers of all kinds and through books and other materials, is yours to keep. No one can take away your knowledge. It is another key you hold.

Nick Thomas (Executive Editor, Levine Querido) is a miracle worker. Or perhaps he's just a wizard. He fell in love with a picture book manuscript and then coaxed this novel out of me. I will be forever grateful for his friendship and collaborative stewardship. Irene Vázquez (Assistant Editor and Publicist, Levine Querido) was an early champion of this novel, particularly because of the rare depictions of colorism in children's literature and beyond. Thanks as well to the rest of the Levine Querido team: Arthur A. Levine, Antonio Gonzalez Cerna, Madelyn McZeal, and Arely Guzmán.

I feel blessed to have had Will Morningstar meticulously copyedit this manuscript.

I am so grateful to Julie Kwon for her beautiful artwork, both on the gorgeous cover and in the interior illustrations that capture the love, joy, hope, and resilience in Pedro and Daniel. Many thanks to Semadar Megged, the designer.

My picture book manuscript mentioned above broke all the rules of picture book writing. It is simply the way I write. This novel has elements of picture book, chapter book, verse novel, middle grade, young adult, new adult, adult fiction, short story, nonfiction, and memoir.

Perhaps that's why I'm working on a graphic novel for my next project. It is another testament to having an editor who is open to the possibilities beyond conventions.

Rules were meant to be broken, conventions were meant to be challenged.

A collective thank you to agents and editors who see the potential when the arbitrary rules of "how to tell a story" aren't followed. There are many ways to tell a story, or a folktale.

When the unusual captures my attention, my imagination is set free.

I was taught English as a second language, first by siblings and neighborhood children, then later in parochial and public schools. I paid particular attention in English classes. It was my key to an expedited assimilation, which allowed me to blend in and disappear when my skin tone didn't offend.

Teachers seem undervalued and underpaid in our society. I value all my teachers, from kindergarten to present day. I honor you with a virtual hug and a full-throated *Thank You!* I try to pay-it-forward when possible.

A special thanks to the Mrs. Davidsons and Mr. Merles of the world.

I am indebted to various writing communities:

My #50PreciousWords submission in 2021 represents *the first* 50 words I wrote about Pedro and Daniel's remarkable relationship. It is particularly poignant that those are *the last* 50 words in this novel. That contest submission became the picture book manuscript Nick Thomas read just weeks after I wrote it. That picture book manuscript, "Caution in the Wind," has transformed into the first chapter of *Pedro & Daniel*.

The seventeen stories I wrote in 2021 for the #12x12PictureBook-Challenge were shaped in part by my co-members, who offered invaluable critiques, comments, and suggestions. Those seventeen stories have transformed and are now incorporated into *Pedro & Daniel*, Part One.

I am grateful for the partnerships and support from Boston's GrubStreet, Porter Square Books, All She Wrote Books, and Poets & Writers, Inc.

The Society of Children's Book Writers and Illustrators (SCBWI) and *Kweli Journal* played roles in this writing journey.

Many thanks to the countless critique partners who have read my stories and offered indispensable feedback. CK Malone, Yolimari García, and Andrew Hacket stand out as insightful, meticulous, and generous editors of this work.

Last, I wish to acknowledge my many families, both given and chosen. My husband James J. Jordan has been extraordinarily considerate and patient with me during this writing journey. Cristian 'El Socio' Tobar, thank you for many faithful years with FEWorks.

I cherish all my four-legged family members. Lola, Jonah, Hector, Felix, and Max still hold my heart. Bela and Oscar are my constant companions, my diversions, my comforts. Pepito The Squirrel was the catalyst for my latest (and last?) career choice; he left an indelible mark on my simply-human heart; he changed me at a chemical level, which I celebrate in my *Pepito The Squirrel* picture books.

AUTHOR'S NOTES

THERE IS A certain irony that the concern for a potentially disastrous Swine Flu pandemic in 1976–77 and the devastation of the HIV/AIDS pandemic are featured events in this book, written during the COVID-19 pandemic, and in the midst of the Global Climate Crisis.

It is estimated that the proportion of time that humans have been in existence, when compared to earth's age, is about 0.004 percent. If humankind were to believe in, and use science, and learn to work together, the human race might prolong its survival. Otherwise, nature will find a new species successor to take our place; she always has.

This book deals with many serious topics.

These stories detail various forms of abuse. Their depictions were necessary to show their authentic effects on Pedro and Daniel. With only a sliver of hope, children can sometimes survive atrocities. But the emotional and physical scars can last a lifetime.

Colorism may be a new concept for readers. It is a form of racism in which prejudice or discrimination is levied against others because of their skin tone or physical and facial features deemed unattractive or inferior. Colorism views are often held by people within the *same* ethnic or racial group. In *Pedro & Daniel*, some lighter-skinned Latinos hold colorist/colorism attitudes against other Latinos of darker complexion.

In addition to blatant discrimination, colorism has an insidious effect on people's opportunities throughout life, ultimately affecting their wealth, health, and even their life expectancy.

Persons of all ages, races, ethnicities, religions, gender identities, sexual identities, and socioeconomics have been subjugated and enslaved throughout human history. This can take many forms. It may occur within a private home, but in plain sight *and* sound.

As mentioned in the novel, the Pope and the Catholic Church used papal bulls, including those known as the Doctrine of Discovery, to normalize atrocities, including the enslavement of Indigenous Peoples on several continents, and land thievery throughout the world.

I will let their words speak for themselves.

Later, Thomas Jefferson, the Monroe Doctrine, and US Supreme Court Chief Justice John Marshall used these bulls as a foundation to justify American Imperialism, strengthening colonial power over Indigenous Peoples in America.

The Catholic Church was instrumental in the formation of Indian residential schools in the United States, then later in Canada. On July 30, 2020, onboard the papal plane leaving Canada, Pope Francis acknowledged that the systematic abuses against Indigenous children and their families was a culture genocide. He had not used the word genocide during his six-day visit.

The horrors committed against Indigenous children in these schools are well-documented, and were recently recognized by the Canadian House of Commons as genocide.

The sexual abuse of children at the hands of Catholic clergy was given media attention in the 1980s and twenty years later were regularly covered following a Pulitzer Prize–winning series in the *Boston Globe*.

We may never know when the physical and sexual abuses against children at the hands of Catholic clergy actually started, or the enormity of their inhumanity, but there are clues in the church's actions over centuries.

To be clear, the Catholic Church is only one of many Christian churches that share these inexpungible stains on their history.

Since the 1990s, the Catholic popes have been petitioned to formally revoke the Doctrine of Discovery and to recognize the human rights of Indigenous Peoples.

Some theologians state that the church has already removed and replaced those edicts; that the doctrine has no legal or moral authority. This may be technically true. But it is a disingenuous argument against actions the church can take that might lead toward healing, restitution, and/or reparations.

The Doctrine and other papal edicts directly *and* indirectly caused what they intended, and those effects continue to this day.

Justice Marshall used the Doctrine of Discovery in his arguments in the unanimous decision of the 1823 Supreme Court case *Johnson v. M'Intosh*, which laid the foundation for determining who owned Indigenous land.

The Rescind the Doctrine movement should continue until the Pope formally rescinds the papal bulls that comprise the Doctrine of Discovery, issues a formal apology to all Indigenous People of the world affected by the Doctrine, returns Indigenous artifacts in the Vatican Museums, and meets all other reasonable requests.

I believe that the Catholic Church cannot hide behind the mantra that the mother church is not responsible for the sins committed by her children. The Church must be instrumental in teaching its followers about these papal bulls and their continued effects, including institutional racism and colorism, on Indigenous Peoples throughout the world.

APPENDIX OF DICHOS USED IN PEDRO & DANIEL

THE DICHOS/PROVERBS USED in this book do not necessarily have a Mexican origin. I have attempted to discover the identifiable origin when possible.

Some have Spanish wording that differs significantly from the understood English proverb to which it is paired; this implies a unique Spanish origin, but the proverbial meaning may have originated in a different form, in a different language, elsewhere.

Many of the dichos/proverbs have no discernible origin, or they may be attributed to multiple persons. These I list as Origin Unknown.

Key:
Spanish dicho.
English translation.
English interpretation/proverb.
Known author of dicho/proverb, if identifiable.

MAY 1968

Más vale pájaro en mano que cien volando.
A bird in hand is worth more than a hundred in flight.
A bird in hand is worth two in a bush.
John Ray, *Handbook of Proverbs* (1670)

Piensa en todo la belleza en tu alrededor y sé feliz.
Think of all the beauty around you and be happy.
Think of all the beauty around you and be happy.
Anne Frank (1929–1945)

La rueda que chilla consigue la grasa.

The squeaky wheel gets the grease.

The squeaky wheel gets the grease.

Josh Billings, "The Kicker" (c. 1870)

CAUTION IN THE WIND

Quisiera matar dos pájaros en un tiro.

I'd like to kill two birds with one strike.

Kill two birds with one stone.

Origin unknown

__Son tal para cual.__

They are one for the other.

They deserve each other. / They are peas in a pod. / They are two of a kind.

John Lyly, *Euphues and his England* (1580)

Querer es poder.

Wanting is being able to.

Where there's a will there's a way.

George Herbert, *Outlandish Proverbs* (1640)

El que no llora, no mama.

He who doesn't cry, doesn't suckle.

The squeaky wheel gets the grease.

Origin unknown

A canas honradas no hay puertas cerradas.

There are no closed doors to honorable grey hairs.

There are no doors closed to wise elders.

Origin unknown

Media verdad es media mentira.
A half-truth is a half-lie.
A half-truth is often a great lie.
Origin unknown

La amistad sincera es un alma repartida en dos cuerpos.
Sincere friendship is one soul divided into two bodies.
True friendship is one soul shared by two bodies.
Aristotle (384–322 BCE)

JUNE 1968

Más vale paso que dure, y no trote que canse.
A pace that lasts is worth more, and not a trot that tires.
A pace that lasts is better than a trot that tires you.
Origin unknown

Lento, pero seguro.
Slow, but safe.
Slowly but surely. / Slow and steady wins the race.
Aesop (c. 620–564 BCE)

A HIGHLIGHT FOR PEDRO

Apretados pero contentos.
Cramped, but content.
The more, the merrier.
Origin unknown

No se puede tener todo.
One can't have everything.
You can't have everything.
Origin unknown

Fuera de vista, fuera de mente.

Out of sight, out of mind.

Out of sight, out of mind.

Origin unknown

El que la sigue, la consigue.

The one that pursues it, gains it.

If at first you don't succeed, try again.

Thomas H. Palmer, *Teacher's Manual* (1840)

JULY 1968

Quien más mira, menos ve.

He who looks more, sees less.

The one who looks the most sees the least.

Origin unknown

Vísteme despacio que tengo prisa.

Dress me slowly, I'm in a hurry.

More haste, less waste.

Napoleon Bonaparte (1769–1821)

Más de prisa, más despacio.

Quicker, slower.

More haste, less speed.

Origin unknown

HERMANOS DE DOBLES SENTIDOS

Otra cosa, mariposa.

Another thing, butterfly.

Do something else, butterfly. / Let's change the subject.

Origin unknown

El mismo perro con distinto collar.

The same dog with different collar.

Same dog different collar.

Origin unknown

Hay que hacer de tripas corazón.

One has to make guts a heart.

When life gives you lemons, make lemonade.

Origin unknown

AUGUST 1968

Cuando en duda, consúltalo con tu almohada.

When in doubt, consult it with your pillow.

When in doubt, sleep on it.

Origin unknown

Duerme en ello, y tomarás consejo.

Sleep on it, and you will receive advice.

Sleep on it, things will be clearer in the morning.

Origin unknown

El que no oye consejo, no llega a viejo.

He who does not hear advice does not live to old age.

Advice most needed is least heeded.

Origin unknown

FAMILIA EN MÉXICO LINDO

El amor y la felicidad no se pueden ocultar.

Love and happiness cannot be hidden.

You can't hide love or happiness.

Origin unknown

Desgracia compartida, menos sentida.
Shared misery is felt less.
Misery loves company.
Origin unknown

SEPTEMBER 1968

Para tonto no se estudia.
To be a fool, it is not studied.
One need not study to be a fool.
Origin unknown

No estudio para saber más, sino para ignorar menos.
I don't study to know more, rather to ignore less.
I don't study to be smarter, but to be less ignorant.
Sor Juana Inés de la Cruz (1648–1695)

Dios nos libre del hombre de solo un libro.
God free us from the man with just one book.
God save me from the one-book man.
Thomas Aquinas (1225–1274)

WRITINGS ON THE WALL

Entre padres y hermanos, no metas tus manos.
Between fathers and brothers, don't stick your hands.
Don't get involved in family arguments.
Origin unknown

Donde hay humo hay fuego.
Where there's smoke, there's fire.
Where there's smoke, there's fire.
John Heywood, *Proverbs* (1546)

Quien espera, desespera.

He who waits, despairs.

One who longs finds despair. / A watched pot never boils. / Waiting is the worst.

Origin unknown

OCTOBER 1968

Más vale gotita permanente que aguacero de repente.

A permanent drip is worth more than a sudden waterfall.

Better a steady drip than a sudden deluge.

Origin unknown

La mejor salsa es el hambre.

The best sauce is hunger.

Hunger makes the best sauce.

Origin unknown

TELLTALE TRICKS AND TREATS

Sobre gustos no hay nada escrito.

With regard to taste, nothing is written.

There's no accounting for taste.

Origin unknown

A beber y a tragar, que el mundo se va a acabar.

Drink and eat because the world is going to end.

Live for today, we may not get tomorrow.

Origin unknown

NOVEMBER 1968

Un hombre sin alegría no es bueno o no está bien.
A man without happiness is not good or is not well.
A sad man is neither good nor well.
Origin unknown

Una manzana al día para mantener alejado al médico.
An apple a day keeps the doctor away.
An apple a day keeps the doctor away.
Origin unknown

SHADES IN OUR COLORS

Es peor el remedio que la enfermedad.
The remedy is worse than the illness.
The cure is worse than the illness.
Origin unknown

DECEMBER 1968

No dejes para mañana lo que puedas hacer hoy.
Don't leave for tomorrow what you can do today.
Don't put off for tomorrow what can be done today.
Origin unknown

En la tardanza está el peligro.
In the lateness is the danger.
The danger is in delay.
Origin unknown

El perezoso siempre es menesteroso.
The lazy one is always needy.
The sloth is always needy.
Origin unknown

LA VIRGEN DE GUADALUPE

Los niños deben ser vistos y no escuchados.
Children should be seen and not heard.
Children should be seen, but not heard.
Origin unknown

Hay ropa tendida.
There are clothes hanging.
The walls have ears. / Watch what you say.
Origin unknown

La mejor palabra es la que no se dice.
The best word is the one that isn't said.
The best word is the one left unsaid.
Origin unknown

Más vale paso que dure, y no trote que canse.
A pace that lasts is worth more, and not a trot that tires.
Better a pace that lasts than a trot that tires you.
Origin unknown

Algo es algo, menos es nada.
Something is something, less is nothing.
Better than nothing.
Origin unknown

JANUARY 1969

Aunque la jaula sea de oro, no deja de ser prisión.
Although a cage is made of gold, it does not stop being a prison.
A gilded cage is still a jail.
Arthur Lamb, "A Bird in a Gilded Cage" (1900)

Prefiera libertad con pobreza que prisión con riqueza.
Prefer freedom with poverty over prison with wealth.
Prefer freedom with poverty over prison with wealth.
Origin unknown

La libertad es un tesoro que no se compra ni con oro.
Liberty is a treasure that isn't bought, not even with gold.
Liberty is a treasure that isn't bought, not even with gold.
Origin unknown

WORDS IN HIS HEAD

Mejor la verdad que la mentira.
Honesty is the best policy.
Honesty is the best policy.
Sir Edwin Sandys, *Europa Speculum* (1599)

FEBRUARY 1969

Una onza de alegría vale más que una onza de oro.
An ounce of happiness is worth more than an ounce of gold.
Better an ounce of happiness than a pound of gold.
Origin unknown

Más vale un presente que dos después.
One present is worth more than two laters.
One present is better than two laters.
Origin unknown

PAST, PRESENT, AND FUTURE

Hay ropa tendida.
There are clothes hanging.
The walls have ears. / Watch what you say.
Origin unknown

Siempre tranquilo antes de la tormenta.
Always calm before the storm.
It's alway calm before the storm.
Origin unknown

De músico, poeta y loco, todos tenemos un poco.
Of musician, poet, and crazy, we all have a little.
We've all done foolish things.
Origin unknown

El que mucho mal padece, con poco bien se consuela.
He who knows much bad, with little good is comforted.
He who suffers many evils is satisfied with little good.
Origin unknown

Cuando hay hambre, no hay pan duro.
When there is hunger, there is no hard bread.
When one is hungry, everything tastes good.
Origin unknown

MARCH 1969

Todo por servir se acaba.
Everything that serves, ceases to exit.
Things of service wear away. / It was good while it lasted.
Origin unknown

A SMORGASBORD OF DELIGHTS

La vida no es un ensayo.
Life's not a rehearsal.
Life's not a dress rehearsal
Origin unknown

Para tonto no se estudia.
To be a fool, one does not study.
One need not study to be a fool.
Origin unknown

APRIL 1969

El que ansioso escoge lo mejor, suele quedarse con lo peor.
He who anxiously chooses the best, ends up with the worst.
He who is anxious to get the best, tends to be left with the worst.
Origin unknown

Anda tu camino sin ayuda de vecino.
Walk your path without the help of your neighbor.
Walk your path without the help of your neighbor.
Origin unknown

Más vale dar que recibir.
It's worth more to give than to receive
It's more blessed to give than to receive.
Bible, *Acts 20:35*

APRIL SHOWER MAY FLOWER

Camarón que se duerme, se lo lleva la corriente.
A shrimp that falls asleep will be carried away by the current.
Don't fall asleep at the wheel.
Origin unknown

MAY 1969

Contestación sin pregunta, señal de culpa.
An answer without a question signals fault.
An answer without a question is a sign of guilt.
Origin unknown

No pidas perdón antes de ser acusado.
Don't ask for a pardon before being accused.
Don't request a pardon before an accusation.
Origin unknown

Excusa no pedida, la culpa manifiesta.
An unsolicited excuse, fault manifests.
An unsolicited excuse is a sign of guilt.
Origin unknown

SADNESS IN THE WOODS

Haz el bien sin mirar a quién.
Do what's right without looking to whom.
Do good, without looking to whom.
Origin unknown

JUNE 1969

Hay que aprender a perder antes de saber jugar.
One must learn to lose before knowing to play.
You must learn how to lose before you can know how to play.
Origin unknown

Nada arriesgado, nada ganado.
Nothing risked, nothing won.
Nothing ventured, nothing gained.
Origin unknown

No da el que puede, sino el que quiere.
It's not who can who gives, but rather he who wishes.
The true giver is the one who gives willingly, not the one who gives reluctantly.
Origin unknown

OUT OF THE SHADOWS

Fuera de vista, fuera de mente.
Out of sight, out of mind.
Out of sight, out of mind.
Origin unknown

Hay ropa tendida.

There are clothes hanging.

The walls have ears. / Watch what you say.

Origin unknown

No hay más que temer que una mujer despreciada.

There isn't anything worse to fear than a woman disregarded.

Hell hath no fury like a woman scorned.

William Congreve, *The Mourning Bride* (1697)

July 1969

Las deudas viejas no se pagan, y las nuevas se dejan envejecer.

Old debts aren't paid, and the new debts are allowed to get old.

When old debts aren't paid, new debts get old.

Origin unknown

Gasta con tu dinero, no con el del banquero.

Spend with your money, not with that of the banker.

Spend your own money, not the bank's.

Origin unknown

Más lejos ven los sesos que los ojos.

The brain sees further than the eyes.

The eye looks, but the brain sees.

Origin unknown

LESSONS IN THE FIELDS

El que madruga coge la oruga.

He who rises early gets the caterpillar.

The early bird catches the worm.

William Camden, *Proverbs* (1605)

Donde hay patrón, no manda otro.
Where there's a boss, no one else gives orders.
Where there's a boss, no other commands.
Origin unknown

Nadie puede servir a dos.
No one can serve two.
No man can serve two masters.
Bible, *Matthew 6:24*

AUGUST 1969

El pendejo no tiene dudas ni temores.
A fool has no doubts or fears.
A fool has no doubts or fears.
Origin unknown

Sabe el precio de todo y el valor de nada.
He knows the price of everything, but the value of nothing.
He knows the price of everything, but the value of nothing.
Oscar Wilde, *Lady Windermere's Fan* (1892)

Mal piensa el que piensa que otro no piensa.
He thinks poorly if he thinks that another doesn't think.
He who thinks another doesn't think thinks badly.
Origin unknown

FISH IN THE RIVER

El tiempo lo cura todo.
Time heals everything.
Time heals all wounds.
Menander (300 BCE)

HOME

Como elefante en una cacharrería.
Like an elephant in a china shop.
Like a bull in a china shop.
Frederick Marryat, *Jacob Faithful* (1834)

A palabras necias, oídos sordos.
To foolish words, deaf ears.
Let foolish words fall on deaf ears.
Origin unknown

CHONIES

Con la honra no se pone la olla.
With honor, you don't put the pot.
Honor won't fill the pot. / Honor buys no meat in the market.
Origin unknown

CHISME

La ausencia hace crecer el cariño.
Absence makes affection grow.
Absence makes the heart grow fonder.
Sextus Aurelius Propertius (15 BCE)

Dos oídos, pero una boca. Escucha más y habla menos.
Two ears, but one mouth. Listen more and talk less.
Two ears, but one mouth. Listen more and speak less.
Zeno of Citium (300 BCE)

Guarda la ayuda para quien te la pida.

Save help for those who request it.

I'll keep my advice for those who request it.

(300 BCE)

En bocas cerradas no entran moscas.

In closed mouths, flies don't enter.

Flies don't enter closed mouths. / Silence is golden.

Thomas Carlyle, *Sartor Resartus* (1831)

No hay fuego más ardiente que la lengua del maldiciente.

There is no fire hotter as the tongue of the curser.

There is no hotter flame than the tongue of a gossip.

Origin unknown

Quien comenta, inventa.

He who comments, invents.

Where there is gossip, there are lies.

Origin unknown

COLUMPIOS

El que se fue a Sevilla perdió su silla.

El que se fue a Torreón perdió su sillón.

He who went to Sevilla lost his chair.

He who went to Torreón lost his armchair.

You snooze you lose. / Move your feet, lose your seat.

Dicho version of "Finders keepers, losers weepers": Plautus (200 BCE)

Gusta lo ajeno más por ajeno que por bueno.

They like the foreign more for foreign than for good.

The grass is always greener on the other side.

Ovid, (43 BCE–18 CE)

Consejo no pedido da el entrometido.
Unsolicited advice is given by the busybody.
The busybody gives unrequested advice.
Origin unknown

Lo que no mata, engorda.
What doesn't kill, fattens.
What doesn't kill you makes you stronger.
Friedrich Nietzsche, *Twilight of the Idols* (1888)

De mal el menos.
Of bad, the least.
The lesser of two evils.
Aristotle (384–322 BCE)

El mejor no vale nada.
The best is worthless.
Bad is the best choice.
Origin unknown

DULCE

El que quiere algo, algo le cuesta.
He who wants something, it will cost him something.
One must work for what one desires. / No pain, no gain.
Origin unknown

El que es puro dulce, se lo comen las hormigas.
He who is purely sweet will be eaten by ants.
The good is often taken for a fool.
Origin unknown

No hay que ahogarse en un vaso de agua.

No need to drown in a glass of water.

Don't overreact / make a big deal about it / make a mountain out of a molehill.

Origin unknown

Mientras dura, vida y dulzura.

While it lasts, life and sweetness.

Enjoy the sweetness in life while it lasts.

Origin unknown

FAIR

Más sabe el diablo por viejo que por diablo.

The devil knows more for being old than for being the devil.

The devil knows more because he's old than because he's the devil.

Origin unknown

Si te queda el saco, póntelo.

If the coat fits, put it on.

If the shoe fits, wear it.

Dicho version of "If the shoe fits, wear it."

HOMER

No se puede sacar sangre de piedra.

You can't get blood out of a stone.

Like trying to get blood out of a stone.

Origin unknown

Hierbas malas que nunca mueren.

Bad weeds never die.

Bad influences don't leave.

Herodotus, *Histories*: Only the good die young. (c. 445 B.C.)

El éxito llama el éxito.
Success beckons success.
Nothing succeeds like success. / Success leads to success.
Origin unknown

FANTASY

El hombre que se levanta es más fuerte que el que no ha caído.
The man who gets up is bigger than he who has not fallen.
The man who rises is stronger than he who has not fallen.
Origin unknown

KENNY'S

Lo que no sabes no te hará daño.
What you don't know won't hurt you.
What you don't know won't hurt you.
George Pettie, *A Petite Palace* (1576)

A los tontos no les dura el dinero.
For the fools, their money doesn't last.
A fool and his money are soon parted.
Thomas Tusser, *Five Hundred Points of Good Husbandry* (1557)

Quien poco tiene pronto lo gasta.
He who has little quickly spends it.
The poor man spends his money quickly.
Origin unknown

Quien mal anda mal acaba.
He who goes poorly ends poorly.
Your bad ways will end badly.
Origin unknown

Más vale lo que aprendí que lo que perdí.
What I learned is worth more than what I lost.
Better what I learned than what I lost.
Origin unknown

El que jugó, jugará.
He who played, will play again.
Once a thief, always a thief.
Origin unknown

Dame pan y dime tonto.
Give me bread and call me a fool.
Call me a fool after you've given me what I want.
Origin unknown

Dame pan pronto y dime el tonto.
Give me bread quickly and call me the fool.
Call me a fool after you've given me what I want.
Daniel's version, *Pedro & Daniel* (2023)

De casi, no se muere nadie.
Of "almost," no one dies.
It was a miss, as good as a mile. / A miss is still a miss.
William Camden (1614)

BEST

El saber es fuerza.
Knowing is strength.
Knowledge is strength.
Origin unknown

ALTAR

Con esperanza no se come.
With hope, one doesn't eat.
One can't survive on hope alone.
Origin unknown

Casi, pero no.
Almost, but no.
Almost, but not quite. / Close, but no cigar.
Origin unknown

El que la hace, la paga.
He who does it pays for it.
Actions have consequences. / You've made your bed, now lie in it.
French proverb (1590)

El empezar es el comienzo del acabar.
The start is the beginning of the end.
Starting is the beginning of the end.
Origin unknown

FRIENDS

Borra con el codo lo que escribe con la mano.
He erases with his elbow what he writes with his hand.
He gives with one hand and takes away with the other.
Origin unknown

Cada quien con su cada cual.
Everyone with his everyone.
Everyone has someone. / Each with their own. / Birds of a feather.
Latin proverb

Dime con quien andas y te diré quién eres.
Tell me who you're with and I'll tell you who you are.
Tell me what company you keep and I'll tell you who you are.
Miguel de Cervantes, *Don Quixote* (1615)

BAILE

Al que le pique, que se rasque.
If you've got an itch, you should scratch.
If you've got an itch, you should scratch.
Origin unknown

Como dos y dos son cuatro.
Like two and two are four.
As sure as two plus two is four.
Origin unknown

SCHISM

No es lo mismo hablar de toros que estar en el redondel.
Talking about bulls is not the same as being in the bullring.
Talk is cheap.
Origin unknown

CHAOS

Hombre precavido vale dos.
The cautious man is worth two.
The cautious man is worth two.
Origin unknown

La suerte está echada.
Luck has been cast.
The die is cast.
Julius Caesar (49 BCE)

Cada cabeza es un mundo.
Every head is a world.
Every mind has its own perspective.
Origin unknown

Los genios pensamos iqual.
Geniuses, we think alike.
Great minds think alike.
Origin unknown

CIRCUMSPECTION

La risa es el mejor remedio.
Laughter is the best remedy.
Laughter is the best medicine.
Bible, *Proverbs 17:22*

Todo con moderación, incluso la moderación.
Everything in moderation, including moderation.
Everything in moderation, including moderation.
Hesiod (c. 700 BCE)

Las palabras se las lleva el viento.
Words are taken away by the wind.
Actions speak louder than words.
Origin unknown

Los mirones son de piedra.
Voyeurs are of stone.
Onlookers should remain silent.
Origin unknown

La cabra siempre tira al monte.
The goat always runs toward the mountain.
A leopard cannot change its spots.
Origin unknown

Mala piensa la que piensa que otro no piensa.
Poorly does one think the one who thinks the other does not think.
She's wrong if she thinks another doesn't think.
Origin unknown

MISFITS

Qué bonito es ver la lluvia y no mojarse.
How pretty to see the rain and not get wet.
Don't criticize others.
Origin unknown

HOPE

No hay más que temer que una mujer enfadada.
There is nothing worse to fear than an angry woman.
Nothing is as scary as an angry woman.
William Congreve, variation, *The Mourning Bride* (1697)

Deja de mirar atrás, si no nunca llegarás.
Stop looking behind, if not you will never arrive.
Stop looking back, otherwise you will never get where you're going.
Origin unknown

DOT

Todo llega a su tiempo.
Things arrive at their time.
Things happen when they're supposed to.
Origin unknown

Mejor que nada.
Better than nothing.
It's better than nothing.
Origin unknown.

Donde fueres, haz lo que vieres.
Wherever you go, do what you see.
When in Rome, do as the Romans do.
Dicho version of St. Ambrose quote.

SEMINARY

There are those who seek knowledge for the sake of knowledge; that
   is curiosity.
There are those who seek knowledge to be known by others; that is vanity.
There are those who seek knowledge in order to serve; that is charity/love.
St. Bernard of Clairvaux (1090–1152)

Trata a los demás como te gustaría ser tratado.
Treat others as you wish to be treated.
Do to others as you would have them do to you.
Bible, *Matthew 7:12*

El hábito no hace al monje.

The habit does not make the monk.

The habit does not a monk make. / Clothes don't make a man.

François Rabelais (c. 1494–1553)

Haz lo que bien digo, no lo que mal hago.

Do what I say well, not what I do poorly.

Do as I say, not as I do.

John Selden, *Table Talk* (1654)

BLT

Todo llega a su tiempo.

Everything arrives at its time.

Things happen when they're supposed to.

Origin unknown

Mejor antes que después.

Better before than later.

Sooner rather than later.

Origin unknown

CONFESSIONS

Es como hablar a la pared.

It's like talking to a wall.

It's like talking to a wall.

Origin unknown

Consejo no pedido, consejo mal oído. / nunca es bien recibido.

Unsolicited advice is misheard. / is never well-received.

Unsolicited advice is misheard. / is never well-received.

Origin unknown

No hay peor sordo que el que no quiere oír.

There is no one more deaf than he who does not wish to hear.

There is no one more deaf than he who does not wish to hear.

Origin unknown

Hay ropa tendida.

There are clothes hanging.

The walls have ears. / Others are listening.

Origin unknown

Lo que se mama de niña, dura toda la vida.

What is suckled as a child, it lasts all of their life.

A person is a product of their upbringing.

Origin unknown

SHAME

When the unusual captures my attention, my imagination is set free.

Pedro in *Pedro & Daniel* (2023)

A lo hecho, pecho.

To what's done, your chest.

Own up to what you have done. / Time to face the consequences.

Origin unknown

A cada cerdo le llega su San Martín.

To every pig will arrive their St. Martin.

Every pig has its day. / Everyone gets their comeuppance.

Origin unknown

Al médico, confesor, y letrado, no le hayas engañado.

To your doctor, priest and lawyer, don't deceive.

Don't deceive your doctor, priest or lawyer.

Origin unknown

La hierba mala nunca muere.

The bad weed never dies.

Only the good die young.

Origin unknown

El malo no muere porque tiene buena suerte.

The bad guy won't die because he's got good luck

The bad guy won't die because he's got good luck

Pedro's version of "Only the good die young," *Pedro & Daniel* (2023)

Si no fuera por mala suerte, no tendría ninguna suerte.

If it weren't for bad luck, I'd have no luck at all.

If it weren't for bad luck, I'd have no luck at all.

Origin unknown

JESÚS

Nunca es tarde para aprender.

It's never late to learn.

It's never too late to learn.

Origin unknown

IMPOSTER

El valiente vive hasta que el cobarde quiere.

The brave man lives until the coward wants.

The brave man lives until the coward wants.

Origin unknown

Solo se tiran piedras al árbol cargado de fruto.

People only throw stones at trees full of fruit.
People will criticize those doing well.
Origin unknown

A palabras necias, oídos sordos.

To foolish words, deaf ears.
Let foolish words fall on deaf ears.
Origin unknown

Más vale morir parado que vivir de rodillas.

It's worth more to die standing than to live on your knees.
I'd rather die standing than live on my knees.
Emiliano Zapata, Mexican Revolution (1910–1920)

LIFE

Las desgracias nunca vienen solas.

Misfortunes never come one at a time.
When it rains, it pours.
Origin unknown

Mañana será otro día.

Tomorrow will be another day.
Tomorrow is another day.
Origin unknown

FREEDOM

Quien quiere a Pedro también quiere su perro.
He who loves Pedro also loves his dog.
Love me, love my dog.
Daniel's version of a dicho of unknown origin, *Pedro & Daniel* (2023)

GERARD

A otro perro con ese hueso
To another dog with that bone.
Tell someone who'll believe you.
Origin unknown

GRINCHLY

Vale más huir que morir.
It's better to flee than to die.
It's better to flee than to die. / You live to fight another day.
Origin unknown

OUT

Cuando puede, no quiere; cuando quiere, no puede.
When he can, he doesn't want to; when he wants to, he can't.
When he can, he doesn't want to; when he wants to, he can't.
Origin unknown

Ojos que no ven, corazón que no siente.
Eyes that don't see, heart that doesn't feel.
What the eyes don't see, the heart doesn't grieve.
Dicho version of "Out of sight, out of mind"

El tiempo cura y nos mata.
Time heals and it kills us.
Time heals everything.
Origin unknown

MEDICINE

La salud no es conocida hasta que es perdida.
Health is not recognized until it is lost.
Health is not valued until it is lost.
Origin unknown

HIV

Una golondrina no hace verano.
A swallow doesn't make a summer.
A single swallow doesn't mean summer has arrived.
Ancient Greece

Lo que es moda no incomoda.
What is fashion does not cause discomfort.
One must suffer for fashion.
Origin unknown

MÉXICO

Lo que mal empieza, mal termina.
What starts badly ends badly.
What starts badly ends badly.
Origin unknown

Más vale saber que hablar.
It's better to know than to speak.
It's better to know than to speak.
Origin unknown

MEN

La práctica hace al maestro.
Practice makes a master/teacher.
Practice makes perfect.
John Adams, Diary (1760s)

Para todo mal, mezcal. Para todo bien, también.
For everything bad, mezcal. For all that is well, as well.
Mezcal for the good times and the bad.
Origin unknown

Para todo mal, un refrán, para todo bien, también.
For everything bad, a saying, for everything good, also.
There's a saying for the bad times, and the good as well.
Origin unknown

Una vez al día, es manía.
Una vez por semana, es cosa sana.
Una vez por mes, es dejadez.
Una vez al año, se te oxida el caño.
Once a day, it's mania.
Once a week, it's something healthy.
Once a month, it's neglect.
Once a month, your pipe will rust.
Origin unknown

El que no vive para servir, no sirve para vivir.

Whoever does not live to servie does not [de]serve to live.

One who does not live to serve does not [de]serve to live.

Origin unknown

Sin propósito para servir, no sirves para ningún propósito.

Without a purpose to serve, you do not serve a purpose.

If you have no purpose to serve, you serve no purpose.

Origin unknown.

PROVINCETOWN

El mundo es un pañuelo.

The world is a handkerchief.

It's a small world.

Origin unknown

Primun non nocere.

First, do no harm.

First, do no harm.

Origin unknown

RELIGION

Siempre se hizo lo que Dios quiso.

It was always done what God wanted.

God's will be done.

Bible, *Matthew 6:10*

Más vale tarde que nunca.

It's worth more late than never.

Better late than never.

Geoffrey Chaucer, *The Canterbury Tales* (1386)

Más vale estar solo que mal acompañado.
It's worth more to be alone than poorly accompanied.
It's better to be alone than in bad company.
George Washington, letter to niece (1791)

Es mejor haber amado y haber perdido que nunca haber amado.
It's better to have loved and lost than to never have loved.
It's better to have loved and lost than never to have loved at all.
Alfred Lord Tennyson, "In Memoriam A. H. H." (1850)

Las palabras se las lleva el viento.
Words are taken away by the wind.
Actions speak louder than words.
Origin unknown

Si te acuestas con perros, amaneces con pulgas.
If you sleep with dogs, you wake up with fleas.
If you sleep with dogs, you wake up with fleas.
John Webster, *The White Devil* (1612)

AIDS

No hay miel sin hiel.
There is no honey without bile.
There's always a catch. / Every rose has a thorn.
Origin unknown

PERHAPS

Amor no correspondido es tiempo perdido
Unrequited love is time lost.
Unrequited love is time lost.
Origin unknown

Es hora de cagar o salir de la olla.
It's time to shit, or get off the pot.
It's time to shit, or get off the pot.
Origin unknown

La vida de los muertos está en la memoria de los vivos.
The life of the dead is in the memory of the living.
The life of the dead is in the memories of the living.
Origin unknown

Solo se sabe que nunca se sabe.
The only certainty is that you never know.
The only certainty is that you never know.
Pedro's version of "you never know," *Pedro & Daniel* (2023)

La Muerte: Cuando te toca, aunque te quites. Cuando no te toca, aunque te brinques.
Death: When it's your time, even if you flee. When it's not your time, even if you jump.
Daniel's version of the dicho [substitutes pongas with brinques], *Pedro & Daniel* (2023)

Nunca es tarde si la dicha es buena.
It's never late if the saying is good.
It's never too late if the saying is good.
Origin unknown

Más puede la pluma que la espada.
The pen can do more than the blade.
The pen is mightier than the sword.
Edward Bulwer-Lytton, *Richelieu* (1839)

Recordar es volver a vivir.
To remember is to live again.
To remember is to live again.
Origin unknown

I have nothing, I owe a great deal, and the rest I leave to the poor.
François Rabelais, last will (c. 1494–1553)

I go to seek a Great Perhaps.
François Rabelais, last words (c. 1494–1553)

La adulación no te llevará a ninguna parte.
La adulación te llevará a todas partes.
Flattery will get you nowhere/everywhere.
Origin unknown

Don't let the truth ruin a good story.
Mark Twain (1835–1910)

Al mentiroso, le conviene ser memorioso.
It suits the liar to be memorious.
The liar should remember their lies.
Origin unknown

Hasta el mejor escribano echa un borrón.
Even the best writer makes a blur.
Even the best writer makes mistakes.
Origin unknown

A caballo regalado no le mires el diente.
To a gift horse, don't look at its tooth.
Don't look a gift horse in the mouth. / Beggars can't be choosers.
Origin unknown

A quien dan, no escoge.
To whom is given, they do not choose.
Beggars can't be choosers.
Origin unknown

EULOGY

El que no espera vencer, ya está vencido.
He who does not expect to win has already lost.
He who does not expect to win has already lost.
José Joaquín Olmedo, "La Victoria de Junín" (1825)

Comiendo entra la gana.
With eating desire enters.
Appetite comes with eating. [but thirst vanishes with drinking]
François Rabelais (c. 1494–1553)

La historia la escriben los vencedores.
History is written by the victors.
History is written by victors.
Origin unknown

Solo en la oscuridad se ven las estrellas.
Only in darkness are the stars seen.
Only in darkness can we see the stars.
Martin Luther King, Jr., "I've Been To The Mountaintop" (1968)

• • •

ABOUT THE AUTHOR

FEDERICO EREBIA is a retired physician, artist, woodworker, author, and illustrator. He is on the SCBWI Impact & Legacy Fund Steering Committee, was selected for the Poets & Writers publicity incubator for debut authors, and is an active member of several other writing groups.

Pedro & Daniel is his debut novel.

He lives in Massachusetts with his husband, and their westie and whippet.

SOME NOTES ON THIS BOOK'S PRODUCTION

The jacket and interior art was created by Julie Kwon traditionally, with ink, pencil, and marker, then finished digitally. The text was set by Westchester Publishing Services in Danbury, CT, in Legacy Serif, a type designed by American Ronald Arnholm for ITC. Arnholm was inspired by Garamond and most especially Jenson, whose Roman type is considered the first true example of its kind. The display was set in Bodoni, first designed by Italian Giambattisa Bodoni in 1798, himself heavily influenced by the work of John Baskerville. The book was printed on 78 gsm Yunshidai Ivory uncoated woodfree FSC™-certified paper and bound in China.

Production supervised by Freesia Blizard
Book jacket, case, and interiors designed by Semadar Megged
Editor: Nick Thomas
Assistant Editor: Irene Vázquez

LEVINE QUERIDO